BERLIN

PIERRE FREI

"An ambitious novel, filled with brilliantly
drawn characters, mesmerizingly readable,
and disturbingly convincing."
—*THE SUNDAY TELEGRAPH*

A NOVEL

"As the blasted city is being carved up by conquerors, a killer on a $3.00 carving up blue-eyed blondes in the American sector. As the victims fall, their lives unfold before our eyes . . . a panoramic portrait of a nation seduced and raped by Hitler and his Reich." —*Booklist*

"A winding and gripping whodunit . . . intricately woven and fantastically plotted . . . It is engrossing, addictive." —*Buzz* (UK)

"Heinz G. Konsalik is dead. Long live his far more intelligent heir Pierre Frei." —*Österreichische Zeitung*

"Riveting." —Jake Kerridge, *The Daily Telegraph*

"In this winning mix of mystery and history set in 1945 Berlin, Frei personalizes the horrors of war. . . . [He] maintains the suspense of whether the killer will claim another victim to the final pages. . . . Fine storytelling." —*Library Journal* (starred review)

"Pierre Frei adopts the approach taken by Graham Greene in *The Third Man*, using a postwar setting made more difficult by divided military occupation. Berlin struggles to adapt to the uneasy peace. Rapacious victors possess the place physically (the Russians, with their policy of looting and rape) or by psychological means (the Americans with the superior rations and subtle fraternization), resulting in what the filmmaker Wim Wenders called the colonization of the German unconscious. . . . A jittery, feral sexuality adds to the [book's] foreboding. . . . Entirely readable." —*The Guardian*

"It's a serial-killer whodunit, but it's also a very funny tale of a young man's coming-of-age in postwar Germany, and a series of stories about life in the Third Reich told through the lives of women who lived—and died—there. What's most surprising is that Frei . . . manages to pull all this complicated plotting and character development together. . . . I found *Berlin* very engaging and liked the slow pace and careful characterization. Plus there's a neat twist. . . . Let's hope Frei decides to bring the Dietrichs back for another round." —*The Globe and Mail*

"A gratifyingly original and surprisingly affecting crime novel . . . I'd be hard pressed to name a better researched and more readable crime novel this year." —*Nottingham Evening Post*

"Enormously exciting—your best plan is to keep a whole weekend free to read it all at once." —*Berliner Zeitung*

"*Berlin* by Pierre Frei begins a month after the Second World War has ended. The Allies have divided Germany's ruined capital, and in the American sector young blondes are being savagely murdered. At first it seems that this is going to be another police procedural, with a German detective teamed up with an American military policeman to hunt for the killer. But as the life story of each is told in a series of flashbacks, what emerges is a vivid picture of Germany as Hitler's followers tighten their grip on the country. It's an ambitious novel, filled with brilliantly drawn characters, mesmerizingly readable and disturbingly convincing." —*Sunday Telegraph* (UK)

"The stories of the murder victims, described in flashbacks, are fascinating, and the lively picture of the period, enriched with many details, rings true." —*Blick* (Zürich)

"*Berlin* takes us back to a very different capital in the aftermath of a very different apocalypse. In 1946 Berlin is under occupation by rival powers and hardened to killing, rape, and atrocity. Or so you would think. But when the killing resumes on an individual scale, there is a wholly different climate of horror. The victims are all young, beautiful, blue-eyed, blonde-haired women strangled with a chain and submitted to horrific sexual abuse. It is up to a German police inspector working with a group of American GIs to stop the serial killer. . . . In the end it is Berlin itself, the city and its inhabitants, meticulously observed and depicted, that emerges as the true star of the story, flawed, cruel, seductively engaging and all too human. This is its best evocation since Len Deighton's *Winter*." —*The Times* (London)

"Frei's real strength lies in the presentation of his characters. After each young woman's murder, her life story is described. The result is a fine novel of Berlin, set against the background of German political history." —*Das Echo*

"[*Berlin* is] set in occupied Berlin, where a serial killer targeting young women is on the loose. . . . With each woman's death we spiral back in time, learning about her life and the journey that led her to a lonely railway station or back street. The women's compelling stories run through the book, giving readers a sense of life before and during the war, and their struggles to face the ruin around them, until the killer snuffs out their lives." —*Publishing News* (UK)

"Life is anything but peaceful in postwar Berlin when a serial killer is on the loose. Young, blonde, and beautiful women are at risk as the killer lurks in the vicinity of Uncle Tom's Cabin underground station. . . . Each victim has a story to tell: Karin, a small-town girl turned film star was wooed by Hitler propagandist Joseph Goebbels; Helga fought to protect her handicapped child from the Nazis; Henrietta was an aristocratic diplomat; and Marlene was a high-class prostitute who got married to a high-ranking Gestapo officer. The fifth target, Jutta, has already escaped one attack. Will the authorities stop the killer in time to save her?" —*The Good Book Guide*

BERLIN

A Novel

Translated from the German by Anthea Bell

Pierre Frei

GROVE PRESS
New York

First published in Great Britain in 2005 by
Atlantic Books, an imprint of Grove Atlantic Ltd.

Originally published in Germany in 2003 by
Karl Blessing Verlag, Munich, as *Onkel Toms Hütte, Berlin.*

This novel is entirely a work of fiction. The names, characters and incidents
portrayed in it are the work of the author's imagination. Any resemblance to
actual persons, living or dead, events or localities, is entirely coincidental.

Printed in the United States of America

FIRST PAPERBACK EDITION

Library of Congress Cataloging-in-Publication Data

Frei, Pierre, 1930–
    [Onkel Toms Hütte, Berlin. English]
    Berlin : a novel / Pierre Frei ; translated from the
  German by Anthea Bell.
    p. cm.
    ISBN-10: 0-8021-4329-6
    ISBN-13: 978-0-8021-4329-7
    I. Bell, Anthea. II. Title

PT2666.R359205513 2006
833'.92—dc22   2006043433

Grove Press
an imprint of Grove/Atlantic, Inc.
841 Broadway
New York, NY 10003

Distributed by Publishers Group West

www.groveatlantic.com

07 08 09 10   10 9 8 7 6 5 4 3 2 1

For Catherine-Hélène

CHAPTER ONE

THE BOY NEVER took his eyes off the soldier. The American removed the last Lucky Strike from its packet and tossed the empty wrappings on the tracks. He lit the cigarette and waited for the U-Bahn train coming in from Krumme Lanke station to stop. If the Yank was going only one station up the line to Oskar-Helene-Heim, he'd throw the half-smoked cigarette away as he got out, it would fly through the air in a wide arc, and the boy could retrieve it.

A dozen cigarette butts of that length, once the burnt end had been neatly trimmed away with a razor blade, would earn him forty marks. But if the Yank was travelling further the prospects weren't so good, because then he'd probably tread out that coveted cigarette on the floor of the car or chuck it out of the window, which was open in the summer weather. Yanks were entirely indifferent to such things.

With equal indifference, the US Army quartermaster had ordered that a square mile around the Onkel Toms Hütte U-Bahn station was to be fenced in with barbed wire, leaving only one narrow passage available to German passengers for access. The shopping streets on both the longer sides of the station were off limits too, and had become a centre for the soldiers billeted in the requisitioned apartment buildings around it.

Decades before, the landlord of an inn frequented by people going on excursions to the nearby Grunewald had called his establishment after Harriet Beecher Stowe's affecting novel, *Uncle Tom's Cabin*, and the Berlin Transport Company adopted the name for the new U-Bahn station built in late 1929. 'Uncle Tom' soon became familiar to the American occupying forces when they arrived in 1945.

The U-Bahn train stopped. The Yank boarded it, cigarette in the corner of his mouth, and slouched against one of the upright poles you could hold

1

on to. Another passenger followed him in and closed the door. The railway-man in the middle of the platform raised his signal disc. The conductor at the front of the train knocked on the window of the driver's cab to pass the message on, and swung himself up into the car as it started moving.

The boy watched the train leave. He had decided not to pursue the cigarette end. As soon as the stationmaster with the signal disc turned his back, he jumped down on the tracks to salvage the empty cigarette packet.

The stationmaster's head appeared above him. 'What d'you think you're doing down there?' he barked.

'Looking for cigarette ends.'

'Found any?' The man was thinking of his own empty pipe.

'No cigarette ends. Only a dead woman.' The boy pointed casually to something beside the tracks.

The stationmaster sat on the edge of the platform, put his disc down and lowered himself, grunting. Two slender legs in torn, pale nylon stockings were sticking out of one of the side bays which, if you bent double, enabled you to reach the cables below the platform. The feet were shod in brown, high-heeled pumps with white leather inserts, currently the latest fashion in the USA. The white inserts bore dark-red splashes of blood.

'She's American. Go get the Yanks.' The man clambered back up on the platform and hurried to his booth, where he took the receiver off its rest and cranked up the phone. 'Krumme Lanke? Onkel Tom stationmaster here. We got a dead woman under platform one. Stop the trains coming through from your end. Message over.'

The boy's name was Benjamin, but everyone called him Ben. He was fifteen, dark-blond, and showed no ill effects of the events of the last few months – the British and American air raids, the chaos of the final days of the war, the havoc as the Red Army marched in. He had filed these experiences away in his head, making room for new impressions. New impressions included Glenn Miller, chewing gum, Hershey chocolate bars and automobiles a mile long, first and foremost the Buick Eight, closely followed by the De Soto, the Dodge and the Chevrolet. New impressions included brightly coloured ties, narrow, ankle-length trousers, Old Spice and Pepsi Cola. All these items arrived overnight when, in line with the agreement between the Allies, the Russians vacated half of Berlin and Western troops moved into the ruined capital.

Ben climbed the broad steps to the ticket windows and walked away down the barbed-wire passage and into the dusty summer heat, which instantly made him thirsty. In his mind he pictured a cold sparkling drink, woodruff flavour. When you took the top off there was a promising pop, and the fizz rose into the air like a djinn from its bottle. But there was no woodruff-flavour sparkling drink available, just the dusty heat and a lingering aroma of DDT insecticide and spearmint chewing gum. Even the smells were different now the Yanks were here.

Ben strolled over to the guard on duty at the entrance to the prohibited area. Haste would have suggested dismay. 'Dead woman on the U-Bahn,' he said.

'OK, buddy. It better be true.' The man on duty reached for the phone.

The call came from the Military Police. Inspector Klaus Dietrich took it. 'Thanks, yes, we're on our way.' He hung up and called, 'The car, Franke.'

'Just heating up. It'll take a good half-hour.' Detective Sergeant Franke pointed through the window at an old Opel by the roadside. It had a kind of sawn-off bathroom geyser fitted at the back, into which a policeman was feeding scraps of wood. When they were burning hard enough they would generate the wood gas needed to drive the engine. There was no gasoline available for the Berlin Zehlendorf CID.

'We'll take the bikes,' Dietrich decided. He was a tall man of forty-five, with grey hair and the prominent cheekbones of those who were living on starvation rations. His grey, double-breasted suit, the only one Inge had managed to retrieve from their bombed-out apartment on the Kaiserdamm, hung loose on him. He dragged his left leg a little. The prosthesis, fitted at the auxiliary military hospital in the Zinnowald School where he'd spent the end of the war, chafed in hot weather. His wound had saved him from imprisonment, and he'd been able to go home in May. Inge and the boys were living with her parents in Riemeister Strasse. Inge's father, Dr Bruno Hellbich, had survived the Hitler years in compulsory retirement but otherwise unharmed. He'd returned to his old position as a Social Democrat district councillor at Zehlendorf Town Hall, and he had been able to get his son-in-law a job as a police inspector. The Zehlendorf CID needed a temporary head, and Klaus Dietrich's pre-war work as deputy managing director of a security services firm and his lack of political baggage, compensated for

3

the loss of his left leg below the knee and his absence of criminological training. In any case, he had soon found out that a sound understanding of
human nature was perfectly adequate for dealing with black marketeers,
thieves and burglars.

It took them fifteen minutes to reach the U-Bahn station, where their
police passes got them past the gathering crowd.

'Oh shit, here comes my old man,' muttered Ben, making off.

An American officer was standing on the tracks with a military policeman and the stationmaster. They had laid the dead woman down on her
back. She was blonde, with a beautiful face and regular features. Her blue
eyes stared into space. Strangulation marks suffused with blood were
notched in her delicate neck. Klaus Dietrich pointed to her nylon stockings,
her nearly new pumps, and her fashionable, pale summer dress. 'An
American,' he said, gloomily. 'If a German did this there'll be trouble.'

Sergeant Franke scratched his head. 'I feel as if I've seen her before.'

The American officer straightened up. 'Which of you guys is in charge?'

Klaus Dietrich answered. 'Inspector Dietrich and Sergeant Franke,
Zehlendorf CID.'

'Captain Ashburner, Military Police.' The American was tall and lean,
with smooth, fair hair. His alert, intelligent gaze rested on the inspector. 'And
this is Sergeant Donovan.' The sergeant was a stocky man with broad,
powerful shoulders and a crew cut.

Dietrich raised the dead woman's left arm. The glass of her watch was
shattered; the hands stood at ten forty-two. 'Probably the time of death,' he
commented, beckoning to the stationmaster. 'Who was on duty here yesterday evening, about quarter to eleven?'

'Me, of course,' said the man in injured tones. 'Until the last train, at
22.48 hours, and then again from six in the morning. They hardly give us
time for a wink of sleep.'

'Were there many passengers waiting for the last train?'

'Couple of Yanks with their girls, two or three Germans.'

'Was the dead woman among them?'

'Maybe, maybe not. I had to clear the 22.34 to Krumme Lanke for departure. You don't look at the passengers separately. Nobody kind of caught my
eye. Only that weirdo with goggles and a leather cap. Like a sky-pilot off on
a tobogganing trip, I thought.'

'Goggles and a leather cap?'

'Well, kind of motorcycling gear, I'd say. But I didn't really look close. The lights at the far end of the platform have been a write-off for weeks.'

'So he was standing in semi-darkness.'

'The only one who was, now you mention it. The other passengers were waiting where the lights still work.'

'Did you see him get in?'

'Nope. I have to be up at the front of the train to give the guard the signal to leave. Now excuse me, here's the eleven-ten.'

'Hey, Kraut, take a look.' The MP sergeant handed Dietrich a shoulder bag. 'Not an American, one of yours. Karin Rembach, aged twenty-five. Works in our dry cleaners' shop over there.' He pointed to the shopping centre on the far side of the fence. 'I guess her boyfriend bought her the shoes and nylons in the PX. Man called Dennis Morgan, stationed with the Signal Corps in Lichterfelde.'

Klaus Dietrich opened the bag. Her ID, with a pass for a German employee of the US Army, indicated where the sergeant had gathered his information. He also found a note bearing the soldier's name and his barracks address. 'I'd like to ask this Morgan some questions.'

'A Kraut wants to interrogate an American? Don't you know who won the war?' barked the sergeant.

'I know the war's over and murder's a crime again,' Klaus Dietrich replied calmly.

For a moment it looked as if the beefy Donovan might take a swing at him, but the captain intervened. 'I'll question Morgan and send you the statement. In return you can let me have the results of the autopsy. A Medical Corps ambulance will take her wherever you like. Goodbye, Inspector.'

Sergeant Franke watched the Americans leave. 'Not very friendly, that bunch.'

'Privilege of the victors. Franke, what do you think about this man in the goggles?'

'Either a nutcase, like the stationmaster says, or someone who doesn't want to be recognized. Inspector, why do they keep calling us Krauts?'

Klaus Dietrich laughed. 'Our transatlantic liberators believe we Germans live on nothing but sauerkraut.'

5

'With pork knuckle and pea purée.' A note of nostalgia entered the detective sergeant's voice. A siren came closer and died away. Two GIs with Red Cross armbands carried a stretcher down the steps. The morgue in Berlin Mitte had been bombed out and was now in the Soviet sector, so Klaus Dietrich had the corpse taken to the nearby Waldfrieden hospital, where his friend Walter Möbius was medical superintendent.

'I'll do the autopsy later,' said Dr Möbius. 'I have to operate on the living while daylight lasts, and then until they cut off the electricity at nine. If you really want to watch the autopsy, we'll have the power back at three in the morning.'

A young man clad in the best pre-war Prince of Wales check suiting nonchalantly lit an extra-length Pall Mall outside the U-Bahn station. Ben looked enviously at the thick crêpe soles of his suede shoes. He knew the man slightly. Hendrijk Claasen was a Dutchman and a black marketeer. Only a black marketeer could afford such a sharp suit. Ben wanted a Prince of Wales check suit and shoes with crêpe soles too. He imagined himself appearing before Heidi Rödel in his made-to-measure outfit, on soles a centimetre thick. Then it would be curtains for Gert Schlomm in his silly short lederhosen.

The boy walked home from the station, glad to have avoided his father. Papa would have asked questions. In this case, he would have wanted to know why Ben was finding dead women on the U-Bahn instead of being at school. Papa had a quietly sarcastic manner which hit the vulnerable spot.

Not that Ben had anything against school in itself, only its regularity. The chaos of the recent past had brought with it not only fear and terror but adventure and freedom too, and he was finding it difficult to get used to an ordered existence.

He made for the back of the house, went into the shed at the end of the garden, and fished his school bag out from under a couple of empty potato sacks. His grandmother was weeding near the veranda. She had dug up the lawn months ago to plant tobacco. The district councillor was a heavy smoker and she dried the leaves on the stove for him, filling the house with a horrible smell, which was the lesser of two evils. Hellbich was unbearable when his body craved nicotine.

'There's a special margarine ration at Frau Kalkfurth's. Ralf's down there queuing already. Go and take over from him, Ben – your mother will relieve you later. She's gone to the cobbler's. With luck he can repair your brother's sandals again – the poor boy's going around in gym shoes full of holes.'

'OK.' Ben climbed the steep stairs to the attic room he shared with Ralf, and tossed the school bag on his bed. Before going downstairs again he put the empty cigarette packet away with the razor blade in a drawer. He'd work on it later.

There was no one in the kitchen. He pulled out the left-hand drawer of the kitchen dresser, reached into it, pushed the bolt down and opened the locked cupboard door from the inside. Inge Dietrich kept the family's bread rations in that cupboard: two slices of dry bread each in the morning and again at lunchtime. They ate a hot meal in the evening.

Ben hacked himself off an extra-thick slice and clamped it between his teeth, returned the loaf to the dresser, shut the door and bolted it again. Then he closed the drawer and went off to take his little brother's place in the queue. On the way he ate his looted slice of bread in bites as small as possible. That way you prolonged the pleasure.

Frau Kalkfurth's shop had once been the living room of a terraced house in the street known as Am Hegewinkel, 'Game Preserve Corner'. The surrounding streets, all with brightly painted houses, were named Hochsitzweg, Lappjagen and Auerhahnbalz, suggesting images of hides, hunting and capercaillies. A local mayor who was a keen huntsman had given them these names sometime in the past. The garage built on to the back of the house was used to store goods for the shop. It had once held the family car, for the Kalkfurths had owned a big butcher's shop in eastern Berlin. The butcher's shop had long been in ruins, and the car, an Adler, was only a memory now.

The widow Kalkfurth, having worked in a similar line before the war, was granted the coveted permit to run a grocery store after the fall of Berlin. Now, her former trainee butcher, Heinz Winkelmann, stood behind the improvised counter, while she oversaw the little business from her wheelchair, sticking her customers' ration coupons on large sheets of newspaper in the evenings. Someone from the rationing authority collected them once a week. She lived alone in the Am Hegewinkel house: discreet gifts of butter, smoked sausage and streaky bacon to the people in the Housing Department saved her from having the homeless billeted on her.

The queue outside the shop was grey and endless. Many of the women were dressed in old pairs of men's trousers and had scarves over their heads. There were no hairdressing salons these days. Ralf was standing quite a long way back, brushing a broken-off twig back and forth in zigzags over the pavement, while Frau Kalkfurth's tabby kitten tried to catch it. The game came to an abrupt end when a dachshund at the very end of the line broke away and attacked the kitten, which shot off into the garage.

Ralf grabbed the yapping dog's collar and hauled it back to its owner. 'Can't you keep your dog in order?' he asked loudly.

'None of your cheek, young man. Sit, Lehmann!' The man took the dog's lead.

Ralf went into the garage. Old vegetable crates and broken furniture towered up in an impenetrable wall at the back. 'Mutzi, Mutzi,' he called to the kitten. A plaintive mew came from the far side of the lumber. There was no way through. Or was there? The mouldering doors of a wardrobe were hanging off their hinges, and the back of it was smashed. The boy wriggled through. The little cat was crouching on a shabby eiderdown in the dim light. 'Come on, Mutzi. That silly dachshund's back on its lead.' He picked up the frightened animal, which had dug its claws into the eiderdown so hard that the quilt came up with it, revealing the saddle of a motorbike. Carefully, the boy freed the kitten's claws and put the eiderdown back in place. Then he scrambled into the daylight with his protégé.

'There you are.' Ben greeted him reproachfully. 'Where's your place in the queue?'

'Behind that woman with the green headscarf.' Ralf let the kitten go and strolled away. Reluctantly, Ben took his slot in the queue. He hated standing in line.

He cut the waiting short by imagining a man in a white jacket with a steaming pan full of sausages slung on a tray in front of him, like that time on the Wannsee bathing beach. He had been very small then, and it was before the war. He could almost hear the squelch as the man squirted mustard on the paper plate from a squeezy bottle. It made a delightfully rude noise.

His mother arrived around six. Gritscher the master cobbler had repaired Ralf's sandals for the umpteenth time. 'That man works miracles,' she told the woman next to her. 'Off you go and do your homework,' she said, turning to her son. 'And take your brother with you.'

'What'll it be, Frau Dietrich?' Winkelmann beamed at her over the counter, looking healthy and well fed. He had direct access to all good things.

'A loaf of bread, 150 grams of powdered egg and the extra margarine ration. Can you let me have the powdered egg as an advance on next week's rations?'

'I'll have to ask the boss about that. Come here a moment, will you, Frau Kalkfurth?'

Martha Kalkfurth had dark hair with strands of grey in it, and a smooth, round, ageless face with a double chin. She sat heavily in her wheelchair, steering it skilfully past sacks of dried potato and cartons filled with bags of ersatz coffee.

'Can Frau Dietrich have 150 grams of powdered egg in advance?'

'Please, Frau Kalkfurth, it's only until Monday when the new ration cards begin.'

Martha Kalkfurth shook her head. 'No special favours from me, even if your husband is with the police.' She turned the wheelchair and went back into the room behind the shop.

Ben found his brother outside the Yanks' ice cream parlour. One of the soldiers was leaning down to hand him a large portion of ice cream. Ralf was a successful beggar; few could resist his angelic face. The two boys scooped up the chocolate and vanilla ice on their way home, using the wafers that came with it. Life was OK.

*

The soft strains of 'Starlight Melody' drifted out of Club 48, combining with the tempting aroma of grilled steaks to arouse impossible longings in the Germans hurrying by. The US Engineers had put the building together from prefabricated components in three days, and within a week it was completely fitted out with a kitchen, cocktail bar, tables and dance floor.

The commandant of the American sector of Berlin, a two-star general from Boston, had handed over the club to the private soldiers and NCOs, dancing the first dance with his wife before withdrawing with relief to the nearby Harnack House, where the commissioned officers and upper ranks of civilian staff drank dry martinis.

Jutta Weber, a pretty blonde aged thirty, worked in the kitchen of the Club. She peeled potatoes, washed dishes, and heaved around the heavy pots and pans used by Mess Sergeant Jack Panelli and his cooks to concoct hearty, unsophisticated dishes from their canned and frozen supplies.

At just before eleven she set off for home. Her bicycle light barely illuminated her way back along Argentinische Allee. The buildings were in darkness; there would be no electricity in this part of town until three in the morning. The coal shortage and the state of the turbines in the city power stations, half of them destroyed in air raids, made power rationing essential. Next came Steglitz. A pedestrian emerged from the darkness. Jutta rang the bicycle bell on her handlebars, making a shrill sound, but he kept coming straight at her. She swerved, caught the edge of the pavement with her front wheel and lost her balance. For a moment she lay there in the road, helpless. Headlights approached, lighting up the face above her for a fraction of a second. The lenses of a large pair of goggles flashed. Then the face disappeared into the darkness again.

An open jeep stopped. The driver jumped out. 'Everything OK?' He helped her to her feet, and she recognized a captain's insignia and the Military Police armband. He was very tall, about one metre ninety, she guessed.

'Everything OK,' she told him. 'I'm on my way home. I work at the Forty-Eight.' She showed him the ID card allowing her, as a German employee of the army, to be out after curfew. Somewhere nearby the engine of a motorbike started up. The sound rapidly receded.

'Your light's not very strong. Easy to miss an obstacle.' Obviously he hadn't noticed the man with the goggles. 'I'll take you home.'

'There's really no need,' she protested, but he had already lifted her bike into the back of the jeep, and she had no choice but to get in.

'Where do you want to go?'

'Straight ahead, then right into Onkel-Tom-Strasse.'

He started the engine. She glanced at him, but couldn't make out his face beneath his helmet in the darkness. 'Are you always so late going home?' He had a calm, masculine voice that inspired trust. A bit like Jochen, she thought sadly.

'I never finish before eleven, except on Wednesdays, when I get off at seven.'

'You want to be very careful at night. You never know who may be prowling around in the dark.' He turned into Onkel-Tom-Strasse. Number 133 was one of the two-storey apartment buildings on the right, painted in bright colours in the twenties by an architect with gaudy tastes. He helped her out of the jeep and lifted her bike down.

'Thanks, captain. You were a great help.'

'It was a pleasure, ma'am.' He touched his hand to his white helmet.

Nice American, she thought. She opened the front door of the building, locked it from the inside, and took her bike down to the cellar, where she secured it with a padlock and chain. Then she went quietly upstairs. The little dynamo lamp hummed as she switched it on.

The top apartment on the left had fallen vacant when the Red Army marched in and its tenant, a Nazi local group leader, shot his wife and himself. It had three rooms. The Königs and their twelve-year-old son Hans-Joachim, Hajo for short, lived in one, Jutta had the room next to theirs, and the Housing Department had given the room opposite to Jürgen Brandenburg, just released from a POW camp, a small, dark-haired man in his late twenties who wore clothes made from blue Luftwaffe fabric.

The door of the Königs' room was open. 'Come on in, Frau Weber, sit down, this is just getting interesting,' cried Herr König, in high spirits. He poured out some potato schnapps. 'From my brother's secret still. He has an allotment garden in Steglitz. Like a little drink?'

'No, thank you, Herr König.'

'Well, where were we, captain?'

Brandenburg's dark glasses for the blind reflected the candlelight. Hands tilted at an angle, he was demonstrating one of his countless fights in the air. 'So the Englishman comes down from the clouds. A two-engine Mosquito. Dangerous craft, that, with three guns on board. I swerve aside. He dives down past me, it takes him a moment to regain height. I wait for him to climb past me, then I rake his underside. *Ratatatat* – boing – bull's-eye! He's flying round me in a thousand pieces. My twenty-fifth victory in the air. I got the Knight's Cross for it – presented by *him* personally.'

'Bravo!' Herr König was beside himself. 'The Knight's Cross. Think of that, Frau Weber.'

Jutta's reaction was icy. 'I'd rather think about how it's all over now, and *he* is frying in hell instead of handing out gongs. Haven't you men had enough of this rot, with your murderous games of cowboys and Indians?'

Brandenburg leaped to his feet. 'I'm not taking that about rot!'

'Then don't talk it, OK? Goodnight, everyone.' In her room she lit a candle and took it into the bathroom to clean her teeth. The strong-tasting American dentifrice concealed the horrible chlorine flavour of the tapwater. As she fell asleep she pictured Jochen in her mind's eye. He had been killed at the very beginning of the war. The men's voices next door rose in excitement. She wondered, bitterly, Will it never end?

*

The motorcyclist was disappointed and angry. He had watched his victim for days before deciding she was worthy. Carefully, lovingly, he had chosen her from among a number of blonde, blue-eyed candidates. Not everyone passed the test.

He had been so close to her, and then the jeep ruined everything. Who knew how long he'd have to wait for another opportunity?

He took every precaution, but he had nothing to fear at this time of night. Unseen, he put the bike back in its hiding place, where he also kept the goggles, gauntlets and leather helmet. The rest of his route was hidden in darkness. It was not far to his home.

He went straight to bed, put out the light and waited patiently for the dream. It was always the same: he sank deep into the chosen one's blue eyes, stroked her long blonde hair, kissed her beautiful full lips as she opened them to him. She sighed as he penetrated her. He was a wonderful lover, with strength and stamina. But when he woke up he was an awkward fool again, a clown who had no idea how to approach a girl.

It had been like that with Annie. Annie, blonde and blue-eyed, who worked in Brumm's Bakery and Cake Shop opposite the U-Bahn station. He spent endless Sunday afternoons sitting in the front garden of the café, ordering countless cups of coffee and pieces of cake, following every move she made with his eyes. He financed his generous tips from the till of the family business. She said, 'Thank you very much, sir,' nicely, and bobbed a little curtsey. He didn't realize that she was laughing at him.

He gave her flowers and chocolate and a pair of silk stockings, but she just laughed. 'You're out of your league, kid!' His pink, youthful face belied his age; he was twenty-five. But the diamond ring from his mother's jewel box made a difference. She put it on her finger and said, 'Come up and see me tomorrow evening.' She had an attic room above the cake shop.

He arrived from work on his motorbike late that Monday, still dressed in his butcher's overall. She was ready, waiting for him. Her naked body shone pale in the light of the big candle beside the bed. He stood there with arms dangling, not daring to touch her; not knowing where to look. She helped him out of his overall. Something clinked. 'What's that, then?' Embarrassed, he showed her the cattle chain he'd left in his pocket by mistake.

Quick-fingered, she undressed him. When she saw his tiny prick she spluttered with laughter. All the same, she tried hard. But it was no good, he was too tense. Shrugging her shoulders, she gave up. 'Come back when you've grown up, little sissy!' she mocked him as she dressed.

He didn't want to hurt her. He only wanted her to be his. That was the deal. He grabbed hold of her. She resisted and kicked out at him, like a calf resisting slaughter. He reached for the chain that had tamed so many recalcitrant animals. She soon stopped resisting. He pulled her panties down and took her by force, using the candle in its holder as a substitute for his manhood, imaging her stertorous breathing to be the sound of orgasm. An overwhelming climax shook him as he rooted about in her, letting her go only when she stopped moving.

No one saw him carry her out into the front garden in the dark and sit her at one of the tables, her dress pulled up to show her bloodstained sex. He wanted people to know he had possessed her. He removed the ring from her finger.

It had been like that the first time, and it was the same whenever his craving grew too strong and there was only one way to satisfy it: with a young, blonde, blue-eyed woman and a cattle chain.

*

It was three in the morning. The basement smelled of formalin and decomposition. Gratefully, Klaus Dietrich allowed the nurse to put a mask over his mouth and nose. The body lay on the marble slab, a well-grown young woman with slender limbs.

Walter Möbius had been a medical officer with the Afrika Corps. 'We

13

had refrigeration problems there too. Your Karin must be buried as soon as possible.'

'My Karin! Heavens, what do you think that sounds like? I never knew her. But I'd like to know how and when she died.'

'Last night, around eleven o'clock. Strangled with a chain about the thickness of your finger. Here, you can see the indentations its links left in her neck. But that's not all.' The doctor pointed to the young woman's vagina. Her blonde pubic hair was clotted with blood. He picked up a speculum and gently opened the dead woman's thighs. The inspector turned away. 'The monster,' said Möbius, after a brief examination. 'Some sharp object. Forcibly inserted and then moved back and forth.'

'A chain with a toggle to lock it in place,' said the inspector, thinking out loud. 'Using a chain like that, he could throttle her with one hand while he used the other to . . .' He stopped. 'Around eleven at night? Probably just before the last train left at 22.48. The platform was almost empty and half the lights weren't working. The murderer would have been waiting in the shadows. The chain would have stifled her screams. And when he'd finished with her he pushed the body down on the tracks, jumped after it, hauled the corpse out of sight into the bay under the edge of the platform, clambered up again and waited for the last train, cool as a cucumber. It could have been like that.'

The doctor put the speculum in a dish. 'Nurse Dagmar undressed the body. She wasn't wearing any panties. Does anyone know anything about her?'

'Sergeant Franke thinks he might have seen her before, but he can't remember where.'

'I'm going to open up the body now. Want to stay and watch?'

'No thanks. I can't promise not to keel over. One of our men will come and collect your autopsy report later.'

Dr Möbius looked at the beautiful corpse with pity. 'I wonder who this Karin Rembach was?' He picked up his scalpel.

KARIN

SUMMER SUNDAYS WERE the best thing about Weissroda. The entire
village drowsed off after lunch, and you could make off down the path
through the fields and walk through the tall rye. If you parted the blades
very carefully as you went in, they closed behind you, forming an impenetrable curtain. The wind had made a little clearing in the middle of the rye
field. You could undo your plaits there, shake your long hair loose over your
shoulders, lie down and daydream, looking up at the sky, and sometimes
your hand found its way between your legs, giving you a tingling feeling
which was simply unbearable, and felt so nice that you couldn't stop.

Seventeen-year-old Karin liked to be all alone, with no one telling her
what she was to do, muck out the henhouse or feed the horse. She had been
on the Werneisens' farm for two years now, ever since her mother, Anna
Werneisen's sister, died of heart disease. She'd never been married to Karin's
father. He was English, a steward on a cruise ship plying between London
and Hamburg. When he was in Cuxhaven he spoke English to his daughter.
Then he was posted to the Far East, and they never heard from him again.
It wasn't that the Werneisens made Karin feel aware of her situation. But if
she hadn't closed the pigsty door properly, or she neglected a job, one of
them would say she was a city child and didn't belong here. She knew that
she wasn't like them; she had a different accent, speaking the pure High
German of the north, instead of the local dialect spoken here on the border
of Thuringia, which seemed to have a constant undertone of malice. She was
blonde, with long, slender limbs, and that too distinguished her from her
sturdy relations.

When she had daydreamed enough, she sat up and braided her plaits.
She kept the ends in place with little leather straps that closed with snap-
fasteners, instead of the slides that the village girls wore. She rose, smoothed

15

down her dress, and strolled slowly back along the path through the fields. There was a notice up outside the inn.

THE BLOND-LACE LADY
WITH NADJA HORN AND ERIK DE WINTER

It was an advertisement for a theatrical company from Berlin touring the provinces in the summer break. Karin looked for the umpteenth time at the picture of the leading actress, a beautiful lady with blonde hair sprayed into place and a white fox fur stole, and the photo of her partner beside it. He was a good-looking man in tails, really dishy. She couldn't tear herself away.

Hans Görke was waiting for her outside the blacksmith's forge. He had washed thoroughly, and only his black fingernails showed that he'd been working at the anvil. Hans was three years older than Karin, a stocky, red-headed lad with heavy arms and big hands.

'I went to pick you up.'

'So?' With pointed indifference, she glanced at the swastika flag flying above the forge. Görke senior was a Party member.

She was about to go on, but he grabbed her forearm in a firm grip. 'Where you been, then?'

'That's none of your business.'

'It is so, 'cause you're my girl.'

'Don't you get any ideas.' She freed himself from his grasp by unbending his fingers one by one, and he let her. He could easily have held on.

'How's about a trip to Eckartsberga next Sunday? There's a dance on at the Lion.'

'I don't feel like dancing,' she snapped.

'How's about a little walk now, then?'

'I have to help with the milking.'

In her bedroom, she took off the thin, flower-patterned dress with its white collar, and her sandals and white socks. She avoided looking in the wardrobe mirror, because she hated the sight of her blue, cotton-jersey knickers with elasticated legs and high-necked undershirt. She sat down on the edge of the bed, put on the thick wool stockings lying ready for her, and slipped into the dirty white, cotton-drill overall that was too big for her and had too many buttons.

Anna Werneisen was standing by the stove, cooking oatmeal for supper.

16

The sight of the thick lumps on the surface nauseated Karin. 'Hans was here,' her aunt told her.

'I know.' Karin put on the gumboots standing by the door.

'You don't want to let that Hans get away. He's the lad for you. Plans to go to Kösen and join the cavalry as a farrier. That's as good as a sergeant when it comes to the pay. I heard it from old Riester, he served with the cavalry.' Anna Werneisen was a practical woman.

'Hans has black fingernails and smells of soot.' Karin didn't wait to hear her aunt's reply, but went off to the cowshed, gumboots slapping on the ground. Her cousins Bärbel and Gisela were already sitting with the cows. Karin put her stool down to the right of Liese's rear end and placed the bucket under it. She massaged the cow's udder, took hold of two teats and began milking: gentle pressure with thumb and forefinger, let the other three fingers follow one by one, almost as if you were playing the piano, a slight downward tug at the same time, and the milk came splashing down into the empty bucket with a dull, tinny note that rose in pitch as the bucket slowly filled. Liese turned her head, contentedly chewing the cud. The cousins were giggling together about their romp in the straw with two boys from Braunsroda.

Karin carried the full bucket out and poured it into the milk churn through the strainer. Rosa was mooing impatiently. It was her turn next. Each of the three girls milked four cows twice a day. Father Werneisen fed the cows and mucked them out.

After supper they sat around the People's Radio, a black Bakelite box with three knobs and a round, fabric-covered speaker, from which issued the voice of a journalist enthusiastically reporting from Vienna. The Führer had brought Austria home into the Reich. 'And he ain't finished yet,' prophesied Werneisen darkly.

Karin wasn't listening. She was leafing through a old issue of *Die Dame* magazine, looking at the glossy photos of beautiful, elegant people and dreaming of blonde Nadja Horn and Erik de Winter, that dishy man in evening dress.

One Friday morning in July, a coach containing the theatrical company and a truck with its scenery drew up in the yard of the inn at Weissroda. Karin was mucking out the henhouse when Bärbel burst in with the news. She dropped her pitchfork. This she had to see.

Actors and stagehands got out of the coach, along with the director Theodor Alberti, a gentleman with a leonine mane of hair, a monocle and a Scotch terrier. Erik de Winter the film star got out too.

Karin recognized him at once: dark, wavy hair, soft chin and velvety brown eyes. He was wearing pale flannels and a white tennis sweater, and had a clutch of newspapers under one arm. He laughed and waved; he always laughed and waved when there was an audience in the offing. News of the actors' arrival had not yet spread, so the audience was Karin. Unabashed, she waved back.

Erik de Winter was moved by the sight of the girl's slender figure in an overall much too big for her, her regular features and expressive blue eyes. 'What a young beauty,' he said, helping his stage partner out of the bus.

'You've never fallen for rustic charm before,' Nadja Horn teased him. She bore only the most remote resemblance to the groomed blonde lady in the white fox fur. Her black hair was tied up with a red scarf, and she wore wide-legged trousers in the Dietrich style. 'But as usual, your taste is impeccable.' She walked over to the startled girl with long, energetic strides, and offered her hand. 'I'm Nadja Horn.'

'But you're not blonde!' exclaimed Karin.

'Oh, we actors are whatever the public wants us to be. Black-haired, red-headed, blonde, brunette. May I introduce you to my partner? Herr Erik de Winter – this is Fräulein . . . what did you say your name was?'

'Karin Rembach.' Karin wiped some chicken shit off her face.

A long look from those velvety brown eyes. 'Very pleased to meet you, Fräulein Rembach.'

'Oh, me too! I saw you in a movie. You played an airman.'

'Yes, it was *Storming the Heavens*.' He kept on looking at her. 'Are you coming to the show this evening? We'll leave you a complimentary ticket at the box office.'

Nadja Horn was watching the encounter with amusement. This little country girl seemed to have made a great impression on him. 'Come and see us after the performance,' she suggested. 'Then you can tell us what you thought of the play. Herr de Winter and I would like that.'

'I'll ask Aunt Anna if I may,' she promised, and then could have kicked herself.

By now the yard had filled with curious onlookers. Half the village watched with bated breath as de Winter bent to kiss Karin's hand. Her heart was thudding, but she didn't let it show. 'See you this evening, then,' she said loud enough for everyone to hear, and ran back to the henhouse with a spring in her step.

Later, in the kitchen, she asked her aunt's permission. 'Take them a few roses from the garden, and don't be back too late,' was Anna Werneisen's only comment. 'It won't hurt the child to meet someone new for a change,' she said later, justifying her decision to her husband.

*

The play was a drawing-room comedy, with witty dialogue that went right over the heads of most of the audience. But Karin instinctively understood its subtle irony and *double-entendres*, and she loved the actors' elegant costumes. She wanted to be like them too.

She felt ashamed of her thin summer dress with its little white collar when she went to see her new friends after the show. They had been given the two best rooms in the inn.

'Oh, how sweet of you, my dear.' Nadja Horn came towards her with outstretched arms. She was wearing a flowing house dress. She had taken off her blonde wig, and was black-haired again. 'What lovely roses! Thank you so much. Did you like the play?'

'Oh yes, specially the scene where Verena van Bergen pretends not to have seen Armand for ages, even though he's waiting for her just next door.' Karin picked up a long cigarette-holder from the table and posed, her hand held at a casual angle. 'My dear, whatever are you thinking of? I'm about as interested in Armand as I am in Dr Dupont's dachshund. Or was it a Dobermann?' She'd captured Nadja Horn's tone of voice.

'Bravo!' Erik de Winter applauded. He had exchanged his evening dress for a silk dressing gown and a cravat, and looked captivating. 'A little champagne?' He poured some and handed Karin the glass.

It tickled her nose. Karin couldn't help sneezing. She laughed, not at all embarrassed. 'I never drank anything like this before.' She took another sip, without sneezing this time.

He raised his glass to her. 'I really like your village. Delightful people.' It sounded slightly patronizing.

And he doesn't even know the name of this dump, thought Nadja, putting the roses in a jug, since there was no vase available.

'It's not *my* village. I'm from Cuxhaven.'

Nadja sipped from her own glass. 'So you're visiting your family and helping out on the farm a little?'

'No, I've lived and worked here since Mutti died. But I'm soon going to Berlin.' She believed it as she said it. There was a determined set to her beautiful, full-lipped mouth.

Nadja Horn was observing the girl attentively. She heard her educated German, registered her natural, self-confident bearing. This was no naïve rustic, there was more to her than that. Erik had spotted it, and he was right. She rose to her feet. 'Come with me a moment, my dear. Erik darling, top up our glasses, would you?'

Karin followed her into the next room, where Nadja opened the two halves of a large wardrobe trunk containing a dozen evening dresses. She chose one and tossed it to Karin. 'Try that on.' Karin had never undressed in front of a strange woman, and went into the bathroom, but her hostess followed. She took off her thin summer dress. 'Good heavens, how frightful!' cried Nadja, horrified at the sight of the blue jersey knickers. 'Wait a moment.' She disappeared and came back with a pair of diaphanous camiknickers and other delicious items. 'Come on, child, you want to look pretty,' she enticed her. Karin overcame her shyness and took off her dismal underclothes.

Nadja saw a fully developed young woman with long, slim thighs and beautifully shaped breasts. 'Now, sit down in front of the mirror.' She undid Karin's plaits and brushed her hair until it fell to her shoulders in golden waves. Then she carefully pencilled in the line of the girl's eyebrows and added just a touch of lipstick. That regular young face with its perfect complexion needed nothing more.

'Now stand up.' A cool, fragrant mist of perfume from Nadja's atomizer surrounded her naked body, making her nipples erect. Nadja helped her with the suspender belt and silk stockings. The long dress rustled as Karin drew it over her shoulders and hips. A few hooks and eyes completed the operation. Everything fitted, including the high-heeled silver pumps. Enchanted, Nadja clapped her hands.

'You took your time,' Erik de Winter complained in good-humoured tones. Then he said no more, so overwhelmed was he by the blonde young woman in the close-fitting black evening dress, high-necked in front and plunging right down to her waist at the back. Incredulous, Karin realized that she had bowled him right over.

'Armand, where's that champagne? I'm dying of thirst,' she said, mimicking Nadja's lines from the second act, and she perched on the arm of a chair just like her model, ensuring that the slit in her skirt fell open all the way to her knee.

Erik regained his composure. 'Only if you'll dance with me, my love,' he quoted from his own lines, and wound up the gramophone.

Karin had seen him and Nadja dancing on stage. Now she just melted into his arms and they drifted over the creaking floorboards. She smelled his astringent eau-de-Cologne and felt the silk of his dressing gown. He felt her young body next to his and stopped thinking at all.

There was a knock. Theodor Alberti put his leonine head round the door. 'Come in, Theo. A glass of champagne?' Nadja asked the director in honeyed tones.

The monocle flashed. He looked Karin up and down with pleasure. 'So whom have we here, then? A charming new colleague, by any chance?'

Nadja Horn looked at her protégée. 'Maybe.'

Karin danced home over the cobblestones of the village street in an exuberant mood. Aunt Anna had left the door in the farmyard gate open. As she reached for the doorknob, a hand shot out of the dark and grabbed her arm. 'So you don't mind dancing with that actor fellow,' growled Hans Görke. She could smell the alcohol on his breath. 'You wait, he'll get what's coming to him.' He let her go and moved away, his footsteps heavy.

By the time she was in her bedroom she had forgotten this encounter. She took off her thin summer dress. Nadja Horn had made her a present of the undies. She went to bed in those delicate wisps of nothing, thought of Erik de Winter, and fell happily asleep.

The second and final performance was on Saturday. Görke had put his son under house arrest when Theodor Alberti told him of the young man's threats to a member of his company, and held out the prospect of 'measures that could be taken by the Reich Chamber of Culture. And then, my dear fellow, you'd be kicked out of the Party,' Alberti had said, exaggerating wildly.

So Erik de Winter remained unscathed, and the final performance was another great success. Erik didn't get to see Karin again. 'On Theo's orders,' Nadja told him. 'It's better this way, believe me. For now, anyway.' He thought he detected the hint of a promise in her voice.

On Sunday morning Nadja Horn called on the Werneisens. She was invited into the parlour and asked to sit on the sofa. The Werneisens sat opposite her, waiting to see what she wanted.

The actress came straight to the point. 'I'd like to take your niece to Berlin. Not at once, but next spring. She can stay at my place and keep house for me, and the job will leave her enough time for drama school. The Stage Employees' Co-Operative will send you my character reference.'

'Drama school? That's the idea, is it?' Werneisen repeated, suspicion in his voice.

'Karin doesn't belong in the cowshed, you know that as well as I do. She has talent, and it must be trained.' Acting on intuition, Nadja Horn turned to Anna Werneisen. 'Do please give her this chance.'

The farmer's wife was listening attentively. 'It's not that we want to put obstacles in Karin's way. But what about the expense?' she said.

'She'll have free board and lodging with me. That just leaves the question of the drama school fees.'

'She has a little money of her own that her mother left her. But it's really supposed to be for her trousseau.'

'And you want us to cough that up?' Werneisen narrowed his eyes. 'I dare say you think we're stupid peasants, but we're not *that* stupid.'

'A notary of your own choice would hold the money in trust, and make payments on Karin's behalf, having checked their validity. I assure you, Herr Werneisen, that *I* am not so stupid as to take responsibility for a young girl's money.'

The farmer looked at her in astonishment. 'Well, you're a one! Do we let our Karin go, Mother?' Anna Werneisen nodded. And so it was decided.

It was a long autumn for Karin, and a long winter. She didn't let anyone see her impatience, but worked harder than ever. She was even nice to Hans Görke, although she kept her distance.

Nadja Horn lived in an apartment on the Südwestkorso, where many artists had made their homes. From the window of her room, Karin had a view of the green Breitenbachplatz and its U-Bahn entrance, half-hidden by shrubs and spring flowers. She had been in Berlin for three weeks, and was finding her way around the capital with insatiable curiosity. The notary had allowed her a small budget for clothes, and some presents from her patron Nadja completed her wardrobe. The country girl was quickly turning into a chic young Berliner.

The Lore Bruck School of Drama in Kantstrasse was easily reached by the T-line bus. Nadja had registered her protégée in the beginners' class. 'All we do is breathing exercises until we're right out of puff,' Karin complained.

'You'll be playing Goethe's Gretchen soon enough,' Nadja consoled her.

'With Erik de Winter as Faust,' said Karin dreamily. 'We never hear from him these days.'

'He's making a movie with Josef von Baky on Rügen island.'

'Will he be away long?'

'You'll probably have to possess your soul in patience for a while. They've only just begun the location shots.' Nadja hesitated. 'I think it's time we talked. You're young and beautiful. You're going to meet a great many men, and they'll all try to get you into bed. Including Erik. I assume that as a country girl you know the facts of life?'

'You mean what happens when the cow's taken to the bull? Any child knows that.'

'Yes, but do you know the difference? The cow has no choice. You do. Choose your first man for love. And from then on choose wisely.'

At first Karin didn't understand what Nadja meant. Then she did, and her innermost being rejected the idea. There would be only one man for her, ever. Guessing her thoughts, Nadja smiled.

The beginners' class had fencing that July morning. Lore Bruck cultivated good relations with Heinrich Himmler, the Reichsführer SS, so a sports instructor from the Leibstandarte Adolf Hitler Division taught the aspiring actors. His name was Siegfried, and he was a blond giant who wielded his foil with astonishing ease and elegance. He stood behind Karin and guided her hand. Concentrating hard, she followed his movements. As she did so she pressed her buttocks back against him as if by chance. The other girls giggled. Siegfried blushed.

It was one of the little interludes she introduced into classes. Another was her imitation of Lore Bruck, which was so perfect that everyone fell about laughing. 'Karin, we can see that you have a certain gift for comedy,' her teacher remarked of these flights of fancy. 'All the same, I'd like you to be a little more serious. You can't fool about the whole time on stage.'

Lore Bruck was an ardent National Socialist. She had been in her prime at the German National Theatre in the 1920s, and in the days of the silent movies. The elegant actress of that period had now become a matronly figure who looked after her pupils like a mother hen. The young people adored her, and took all their troubles to her.

'Now I'll show you a tierce,' the fencing master told them. But no one took any notice. Lore Bruck had just come in with Erik de Winter. He was immediately surrounded by the drama students, who besieged him with questions and requests for autographs. He fended off their demands with great good humour. 'Ladies and gentlemen, you'll be the death of me!'

Karin stayed in the background, waiting for him to notice her. He disentangled himself from the group and came over. 'How are you, Karin?' he asked, his tone formal. 'Frau Bruck says you're making good progress.'

'Thanks, I'm fine,' she said, sounding wooden. Her heart was thudding.

'Karin, I'm told that Herr de Winter is a friend of your family,' said Lore Bruck. 'So just this once I'm giving you the rest of the day off.'

'How very kind of you, Lore.' He hugged her and winked at Karin. She relished the envious glances of the others as he took her hand and led her out of the rehearsal room. Down in the street, a cream Wanderer convertible with its hood down was waiting. He helped her into the car. Two passers-by recognized him and stopped. He waved to them, laughing, got behind the wheel and started the engine.

They drove down Kantstrasse to Masurenallee, past the Reich Radio building to Adolf-Hitler-Platz, gathering speed down Heerstrasse, Karin enjoying the warm wind. When they reached the Stössensee bridge they turned left into the Havelchaussee, which wound its way along beside the river.

At the Schildhorn he steered the convertible over to the side of the road and stopped. The resinous scent of pines rose from the Grunewald as it lay in the heat of the sun. White sails glinted on the water. Above them the stout little Odol advertising airship droned away. He leaned over and kissed her. To Karin, it was quite unexpected, and entirely different from the clumsy kisses of the boy next door back in Cuxhaven, or the stage kisses they were learning to exchange in class. Acting on instinct, she opened her lips and met his exploring tongue. Shudders ran through her body, converging on one point. It was like those times she'd touched herself in the field of rye, but much better.

He took her head between his hands. His voice was warm and full of tenderness. 'That's what I wanted to say to you.' Slowly, he drove on. She leaned her head against his shoulder. She was filled with an indescribable sense of happiness. He had put his right arm round her, and let the car cruise on in fourth gear. Only when the Havelchaussee was behind them did he push her gently aside and switch the engine off. 'Do you like *Aal Grün?*' he asked. Green eel? She had no idea what he meant.

On a restaurant terrace looking over the Wannsee, he ordered the local dish of eel with potatoes and chopped parsley, and a green sauce. They drank Mosel with it. 'Tastes delicious,' she said with her mouth full.

How young she is, he thought.

'What's it like acting in a movie?' she asked.

'Oh, a real test of patience. You sit around for hours in the studio until your moment comes. Then you say a few words to your opposite number — who often isn't even there — and the director makes you repeat it a dozen times until he's satisfied.'

'How do you mean, your opposite number isn't there? You mean away sick?'

He explained. 'You stand there speaking direct to the camera, as if it were your partner. And he or she does the same, answering the camera. Except that by then you're far away in the hairdresser's or somewhere. The director cuts the two takes together.'

'You mean apart,' she corrected him.

'No, together — the cinema has its own language.'

She got the idea. 'You see one actor speaking on screen and another actor answering because the director has stuck the two takes together.'

'Of course there are some takes where you see the whole scene with all the actors. Or the camera pans from side to side, from the top of the frame to the bottom, from a close-up to a long-distance shot, or vice versa. It depends on the screenplay. Do you understand?'

She thought about it. Finally she asked: 'Can I have some more eel?' She consumed her second helping with obvious relish. 'So the separate takes aren't particularly long?'

'When we're in full swing we may shoot for a few minutes on end.'

'And if you make a mistake you can just do it again. So nothing can go wrong.'

'You've seen through the trick of it. Would you like an ice for dessert?'

She would. It was extraordinarily erotic to watch the pink tip of her tongue licking the very last of the ice off her spoon. She ate it with rapt attention. 'Where are we going now?' she asked, ready for anything.

'To my place if you like. Or I can take you home if you'd rather.'

'To your place,' she said. Not for the world would she have parted from him now.

Erik de Winter lived in Lietzenburger Strasse, not far from the Kurfürstendamm. Karin marvelled at the bright, elegant rooms, with their Bauhaus furniture and *objets d'art*. She pointed at an oil painting of a woman. 'She looks rather odd, doesn't she?'

'That's a Pechstein,' he explained. 'Degenerate art, they call it these days. The Minister thinks I should hang the lady somewhere less conspicuous. He checks up on me now and then.'

'You know a minister?'

'Dr Joseph Goebbels, Reich Minister for Information and Propaganda. An interesting man who enjoys the company of movie people. He looks in here sometimes when things are getting him down at work. Come on, I'll show you the rest of the apartment.'

The large tiled tub sunk into the marble floor of the bathroom drew cries of delight. 'Oh, may I?' she asked.

He turned the taps on and poured fragrant bath essence into the water before leaving her alone. Karin undressed and climbed into the tub. Deliciously scented foam enveloped her. In high spirits, she squeezed the gigantic bath sponge over her head. 'Come on in, Erik!' she called.

He reappeared in a white dressing gown, carrying a tray with champagne and glasses. He put the tray down beside the tub and let the dressing gown fall to the floor. Not at all embarrassed, she looked up at him, scrutinized his powerful figure, and put her arms out to him. He joined her in the water and took her in his arms, caressing her breasts as he kissed her. She put her hand out to him, becoming bolder. He was aroused. 'Oh, how big you are!' she said naïvely.

He filled their glasses. She emptied hers in a single gulp, while he sipped. Then he took her by the waist and lifted her up on the edge of the tub. She cried out with pleasure as chilled champagne moistened her mount of Venus. Gently, he parted her thighs and buried his face in her sex. A heavenly feeling announced itself, grew stronger, hardly bearable until she reached orgasm.

He knelt down in front of her. 'Look,' he told her. 'I want you to see everything.' Carefully, he penetrated her, and the sight was so new and so exciting that she didn't even notice the pain.

Only when he had carried her from the bathroom to his bed, dripping wet, and had discreetly put on a condom did he let himself come too. He found an apt and willing pupil that sultry August afternoon in Berlin.

Twilight was falling. The scent of roses wafted in through the open window from the Olivaer Platz. A late blackbird sang. From far away came the first faint rumbling of a thunderstorm. Exhausted and happy, they lay side by side. Karin rolled over, propped her chin on his chest. 'Erik?'

'Yes, darling?'

'Erik — I want to be in the movies too.'

'Ladies, ladies. This is not a scene in Bedlam we're acting, this is a Prussian girls' boarding school. A little calm and discipline, please,' called Conrad Jung, the director. Jung was an energetic, grey-haired man of medium height in his forties. He clapped his hands. The young actresses sitting on the benches fell silent.

The man with the clapperboard stepped in front of the camera and trumpeted: '*Love and Duty*, scene eighty-six, take twenty, third shot!' He let the clapperboard sink. Slowly, the camera moved towards the school benches. Karin was sitting half-concealed in the second row, wearing an apron and wrapover dress in the style of 1914 and bending over her exercise book like the other girls. She slid to the left to get into the picture.

'Stop!' cried Jung in annoyance. 'You there in the second row!'

'My name is Karin Rembach, not "you there",' Karin answered.

'Stay where you are and keep looking at your exercise book, please, Fräulein Rembach. We're shooting for a full half-minute, in case you hadn't noticed.'

Karin rose to her feet. 'He didn't strike the clapperboard together, so I thought the camera wasn't rolling.'

'Sit down. Take, please.' Karin remained on her feet. 'What is it now?'

'Wouldn't it be a good idea for the schoolmistress to call me up in front of the class, and then as I stand up I point out of the window in surprise, because Captain von Stechow is riding up?'

'Well, well, did you all hear that? Fräulein Rembach has taken over as director.' Everyone laughed. 'Erik, you landed me with this natural talent, what do you think?'

Erik de Winter was standing to one side. He wasn't on camera for another two takes. He wore the uniform of a cavalry captain in the Yellow Lancers. 'Well, it's a fact, Kalle didn't strike the clapperboard. And I don't think Fräulein Rembach's suggestion is at all bad. You should try it, Conrad.'

'Very well, then let's do the thing properly. La Rembach doesn't just stand up, she tells us what she sees outside, so that we less gifted mortals will know what's going on. Perhaps our star will be good enough to compose her own speech?' He laid the sarcasm on as thick as sour cream.

Karin sat down, looked at her exercise book and then raised her head to look at the schoolmistress, who wasn't in the shot. 'Yes, Fräulein von Ilmen?' She rose to her feet, glanced at the window, looked to the front, realized in surprise who it was she had just seen, and turned her head to the window again. 'Fritz,' she said quietly, a trace of yearning in her voice, and corrected herself at once. 'Captain von Stechow.'

'Not bad,' Jung conceded. 'So why does this schoolgirl call the cavalry captain by his first name?'

'So the audience will guess that Ulrike's in love with him.'

'We'll shoot it again,' Conrad Jung decided.

'He called me "La Rembach",' said the delighted Karin at midday in the canteen.

'You impressed him, although he'll never admit it. You impressed me too. You were really good, no doubt about it.'

'If it wasn't for you I wouldn't be here in Babelsberg.' She raised Erik's

28

hand to her lips. Her moist tongue licked his palm, sending a thrill right through him.

'Conrad owed me a little favour.'

She dropped his hand. 'Is he a good director?'

'He learned his trade as assistant to Fritz Lang, and after Lang had left the country he made a name for himself making some battle movies at the UfA studios. Crowd scenes are his strong point, so he's highly thought of these days. His next project is a big historical film about Queen Louise.'

Karin took a hearty bite of her *bockwurst*. 'Who's playing the Queen?'

'They're thinking of La Hielscher, but she probably isn't Aryan enough for the Minister.'

'What's he like in private life?'

'Jung? A family man. Five children. Malicious tongues say he and Goebbels are in competition in that department.'

'Would you like to have children?'

'You need to be married for that.'

'Yes?'

'Listen, darling.' He avoided her question. 'I'm shooting with Willi Forst at the Rosenhügel. You and I won't see each other for a couple of months.'

'What, a whole couple of months? Then I don't mind if you find a girl among the extras in Vienna,' she joked, covering up her disappointment.

As they were passing the cutting room on the way back to the hall, they heard marching music blaring from the loudspeakers, which were usually kept silent so that sound recordings could go ahead. The German Army was on its way to Poland.

'Erik, do I look Aryan enough?' she asked.

He knew what she was getting at. 'You're as blonde as they come, tall and slim too – and very beautiful. But don't cherish false hopes. Conrad Jung doesn't cast beginners. You've a long way to go yet. Shall we meet this evening?'

He had found Karin a small apartment on the Hohenzollerndamm, on the corner of Mansfelder Strasse, where he visited her as often as he could. She cooked with enthusiasm, and he often stayed the night. But best of all were their love-feasts in his marble bathroom.

'No time,' she told him. She lay awake until long after midnight, thinking.

Nadja Horn echoed Erik in different words. 'Well, yes, you've tricked your way into this little speaking part. And I'll hand it to you, you did it very cleverly. But it doesn't make you an actress just like that. Finish drama school, learn the classic roles, and if you're good success will come of itself. So long as those brown goblins don't wreck everything first.' Nadja made no secret of her opinion of the National Socialists. She poured more tea. 'Are you happy with him, child?'

'He's the best man in the world. Nadja – what did Queen Louise look like?'

'Since when have you been so interested in history?'

'Since Conrad Jung started planning a movie about her.'

'Oh, don't start on about that again. Put it out of your mind.'

'Louise of Mecklenburg-Strelitz, wife of Frederick William III of Prussia. Born 1776. Mother of Frederick William IV and William I. Napoleon was greatly impressed by her noble bearing after his victory over Prussia.' Karin had been reading her up in the big Brockhaus encyclopaedia. 'She must have been very beautiful,' she said dreamily. 'She died when she was only thirty-six. I look older than I am, don't I?'

'What are you planning?'

Karin had thought it all out. 'Jung will be shooting *Love and Duty* for three more weeks. Then he'll be cutting the film. During that time he'll go home to his family on the Scharmützelsee only on Saturdays and Sundays. He'll be staying in town during the week. He has an apartment on Lehniner Platz, right behind the Comedians' Cabaret. I'm going to pay him a surprise visit there in the character of Louise. Will you help me, Nadja?'

'You're out of your mind.'

'But what could happen? He can only throw me out!'

Nadja Horn never drank sweet tea, but now she put sugar cube after sugar cube in her cup. After the sixth cube she burst into a peal of laughter. 'That's the craziest story of the year,' she gasped. 'Let's rope in Manon Arens,' she added, quietening down.

Manon Arens was a hunchbacked, elderly spinster who had been costume designer at the Schauspielhaus since time immemorial. 'An Empire line dress, pale blue trimmed with grey,' she decided, and found her visitors just the thing among the stock costumes, with all its accessories. 'Good luck, little one,' she chuckled, looking up at Karin, who towered above her.

Roland-Roland, star hairdresser at the Komische Oper, did the historic hairstyle and diadem. He paid a special visit to Nadja's apartment. He had not been let in on the secret. 'Have fun at your fancy dress party,' he said to Karin.

Nadja looked Karin over. 'You make an enchanting young queen,' she pronounced, as if sizing up a racehorse. She put a long black evening cloak around her protégée's shoulders. 'Karin Rembach doesn't suit you. You need a new name.'

'Verena van Bergen,' Karin suggested. 'Remember?'

'Of course I remember. Right, why not Verena van Bergen? It sounds Aryan and aristocratic. Just what those brown goblins like. Break a leg, my dear.'

A taxi drove Karin to Lehniner Platz. Conrad Jung opened his door, and didn't recognize his visitor. 'May I come in?' she asked.

'Who are you? What do you want?'

She put back the hood, let her cape fall to the floor, and stood straight and tall before him in her pale blue Empire dress. Her shining eyes rivalled the diadem in her hair. 'I ask it not for myself, Sire,' she said in a warm voice. 'I ask it for Prussia.'

He was amazed. Now he knew who she was. 'Karin Rembach, am I right?'

'Verena van Bergen from now on.'

He scrutinized her with admiration. 'Well staged, Verena van Bergen,' he said appreciatively. 'All the same — why should I give you the part?'

Karin undid a clasp. The dress sank to the floor. She was naked underneath it.

'This is why,' she said with a little smile.

'You're a quick learner. Congratulations on Queen Louise.' Erik de Winter had come back from Vienna to take a bow at the première of Conrad Jung's *Love and Duty* at the Gloria Palast. 'Shall we see each other after the showing?'

'I'm afraid not.' Some instinct warned her against going to the party after the première when both her old and her new lover would be there. 'I have an early-morning driving lesson. I've already ordered my car, a wonderful new convertible, black and yellow with spoked wheels. I still can't believe I can afford such things. Please don't be cross, Erik.'

'Another time, then.' He was a good loser.

She embraced him, her lips close to his ear. 'Thank you,' she whispered. 'Thank you for everything.'

'Take it easy, please, Fräulein Rembach. Let the clutch in slowly. That's right. Light pressure on the accelerator at the same time, treat it like a raw egg.'

The raw egg suggestion didn't quite work, for the driving school car shot abruptly forward and nearly mounted the pavement. Karin was clinging to the steering wheel, but not going straight ahead. The driving instructor calmly put things right. 'There, now take your right foot off the accelerator, left foot down on the clutch again. Keep the clutch pressed down. Now put the car into second gear the way we practised on the dummy model. No, don't look down. Look forward, the way you're going. Good, that's right. Left foot off the clutch, right foot down on the gas. Drive straight ahead. Now, the third and last gear. Clutch, change gear, accelerator.'

An architect called Speer had knocked a breach through the sea of buildings in West Berlin to lay out a street from the Brandenburg Gate to Adolf-Hitler-Platz. It was wide enough for marches, parades and thousands of spectators. This was the street where the driving instructor had chosen to practise. Karin rounded the Victory Column and made for the Brandenburg Gate. As long as she could concentrate on steering without the distractions of letting in the clutch and changing gear, she was all right.

'Well done,' said her fellow-pupil from the back seat. 'I'm Isabel Jordan,' she told Karin after the driving lesson. She was a slender, dark-blonde woman with grey eyes, taller than Karin and a few years older.

'And I'm Karin Rembach.'

'Your first lesson, wasn't it? I've had five already. My husband insists. He says he's tired of driving me to my dressmaker. But really he'd like me to drive him about so that he can study his files on the way to court. He's a lawyer, you see.' Isabel Jordan went on chatting cheerfully. 'What do you do, Fräulein Rembach?'

'I'm a movie actress. I've just ordered my first car.'

'Congratulations. My husband has lots of you movie people among his clients. There he is. Come on, we'll drive you home. Darling, this is Karin Rembach. She's an actress.'

'Verena van Bergen, surely?' Dr Rainer Jordan kissed Karin's hand. 'Conrad Jung's Queen Louise. You're the talk of Babelsberg.'

'It's my stage name,' Karin explained to her new acquaintance.

'So you're a real film star! When does work on the movie start?'

'Next week. Shooting will take almost a year.'

'If the Great Powers don't come to some agreement on Poland we'll be in the middle of a war by then,' Dr Jordan prophesied.

'Don't listen to him. He's a professional pessimist. You must come and have dinner with us some evening soon. I'll call you.'

A guttural voice with an accent that could have belonged to a suburban Viennese pimp issued from the radio set in the dressing room. 'There have been exchanges of fire since 5.45.' It was Friday, 1 September 1939. The German Army had marched into Poland.

'So now we're in the shit and no mistake.' Grethe Weiser turned off the radio. The director had given the popular actress the part of Countess Thann, a lady in waiting who told the young queen home truths in a down-to-earth Berlin accent. Karin liked her colleague. She didn't mince her words outside her role either.

'But after all the Poles have done to us . . . I mean, even *his* patience was bound to crack sometime.' Karin spoke in defence of the ruler of the Greater German Reich. Like most people in the country, she knew nothing about the SS men wearing Polish uniforms who had been ordered to attack the Reich transmitter at Gleiwitz near the Polish border, thus manufacturing the final pretext for a war that was inevitable anyway. Plus she was concentrating on her part far too hard to stop and think of such things. 'We'll have peace again in a few weeks' time.'

'That's what you think, sweetie. Once a guy like him gets a taste for something he's in no hurry to stop eating.' Grethe Weiser waved her powder puff, sending powder flying. 'Never mind that now. You and me, we're making a little movie like the good little Reich film folk we are. And I tell you something, sweetie, I don't mind spending a couple of months with you, I don't mind that one bit.'

'So this is our Queen Louise.' Karin noted the Rhineland accent, the admiring look in the intelligent brown eyes, the smooth dark hair, the high, slightly receding forehead, the charming smile that had been tested out on countless women. An immaculately cut, double-breasted suit and a touch of *Cuir de Russie* completed her host's appearance. Reich Minister Dr Joseph Goebbels was shorter than Karin, but in spite of his deformed foot moved quickly and with elegance. He poured champagne himself. This was a small, intimate party at the Minister's private cinema. Conrad Jung had brought his principal actors to see the preview of the movie. Ten months of strenuous shooting lay behind them.

'Thank you, Minister.' Karin accepted her glass.

That admiring look again. A little too appraising, she thought. 'Now, dear lady, come and sit next to me. I suppose you've seen our friend Jung's work already?'

'Only the odd scene on the cutting table.'

'Then this is a première for you too, and I can sense that your heart is beating faster. I can't wait. Shall we start?'

An adjutant in the brown Party uniform gave the signal. The wall lights went out. The UfA logo appeared on the screen, and the film began. It was a mixture of courtly splendour, impressive crowd scenes and touching episodes from the life of the young queen. Conrad Jung and his cameraman had given Karin the simple, neo-classical beauty of the real Queen Louise. Her scene with Napoleon, when she begged him to have pity on the people of her country, was the climax of the film. The music rose to a crescendo, and the lights came on again.

Karin kept her head bent as she waited in trepidation for the verdict that would make or break her. There was silence all around. No one dared say a word before the Minister had given his opinion. She glanced at her neighbour out of the corner of her eye. Goebbels picked up his glass, turned it thoughtfully back and forth by the stem and took a small sip, clearly enjoying the tension he was creating.

Finally he turned to her, raised his hands and applauded. 'A wonderful artistic achievement! My congratulations.' Everyone clapped. Karin breathed a sigh of relief. 'Verena van Bergen, I can see you have a great future before you.'

He kissed her hand, careful to meet her eyes. The attention he was paying her made her uncomfortable, but she hid it with a radiant smile. 'Thank you, Minister.'

'And let me congratulate you too, Conrad Jung, and everyone else involved. A great movie! We'll send it to the Biennale after the final victory. Now that we're in the second year of the war, and our soldiers are fighting in France, we can't expect them or the German people even to contemplate any idea of a French victory and a Prussian defeat. I'm sure you'll agree that such a thing would be treasonable.'

'Yes, indeed – quite right – how far-sighted . . .' They never stopped crawling to him.

'What do you think, Frau van Bergen?' There was an ironic twist to Goebbels' mouth.

'I think you should enter the film for Venice next year.'

An uneasy silence fell. Had she ventured to contradict this powerful man?

Goebbels raised his glass to her. 'Your very good health, my dear.' He had understood what she meant at once.

It was draughty in the kitchen. Two window panes had broken during the last air raid, and the cardboard in them was a poor substitute. Karin was grinding coffee. Erik had sent it, along with a pair of silk stockings. He was filming in Paris.

'I don't have any cream. And only one sugar cube,' she called.

'Not surprising now the war's in its fourth year.' Conrad Jung came out of the bathroom, dabbing the last of his shaving foam off his chin. 'Keep the sugar for the horse. You play a brave young estate owner whose husband is fighting at the Eastern Front while she's left at home to deal with Polish and Russian farm labourers, riff-raff who sabotage the harvest. The authors wanted you to die a heroic death at the end, but I changed it.'

'Oh, thank you, Conrad. I hate death scenes.'

'Goebbels wants you to play the part. You made a great impression on him as Louise, and he liked your last two films too. He hasn't forgotten you.'

'I'm touched.'

'I'll leave the screenplay with you. He'd like to discuss it with us some-time soon, but he's not expecting me to be able to come. He wants to sleep with you. You've not been added to his collection yet.'

'Am I supposed to feel insulted or flattered?' Karin poured coffee.

'It depends what you want.'

'How about you?' She spread a roll with honey for him.

'We haven't seen each other much recently. I'll be at home more often from now on. Lore's expecting our sixth. She's a wonderful wife. And you don't need me any more, you haven't for a long time. Of course we'll still be making movies together.' He went into the bedroom to get dressed. 'Whatever way you decide, it's up to you. Goebbels can do your career a great deal of good – so think about it.'

Nadja Horn was the only person Karin trusted. Nadja would know the right thing to do. Karin parked in Breitenbachplatz and walked the few steps to the Südwestkorso. The pressure of a bomb blast had knocked the front door of the building off its hinges. She climbed to the first floor and rang the bell. Nadja was in a negligée.

'You must forgive me arriving out of the blue. I need your advice,' said Karin.

'Come on in.' Splinters of glass sparkled on the ivory, matt-lacquered furniture in the drawing room. 'Frieda hasn't cleared up yet,' Nadja apologized. 'Another window gone. Even cardboard's in short supply. Would you like a sherry?' She always had some little luxury from pre-war days on hand.

'No, thank you. Listen to this.'

'So your lover Conrad Jung is not only leaving you, he's telling you who to sleep with,' Nadja Horn said dryly, summing up what she had just heard. 'Still, that's no reason to feel insulted. Don't forget why you went to bed with him in the first place.'

'You could put it a little more tactfully.'

'Be on your guard with Goebbels. He's short, he's ugly, and he's had a club foot from birth, though he makes out it's a war wound. He compensates for his inferiority complex by making new conquests. And since he's overlord of the movies too, he helps himself lavishly from the cast lists of the UfA, Terra and Tobis studios.'

'Nadja, what should I do?'

'I'd say avoid him, but don't dent his ego in the process. My friend Kurt Hoffmann is shooting a comedy in Prague. You'd be well out of the firing line there.'

'A comedy? I don't want to be in some stupid comedy, I want a dramatic, modern role.'

'As a blonde Germanic estate owner left to deal with the Eastern scum on her own, shooting down a few of those subhumans in cold blood?' Nadja had read the screenplay. 'The war's lost. You'll have to explain yourself later if you accept a tendentious part like that. Don't be silly. Go to Prague. I'll talk to Hoffmann.'

Karin heard a sound behind her and turned. Erik de Winter was standing in the bedroom doorway. He wore a dressing gown, and looked like one of his own drawing-room comedy characters.

'Erik?'

'I got back from Paris yesterday. General von Choltitz ordered it to be evacuated without a fight. So the most beautiful city in the world still stands. How are you, darling?' He drew her to him and gave her a kiss on the cheek. She smelled Nadja's perfume on his shoulder. All at once she knew that she was still in love with him.

'I didn't know you two had got together recently. Congratulations.'

'Recently? Did you hear that?' Nadja gave her husky stage laugh. 'We were a couple before you ever came along, my dear. With interruptions, I admit. Ultimately a change did us both good, isn't that so, Erik?' It was Nadja's little triumph over the younger woman.

'Well, I must go. Thanks for your advice, Nadja. And thank you very much for the parcel you sent, Erik.'

Her car wouldn't start. Karin tried the choke and the starter in vain. Like other outstanding figures in the world of the arts, she had the coveted red chevron on the number plate indicating that she was allowed to drive a motor vehicle.

'Hello, Fräulein, so the little miracle won't oblige!' A young man grinned at her. He was swinging himself nimbly along on two crutches; his left leg ended just below the hip. He wore a gold Wounded badge on his jacket. 'Let's have a look.' He opened the bonnet, rummaged about inside the engine and called, 'Try starting it now.'

The engine caught, chugging. Karin leaned out of the window. 'What was it?'

'Fuel connection worked loose. I tightened it up for now, but you'll have to get it seen to by a garage or it'll come off again. Hey, don't I know you? Yes, wait, I remember. You're Verena van Bergen. I've seen you in the movies.'

'Nice to be recognized! And what's your name?'

'Paul Kasischke.'

'Pleased to meet you, Herr Kasischke. Come on, get in. Where can I take you?'

'To my mother. She works with the cows.'

It was not far from Breitenbachplatz to Dahlem City Farm, a state property that had survived the merging of the village with the city of Berlin. Karin let the Number 40 tram pass, then turned into the farm and helped her passenger out of the car.

'Got a moment to spare? Ma would just love to meet someone from the movies.'

Karin followed him awkwardly. Her fashionable wedge heels made walking on the cobblestones difficult. It was easier in the cowshed. Six women looked up from the cows they were milking at the elegant apparition in a hat and silk stockings. She didn't fit this setting.

'Ma, this is Verena van Bergen. She gave me a lift and now she'd like to say hello to you.'

Karin offered her hand with unaffected good humour. 'Good day, Frau Kasischke. Your son has been most helpful. My car wouldn't start.'

Frau Kasischke looked her up and down. 'I've seen you in the pictures. Thanks for giving my boy a lift. He can't walk too well. They gave him a nice gold medal, though.' There was no missing the bitterness in her voice.

'I'm really sorry. If there's anything I can do to help . . .'

'Maybe the pretty lady from the movies can give us a hand with the milking?' joked one of the women.

'In her smart gloves,' said another.

'Here, hold these.' Karin stripped her gloves off and handed them to Frau Kasischke. Without any embarrassment, she hitched her dress up well above her knees and sat on the milking stool with her legs wide apart. A steady stream of milk gushed into the bucket.

'What do you know, she's one of us!' someone said, impressed.

Karin stood up. 'Goes to show how easily you can be mistaken, right? Good day, ladies, and many thanks, Herr Kasischke.' She turned the car and drove off. What would become of him after the war?

She heard Nadja saying, 'The war's lost.' Was she right? Should she go and make that comedy in Prague? Conrad's offer was tempting. She had a date with a photographer at three o'clock. There was time for a flying visit to Lore Bruck. A second, independent opinion wouldn't hurt.

'How nice of you to visit your old teacher.' Lore Bruck was touched. 'It's so quiet here now. All our young lovers and future character actors are at the Front. Imagine, Karin, Erwin Meinke from your class is a lieutenant-colonel now. And the girls have almost all been recruited for war work too. But your work is just as important. Now of all times we need actors who can personify the essence of the German nature.'

'That's why I'm here. I want your advice, Frau Bruck. The Minister would like me to take a dramatic role in a movie directed by Conrad Jung, as a German estate owner's wife. Nadja Horn thinks the war's already lost, and if I play a part like that it could count against me later. Would you give me your honest opinion?'

Lore Bruck laughed the warm, motherly laugh that had comforted a whole generation of students. She took Karin in her arms. Her generous bosom was warm. 'Oh dear, oh dear,' she sighed. 'Fancy my little girl facing such a dilemma!'

Just as quickly, she pushed Karin away again, crying, 'Let's open my last but one bottle of Rheinhessen and talk about old times. Do you remember how you always used to imitate me? Your impersonations were little masterpieces, though I didn't like to tell you so straight out.' Lore Bruck chuckled. 'I recognized your talent even then.'

They leafed through old albums full of press cuttings from Lore Bruck's days on stage. Karin pointed to the photograph of a striking male profile, inscribed to Lore. 'He looks interesting. Who is he?'

'A man called Max Goldmann. As a director he hid behind the Aryan name of Reinhardt. Went off to America some time ago.'

'About my question . . .' Karin reminded her old teacher as she left.

'It will all work out, I'm sure. Just follow your own instincts, my child.' Lore Bruck pushed her out of the door, and then hurried to the telephone.

*

A British air raid that went on for hours kept the tenants of Number 25 Hohenzollerndamm down in the cellar half the night. Karin was still fast asleep when her bell rang at eight in the morning. Two men in long, grey leather coats and felt hats were standing outside. *Geheime Staatspolizei.*

They showed their badges. 'Frau Karin Rembach, known as Verena van Bergen?'

'Yes?' An odd feeling came over her. She had heard of the Gestapo, as you might hear of a shadowy phantom. And now its envoys were at her door.

'May we come in?'

'You can see I'm not dressed yet. Can't you come back later? What's it about, anyway?'

'Urgent business. So if we may . . . ?'

Reluctantly, Karin let her visitors in. 'Please sit down. Excuse me for a few minutes.' She disappeared into the bathroom, and quickly dressed in the adjoining bedroom. 'There, I'm at your disposal now.'

'We must ask you to come with us,' said the elder of the two men.

'Why? Have I committed a crime?' She received no answer. 'I shall complain to Reich Minister Dr Goebbels.'

'That's up to you. Come with us, please.' Downstairs a black Mercedes was waiting, and took them to Prinz-Albrecht-Strasse. They went up flights of stairs, and along corridors with well-polished floors. A tall, double door opened. A young man with short, dark-brown hair rose from behind a large desk. He was wearing a well-cut, dove-grey uniform with a black collar and silver tabs, and elegant boots. 'Thank you so much for coming, Frau van Bergen. I am Standartenführer Hofner.' His accent was Bavarian. He clicked his heels as if he were in a Prussian officers' mess and kissed her hand. 'Please sit down, dear lady.'

Karin breathed again. This didn't sound like an arrest.

Hofner sat down at his desk again. 'I enjoyed your last film. We need something cheerful to help us relax in these difficult times.' He carefully drew a long-stemmed rose in a slender crystal vase closer to him. 'But we also need firm confidence and an iron will to victory. Those are the very words of Reichsführer Himmler, who called me this morning.' He breathed in the scent of the rose. 'It has been reported to him that the actress Nadja Horn gave it as her opinion that the war was lost. Can you confirm that Nadja Horn made such a comment to you?'

'Lore Bruck!' Karin exclaimed.

'Frau Bruck is an upright National Comrade and a good friend of the Reichsführer. There can be no doubting her word. Or yours either, I assume,

Frau van Bergen.' There was a dangerous undertone to the Standarten-führer's words.

Karin had bent her head. She said nothing. Hofner wasn't letting go. 'I put it to you that yesterday, in her apartment on Breitenbachplatz, Frau Nadja Horn said to you, word for word, "The war is lost".'

'Nadja Horn didn't mean it like that. It was just idle chatter. She hadn't thought about it, she was talking at random. That's how we actresses some-times are.'

The Standartenführer handed her a formal document. 'We have prepared your witness statement. Kindly read it and confirm its accuracy by signing.' Karin read the few typed lines. They were indeed accurate. 'The authorities concerned will consider your interpretation of Frau Horn's behaviour, to the effect that it was thoughtless rather than malicious,' added Hofner in a detached voice. Karin signed. Hofner countersigned the document, and put an official seal on it. 'Please wait a few minutes.' The Standartenführer left the room.

Karin thought of her friend and patron. This couldn't be too serious. Lively Sabine Sanders had got off with just a fright. At Theo Alberti's birth-day party, she had persuaded a make-up artist to stick a little moustache on her upper lip, and acted a take-off of Hitler that had everyone bent double with laughter. But someone had reported it to the Gestapo. The rising young actress had spent an uncomfortable half-hour with the police, and was reprimanded by the Reich Chamber of Cinema. Karin felt sure that Nadja would get no worse than a similar reprimand.

It was ages before Hofner came back. Once again, he was civility itself. 'We disturbed you very abruptly, I'm afraid. Please forgive us. May I invite you to breakfast at Borchardt's?'

'That's very kind of you, Herr Hofner, but unfortunately I have to go for some sound recordings in Babelsberg.' Karin forced a smile.

'I understand. Professional duties take precedence. My men will escort you home.' A kiss of her hand, a click of his heels, and she could go.

Back home, she went straight to the telephone to tell Nadja about Lore Bruck's infamous behaviour. The housekeeper answered, in great distress. 'They've taken Frau Horn away. Handcuffed like a criminal.'

Karin realized what had happened. Standartenführer Hofner had kept

41

her waiting so that she couldn't warn Nadja. 'Calm down, Frieda. It won't be as bad as all that.'

But how bad would it be? Karin fetched her car from the garage. Dr Jordan would know what to do.

Diggers were at work in Brandenburgische Strasse. 'A British air mine,' she was told. 'A four-engined Lancaster can't carry more than one of those things. They weigh about four tons.' The bomb had flattened three buildings. 'There wasn't so much as a little finger left of the folks down in the cellar,' the policeman on duty told her, diverting her along Konstanzer Strasse.

Jordan's legal chambers were on the first floor of a grand building in Lützowstrasse, which was still unscathed, other than by the impact of an anti-aircraft shell which had failed to explode at a height of three thousand metres.

'I'm afraid you don't have an appointment, Frau van Bergen. I'll see if I can fit you in.' The secretary spoke quietly into the intercom.

She had to wait quarter of an hour before the padded double doors opened. Jordan showed his visitor out. It was Heinrich George. Karin recognized her famous colleague at once. George shook hands with all the ladies in the outer office, including Karin herself. The great thespian had taken her for one of the typists.

'Frau van Bergen, how are you? Come in. I'm rather pressed for time, but how can I help you?'

Karin came straight to the point. 'Nadja Horn has been taken away by the Gestapo because of something silly she said. I'd never have thought that Lore Bruck would pass it on.'

'Lore Bruck and her friend Ida Wüst are the most notorious informers in the business,' said the lawyer, with scorn in his voice. 'Well, I'll undertake Nadja Horn's defence.'

'Her defence? Will such a silly thing come to court?'

'I'm afraid so.'

'Will she be fined?' Dr Jordan said nothing. An unpleasant presentiment formed in Karin's mind. 'Expulsion from the Reich Chamber of Cinema and a ban on practising her profession? No, they'd never dare. Nadja is very popular with the public. There'd be a storm of protest.' Jordan still said nothing. 'Surely not prison?'

'I shall call you as a witness to exonerate Frau Horn, Frau von Bergen.

But you won't be able to avoid giving evidence under oath.' The lawyer looked gravely at her. 'I can't hold out much hope. A remark like that is regarded as high treason.' He struggled for words. 'And the penalty for high treason is execution by the guillotine.'

*

'They come early in the morning, two wardresses, one warder. They don't need to wake you, you've been lying awake, night after night. The women help you into the smock, put the wooden clogs on your feet. The warder handcuffs you. Then they cut your hair off to leave your neck free. You walk down long corridors, past pale faces staring silently at you through the peep-holes in their cell doors.

'They lead you down a staircase into a basement, open a door, push you in front of a lectern. There's a burning candle and a crucifix on the lectern. Behind it you see the public prosecutor who demanded your life in court and now is going to get it. Beside him, your own lawyer and a lay assessor. Three men not involved in the case stand around the room in black suits. To your left there's a black curtain from ceiling to floor of the basement. You hardly notice it.

'You see the public prosecutor. He reads the verdict out to you again, you don't know why, you know it by now. You hear his final words: "Executioner, do your duty."

'The black curtain is hauled up. Bright light fills the white-tiled space behind it. You see the scaffold. It's smaller than you expected. One of the black-clad men takes hold of your ankles from behind, pulling your feet from under you. Another holds your hands behind your back. The third holds your upper arms and body. They drag you to the scaffold and push you forward over it, like a loaf of bread going into the oven. You look down into the basket which will soon catch your head. You feel the hard wood of the frame closing over your neck. The executioner pulls the cord. The guillotine falls. It falls for an eternity, and then finally brings you release.'

Karin raised her face, wet with tears. 'I didn't want that to happen,' she sobbed, shaken by convulsive weeping.

'Lore Bruck did. She had an old score to settle with Nadja. An everyday tale of jealousy.' Erik de Winter was lying beside Karin on the grass. 'I once had to attend an execution as lay assessor. I had to tell you what it's like, I couldn't spare you. Even if it happened nearly a year ago. You can't come to terms with something unless you know all about it.'

Alongside films designed to encourage the population to hold out, Goebbels had decreed light fare to divert their minds. Theodor Alberti was directing an amusing love story, *Springtime Games*, starring Karin and Erik. This warm, sunny spring of 1945 was ideal for location shots beside the river.

The rumble of guns from the East had been coming closer and closer these last few days. Since yesterday columns of German soldiers, gaunt figures, had been moving along the nearby road in the vague hope of reaching the Western lines on the other side of the Elbe. It would be better to be taken prisoner there than fall into Bolshevik hands.

'Go over to make-up and get your face repaired.' Erik helped her to her feet, but then immediately threw her to the ground. A low-flying Russian aircraft swooped past close above them, engines roaring. They heard the staccato tack-tack of its machine guns. Earth sprayed into the air around them. Then it was quiet again. A lark sang high in the sky against the distant thunder of the guns.

'All right, ladies and gentlemen,' called the director from the river bank. 'Come on, children, time to shoot the bathing scene.'

'Not with me, Theo,' called the chief cameraman from the slope.

'What's the matter, Erwin?'

The cameraman pointed to the opposite bank. 'Oh, nothing much, just a Russian tank on course for the Greater German movie industry. *Adios, amigos*, I'm off.' He settled his peaked cap firmly on his head and disappeared over the far side of the slope.

Now they could hear the drone of a diesel engine and the rattle of tank tracks. A T34 came slowly into view on the other side of the river. 'Come on, this way.' Erik rolled down the slope and dived into the reeds. Karin clutched her shoulder bag and followed him. She was wearing trousers, a sweater and stout shoes, because the screenplay had provided for a hiking scene before the river-bathing. She landed beside him. In single file, they waded knee-deep through the mud. They clambered back on land once they were past the next bend in the river.

Erik pointed to a hayrick. 'We'd better dry off a bit there before we go on. I have an aunt in Nauen. We can stay with her until the proud victors have finished running riot.'

'No, Erik, it'll be better if we part company.' She hugged him. 'See you at four-thirty after the war.'

Going by roundabout ways, Karin reached Berlin ahead of the Russians, and spent the final days of the war in the cellar with the other tenants of her building. When the firing finally died down outside, she picked up her small suitcase. 'Hey, where d'you think you're going?' snarled Herr Krapp. He was a Party member and air-raid warden, and very full of himself.

'Up to my apartment to celebrate the final victory,' she replied.

'Better stay here, Frau van Bergen,' Dr Seidel the dentist warned her.

'I've been hiding long enough.' Karin opened the cellar door.

'Nobody leaves this shelter without my permission,' barked Herr Krapp.

'Oh, shut your big mouth, Krapp, and you'd better take your helmet off,' Seidel said. 'Your headgear might give our liberators the wrong idea.'

She climbed the stairs to the second floor. Apart from a little damage caused by shell splinters, her apartment was intact. She went into the kitchen, where she could look down on the Hohenzollerndamm through a chink in the boards nailed over the window frame.

There were troops who looked like Mongolians in the street, with horse-drawn, tarpaulin-covered carts. The soldiers were shouting and pushing a naked young woman back and forth, and finally pulled her into one of the carts. One by one they clambered up under the tarpaulin. There were at least twenty men standing in line. The screams of their victim rose up to Karin. Then they turned to whimpering, and soon died away. You'll be next, she thought. Everything within her rebelled against this dreadful idea.

She remembered the chrome-plated pistol, a prop from one of her films, which Conrad Jung had given her at the première as a souvenir, with its magazine full. 'In case a bad man comes your way,' he had joked. She took the little weapon out of its hiding place and put it in the pocket of her track suit. She'd account for at least one attacker before she ended it all.

A dirty jeep braked sharply. The officer beside the driver rose to his feet and shouted an order. Reluctantly, the Asiatic soldiers obeyed. They climbed into their carts, cracking whips. The shaggy little horses moved slowly on. The raped woman was thrown out of one of the covered carts and landed in the road, where she lay with her limbs skewed awkwardly. Her vulva was nothing but bloody mush. The officer jumped out of the jeep, drew his pistol and signed to the two soldiers in the back seat to follow him. Bending low, he ran to the door of the building and disappeared from Karin's view.

The driver got out. He aimed his sub-machine gun at the naked, lifeless piece of humanity. The victim's body arched under the force of his salvo, and then collapsed.

Karin heard them searching the apartments. First the ground floor, then the first floor. All front doors had remained unlocked during air raids, to make fire-fighting easier, so there was nothing to bar the intruders' way.

Standing very straight, she waited for the three Russians in the doorway of her apartment, holding the small gun in her pocket. Instinctively, the officer raised his pistol. Very well, thought Karin, shrugging.

The soldiers pushed past her. Next moment they reappeared. One of them said something in guttural tones, obviously reporting that there was no one else in the apartment. The officer put his pistol in its holster. A brief command, and the soldiers went away.

Karin looked at the man opposite her. He was tall and lean, with grey eyes and a firm chin. He wore the clasp of some decoration on his dusty uniform tunic, and broad epaulettes. Closing the apartment door behind him, he took his helmet off, revealing a well-shaped head and wiry fair hair. He took a cigarette case out of his breast pocket.

'Like a cigarette?'

She didn't smoke, but this wasn't the moment to decline the offer. 'Yes, please.' She took one.

He gave her a light. 'The first few days will be the worst,' he said, apologetically. 'After that things will gradually calm down.'

'You speak German,' she cried in surprise, and coughed. She had only just registered his fluent, educated German.

'You're not used to smoking, I guess?' He laughed. 'We people from the Baltic speak many languages. Pure self-defence. I'm Major Maxim Petrovich Berkov.'

'Karin Rembach.'

'Nazi?'

'I'm an actress. I'm not a Party member, if that's what you mean.'

'We Russians like art and artists. Will you wait a moment? I have bread, sausage and vodka in the vehicle. Close the door behind me.'

46

When he came back she was wearing a lightweight if crumpled summer dress, much more suitable for this warm May day than her tracksuit. His glance penetrated the thin material. With an unexpected, quick movement he drew her close to him and raised the skirt of the dress. Then he had the little pistol in his hand. Karin had put it in the elastic waistband of her panties. 'Better this way, I think.' He smoothed her dress down again. '*Nasdrovye*.' He handed her the vodka bottle.

She drank only a little, but devoured the smoked sausage and coarse wholemeal bread. She hadn't had anything proper to eat for days.

'You'll stay with me,' he said suddenly. 'I like you.'

His decision matched her own wishes. She needed a protector, and this one had made a civilized impression on her. Karin was a realist. He could have taken her by force and then left her to his men. The question wasn't whether she wanted him but whether she could keep him long enough, until the worst was over.

'Come here, Maxim Petrovich.' Her voice promised him what he was waiting for.

It was a sensible arrangement, and the whole building profited by it, although some of the women sniffed in a superior way. The major was interpreter to General Bersarin, who had just been appointed city commandant. He stationed a tanker of drinking water and two guards outside the corner house of Karin's street. He brought food, which Karin shared with the other people in the building, and had glass put into the windows of her apartment. He was a passionate and a thoughtful lover.

On 1 July 1945 the Western Allies moved into Berlin. There was water in the mains again, although it was highly chlorinated, the transport system was more or less up and running, and the theatres were putting on more and better performances than they had for the last twelve years. The building on the Hohenzollerndamm on the corner of Mansfelder Strasse was now part of West Berlin. Maxim Petrovich Berkov did not come back.

The tribunal for artists of stage and screen met in a classroom. Its chairman was an old Communist whom the Russians had freed from a concentration camp. He tried hard to be objective, and listened to all Karin had to say.

'It is true that I made three films with Conrad Jung. *Queen Louise* was suppressed by Goebbels, *Midsummer Night* was a love story from a

Scandinavian novella, and *St Elmo's Fire* was the tragedy of a seaman's wife in the last century. Working with Jung was very important to me. He is a director of high standing.'

'Note that the defendant calls the maker of the propaganda film *The Wandering Jew* a director of high standing,' said the tribunal member on the left, a stout woman in her fifties, who disliked Karin for her youth and beauty.

'Did you act in that film?' asked the chairman.

'No, I was shooting a comedy in Prague at the time, and then a harmless love story for UfA, with Erik de Winter, directed by Theodor Alberti. The Russians interrupted our location shots on the banks of the Havel.'

'Thank you for your full account.' The chairman turned to the other members of the tribunal. 'The defendant's professional opinion of the director Conrad Jung and the fact that he made an anti-Semitic film should not influence our ruling.' He leafed through his papers before going on. 'Frau Rembach, we now come to a very grave charge.'

Karin bowed her head. She spoke in a low voice. 'My patron and friend Nadja Horn, to whom I owe everything, and whom I carelessly and unthinkingly destroyed.' She looked up. 'I did not intend to do it, Mr Chairman, but it will haunt me all my life.'

'Didn't intend to do it? That's an outright lie,' said the woman tribunal member. 'We have before us the text of your evidence, given in court, which sent Nadja Horn to her death.'

'But we also have the decision of the present public prosecutor's office,' said Dr Jordan. Karin had asked him to speak for her. 'The case against Frau Karin Rembach, known as Verena van Bergen, was dropped a few days ago. I myself heard Lore Bruck admit that she told the Gestapo about Verena van Bergen's thoughtless repetition to her of Nadja Horn's opinion that the war was lost. It was not Verena van Bergen who denounced Nadja Horn, but Lore Bruck. Unfortunately we can't call her to account for it now. She died in an air raid.'

'We're concerned here not with the criminal but with the human aspect of the case,' the stout woman insisted. 'The accused profited by her good relations with the Nazi regime and caused the death of a colleague, at least through negligence.'

'Is there anything else you would like to say about this, Frau van

Bergen?' Karin shook her head, hating the whole episode.

After a short consultation, the tribunal delivered its ruling: a three-year ban on working in her profession.

'And what am I going to live on meanwhile?' she challenged them.

'Try the Labour Office,' they suggested, indifferent to her plight.

The Labour Office had nothing for her, but a helpful official told her: 'If you happen to know a little English, the Yanks are looking for people to work for them.'

Her father had spoken English to her before he went to the Far East and never came back. That was twelve years earlier, but a little of it had stuck. 'I want work' sounded all right. There was a nameplate on the desk in front of her: CURTIS S. CHALFORD. The man behind the desk was friendly, in his thirties, with thinning fair hair, a round, rosy face, and pale-blue eyes. Mr Chalford was head of the German-American Employment Office in Lichterfelde.

Washington had advertised positions in occupied Germany. Applications came in from people all over the United States who were unemployed or hoped to improve their prospects – the adventurous, the curious, many emigrants. It was not always the *crème de la crème* who were sent off to the defeated enemy country without much in the way of examinations. They were all put in uniform, darker than an officer's US Army uniform but of the same cut, and with a triangular badge bearing the inscription US CIVILIAN on the upper left sleeve.

Mr Chalford was obviously one of the better sort. 'Well, Fräulein Rembach, let's see what we can do for you.' He opened a file and slowly turned the pages. 'Housekeeper for Major Kelly? Waitress at the Harnack House? Cleaning lady in the Telefunken Building?' He spoke German with a heavy American accent. 'No, all gone already.'

Curiously, Karin looked at the little black marble obelisk garlanded with barbed wire. 'A genuine Barlach,' explained Mr Chalford proudly, noticing her interest. 'Considered "degenerate art" by you people until recently. Spent the Hitler years in a pigeon loft. I managed to acquire it for a few cartons of Chesterfields. Now, about you, Fräulein Rembach. I think I have something for you. Our dry cleaners' shop at Uncle Tom's needs staff. Sergeant Chang will show you the ropes. A hundred and twenty marks a week, army food, half a CARE parcel a month. Girls who smile at the customers sometimes get given a few cigarettes too. OK?'

She didn't need to think about it long. Army food and the coveted foodstuffs from a CARE parcel made up her mind. Mr Chalford nodded, satisfied. 'Now, off you go to the photographer and for a medical examination. We don't want any TB or VD brought in.'

Sergeant Chang was a friendly Chinese man from San Francisco who tried in vain to initiate Karin into the mysteries of several dozen little bottles for treating fruit, wine, grass, grease and various other stains before the item of clothing was put into the big, chemical dry-cleaning machine. Karin got the tinctures hopelessly confused, and from then on Sergeant Chang employed her at the desk, taking in and returning the garments.

Mr Chalford's prediction had been correct – a smile often brought her chocolate or cigarettes from the customers. Some of them also wanted a date. Karin made her American boyfriend an excuse for declining. A young soldier in the Signal Corps was just what she needed. Dennis Morgan was a harmless boy from Connecticut. He invited her to Club 48 and gave her nylons and shoes from the PX. She had enough clothes; her wardrobe had survived the chaos. She was nice to Dennis, no more. He was satisfied with being envied by his friends for his beautiful German Fräulein.

Less agreeable was Otto Ziesel, the German driver from the motor pool who collected the garbage in an army truck and emptied the big garbage bins behind the shops. He wore GI clothes died black, and was a repulsive creature. He called Karin and the other women in the dry cleaners' Yankee floozies.

'Sooner a good strong Yank than a German wimp like you.' Karin's colleague Gerti Krüger was never at a loss for an answer. She had found herself a black sergeant, tall as a tree, from the Transport Division.

'You want your cunt burning out,' Ziesel spat.

One Tuesday morning in August, Sergeant Chang called Karin round behind the shop. The guard at the main gate was on the phone. There was a German there who insisted on speaking to her. 'Five minutes, no more,' Chang told his employee.

Erik de Winter was waiting at the gate. He had lost weight and wore a shabby suit, but his youthful laugh was still the same. 'Erik!' Shedding

50

tears, she ran to him, and they were in each other's arms. 'You're alive.' She could manage no more.

'The Russians let me go.' They had found him at his aunt's place in Nauen, and interned him in a camp for a while. 'The old lady in your apartment told me where to find you.'

'Fräulein Bahr. The Housing Office billeted her on me. It seems two rooms are too much for one person. What about you?'

Erik's apartment in Lietzenburger Strasse had been destroyed. 'A direct hit at the last minute. I'm staying with friends on Fasanenplatz. Fräulein Bahr says you've been banned from stage and screen work?'

'I'll tell you about it later. The sergeant only gave me five minutes.'

'Listen, my angel. The old UfA head of production is back. The Nazis chased him away, but Erich Pommer is back now as US film officer, and very powerful. We know each other well. He's invited me to dine with him this evening. I'll talk to him. I'm sure he'll get your ban lifted if I speak up for you.'

'Oh, Erik, that would be wonderful.'

'Come and see me after work tomorrow. Then I'll know more.' He wrote his new address down for her.

'See you tomorrow evening.' She embraced him passionately.

The military governor was expected. The army band's gala uniforms had to be cleaned. Sergeant Chang had told his staff to work a late shift. Karin helped to sort the items of clothing, and thought of Erik. He would be having dinner with his friend now. Tomorrow she'd know if he could do anything for her.

She was tired of cleaning clothes for the Americans. The cinema was her world. The studios in Babelsberg were up and running again. UfA was now known as DEFA. And a man from Poland was shooting his first production in a former poison-gas factory in Spandau. He had brought a case with him, full of dollars from heaven knew where, to finance it.

She was on the station platform in time to catch the last U-Bahn train. A couple of GIs and their girls were standing at the far end; the rest of the platform was in darkness. A figure emerged from behind the newspaper kiosk, long closed at this time of night. Why, she wondered in surprise, was he wearing a motorbike cap and protective goggles? Then a chain came around

51

her neck, clinking. She tried to scream, but the chain constricted her throat. Her attacker dragged her behind the kiosk as if she were livestock.

She flailed her arms helplessly. A barely audible rattle came from her throat. Avid fingers pulled up her dress, pulled down her panties. Burning pain tore her vulva. Her tormentor was gasping with excitement. With relief, she felt herself losing consciousness. Her last thought was: I hate death scenes.

CHAPTER TWO

INGE DIETRICH SERVED out breakfast: two thin slices of rye bread each. With it the family drank brownish ersatz coffee made from roasted chestnuts, with half a spoonful of powdered milk which refused to dissolve and floated on top of the coffee in little lumps. 'Funny, I thought we had more left,' she said in surprise as she cut the bread.

'That's the way with rations,' said her husband equably. 'Well, at least you boys get school dinners.'

'It's always bean soup,' complained Ralf.

'I had a real bit of bacon with the rind on it in mine the other day,' Ben said, glad that his mother wasn't pursuing the subject of the bread.

'Have you packed your school bags?'

'Sure. Come on.' Ben hauled his brother off his chair. He had decided to go to school today for a change. On Wednesday they had physical education, art and geography, which left gratifyingly little time for Latin and maths. Most important of all, the sixth lesson was religious instruction. He was going to turn the pathos on for Pastor Steffen. He urgently needed a New Testament.

Captain John Ashburner put down the piece of paper and leaned back in the chair at his desk. Outside his window, which had a view of Garystrasse, two adolescents were washing a few of the Military Police jeeps. Sergeant Donovan had come up with a practical method of recruiting youths for car-washing; he simply arrested a few of them for hanging about. 'Gives those damn Hitler Youth kids something sensible to do,' he announced, pleased with himself.

The captain went on reading. It was upsetting. The German inspector had kept his promise, and sent him not only the results of the autopsy but a translation too. Not particularly edifying reading. He thought of home, where these dreadful things didn't happen, where the worst you got was a straightforward murder because someone was jealous or drunk, and even that was a rare occurrence. He had been elected sheriff in Venice, Illinois for the fourth time when he had to report for army duty. But he hoped to be home again soon. Not that he was missing Ethel; she'd be fully occupied running the fan club of the local baseball team. What he liked was making sure folks in his county were law-abiding, going out and about talking to people, looking in at Bill's Bar for a quick coffee.

Donovan's jeep braked outside the door, squealing. The sergeant was a jerky driver, possibly because he was more used to handling bridle and reins back home on his ranch in Arizona. He got out and nodded to his passenger to follow him.

'Morgan, sir,' he announced a few moments later.

'Read that, sergeant.' Ashburner handed Donovan the autopsy report. Donovan read it, his expression grim. Ashburner turned to the young soldier. 'Dennis Morgan, Army Signal Corps, is that right?'

'Yes, sir.'

'You know a German Fräulein called Karin Rembach?'

'Yes, sir. Karin works in the dry cleaners' at Uncle Tom's.'

'Your girlfriend?'

'Yes, sir.' The young soldier continued standing to attention.

'Sit down, boy, sit down. Do you know why you're here?'

'No, sir.' Nervously, Morgan took a chair.

'When did you last see Karin?'

'Four days ago. We went to the movies.'

'Will you be seeing each other again soon?'

Dennis Morgan hesitated. 'Tomorrow, sir, I hope.'

The captain noticed the almost imperceptible hesitation. Was it the soldier's uncertainty at facing a superior officer? Or did he know that Karin Rembach was dead? That would be a very suspicious factor. Neither the military newspaper *Stars and Stripes* nor the military radio station AFN had reported the murder. The US Army media weren't interested in dead German girls, and it was unlikely that Morgan read the German papers.

Sergeant Donovan intervened. 'Your Karin's very pretty, eh?'

'Yes, sergeant, very.'

Donovan adopted a confidential tone. 'Good in bed, is she, Dennis?'

The young soldier blushed. 'I don't know, sergeant. I mean, yes, I guess so.'

'What do you mean, you don't know?' Donovan persisted.

'I meant to say I don't know what you mean by "good in bed", sergeant.'

'Because you're not sleeping with her. We know that from her colleague Gerti. Because she won't let you touch her. In spite of your invitations and gifts. Because that makes you disappointed and furious. Because you're afraid it might get out. A word from her would make you look ridiculous, right?'

'I don't know, sergeant.'

'Am I right?' bellowed Donovan.

Dennis Morgan bent his head. 'We're good friends,' he said quietly. 'Captain, what does all this mean? Why am I here?'

Sergeant Donovan took him by the shoulders. 'Because your Karin is dead.'

'Dead? Karin's not dead. We have a date tomorrow, see, it's at seven, we're meeting by the guard on the main gate in Uncle Tom's.' Morgan spoke fast, as if trying to convince himself.

Donovan shook him. 'She's dead. And you know why? Because someone murdered her. In the most brutal way. Who was it, Morgan? Who killed Karin?'

The young soldier was weeping soundlessly. 'Go easy, sergeant,' Ashburner told him. 'That's all, Morgan,' he said mildly. The GI jumped up and stood to attention. He saluted, tears running down his face, stiffly did an about-turn, and left. John Ashburner leaned back again, thoughtfully. 'He seemed genuinely shocked.'

'Or else he's putting on a cold-blooded act for us.'

'You think he killed her?'

'It's possible, sir. I checked his alibi. Morgan was on guard duty in McNair Barracks from 21 hours to 3 hours on Tuesday. Alone, by the back fence of the motor pool. He could easily have borrowed a car, and he'd have been back in plenty of time before the guard changed.'

'The question is whether he really did it. And why.'

'I see it this way, sir: she won't let him touch her. First he's disappointed, then he's furious, finally he starts to hate her. If he can't have her, then no one else will.'

'With all due respect to your home-grown psychology, Mike – that lad's probably as innocent as you or I.'

'Maybe, captain. And anyway, one Fräulein more or less, what's the difference? They all sleep around, and not just with our boys. Why wouldn't it have been a German?'

'Why not, indeed?' Ashburner agreed. 'Draw up a short report detailing Morgan's alibi and send it to that German inspector. And then we've done our bit. Let the German police figure it out.'

'Will do, sir.'

The captain rose to his feet. 'Don't know when I'll be back. You mind the shop here meanwhile.' He turned to go.

'Sir.' Sergeant Donovan indicated the white helmet and the holster with the heavy Magnum on the coat rack, but Ashburner shook his head and took his garrison cap instead.

Ben met Heidi Rödel as he was coming out of the U-Bahn. Heidi was sixteen. She wore sandals with home-made wedge heels and a blouse that her father had made her from the parachute of an English airman who had been shot down. Her breasts swelled gently under the silk. Ben kind of liked to look at them. Touching would have been even better, but presumably that was off limits. Though you couldn't ever be sure what was or wasn't off limits, not with girls.

She threw back her dark-brown hair with a brief toss of her head. 'The Yanks have opened a German youth club in Bruckstrasse. You can do hand-icrafts and painting there, and have debates, and they give you chocolate bars too.'

Someone in Washington had decreed that particular emphasis should be placed on bringing the joyful message of freedom and democracy to the young people of conquered Germany who had suffered under the Nazi regime. And since the US Army was on the spot already, and was success-fully Americanizing those quick learners the Germans with chewing gum, instant coffee and Bing Crosby – even if the first of those items was French, the second Swiss and the third of Irish origin – it fell to them to organize the matter.

There were plenty of requisitioned villas in excellent locations. Games, tools, musical instruments, anything else that might lure the youngsters in – the US Army, better equipped than any other outfit in the world, had all these things in abundance. Hence the rise of German Youth Activities, or GYA, with each branch of the service competing to set up the best GYA Club.

'Why don't we go along together?' Ben saw an opportunity.

'I already have a date with Gert Schlomm. He's started a drama group at the club, and I get to play the leading role.'

Ben couldn't compete with the leading role in a drama group, at least not until he outdid Gert Schlomm's lederhosen with his own made-to-measure suit in Prince of Wales check. 'Well, I may look in sometime,' he said, negotiating a tactical retreat. 'Although I'm pretty busy right now.'

Pastor Steffen had come up with a New Testament, exactly the India paper edition that Ben needed. He happily climbed the narrow stairs to the attic room. Ralf finished school an hour earlier and had gone round to his friend Hajo König in Onkel-Tom-Strasse, so the coast was clear.

Ben took the razor blade and the empty packet of Lucky Strikes from the desk drawer. The Yanks usually just tore off a piece of the silver foil to get at their cigarettes, so the outer packet and the seal remained intact, which was the case with this one. Using the blunt side of his penknife, he carefully levered up the bottom of the packet where it was stuck together and removed the silver paper without changing its shape. He put it back in the wrapping the other way up, pushing it up to the level of the seal.

Carefully, he placed the packet on the table. From the top, it looked virginal again. He opened the New Testament at the Gospel According to St Luke, and cut rectangles the size of the cigarette packet from the paper, going through no more than ten pages at a time.

Now he had to fill the packet to the right strength and elasticity, round off the long sides around the cigarettes it would appear to contain, and close it with a little glue. Ben weighed his successful piece of work in his hand, satisfied. When his brother came clumping upstairs, he put it in his pocket.

Ralf was two years younger than Ben. He had an angelic face, but it was deceptive. 'We're going up to the woods at Krumme Lanke tomorrow. Want to come?'

'What for?' Ben asked cautiously.

'Hajo knows a hollow in the ground where people go to screw.'

57

Ben decided to postpone putting his cigarette packet on the market until the day after tomorrow. 'OK,' he said magnanimously.

*

Jutta Weber rubbed dozens of veal schnitzels with garlic, seasoned them with salt and pepper and dusted them with flour, then dipped each in beaten egg and tossed it in breadcrumbs.

'Garlic, that's a good idea,' Mess Sergeant Jack Panelli said with approval, putting the breadcrumb-coated schnitzels in hot oil. They hissed violently.

'A real Wiener schnitzel should be fried in lard,' she told the chef.

'What, and have Major Davison thump me round the head with his Torah?' Major Davidson was the garrison rabbi; there were many soldiers of the Jewish faith here. Jack Panelli grinned. 'Now me, I'm a good Catholic, so you're welcome to make me a real Wiener schnitzel after the kitchen closes. That was a brilliant idea I had, taking you off dishwashing and putting you on the stove. Did I ever tell you you're a damn good cook?'

'Thanks for the compliment, Jack. My parents run a bar and café in Köpenick. They used to serve good home cooking there, and I often helped Mother in the kitchen.'

Jutta went on with her work. The soldiers came flocking into Club 48 for lunch. Last orders were around one-thirty. Then came the dishwashing, and next preparations for dinner, which took all afternoon. She automatically looked at her watch, but since the beginning of May it had been on the wrist of a pockmarked little Russian who hadn't raped her only because he'd failed to get an erection.

Sergeant Panelli noticed her glance. 'It's five o'clock.'

'Five o'clock . . .' Diana Gerold had said that when it was time for Jutta to make tea – Ceylon Orange Pekoe, a thing of the distant past the final year of the war, although now and then she got some from a woman she knew at the Swiss Embassy. Back then, they would sit in the back room of the bookshop in the shopping street, listening to the U-Bahn trains going in and out, while Frau Gerold talked about the new books she had read. There were fewer and fewer of them. Sometimes Jutta thought about Jochen, who was dead.

Jochen . . . A melancholy feeling came over her, but soon changed to business-like determination. She'd go and fetch him home. This was her evening off. A good opportunity.

As seven approached she took off her white overall, and slipped on the threadbare jacket that had once been part of an elegant tailored suit. She wore it now with a light, pale-blue summer dress that set off her slender brown legs prettily. She cycled the few minutes to Onkel Toms Hütte, and showed her pass to the sentry at the barrier. As a German employee of the US Army she had access to the prohibited area.

In the early thirties, a large real-estate company had built a rectangular housing project of two-storey, cast concrete apartments around the U-Bahn station. Schlieffenstrasse formed one of the two long sides of the rectangle. When completed, it was thought too small for the Kaiser's Field Marshal Schlieffen, so it was renamed for a comparatively unknown general called Wilski. She and Jochen had had the two-roomed, ground-floor apartment on the right. Number 47 Wilskistrasse. Today the whole block had been requisitioned.

Her name was still beside the bell: WEBER. She rang it. The automatic door opener buzzed. A tall, lanky American in shorts and T-shirt appeared at the door of the apartment. 'Hey, it's you,' he exclaimed, with pleasure. 'I'm John Ashburner, remember me?' Without his martial helmet and gun, he looked much more attractive than he had on their first, nocturnal meeting.

'Of course I remember you, captain. I'm Jutta Weber.'

'You came to see me?'

'Well, I didn't know you lived here. This used to be our apartment.'

'Sorry, not my fault. I hope you've found good accommodation somewhere else?'

'The housing department has given me a little room in Onkel-Tom-Strasse.'

'So what can I do for you?'

'I'd like to have the photo of my husband with his pupils. If it's still here I'd like to take it with me.'

'Come on in.'

The picture hung on the left beside the door to the balcony, a group photo in front of the Kaiser Wilhelm Tower in the Grunewald. 'The 1939 class outing. It was his last.'

'He was a schoolteacher?'

'Yes. There in the middle, that's him. He never came back from Poland. And that was Didi, one of his pupils.' She was about to add something, but decided against it.

Ashburner took the photograph down from the wall. 'I don't have any right to dispose of requisitioned property, but I'm sure the quartermaster won't mind. Cigarette?'

'No thanks, I don't smoke.'

'Would you like a couple of packets all the same?'

'Why?' she asked coldly.

'Because you're a pretty young woman.' He didn't hide his admiration.

'I told you, I don't smoke. And if that's meant as payment in advance for sex, then a couple of packets isn't enough.'

'Oh, don't be silly. I like you, that doesn't mean I'm about to rape you. I thought we might talk a little, that's all. How about a coffee?' Jutta hesitated. 'This building has six apartments. Most of the tenants are at home at this time of day, so you could easily call for help or jump out of the window. We're on the ground floor here, remember?'

She laughed because he kept such a straight face. 'Right, a coffee, then. And forgive my reaction. We Germans are over-sensitive these days, it's not easy to get on with us. We're full of self-pity. What did you want to talk to me about?'

'Oh, you and your life. I know almost nothing about the Germans.'

While he was boiling water in the kitchen Jutta looked around. The dining table was still there, and Jochen's armchair by the window. The rest was a motley collection of furniture confiscated from elsewhere. The picture over the sideboard showed a younger John Ashburner and an averagely pretty young woman.

'My wife Ethel. We've been married ten years.' The captain put a tray on the table bearing hot water, cups and a can of condensed milk. There were brown tinfoil one-cup sachets of Nescafé on a plate. 'Take two, that'll make it stronger,' he advised, but Jutta was happy with one. The condensed milk was thick and sweet, so there was no need for sugar. Her host opened an olive-coloured ration tin of biscuits. The lid came off with a sharp crack.

'What do you do?'

'I'm a bookseller. What about you? Have you always been a policeman?'

'Yes, but I'd rather have opened a little restaurant.' He had a dreamy look in his eyes. 'Red check tablecloths, candles in wine bottles on the table. Do you know, I inherited my great-great-grandma's cookbook — she came from Breslau. Tweak the recipes a bit and they'd be sensational today. The real old-fashioned stuff. People like that kind of thing.'

'So what came of your idea?'

'Nothing. Ethel was against it. She thought serving other people was beneath her.'

'Oh, I'm sorry, captain.'

'Just call me John. We Americans like to use first names.'

'OK, John then — and call me Jutta.'

He sipped his coffee and put the cup down. 'What was it like for you, Jutta, when Hitler came along?'

'We had to throw out a lot of books. Most people didn't notice because they didn't read anyway. Otherwise life went on as usual.' She didn't feel like explaining the last few years to him. He wouldn't have understood anyway. 'And then the war came.'

'The Nazis began it.'

'Could well be.'

'What were they like — the Nazis?'

'My father's brother was a PG.'

'What?' Ashburner didn't know the term.

'*Parteigenosse* — Party Comrade. And Uncle Rudi was no cannibal. A lot of people were in the NSDAP. Perfectly ordinary people. My husband was going to join the Party. He hoped it would get him promoted in the teaching profession faster.'

'What about those camps?'

'Look, if this is going to be an interrogation, you'd better ask how we liked your air raids. When you heard a rumbling overhead like a furniture van coming closer, you knew there was a plane almost right above you, and when the rumbling stopped you could only pray the bombs would land next door.'

'Must have been bad,' he conceded. 'Another coffee? Or would you rather have a whiskey?'

'Neither, thanks. Why are you so interested in us Germans?'

'Because you're one. Because you're so different from the women back home.' She felt a pleasant sensation which she tried in vain to suppress. He stood up, as if he was afraid he'd said too much. 'Where can I drive you?'

'I have my bike with me. It's not far. Thank you very much for the coffee. Shall we see each other again? I have Wednesday evenings off.'

He liked her directness. 'Seven o'clock beside the guard at the gate?' he suggested.

'OK, John.' She stood on tiptoe and gave him a kiss on the cheek.

The clock at the U-Bahn station said just before eleven. Jutta wondered whether to ride straight home, but decided to look in on the Schmidts for a moment. Herr Schmidt was usually up until after midnight. He was a pharmacist, and at the beginning of the war he had buried a crate full of bottles of *eau-de-parfum* in his cellar. Now he was gradually selling or bartering them. Six hungry children had to be fed. Jutta had wheedled a half-pound can of real coffee out of Jack Panelli. It didn't hurt the sergeant, and she got a bottle of genuine eau-de-Cologne in exchange.

The Schmidts lived on the other side of the prohibited area. It was drizzling slightly. Jutta pushed her bike along the tall fence. Behind it, the electricity was on day and night, people had well-fed faces, young women of the Women's Army Corps wore high-heeled pumps and unladdered stockings, and smoked in the street. She thought of lanky John Ashburner and wondered if she liked him enough to sleep with him, but came to no conclusion.

A motorbike started up nearby. She jumped back as it rattled past very close to her, headlight suddenly flaring on.

There was a roll of barbed wire propped against a post. It had probably been left over from building the fence. Jutta screamed. A woman's face, waxen and pale, was staring at her through the coiled wire with wide, dead eyes.

They ate a hot meal in the evening: dehydrated potato sticks from US supplies, you had to soak them for two days before you could cook them. With a roux made of a little flour and home-grown onions, the dish bore some distant resemblance to potato soup. The family sat around the table and spooned it up in silence.

Dr Bruno Hellbich tapped his spoon on the side of his plate with annoyance. 'The neighbours grow real potatoes. They have their own carrots too. And lettuces. Setting you all an example.'

'Papa, please don't be unfair. We're using every patch of earth in the garden to grow your tobacco,' Inge Dietrich reminded her father.

'I suppose you'd rather I went and sold the last little bit of our silver on the black market for a few Yank cigarettes?' asked the district councillor, indignant.

'You could smoke less,' suggested his son-in-law in neutral tones.

For a moment it looked as if they were in for one of Hellbich's furious tirades, which the family found ridiculous rather than terrifying, but his daughter changed the subject. 'Frau Zeidler was in Kalkfurth's, queuing for margarine. She keeps her bread coupons in the drawer of the kitchen table. When she pulled out the drawer the other day all that was left was a heap of tiny shreds of paper. A mouse had been at them. The month's ration for the whole family was gone. She didn't have much hope, but she put the remains in an envelope and took them to the head of the ration-card distribution centre. He laughed like a hyena and gave her replacement coupons straight away, saying he was sure no one would make up a thing like that.'

It was not a particularly funny story, but it mollified her father. 'Sensible man,' he said. The power went off, and he lit a candle.

'That Frau Kalkfurth is hard as nails.' His daughter told them about her attempt to get the powdered egg in advance.

'She's bitter. You can't blame her. Not a very lucky family, the Kalkfurths. They bought the Am Hegewinkel house in '29. It was a better place than the Prenzlauer Berg where their butcher's shop was. They had sausage stalls all over town. "Kalkfurth Sausages", that's how everyone knew them at the time. Not that success in business did them much good. An ox kicked Adalbert Kalkfurth in the belly when he was slaughtering it, tore his guts to pieces. Heinz Winkelmann carried on the business, with Kurt the son helping him. He was going to take it over some day. Big, strong lad with a baby face. Always chasing around the district on his motorbike. Volunteered for the Motorcycle Corps and was killed at the very beginning of the war in the Polish campaign. Martha Kalkfurth had a stroke when the news came, she's been in that wheelchair ever since. Any more potato soup?'

'Half a ladleful for everyone.' Inge Dietrich concentrated on dividing up what was left. She was thirty-six and had a few silver threads in her thick brown hair, mementoes of the countless nights she had sat in the cellar holding her sons close, listening to the deep hum of the aircraft and the sound of bombs dropping.

Her face glowed softly in the candlelight. How beautiful she is, thought Klaus. She smiled a little, as if she knew exactly what he was thinking.

The district councillor had finished. He rolled himself a cigarette with the tobacco that they dried green, and was thoughtful enough to go and smoke it in the garden. 'A lovely warm night,' he called. 'Come on out.'

'We're going up to bed,' his daughter called back. 'Goodnight, Father. Ben, Ralf, help Grandma clear away and don't stay up too long. Coming, Klaus?'

He picked up the dynamo lamp that was part of every household's equipment and lit the way upstairs. They undressed in silence. In spite of the slight drizzle, the night was light enough for him to see her figure – medium height, with breasts still firm and a slender waist above the feminine curves of her hips. He sat on the edge of the bed, undid his prosthesis, and put it aside together with its shoe and sock. She knelt in front of him and took him between her warm lips. Then they sank back on the bed. Their lovemaking was calm and satisfying.

The telephone rang in the middle of the night, its sound muted because Klaus Dietrich had wedged some cardboard between the bell and the beater so that it wouldn't wake Inge. Sergeant Franke was on the line. 'Another murder, sir. This time right up by the fence of the Yankee zone.'

'Where exactly?' Dietrich kept his voice low.

'Right at the back, where the weekly market used to be. I'll wait for you there. Over.'

He dressed quietly, but the prosthesis slipped from his hands and clattered to the floor. 'What is it, darling?' asked Inge sleepily.

'Business.' He fetched his bike from the veranda and cycled off. The direct way through the prohibited area was out of bounds to him, so he went the long way round, over Waltraudbrücke and through the Fischtal park. An owl hooted among the fir trees. A duck, waking early, quacked on the pond. The first hint of dawn shimmered in the east. It was infinitely quiet and peaceful.

Franke had parked the gas-powered Opel so that its headlights illuminated a place in the fence. A Military Police jeep stood slightly to one side, and Sergeant Donovan was leaning against it with his arms folded. The inspector parked his bike and nodded to him, but Donovan ignored him. Franke pointed to the fence. At first all Dietrich could make out was a roll of barbed wire. Then he saw its ghastly contents.

'Woman called Jutta Weber found the body,' his sergeant told him. 'Cycled to the Zehlendorf-Mitte police station to report it. I've asked her to come and see us this afternoon.'

Klaus Dietrich looked at the pale face, surrounded by strands of blonde hair. Lifeless blue eyes stared at him through the coils of wire. 'What do we know about her?' he asked, without turning round.

'Her name's Helga Lohmann, she's thirty-five and works for the Yanks. Her shopping bag, containing her pass and four cans of corned beef, was lying by the fence here.'

'Clues?'

'Maybe that rag?' Franke pointed to a piece of fabric caught in the barbed wire.

Dietrich took it from him and held it in the light to examine it. 'Olive-green gabardine. Could come from an American trench coat.'

A hand reached into the beam of the headlights and removed the fabric from his grasp. 'Confiscated,' said Sergeant Donovan, adding it in German. '*Beschlagnahmt.*' The word tripped off his tongue so fluently it was clear he'd used it many times before.

'But we need it as evidence,' Dietrich protested.

'Shut up, you goddam Kraut!' Donovan barked, and put his hand on his Magnum. Then he swung himself into his jeep and raced away, tyres squealing.

'What are we going to do with her?' asked Franke, a little helplessly.

Dietrich pointed to the luggage rack on the car roof. 'If we strap her firmly in place we can get her to Waldfrieden hospital in one piece.'

'It's all the same to the lady now,' muttered Franke, lending Dietrich a hand.

Dr Möbius set to work with the wire-cutters. 'And regards from the caretaker,' he said. 'The old boy wasn't best pleased when Nurse Dagmar woke him and asked to borrow these.' It was four in the morning. The power had been back on at the hospital for the last half-hour. 'All in the course of normal surgery,' said the doctor sarcastically, beginning to cut through the barbed wire. He bent back coil after coil until the dead woman lay exposed before them. She was wearing a simple, grey dress with a white collar. Her stockings were torn. With the nurse's help, he undressed her. The police officers stood back a little, the sergeant shifting uneasily from foot to foot. In spite of the surgical mask he wore, the smell of formalin and decomposition bothered him. 'No panties, just like the other one,' said Dr Möbius in matter-of-fact tones. 'Come closer, would you?' Only Dietrich came forward.

The dead woman was well built, with full breasts and stretch marks on her stomach. 'Strangulation marks from a chain on the throat again.' Möbius went on examining the body. 'Traces of blood in her pubic hair and on her thighs. The murderer tortured this victim with a sharp object too. Do we know who the woman is?'

'Helga Lohmann, aged thirty-five. Works for the Americans. That's all we have so far. When did death occur?'

'Subject to an autopsy, I'd say two to three hours ago.'

The inspector worked it out. 'Between ten and eleven, then. It was still raining at the time. That would explain the trench coat. What do you think, Franke?' But he received no answer. His colleague, green in the face, had collapsed on the floor.

HELGA

THE BUILDING WAS on the outskirts of the Onkel Toms Hütte, in Sophie-Charlotte-Strasse: six spacious apartments occupying the ground floor and the two floors above. Helga Lohmann had inherited it from her parents when they died on a skiing vacation, buried under an avalanche. The Lohmanns lived in the ground-floor apartment on the right, where Reinhard Lohmann also had his tax adviser's office. Down in the cellar he had set up a small-bore rifle range for his Sturmabteilung group. Once a week the sound of shots echoed through the apartment building. The attitude of its inhabitants to these SA Brownshirts, family men who were no longer as slim as they had been, was one of amused tolerance.

'Your husband doesn't care for target practice?' Helga asked her tenant, pretty black-haired Frau Salomon from the second floor, one Wednesday evening in the entrance hall. She learned from his wife that Leo Salomon was a good shot himself. He had often gone deer stalking with his late father, and so he had applied to join the Brownshirts' rifle squad.

'All our big boys like to play with guns, don't they?' said Helga cheerfully.

'They turned him down,' Frau Salomon confided. 'We're Jewish, you see.'

'Such nonsense,' said Helga firmly. 'I mean, you both go to church at Easter and Christmas, just like us, and you give to the Führer's Winter Aid fund. I'll have a word with my husband.'

'They're nice people, and they pay their rent on time. Herr Salomon's not a novice either. I mean, he often went shooting with his father,' Helga said to her husband at supper.

Reinhard Lohmann carefully put three slices of sausage on his bread and butter. He was a powerful man of thirty-six, with thinning hair and moles on his forearms. He had married Helga, a nurse ten years his junior, in 1930.

Until then Helga Rinke had worked on the children's ward of the Charité hospital, where she became pregnant by a doctor. Lohmann knew about it, but her ownership of the apartment building and the rental income it brought in promised security. He was not a particularly successful tax adviser.

'No, not Salomon, can't be done.' He put a fourth slice of sausage on his bread, although there was really no room for it. It hung over the edge.

'Why not? You could do with another good marksman for the next regional match, you said so yourself.'

'Yourself – yourself,' babbled little Karl, bringing his spoon down vigorously on his semolina, which his mother had decorated with swirls from a jug of raspberry syrup.

Karl was six. He had been born after the Lohmanns married, and Reinhard Lohmann had unhesitatingly acknowledged him as his son. That was before the baby showed signs of mongolism: a large round head, slanting eyes, small, podgy, deep-set ears, a flat nose and a thick tongue. After that Lohmann avoided being seen with the boy in public.

To Helga, her son was the most normal child in the world. She simply ignored stares or tactless remarks, and there were not many of those in her small world between the U-Bahn station and the Riemeister Eck. People had long ago become used to the child's looks, and they liked his blonde young mother.

'Why not?' Helga repeated, mopping a few splashes of semolina off the waxcloth table cover beside Karl's plate. 'Eat properly,' she told her son.

'I did try to recruit Salomon,' Lohmann defended himself. 'But there was a query from higher up – was I crazy, trying to sneak a Yid into our ranks?'

'You mustn't call him that – he's a good German citizen. You should have a word with your school friend Olbrich.'

Günther Olbrich and Reinhard Lohmann had both volunteered for the army in the last year of the Great War, while they were still at school. They never got as far as the Front, and were soon sent home to take their school-leaving exams. Olbrich studied law and became a legal adviser to the National Socialist party. After Hitler came to power, the Party leadership appointed him head of the legal department in the administrative region of the Berlin Gauleitung. He had excellent connections with senior Party members, and had even once been a guest at the Obersalzberg.

Lohmann joined the Party as soon as the Nazis won their electoral victory, hoping for professional advantages which somehow never came his way. With his friend's help, he made it to Deputy Sturmführer in 'that comic band of warriors,' as Helga called the SA, but such a position was hardly a profitable career.

He changed the subject. 'Günther's given us two tickets for the Olympic Games. We could get the car out on Saturday.' Helga had inherited the Brennabor along with her parents' apartment building, but she got behind the wheel only when Reinhard insisted. He couldn't drive.

Helga was radiant. 'Oh yes, let's take a picnic. We can leave Karl with the Salomons. He'd be happy, wouldn't you, Karl? You like little Ruth.'

'Little Ruth,' the boy echoed her. His eyes shone.

They drove out to the Reich Sports Stadium on Saturday morning. Beautiful weather contributed to the festive mood. Everyone seemed happy and care-free. Several swastika banners fluttered in the summer breeze, but the flags of the guest countries were in the majority, and the scene was dominated by the elegantly clad ladies of Berlin rather than brown uniforms.

The newly built stadium was an impressive architectural achievement. 'This really shows the world what we can do!' said Helga, focusing her grandmother's opera glasses on the government grandstand. She saw the Führer, in good spirits and wearing his white uniform jacket, and Göring gesticulating with animation, his round face gleaming in the sun. She could identify Hess, the Deputy Party leader, by his thick eyebrows. The other Nazi grandees were unknown to her.

She looked down at the arena. 'That American, Jesse Owens – doesn't he look just fabulous? Such a lovely brown. Wow, they're off! See how fast he runs! Yes, yes, yeeees! He won!' She jumped up in delight.

'If our colonies hadn't been stolen from us it'd be a German black winning the medals now,' muttered Lohmann in annoyance.

Helga opened the picnic basket. 'Like a sausage sandwich and a beer? The bottles should still be cold. I wrapped them in the *Morgenpost* down in the cellar.'

'Do we get a beer too?' It was Günther Olbrich. He introduced his companion. 'Meet Ulla Seitz.' The young woman with the dark bob greeted them with some reserve. 'Have we missed much?'

'The hundred metres,' said Lohmann, pouring the beer. 'You're late.'

'Couldn't make it any earlier,' explained his friend. 'A final fitting at my tailor's. White tie and tails are compulsory at the Staatsoper tonight. The Reich Government is giving a reception for the Games. The King of Bulgaria and the Crown Prince of Italy will be there – think of that!'

'What colour is your evening dress?' Helga asked Ulla Seitz with interest. The question earned her a nasty look and the sharp answer, 'I'm not invited.'

'You could have been a bit more tactful,' her husband reprimanded her when they were home. 'Ulla Seitz is Olbrich's secretary and his mistress.' They were listening to the latest results of the games on the radio. Helga had fetched her son from the Salomons on the top floor, and he was nestling close to her, listening open-mouthed to the words he didn't understand coming from the Bakelite box. Now and then he gurgled happily. Automatically, she wiped the dribble from his lips.

Lohmann was making notes with a pencil. 'If this goes on we'll have more gold medals than the Americans.' Karl moved away from his mother to clamber up on his father's lap, but Lohmann pushed him away. 'Time to go to sleep,' he said brusquely.

'If only you could love him,' Helga sighed later in bed.

On 10 May 1940 German troops marched into Holland, Belgium and Luxembourg, Winston Churchill became Prime Minister of Great Britain, and the German authorities in occupied Poland sent the first prisoners to a new camp called Auschwitz. The war was nine months old, and it was Karl's tenth birthday.

In the morning, mother and son went to the shopping street near the Onkel Toms Hütte U-Bahn station. Helga was making for Frau Gerold's bookshop. She sometimes went there to borrow a book from its lending library department.

'I think I have something for you – you like historical novels, don't you?' The bookseller's assistant took a large tome off the shelves. 'Try this – *The Queen's Physician*. The story of Dr Johannes Angelus Weiss, physician to Queen Christine of Prussia, Frederick the Great's wife. Very exciting, lots of love interest.'

'Yes, thanks, I'll borrow it.' Helga smiled shyly. 'We've been meeting here for years, haven't we? And I don't even know your name.'

'Jutta Weber. And you're Frau Lohmann, aren't you? Your name's in the card index. You can keep the book for three weeks without extra charge because it's so long. And what do *you* like to read?' Jutta Weber stroked the boy's bulky head. She had known him since he was in his pram, and was used to the way he looked.

'It's Karl's birthday, so I brought him to choose something for himself.'

'Happy birthday, Karl.'

Karl gurgled, and stuck the Walt Disney version of *The Three Little Pigs* under his arm.

They had a birthday party in the afternoon. Helga made coffee, and milky cocoa for Karl. She lit the ten candles round the birthday cake, and Karl enthusiastically blew them out. 'Again!' he demanded. Helga humoured him and lit them again.

'And now for some shooting.' Reinhard Lohmann had bought his son a simple airgun. They took it down to the cellar. After a little instruction Karl, shrieking with delight, handled the gun with unexpected skill. He had been making a certain amount of progress since he started at a special school. The lead projectiles were shaped like tiny hourglasses and struck the tin target with a dry click. Lohmann took the airgun and immediately hit the bull's-eye, but Karl scored an eight. There was more of a bond between father and son than ever before.

'Come on up, you two!' Helga was waiting impatiently. 'Now for Mama's present.' She took Karl into the bedroom, and ten minutes later they reappeared, Karl in black shorts and a brown shirt, with a belt, shoulder straps and a cravat. It was a uniform copied from the Boy Scouts, and was worn by the Hitler Youth boys aged ten to fourteen, who were known officially as the *Jungvolk* and affectionately as Pimpfs, 'little squirts'. Karl looked grotesque.

At first Lohmann was speechless. Then he managed to utter a strangulated, 'Out of the question.'

'What's out of the question?' asked Helga defiantly. 'They all join the *Jungvolk* at ten. I want our son to join in and be a Pimpf like everyone else.'

'Join in!' Karl said eagerly, grimacing because he couldn't control his facial muscles. 'Pimpf,' he added.

'Think of his condition,' said Lohmann, trying again.

'He's strong and healthy. Come on, Karl, let's blow those candles out again. And on Monday we'll go and register you with the *Jungvolk*.'

Lohmann disappeared into his office without another word. When Helga went to ring her sister, she heard his voice on the phone: '. . . got up as a Pimpf, would you believe it? That little monster will make us a laughing stock.'

'No, no, of course that won't do,' Günther Olbrich agreed. 'We'll find some solution, don't you worry.'

She quietly put the phone down. He *will* be a Pimpf, she thought.

On Saturday Helga Lohmann visited her sister, who was pregnant and in her ninth month. She stayed overnight and went home on Sunday afternoon. Reinhard was waiting for her. He had Günther Olbrich with him.

'Dr Olbrich, how nice! I'll make coffee. Would you like a piece of birthday cake? Where's Karl?'

'That's what we want to talk to you about.' Olbrich cleared his throat. 'You see, your husband has volunteered for an officers' training course. After completing it he'll be commissioned and go to the Front as a lieutenant, so he decided that Karl would be better off in a home than here with only one parent.'

'Lieutenant Lohmann – that sounds fabulous!' Helga said happily. 'You'll look really dashing in an officer's uniform! And you don't have to worry about me and our boy.' Then the full meaning of Olbrich's words dawned on her. 'You surely haven't . . . I mean, Karl isn't . . . ?'

'He's been in the home since yesterday. Believe me, it's for the best,' murmured Lohmann.

'What kind of home? I'm going to fetch him back at once.'

'I'm afraid that's not possible without his father's permission,' Olbrich said. 'And in view of the medical records, his father has made a sensible decision.'

'He's not Karl's father!' she screamed. 'He's a useless failure living on my money. Show your friend the account books, Reinhard, show him how little you earn. Decision? What kind of decision? Since when did you make the decisions?'

Lohmann rose to his feet. 'We must go now. Günther's driving me to

Döberitz. After the course I'll be home on short leave. We can talk it over then.' He picked up his suitcase. He had planned it all down to the last detail, and now he was running away to avoid an argument.

'You coward!' she shouted after him. 'Where's my son?' Her cries echoed through the stairway of the building until her voice grew fainter, and at last all she could do was weep inconsolably.

The Salomons were taken away on Monday, in an open flatbed truck with some twenty other people crowded together inside it. Herr Salomon had his arms protectively around his wife and child. He wore the Iron Cross First Class on his jacket, and his face was set like stone. Frau Salomon had her eyes lowered, as if she felt ashamed. Little Ruth waved. Helga waved back, indifferent. Only a few days ago she would have protested vehemently against such injustice, she would have said she'd write to the Führer about it. Now all her thoughts were for her son who had been taken away from her.

She sat down and dialled the next number in the phone book. An impersonal female voice answered, listened briefly, and then said what Helga had already heard a dozen times that morning: they had no ten-year-old called Karl Lohmann in that establishment.

'This isn't getting us anywhere,' she murmured, and looked up the District Court. The District Court passed her on to the Family Court, where they listened to her patiently and put her through to the judge who dealt with such cases. He said, in reserved tones, 'When the father of the child has consulted a senior Party authority, and that authority has approved his decision, then under our new guidelines, that decision replaces all other legal factors affecting the child's commitment and admission to an institution.'

'You mean that as his mother I don't have any say?'

'You'd better talk to your husband, Frau Lohmann. Try to persuade him to change his mind. Bear in mind, above all, that he can tell you where your son is. Then at least you can visit.'

That was it! She'd speak to Reinhard. He would cave in at once without Olbrich's support. An hour later she was on the S-Bahn train to Döberitz, where she made her way to the officers' training course.

'Lady called Helga Lohmann,' the guard on duty at the camp gates announced by phone. 'Wants to see Reinhard Lohmann, an officer cadet on the training course.'

Soldiers dressed in heavy cotton drill were doing pointless exercises among the huts, with an NCO shouting at them. Was Reinhard there? She couldn't make out the faces. A young officer hurried up to her. 'I'm Lieutenant Hartlieb. Please come this way. Colonel Marquardt is in his office.'

The colonel was a grey-haired man in his fifties. 'We didn't expect you quite so soon, Frau Lohmann.'

'You were expecting me?' Helga was puzzled.

'Didn't our messenger reach you?' It was the colonel's turn to seem baffled. 'Well, never mind. My deepest sympathy, dear lady. A dreadful accident, and on the very first day of the course.'

An exploding gun barrel had shot away half of Officer Cadet Reinhard Lohmann's head during target practice.

'They sent us rifles captured from the Poles for training purposes. Poor quality arms. Your husband would have made a good officer. Of course we'll give him a military funeral. Again, let me express my condolences. If there's anything else I can do for you . . . ?'

Helga shook her head in silence. Relieved, the colonel escorted her out.

On the way home she sat alone at the very back of the S-Bahn train. She imagined Reinhard's face before her, young and laughing, the way he was when she first met him. But the grief would not come. Her only thought was, now he can't tell me where Karl is.

One person could tell her, though. Helga Lohmann hoped to see him at Reinhard's funeral, but Reinhard's old school friend preferred to send a large wreath and a note of condolence on hand-made, deckle-edged paper. He had Party business in Munich, he explained in an accompanying note. On the day of his return she went straight to see him.

National Socialist Legal Adviser Dr Günther Olbrich was in the Berlin Gauleitung offices in Hermann-Göring-Strasse. Helga gave her name to the doorman, and was sent to a first-floor waiting room furnished with comfortable, upholstered chairs.

When the door of the adjoining office finally opened a half-hour later, she leaped hopefully to her feet. It was Olbrich's secretary. She had lost weight, and there was a hard set to her mouth. He's dumped her, thought Helga.

'Fräulein Seitz, am I right? Helga Lohmann – we met at the Olympics, remember? Goodness me, that's nearly five years ago. How are you?'

The secretary's manner remained cool. 'My condolences. I know Dr Olbrich has already sent you his. He asks you to forgive him – he can't spare any time at the moment.'

'Never mind. I can wait.'

'As you like.' A cold glance, and Ulla Seitz disappeared into the office next door.

Endless waiting. She played mind games. Was the farmer in the oil painting behind her sowing seed with his right hand and putting his left foot forward, as she thought? She turned to check. He wasn't sowing seed at all but scything wheat. Remembering what was in pictures, a game she often played with Karl. Dr Weiland, their old family GP, had recommended it. 'Good memory practice for the boy.'

She could see Karl before her, hands over his eyes, guessing what was in the reproduction of Rembrandt's *Man in the Golden Helmet* that hung over the sideboard. 'He's got – got a green hat with a feather in it, 'n there's a – a sparrow sittin' on it, 'n the sparrow – the sparrow got a choccy in its beak.'

'Really?' she used to ask in mock amazement. And he would laugh and laugh, because he'd managed to lead her up the garden path. She couldn't help smiling. Then reality came over her again like a cold shower. They'd taken her Karl away from her.

Her watch showed five o'clock. Had she dozed off? Had Dr Olbrich called for her? Hesitantly, she opened the door of the office. Ulla Seitz was putting on lipstick in front of the mirror. 'The office is closed.'

'Dr Olbrich?'

'Gone home. He's had a very stressful day. Come back tomorrow.'

She was there just before nine next morning and intercepted him at the entrance. He stopped for a moment. 'Frau Lohmann, what a terrible accident. I really am so sorry.'

'Please tell me where my son is.'

'I'm in a hurry. The Gauleiter's expecting me. Get my secretary to make you an appointment.' And he got into the lift.

She went slowly upstairs. Ulla Seitz was just pouring tea. 'Would you like a cup?'

'No, thank you. I'm supposed to ask you to make me an appointment. I don't need an appointment. I want Dr Olbrich to be good enough to tell you where they've taken my son, and then I want you to tell me. I have to find him. He's so helpless without me.'

'I don't know that I can help you.' Yesterday's chilly tone was back in her voice.

Helga bent her head. She said, quietly, 'It grows inside you, you see, and you're so happy when it begins to kick in the womb. You just can't wait for it to arrive. And at last there it is. Your own baby. The most beautiful baby in the world, even if he isn't the same as all the others. You love your child, you'd do anything in the world for him. He needs you, just as you need him, but they take him away from you.' She raised her head and sought the secretary's eyes. 'You don't know what it's like – everything's suddenly so empty.'

Ulla Seitz was not evasive this time. 'Empty,' she repeated bitterly. 'So empty.' She paused for a moment. 'He made me have an abortion. Surely I must understand that a man in his position couldn't have a pregnant secretary. Oh yes, I understood. Most of all I understood that he wanted someone younger. She's eighteen and works on the switchboard. A pretty, naïve little thing. In return I keep my position of trust, with a good salary and pension. Your son is in Klein Moorbach hospital. It's a private mental hospital with a department for children who don't fit in with today's ideas. Be careful. You won't get anywhere as a mother wanting her child back. One wrong step and you'll never see your son again.'

'Thank you.' Helga reached for her hand, but Ulla Seitz drew back, and spoke in a loud voice. 'Dr Olbrich is a very busy man. Please don't come here any more. I suggest you write to him.' Olbrich had entered the room.

Klein Moorbach was a remote hamlet on the borders of the Spreewald. Helga had brought her old bicycle on the train with her. She cycled along country roads. Bright-green birch trees, larks in the blue sky, flowery meadows – and on the path through the fields a tractor noisily spreading its stink of diesel. She took no notice of this springtime idyll. As camouflage, she had brought her easel and painting things with her. Helga had a moderate talent for water colours.

She went into the Klein Moorbach village inn. On the radio, fanfares prepared listeners for a momentous announcement: France had surrendered.

The men sitting at the tables raised their heads. 'Whole damn thing'll soon be over, then,' said one of them.

A smell of vegetables freshly cooked in butter and fried meat came from the kitchen. 'Meat loaf,' the plump landlady told the new arrival. 'You'll need to let me have meat coupons, fifty grams' worth.'

'Hey, Frieda, don't you mean bread coupons?' called a farm worker from the bar. The men laughed. Helga laughed with them.

'You lot don't have to count up those damned snippets of paper,' the landlady retorted, unfazed. 'You can have vegetables and mashed potato here off the ration,' she said to Helga. 'Like a beer?'

'No, thank you. A seltzer water, please,' said Helga.

'On holiday?'

'My day off. I thought I'd do a little landscape painting. Anywhere specially pretty around here?'

'There's Moorbach, on the edge of the forest,' one of the farmers at the next table suggested. 'Only it's not safe right now. Some nutcase broke out of the loony bin.'

'Loony bin?'

'Klein Moorbach, a psychiatric hospital, they call it. Easier to get in than out again. They call you crazy these days if you so much as squint. But that chap really is a danger.'

The door opened, and a moustached police sergeant in a green uniform marched in. 'Hey, Erwin, got him yet?' someone asked.

The sergeant took off his cap and sat down. 'One of the task force shot him. Trying to do a bunk in a boat. Bullet through the head at a hundred metres. If they'd chopped his head off right away we'd have been spared the expense. But no, they put the likes of him in a padded cell instead. He abused and killed a dozen boys, I hear.'

Helga was horrified. 'But there are children in the hospital too.'

The sergeant cast her a suspicious glance. 'How d'you know that?'

Helga corrected herself at once. 'I mean, it would be so irresponsible to put a brute like that anywhere near children! High time the Party did something about it.'

'Let's have a beer, Frieda,' the sergeant called. He didn't want to know about the Party.

After her meal Helga set out, leaving her bike at the inn. It would not have been much use anyway. Waterways threaded the densely forested land-scape, but there was always a tree trunk or a footbridge somewhere to help you across them. After going half a kilometre she reached a wall twice the height of a man, and made her way along it to the entrance. A notice on the railings of the gate announced:

KLEIN MOORBACH HOSPITAL
RACIAL HYGIENE RESEARCH INSTITUTE BRANCH

The battlements of an ugly, late-nineteenth-century building rose menac-ingly beyond the gate. The hospital had been the country house of some family of the minor aristocracy. A man with a peaked cap came out of the porter's lodge with a German shepherd dog on a leash and began going his rounds. The gravel of the forecourt crunched under his boots.

Helga closed her eyes and sent her thoughts flying to the yellow-brick building. Mama is here, Karl, she thought. She felt his warmth, as always when he clung to her for protection. He was a good boy, not at all difficult. But he was twice as helpless as his contemporaries, and thus far, far more vulnerable.

She set up her easel under a tree so that she had the place in front of her. 'Mama will get you out of there,' she said firmly.

Back home, she took up her position in Reinhard's old office and embarked on a pitched battle with the authorities. She made phone calls which gener-ally got no further than an underling's office. She sent letters enclosing a report from Dr Weiland on the harmless nature of Karl's condition. '. . . Care by his mother at home is all that is required. There is no need for hospital-ization.'

Some of her petitions and appeals were even acknowledged, weeks later. The reply was always negative. '. . . Must therefore inform you . . . not the department responsible . . . have read your letter . . . we suggest you apply to . . . your complaint is not upheld . . . With German greetings, signed . . .'

Month followed month. New theatres of war opened up. The German Army marched from victory to victory. Helga took no notice. She racked her brains during sleepless nights. Where there's a will there's a way – the old saying kept hammering inside her head. But there seemed to be no way to reach Karl.

She left the apartment only for the most essential purposes. Most of the time she sat there apathetically, waiting in vain for letters and phone calls that never came.

'This can't go on,' her sister Monika said on one of her rare visits. 'Doing nothing like this doesn't suit you at all.'

'What's the alternative, then?' asked Helga, feeling hopeless.

'Well, at least don't sit around like an old lady. Do something!'

And so, one Monday, Helga Lohmann pulled herself together and went to her old place of employment in Luisenstrasse. She had made an appointment to see the matron. The red-brick building of the famous hospital, which King Frederick William I of Prussia had named the Charité in 1727, intending it to provide free medical treatment for the poor, basked cheerfully in the sun.

Things were less cheerful inside. Young men in striped dressing gowns thronged the corridors. One-legged cripples on crutches, legless men in wheelchairs, a blond giant with burns on his face and bandaged stumps for hands – the human debris of victorious battles.

A squad of white coats hurried past. 'Eugen!' she exclaimed.

The tall, grey-haired man leading them stopped. 'Helga!'

'Your rounds, Professor,' someone reminded him.

'In a minute.' He took her hand. 'At twelve in my office – in Neurosurgery. I'm so pleased to see you.' The smile on his tanned face was radiant.

Her interview with the matron was brief and positive. 'Oh yes, we certainly need nursing staff everywhere. A week's refresher course, and I can use you as a fully qualified nurse. I can't promise it will be in the children's ward, but will you come all the same?'

'Oh yes, Matron, I'd be glad to.'

'Good – go down to the personnel department, then, and they'll see to the paperwork. I'll ring and let them know you're coming.'

'In half an hour's time, if that's all right. I want to look in on a friend in Neurosurgery for a few moments first.'

Helga was received by a middle-aged secretary. 'The professor's expecting you.' Professor Eugen Klemm was head of the Neurosurgical department at the Charité.

'Helga . . .' He took her in his arms. 'I can't tell you how good it is to see

79

you. How many years has it been? No, don't tell me, it'll make me seem even older. Unlike you – you haven't changed a bit.'

'Flatterer!' Warmth flooded through her, and an unassuaged longing. She drew away from him. 'You're a great man now, aren't you? What about your private life? Married? Children?'

'Married eight years, a daughter aged seven, a son aged five. And you?'

'Married for ten years, widowed a year ago, one son. Our son, Eugen.'

It was a few seconds before he took it in. 'Why didn't you tell me? It would have changed everything.'

'We had a few blissful weeks together. We never planned anything more. An ambitious, up-and-coming doctor and a little probationer nurse – it would never have worked. You wouldn't be where you are now. And I should tell you that my husband acknowledged the baby even before he was born, and I had money of my own too, so I didn't need any help.'

'As simple as that?' There was a note of disappointment in his voice.

'No, Eugen, it wasn't simple. Karl's eleven now. He's a dear boy.' She hesitated, and then came out with it. 'They've taken him away from me. He's mongoloid, he doesn't fit in with today's ideas of society. They've put him in Klein Moorbach. He won't survive there without me. Help us, Eugen.'

She could see that her revelation hit him hard, but he remained calm and matter-of-fact. 'Klein Moorbach is a private clinic. Its medical superintendent is Dr Ralf Urban. He is an outstanding psychiatrist and neurologist. An expert on severe mental disturbances.'

'Karl's not mad,' she said earnestly. 'Just slower to develop than other children.'

'I know,' he said. 'But, well, things are seen differently in some quarters. Klein Moorbach is a branch of the Racial Hygiene Research Institute.'

'Yes – what exactly does that mean?'

'I'd rather not go into detail. Listen, Helga, I know Urban. I can ask him to take you on as a nurse in the children's section. I'll think of some plausible reason. You'd have to use your maiden name. In no circumstances must it emerge that you're Karl's mother.'

'How do you think I can prevent that? He'll rush at me shouting "Mama!"'

'You must think of something. I can't help you there.'

'And then?'

'You're a good nurse, you get on well with children. Make yourself indispensable. Stay in Klein Moorbach – with our son. I don't know how long it will be – a year, two years? But some day these horrors will be over – the Party, the Brownshirts . . .'

'Eugen, you mustn't talk like that. Of course some of the things that happen aren't right – like with my tenants the Salomons. The Führer doesn't know everything that goes on. But he'll make sure it turns out all right in the end.'

'Is that what you really believe?' he asked, his voice filled with pity.

An oversight in the personnel department worked to Helga's advantage. 'Heil Hitler,' the man at the registration desk greeted her. He wore a Party badge. 'Matron rang through. Let's see. It was in 1929 you left? We should still have your file. Yes, here we are – Nurse Helga Rinke from Zehlendorf, correct? Given your blonde German looks, we won't need a certificate of Aryan origin. Have any of your particulars changed? Surname, address?' Helga said no, and two days later went to the hospital to collect an identity card with a photograph, made out in her maiden name.

The summons from Klein Moorbach took a little longer. Eugen Klemm had to invent a story for Dr Urban. 'Helga Rinke is an outstanding paediatric nurse. She would certainly be useful to you at Klein Moorbach. Young and very pretty. We know each other a little – privately, if you see what I mean. Unfortunately she's been getting rather possessive. I wouldn't like my wife to be involved. In fact I'd be grateful for your help, Dr Urban, if you understand me.'

Urban did understand him. One grey Tuesday in November, Helga was standing outside the wrought-iron gates of Klein Moorbach hospital. A German shepherd dog barked inside the porter's lodge and a man with a peaked cap appeared. 'Nurse Helga Rinke. I'm expected.'

'Got a pass?'

She showed her ID, and was let in. The gates closed behind her with an ugly screech. Gravel crunched under her feet as she approached the yellow-brick building, with its barred windows.

'You've had experience in nursing children at the Charité?' Dr Ralf Urban was an elegant man in his mid-forties, and wore his tailor-made white coat buttoned high to the neck like an officer's tunic.

'Yes, sir. Dr Sauerbruch had me nursing post-operative cases in particular.'

'Surgeon General Sauerbruch,' he corrected her.

'He was a wonderful boss.'

'My colleague Klemm thinks highly of you, Nurse Helga. As you know, our little patients are not normal children. They are mentally and physically damaged.' Urban pressed a bell. 'Nurse Doris is leaving us today. She'll show you your room and take you to your ward.'

'May I ask why Nurse Doris is leaving, sir?'

The woman entering the room had heard her question. 'Because I've volunteered for a field hospital at the Front. Our brave boys there need me more than the worthless creatures in this place.' Nurse Doris was a strong young woman with nut-brown hair which she had wound around her head under her cap. She wore the Reich Sports badge on her blouse.

'Show Nurse Helga round and give her the key,' Dr Urban told her.

'Yes, sir.' Doris took Helga's arm.

'One more question, sir.'

'Yes?' Urban looked the young woman up and down.

Helga had been thinking of a way to get Karl's joyful greeting over without witnesses. 'I'd like to see my new charges on my own the first time I meet them, to make sure I establish my authority from the start.'

'What do you think, Nurse Doris?'

'Not a bad idea, sir. Then Sister Helga can show the little beasts who's in charge straight away.'

'Very well, then.' Urban immersed himself in some papers.

Nurse Doris marched ahead, leading her over the gravel of the forecourt to the side wing where the nursing staff had its accommodation. The first-floor room was bright and welcoming, with a small bathroom and a view of the autumnal park. Helga put her case down. 'Student Nurse Evi has the room next to yours,' Doris told her. 'A willing young thing, but not his type.' She was relishing her words. 'You'd be more to his taste. Urban sometimes has his quirky little wishes. If you want my advice, don't be prudish. He can easily make life difficult for you.'

'Speaking from experience?' Helga couldn't help but ask.

'I'm not his sort either. I'll take you to the children's ward. Here's your key – it fits every door in the building. You must keep it on its chain and lock everything behind you. We have some very dangerous inmates here. Never forget that. And as for your own patients — well, I advise you to keep the little horrors immobilized.'

Helga wasn't listening. Karl, she thought, little Karl, Mama will soon be with you.

A steel door separated the accommodation wing from the main building. Sister Doris unlocked it, and they entered a corridor. Men in dingy grey hospital clothing shuffled slowly past, without a glimmer of comprehension in their pale faces. Two hefty male orderlies were dragging along a patient in a straitjacket who was screaming his head off. Helga forced herself not to show her dismay.

A barred door at the end of the corridor led into the stairwell. 'The children's ward is one floor higher up. I'll leave you to it now.' Doris locked the barred door behind her. Heart thudding, Helga climbed the stairs. She came to another barred door and then a long passage. Children's voices told her which way to go.

A white door with a window at the top of it, also barred. She put her key in the lock and opened it. A dreadful stench met her. 'My God,' she said, her voice toneless. Two rows of beds were lined up in military order, with children of various ages lying in them, their hands and feet tied to the bedsteads with muslin bandages. She counted twenty boys and girls at different stages of infantile dementia. Some of them looked childlike and almost normal, others showed clear symptoms of their malady, one was a bad case of hydrocephalus. They all had bedpans pushed under them and were lying in their own excrement. She could hear Doris saying, 'Keep the little horrors immobilized.'

She found her son in the last bed. His once twinkling eyes were dull, his face bloated. He didn't recognize her. She untied him and helped him up. 'Karl,' she murmured, kissing his vacant face. 'Everything will be all right now, Karl.' She hugged him tight, with a whole year of desperate struggle in her embrace. He did not react.

There was soft weeping beside her. The girl in the next bed was about twelve or thirteen. She was pretty in an odd way, and looked normal at first glance. Helga untied her. The child crept under the grubby bedclothes, her knees drawn up. 'Don't be afraid, I won't hurt you. Can you tell me your name?'

'Lisa,' said a faint voice from beneath the covers.

'Excellent, Lisa. And I'm Nurse Helga. Did you hear that, children?' she called. 'I'm Nurse Helga, but you can all call me Mama. All together now: Ma-ma.'

'Ma-ma, Ma-ma,' they babbled, until their voices came together in unison. 'Ma-ma!'

'Mama, Mama,' Karl suddenly said thickly, putting his hands out to her. He knew who she was. She hugged her son, wanting never to let go of him again, and let her tears flow freely.

Then she pulled herself together. 'Lisa, is there a bathroom here? And lavatories?' The girl climbed out of bed and pointed to a door at the back of the ward. Beyond it was a sparkling clean, white-tiled bathroom with a big tub and several showers. Next door were a lavatory and a large sink. 'Looks as if these aren't often used.'

Lisa shook her head. 'Nurse Doris wouldn't let us.'

'Well, we're going to change that.' Helga turned on one of the showers. There was plenty of hot water. 'Get undressed, get under the shower and have a good wash.' Lisa happily obeyed. Her pretty little figure was already beginning to develop. It was only if you looked closely that you could see the signs of her disturbance, which was obviously mild. There were piles of bedlinen and clean hospital clothing in a big built-in cupboard. Beaming, Lisa dressed herself again.

Karl came next. Helga soaped him down, her gestures expressing infinite love. She rubbed him dry, helped him into pyjamas and a dressing gown, and combed his wet hair. 'We'll cut that later,' she said. 'Go and strip your bed. You help him, Lisa. We'll make up all the beds with clean sheets. Now for the next child.' Helga was about to untie the bonds of a boy of about six, whose face showed signs of advanced dementia, but Lisa put a hand on her arm. 'No, don't,' she said softly. 'Hans will run wild and hurt himself.'

She washed the little boy in his bed and put clean clothes on him without undoing the soft bonds. She had experience of bedridden patients. 'Is there anyone else who had better not get up?' Lisa said no. An hour later all the children and their beds were clean, and the ward was aired. Clean bedpans were stacked under the sink in the lavatory. 'We're old enough to go to the loo now by ourselves,' Helga announced cheerfully.

Her loving glances kept returning to her son. He had grown taller and older, yet he still seemed like a little boy. She knew he would never develop beyond the mental age of six, and would live only until he was about twenty. Dr Weiland had gently explained that to her soon after the birth, and she had found confirmation in medical textbooks.

He nestled close to her. 'Mama, Mama . . .' All the children came crowding around her. 'Mama . . . Mama . . .' their little voices babbled.

There was a rattling of keys. It was Nurse Doris, and she had a man in a white coat with her. 'Ah yes, at first you think you can improve everything here – but believe me, they're still little monsters.'

'Left wallowing in their own filth.'

Nurse Doris shrugged, without showing any interest. 'Do as you like. My stint here is over. This is Herr Götze, our ward orderly.'

Helga shook his hand vigorously. 'Pleased to meet you, Herr Götze.' She looked at the time. It was midday. 'Where do the children eat?'

'We feed them in their beds. Then they can only get themselves dirty,' explained Doris, with indifference.

'Perhaps you'd rather take them to the dining room?' suggested Götze, earning himself a venomous glance from Doris.

'Oh yes, I would, Herr Götze,' replied Helga, pleased. 'And I'm sure you can tell me if there's a village inn here? We could all go and have a drink – to celebrate my arrival.'

'Yes, sure, there's Bredewitz in Gross Moorbach. I'll tell the others. And if you need any other help, I'm always here. Isn't that right, Lisa?' The child was crouching in a corner, and didn't reply.

On her second Saturday, Helga had the afternoon and evening off. She took some things to the laundry and ran the vacuum cleaner over her room. She finished around five. She put her warm, lined boots on, and her thick loden coat. The cold November air in the park cleared her head. She had a lot to think about: her new job and the responsibility for her little charges that went with it; Karl and herself. How long would she have to stick it out with him here?

'Some day these horrors will be over – the Party, the Brownshirts . . .' she remembered Eugen's words. She longed for that day, and at the same time she felt like a traitor because it meant wishing for the Führer's fall from power. Then he'd probably have to go into retirement in Braunau.

85

She almost fell into a freshly dug pit behind some luxuriant rhododendrons. She remembered that Nurse Meta, who worked in the kitchen, had said it was difficult getting rid of the garbage. The garbage disposal truck hadn't been allotted enough fuel. 'We bury our own rubbish,' the nurse had said, in her strong Saxon accent.

Helga walked as far as the small, barred and locked gate in the park wall. A little stream bordered with reeds, a branch of the river, rippled along outside the gate and then was lost in the dense woodland. A pair of ducks came down and swam towards the bank, quacking. It soon grew dark, and she set off back to the house. The warmth of her room enveloped her pleasantly. She pulled her dress off over her head, put on her dressing gown, and was about to take her boots off when there was a knock at the door.

'Yes?' she called, surprised.

It was Dr Urban. Well, she had been expecting him to turn up sometime, and was even prepared to sleep with him. A boss with his vanity wounded by rejection could be dangerous to her and little Karl. Worse things happen, she'd thought, shrugging.

He had brought flowers and champagne. 'My personal welcome.'

'That's very kind of you, sir. You must excuse my dressing gown. If I'd known you were coming . . .'

'Oh, never mind that.' He dismissed her apology. He kept staring at her boots. 'You've settled in nicely, and you have your ward well under control. My compliments, Nurse Helga.' He still hadn't taken his eyes off those boots.

She remembered what Nurse Doris had said, and it dawned on her that she might not have to sleep with him at all. 'Go and get champagne glasses,' she ordered. He returned with two ordinary wine glasses. 'No, I said champagne glasses, the shallow ones,' she instructed him.

Without demur, he went off a second time but came back empty handed. 'I couldn't find any proper champagne glasses.'

To make quite sure, she took the game a step further. 'Because you didn't look properly. Go off again at once.'

Any other man would have refused. He eagerly obeyed. She was almost certain of it now: he was one of those men who found satisfaction only in submitting to a dominant woman. She had learnt about it in a seminar on sexuality given to the nurses.

'I'll let it pass this time,' she said sternly when he came back without champagne glasses again. 'Open the bottle and then sit down.' She arranged herself so that her dressing gown fell slightly apart, exposing one knee above the top of her boot. He looked at it avidly.

Gradually they fell into conversation. He told her about his wife and daughter, who lived in Berlin. 'The air here doesn't suit Gertraud, and Gisela's at school at the Luisenstift in Dahlem. So I'm alone in the villa.' Helga had seen the former estate manager's house in the park. It was as ugly as the old manor house. 'Would you visit me there sometimes?' It sounded almost pleading.

'We'll see,' she told him coolly.

'May I touch your boots?' he asked as he left.

Her instinct had not let her down. 'Next time.' It gave her a curious satisfaction to make him wait.

'Cuckoo, cuckoo!' Karl had hidden behind a stout oak, and the other children were looking for him. The grounds of the hospital rang with their shouts and laughter. Karl ran out of his hiding place and over to the bramble bushes. 'Cuckoo!' Little Hans was the first to find him. He puffed with excitement, let go of Helga's hand and ran towards Karl, clinging to him and crowing with delight. Only two weeks earlier she wouldn't have dared let him out of bed – he had laid into her with his fists and banged his head against the wall when she'd first tried it. But her cheerful storytelling, with the children gathered round her, interested him so much that he hadn't noticed when she untied him a second time. Even when he became aware that he could move, he went on listening calmly. A new life was opening up for this severely disturbed child; at best he had been ignored in the past, and more often he was restrained and punished. Now the others helped by including him in their games.

Lisa in particular had a calming effect on him. She persuaded him to join in, as Helga patiently practised with the others for days on end, until the nursery rhyme about 'Little Hans' echoed through the children's ward. Helga was proud of this and many other small successes, and felt happy with the children. No one noticed that she paid a little extra attention to Karl, because no one paid any attention to her and her ward anyway.

In practice, she was mistress of her own domain. Dr Urban let her do as

87

she liked. Now and then he called to ask if everything was all right in the children's ward. She visited him sometimes at the villa, reluctantly acting the part of stern dominatrix in words and gestures.

Götze the orderly was not much help. He spent most of his time in the former coach house where Helga kept her bicycle, tinkering away at a green truck. 'For the boss,' he explained, sounding self-important.

On this particular morning, as so often, he was lying under the vehicle, an Opel Blitz, busy with a spanner. The children watched with curiosity. Little Hans was all excited, because Götze let him hand him a pair of pliers.

The telephone on the wall rang. Götze scrambled to his feet. 'Yes, sir, I'm through with it. The flange on the exhaust needs replacing; I'll get a new one tomorrow. I'll bring the vehicle round right away.' He hung up and took the ignition key off the nail beside the telephone.

Helga clapped her hands. 'Come along, children, we're going to visit Papa Zastrow.' She picked little Hans up and led the group away. The children sang 'Little Hans' as they walked right across the park to the porter's lodge. Zastrow had opened the wrought-iron gates. 'Big car!' cried Karl in excitement. An open Horch rolled past them with two officers in the back. They had a great deal of silver braid on the black collars that stood out from the pale grey fabric of their uniforms.

The porter closed the gates again. 'Visitors for the boss,' he grunted. 'I've a feeling this bodes no good.'

Helga patted Jule, the German shepherd, who had turned out to be a harmless elderly lady. 'You do? Why?'

'Because these death's-head fellows never do bode any good. Bunch of crooks, that's what they are.'

'Are you out of your mind, Zastrow? Stupid talk like that could cost you your life.'

The porter grinned. 'Not if you don't pass it on, Nurse Helga. What's more, your concern for me shows you're not so sure of the purity of the firm of Greater Germany Limited yourself.'

Helga wasn't falling into that trap. 'And you really have no idea what's up?'

'They say there's a few patients going to be transferred. Only the boss knows where. Daresay I'll soon find out.'

The children were getting impatient. Karl was pulling at her coat and little Hans tugging her arm. It was time for lunch. 'Bon appetit, Papa Zastrow.' Helga led the children back to the house. The green Opel Blitz was standing on the gravel of the forecourt, with the medical director and the two uniformed visitors beside it. They were listening to Götze's explanation, which he accompanied with many gestures. Dr Urban waved to the children, and the children waved back.

Helga came across the green Opel Blitz again two weeks later, on her afternoon off. It was standing behind the main building, near the tradesmen's entrance. The head orderly, Grabbe, and two assistants were putting a dozen patients into the load area of the truck. They were severe cases, mostly old men and women, not an attractive sight. Götze, meanwhile, was checking something at the back of the vehicle. He bolted the back door and climbed into the driver's cab. The truck drove off, engine roaring. 'Where are the patients being taken?' Helga asked the head orderly.

'You'll have to ask the boss.' Grabbe jerked his head upwards. Dr Urban was watching the truck from his study window.

She set off on her usual walk through the park, wondering whether to order him to walk barefoot through the snow to fetch her leather gloves this evening. Then she would put the gloves on, very slowly, and he would watch, fascinated. He kept asking her to be really strict with him. She ignored his longing glances at the dog whip on the mantelpiece, and this excited him even more. Instead, she ordered him to spend all evening on his knees in front of her, or humiliated him with a few well-chosen words. She hated this game, but she knew that it gave her power over him. Power that she used to demand privileges for the children. That way they got toys, books to read and painting materials, and the kitchen was told to send desserts and cakes to the children's ward more often. Helga asked for nothing for herself.

In 'normal' moments, he was an interesting conversationalist. It was during one of their discussions that she mentioned the subject of mongolism. 'Take little Karl, for instance. The boy is twelve and very independent. He'd be all right in his parents' care, and that would give us room for a more severe case.'

'Children like him don't belong in a healthy community,' he told her.

The sound of an engine brought her back from her thoughts. It must have been a good half-hour since she'd begun. The green truck was approaching from the depths of the park and driving towards the wall. Curious, she made her way through the undergrowth, and saw the vehicle reversing towards the pit she'd almost stumbled into, two weeks before. Götze got out in a leisurely fashion, climbed up on the step behind the truck and peered through the peephole. Then he unbolted the door and got back into the cab.

The engine roared, raising the load area. The back doors fell open. Human bodies with mouths wide open and limbs akimbo slid off the sloping floor of the truck into the pit. Helga's cries of horror were drowned by the noise of the engine. The load area was lowered again. Götze jumped out of the driver's cab, spat on his hands and picked up a shovel. Clods of earth thudded down on the dead men and women. Later, she couldn't remember how she had made it back to the house.

Helga had to watch twice more as the orderlies loaded helpless patients into the green Opel Blitz. By now she knew that the poisonous exhaust gases from the engine were funnelled through a hosepipe straight into the air-tight load area, while Götze drove his cargo of human beings twitching in their death agonies around the park for half an hour, before tipping them into the mass grave.

'Running like clockwork, sir,' she heard him report on the coach-house telephone after one of these drives. She was overcome by a feeling of impotent rage. She was an accessory to an unspeakable crime, and there was nothing she could do about it. Or was there? Perhaps she could send word to the Führer about this monstrous thing? Only how was she to get a message through to him? And ought she to expose herself anyway? If the perpetrators of this crime found out what she was planning to do, and anything happened to her, it would be the end for Karl too.

One morning just before Christmas she found that she could no longer avoid a decision. She was explaining a simple sum to Karl. Lisa was brushing little Hans's hair. Her other charges were busy painting, getting into a colourful mess with spots of bright paint everywhere. They were all enjoying themselves. Helga felt happy in the bustling activity of this self-contained little world, and suppressed thoughts of what was going on outside.

Evi, the young student nurse, came hurrying in. Helga had sent her to the storeroom to find some pairs of woolly socks for the children. Evi was in a state of great excitement. 'The stores manager says we can't have any more new things. The whole children's ward is going to be moved in the New Year.' Everything went round in circles before Helga's eyes. Evi chattered on. 'Do you know where to, Nurse Helga? Hartheim would be nice. They say it's a modern, open asylum for the less serious cases. I expect we'll both be going too.'

Summoning up all her strength of will, Helga managed to appear calm and cheerful. 'I've no idea where to, Evi. We'll find out in due course. You take the children to lunch. There's something I have to do.'

She put on her loden coat. It was wet and cold outside; the snow had melted. She left the building, walking the long way round through the park so as to reach the porter's lodge unseen. Papa Zastrow was sitting by the roaring iron stove with Jule. 'Whatever's the matter, Nurse Helga? You look terrible.'

She ventured everything on a single throw. 'They're going to kill the children.'

The old man nodded. 'In Götze's gas-powered truck, like the others. They call it "elimination of worthless life", those murderers do. Urban's the worst. He's a member of the Racial Hygiene Research Institute staff. An SS institution "for preserving the purity of the Germanic race".'

'The Führer must be told at once!'

Zastrow's barking laughter turned to a coughing fit. 'The Führer?' he croaked when the coughing had died down. 'Him? He gets his executioners' reports fresh off the press on his desk.'

'He knows about it?'

'He laid the foundations for this madness. You can read all about it in his book – Mein Kampf, it's called. He leaves other people to carry out his plans.'

Helga returned to the immediate problem. 'Papa Zastrow, I have to get away from here, only – only not on my own. Please help us!'

'Us?'

'Karl and me.' Quickly, she filled him in.

Zastrow thought for a moment. 'Do you know the branch of the river that runs outside the little gate?'

'Yes.'

'On Christmas Eve they'll be celebrating.' He gave her a large iron key. 'The spare key. No one knows about it. The lock will be oiled. Slip away around seven that evening. When you're out there, signal with a light. Mato will strike a match to show you where the boat is. He's my youngest. He'll take the two of you to safety.'

Götze was being Father Christmas, handing out sugar stars and gingerbread. Some of the children were frightened of his white beard, others were stuffing themselves happily. Candles burned on the wooden Yule pyramid. Dr Urban had installed this piece of pseudo-Germanic folklore in person, before setting off to join his family in Berlin. Helga could have screamed with fury and outrage at the murderer's cynicism.

Nurse Evi had taken little Hans on her lap and was singing, 'Silent Night'. Her young face wore a childlike, devout expression. Karl was looking at her with the awakening interest of puberty.

Helga glanced at the clock. Time to get moving. She sniffed, wrinkled her nose, and drew her son closer to her. 'Oh, Karl, a big boy like you, having an accident!'

Karl protested. 'Didn't dirty my pants!'

'We'll see about that. Evi, we're going to freshen up. It may take a little time.' The student nurse raised her hands and struck up 'O Tannenbaum'.

Helga took her son's arm. The corridor and the stairs were deserted. She heard a babble of voices from below. The staff were celebrating in the hall, along with those inmates who were in any state to do so. In her room she put woollen stockings on her son, socks, a track suit and a thick sweater, as well as gumboots and a woolly hat, items that she had removed one by one from the stores. 'Didn't dirty my pants,' Karl insisted.

'No, no, you didn't,' she soothed him. 'Now, listen hard. You and mama are going away from here. You must keep very quiet so that nobody notices anything. There's nothing to be frightened of. Mama is with you.'

'Didn't dirty my pants. Not frightened either,' Karl announced.

She slipped into her boots and loden coat, and tied a scarf round her head. She put a small torch in her pocket. Her few things were packed in her case, around which she had put a leather strap. She slung it over her shoulder and took Karl's hand. They went quietly down the stairs. Helga opened the front door of the building – and immediately flinched back. Grabbe stood before them, a bottle of schnapps in his hand. His alcohol-laden breath wafted towards them.

Helga forced a smile. 'Happy Christmas, Herr Grabbe,' she said cheerfully.

'Happy Christmas,' Karl echoed her.

'Same to you,' replied Grabbe thickly, patting Karl's head.

It was snowing. The wind drove large, wet flakes into their faces. Helga avoided the forecourt, which was brightly lit. They took the path to the coach house and then went on through the bushes to the barred gate in the wall. The lock was well oiled, as Papa Zastrow had promised.

'Mama, I'm cold,' Karl said in a loud voice.

Alarmed, she put her hand over his mouth. She pointed her torch in the direction of the water, switched it on, and waited for a response, her heart thudding. A thousand thoughts went through her mind. Suppose Zastrow's son didn't come? They couldn't go back to the hospital. They would have to flee into the unknown. If it went wrong, she would put her scarf around Karl's neck as if she were applying a tourniquet. It wouldn't take more than twenty seconds. And then she would follow him.

A match flared up, illuminating a face. Through the driving snow, she saw the indistinct shape of a rowing boat in the reeds. She took her son on her back. He was heavy, his weight pushed her down into the icy mud until it came over her knees. It was a torment to haul her feet, step by step, from the suction of its embrace. Then strong arms heaved her into the boat. 'Get under the tarpaulin,' her rescuer told her.

How long the boat journey lasted she didn't know. It seemed as if she lay freezing under the tarpaulin for an eternity, her son, shivering with cold, in her arms. She heard the monotonous splash of the oars dipping in and out of the water. When the boat turned right she peered out. The driving snow had stopped falling, and the night was clear enough for her to see a few metres ahead. Her ferryman was punting the boat with one oar, towards a place in what looked like an impenetrable wall of reeds. They parted. Willows bent low, their branches lashing the tarpaulin. Driftwood scraped the outside of the boat with a dull sound as they glided into a narrow arm of the waterway. The branches of alders reared aloft like ghosts.

It was another quarter of an hour before the boat came up against a landing stage. Their rescuer made it fast and helped them out. They climbed a slope, a house towering black above them. Everything around it was wet and cold, and Karl clung to his mother for protection. My God, where have we ended up? Helga thought desperately.

The door of the house was opened. Golden light streamed out to meet them. Inside, the place was warm and comfortable. There was a scent of baked apples and cinnamon in the air, and a Christmas tree with burning candles lit the parlour. Five people, four women and a man, surrounded the new arrivals. The women wore festive costumes, elaborately winged caps and finely embroidered shawls. The man was wearing a blue and white patterned smock. He had dark hair streaked with grey, and a ruddy complexion. He stepped forward and said solemnly, '*Witamy was wutsobnje w Blotojskem.*'

Helga was at a loss, but her host repeated it in German. 'You are very welcome to the Spreewald. My name is Fryco Hejdus. This is my wife Wanda, these are my daughters Marja, Slawa and Breda, and you know Zastrow's son Mato already.'

Her ferryman turned out to be a handsome man of twenty with nut-brown hair, who was watching her admiringly. She gave him her hand. 'Thank you, Mato. Thank you all. Karl, say thank you.' Karl obediently shook hands with everyone. The girls giggled and kissed him on the forehead. They were somewhere between fourteen and eighteen years old. Helga was surprised to see how naturally they accepted the boy, although they had probably never seen a mongol child before.

In the bedroom next to the parlour, Hejdus's wife Wanda gave them dry clothes to put on. Then they found a large, steaming bowl of punch waiting in front of the Christmas tree to warm them up. The master of the house filled wooden mugs with a wooden ladle. It was all done in as friendly and natural a manner as if they were old acquaintances.

Helga was anxious. 'Suppose they come looking for us?'

Hejdus dismissed the idea. 'They won't, not on Christmas Eve. And certainly not in this filthy weather. We can talk in peace tomorrow.'

There was baked carp with boiled potatoes and green Spreewald sauce, and pickled cucumbers with dill on the side. Karl ate tidily and with obvious pleasure. The girls mothered him. Helga couldn't remember when she'd felt as relaxed and as much at home, as she did here, at the table of these strangers. They spoke fluent German but occasionally lapsed into their native Sórbian. The fact that young Mato had eyes only for her both amused and flattered her.

Wanda Hejdus had made up the bed in the room next door for them. Mother and son fell asleep holding each other close.

A bright, sunny Christmas Day emerged from the mist. The Hejdus family had already gathered around the breakfast table when Helga and Karl appeared. There was *gugelhupf*, yeast cake baked in a ring mould, and cocoa with milk for the young people, and real coffee for the adults. Wanda Hejdus had bartered several dozen eggs for the coffee in Lubnjow.

'To think we have to do such things,' said Hejdus. 'This damn war.'

'Nonsense,' said his wife. 'Our grandparents and great-grandparents bartered goods whether it was war or peacetime. Money's always been in short supply in the Spreewald.'

After breakfast they went out. The house that had looked so forbidding the night before lay bathed in sunlight. A little way behind it stood a reed-thatched cottage. 'That's where Zastrow and his son live,' Hejdus explained. 'We farm the Kaupe together. The Kaupe? That's what we call the sandy island enriched by the waters of the Spree that our ancestors settled and reclaimed for cultivation three hundred years ago,' he told his guest with pride. 'We grow cucumbers, onions, horseradish and buckwheat, and of course potatoes. Our catches of fish make a great contribution to the final victory, that's what the local Party leader says, and he has the fattest carp parcelled up for himself.'

'Repaying us by turning a blind eye if we forget to fly the Party flag on the Führer's birthday yet again,' added his wife.

Mato waved up at them, smiling. He was sitting in the rowing boat, fishing. Karl ran down to him, and Mato helped him into the boat.

'He ought to be on the Eastern Front,' Hejdus muttered. 'But he won't fight for a regime that ranks us as second-class citizens. We Sorbs are Slavs and don't belong to the Germanic master race.'

'Suppose someone sees him? A healthy young man, not in uniform . . . ?'

'Then he'll end up like young Lenik. Lenik was a rebellious lad even at school. He tore up his call-up papers in front of Lübben Town Hall, said he had better things to do than go to war for those madmen. The SA fetched him from his bed at night. We found him in the morning. He was in a cucumber barrel, head down in the brine.'

Hejdus's eldest daughter sobbed. 'They were engaged, Marja and Lenik,' said her mother sadly.

A duck quacked in alarm some way off. 'Quick, come indoors.' Hejdus took Helga's arm, and Mato followed from the landing stage with Karl. In the kitchen, the master of the house opened a trapdoor. Helga looked down a shaft, and saw her face reflected in water a metre below. A couple of rungs led down the shaft. Hejdus pulled a chain, and there was a rushing, gurgling sound. The water flowed away, revealing a hatch secured by four large, wing-nut screws. Mato let himself down, undid the screws and raised the hatch. 'Right, you and the boy go down there,' Hejdus told them.

Helga helped Karl into the shaft and climbed down after him. Mato caught mother and son at the bottom. A ladder led from the hatch into a room measuring about three by three metres, and the height of a man. Mato lit an oil lamp on the table. In its dim light, Helga saw stools and camp beds. Meanwhile, Hejdus was screwing the hatch back into place overhead. They heard rushing water. 'It will rise to a height of half a metre,' explained Mato with satisfaction. 'Don't worry, the way down is well sealed. The inner tubes of bicycle tyres stuffed with women's hair are the best seal there is. They even use something similar to make U-boat hatches watertight.' The young man pointed to an opening halfway up the wall. 'The ventilation pipe. It ends in a tree stump outside. We have plenty of food and drink, and as long as we keep quiet no one will find us here.'

'How do you know when someone's coming?'

'You couldn't see it in the dark yesterday, but there's an old raised hide for duck shooting at the mouth of the channel. One of us is always on the lookout up there. When someone's coming he quacks like a teal on the decoy whistle. That gives us a good ten minutes to disappear.' The sound of an engine was heard, buzzing angrily like a hornet. Mato raised a warning hand. 'It's Barsig.'

Helga held Karl close, ready to bury his face in her lap to suppress any sound. But the boy looked slyly at her with his narrow, mongol eyes and put a finger on his lips. He had understood.

Deadly fear rose in her, as if icy fingers were tightening around her neck. The sound of the engine cut out. Indistinct voices came down to them. Sweat ran down the back of her neck, and she struggled for air. Mato moved his stool under the opening of the ventilation pipe, and indicated that she should climb up on it. The cool air was a great relief. She took several deep breaths.

Up above, the engine came on again, and quickly receded. Long minutes of anxious waiting followed. Waiting for she didn't know what. At last the water flowed away, gurgling. The hatch was opened, and she saw Hejdus's head. 'All clear, you can come up now.'

The girls took Karl out of doors with them to play hide and seek. Helga sat down at the table with the others. She was trembling. A glass of juniper spirit helped to calm her. 'Who's Barsig?'

'The sergeant from the police station in Lubnjow. Tough as they come. He turns up unexpectedly all over the place in that boat of his, with its outboard motor. He was probably hoping we wouldn't be reckoning on a Christmas Day visit. That's how he took the Siwalniks by surprise last Easter when they were killing a pig on the quiet. Now they're all in jail in Cottbus.' Hejdus clasped his hands so hard that the knuckles turned white. 'If it didn't mean everyone would be in trouble, we'd have done for him and a few others long ago.'

'Are there many like him around, then?'

'Othmar the postman is a rabid Nazi. And Kaunitz the local Party leader. He sent old Wicaz to the guillotine for listening to enemy radio stations.'

Papa Zastrow came in the afternoon. He had two days off. 'They're looking for you and the boy,' he told Helga. 'The medical director has told the Gestapo. Just as a precaution to shield his own back, if you ask me. They think your trail leads to Berlin.'

'Good,' said his son, pleased. 'No one will look for you in the Spreewald.' He took her hand and patted it clumsily. 'You mustn't be frightened.'

'So Urban is back,' said Helga. She tried to remain calm, but the fear in her voice gave her away. 'What about the children?'

Zastrow lowered his voice. 'They're being transferred on the fifteenth of January at three in the afternoon.'

'I must go to Klein Moorbach,' Helga decided. 'Who'll take me?'

'Not me,' said Mato firmly. 'One suicide mission is enough.'

'You'll never find the way alone. What do you want to do there anyway?' asked Hejdus, sounding troubled.

'See what happens. Be a witness for when the day of reckoning comes.'

'If they catch you they'll take you to the Gestapo head office in Cottbus. They'll get you to talk there sooner or later, and we'll all be done for. They're just waiting for an excuse to put all us Sorbs in a camp, like they did with the gypsies.'

Wanda Hejdus spoke up, smoothing things over. 'Please stay here, Helga. Your Karl needs you. All these horrors will soon be over, and then you can go wherever you like.'

Zastrow tried to be optimistic too. 'Now that the Americans are joining in, I'm glad to say it's purely a question of time.'

'You're right. How stupid of me. I'm grateful to you all for letting Karl and me stay here,' said Helga, mollifying her hosts. But secretly she hadn't changed her mind.

The girls were playing on the landing stage with Karl. Hejdus was mending fish-traps in the winter sunlight. Wanda was in the kitchen. Helga strolled over to the Zastrows' cottage.

Mato was sitting by the window, practising his accordion. His father had gone back to the porter's lodge the day before. Helga came up behind the young man and stroked his head.

'Don't give yourself the trouble, I'm not taking you.' She began massaging his neck gently. 'Anyway, what do you want to go back to that nuthouse for?' She slipped the strap of the accordion off his shoulders, and the palms of her hands circled on his chest through his shirt. She felt his nipples hardening. He put the accordion down on the table. 'Hejdus will murder me if I take you.'

'Hejdus doesn't need to know.' She pulled him to his feet and turned him round to face her. Her lips tenderly touched his mouth as she spoke. 'You will take me, won't you?' She pressed close to him. Seducing this good-looking boy was rather intriguing, she thought, surprised at her own frivolity.

She kissed him. Her tongue flickered, like a little snake on the attack. Her sex rubbed against his, and she could feel his erection growing. Gently, she drew him down on the bed, and they fell back on the check pillows.

Once he had overcome his initial shyness they made passionate love. She reached orgasm three times before he climaxed with a loud cry. Then they lay peacefully side by side. 'All that for a boating trip?' He laughed, happy.

'How far is it from Klein Moorbach to the nearest town of any size?'

'Lubnjow, that's Lübbenau to you, is ten kilometres from the hospital. If you want to know exactly, I'll show you on the map – later.' He tried to draw her towards him again, but she pushed him away. He got the map out of the table drawer and unfolded it on the bed. 'Right, so you want to pay a quick visit to the loony bin, heaven knows why. But why Lübbenau afterwards?'

'Those who ask no questions and do as I want will get their reward,' she whispered in his ear. Then her warm lips encircled his prick.

Hejdus was fiddling with the People's Radio. He switched it on only for the midday news, in order to save the bulky battery. Mains electricity ended in Lübbenau. No fanfares announcing special victory bulletins had been broadcast for some time now. Instead, the newsreader reported on the heroic battle for Stalingrad and Rommel's correction of the Front in North Africa, which the informed listener could decipher as the beginning of the end. Karl was sitting at the table with the girls, looking at a picture book. Wanda Hejdus was standing at the stove. Helga did not want to tear herself away from this peaceful scene. She went out, telling them she'd see whether the washing on the line was dry. Mato was waiting in the rowing boat.

Soundlessly, they slipped along the waterway in the midday sun. It was warm for this time of year. The muted boom of an early bittern could be heard across the water. Out in the channel, they met a couple of other boats. Only a brief nod of the head was exchanged. Better to keep to yourself in these uncertain times. Just before three in the afternoon they pulled into the reeds by the park wall. Zastrow's spare key let her through the little gate. She reached the hospital unseen.

The green Opel Blitz was waiting at the tradesmen's entrance. Götze was leaning on the bonnet, looking bored, smoking a cigarette. Three orderlies were lounging around nearby. Children's voices were raised in song: 'Little Hans, on his own, went out in the world alone . . .' Nurse Evi appeared, with the children in a crocodile behind her. They were holding hands and singing: '. . . With hat and stick, he sang a song . . .' The orderlies lifted them into the truck one by one. '. . . As merrily he walked along.'

Helga thought of the hours she had spent teaching them that rhyme. Her heart constricted. She forced herself to watch and do nothing. If she intervened she would be arrested, and they would get everything out of her. Then Karl would die, and Mato, and many more, and the Sorbs would be put in a concentration camp.

'But his mother wept all day . . .' Nurse Evi was singing along with them. She was about to get into the truck with her charges, but Grabbe stopped her. Götze trod out his cigarette and slammed the two halves of the door shut. '. . . When little Hans had gone away.' Their childish voices were muted inside the closed truck. Götze bolted the doors, climbed into the driver's cab and started the engine. The truck began to move. Helga saw Dr Urban's face at a first-floor window. He showed no emotion. You brute! cried a voice inside her. Child-murderer! The tears were flowing down her face.

She went back to the boat. Mato was surprised. 'That was quick. Let's get going.'

'We must wait until dark. I still have something to do.' She crept under the tarpaulin and fell into sleep as if in a deep faint. In her dreams she heard children's voices singing, 'Little Hans, on his own . . .'. When she woke, night had fallen.

She pushed back the tarpaulin. 'Wait till I'm back.'

'This is crazy,' Mato protested. 'If they catch you it's the end for all of us. Come on, see sense and let's be off.'

She had no intention of doing such a thing, but she put her arm around him. 'Be a dear boy,' she breathed in his ear. 'It will be lovely again once we're home.'

Sleet drove into her face as she struggled through the undergrowth to the coach-house. She put on the light. You couldn't see the coach house from the hospital. The green Opel Blitz was standing in its place, with her bicycle propped nearby. She picked up the telephone and dialled Urban's extension. He answered in forbidding tones. 'Yes, what is it?'

She slipped into the role she hated. 'You know who this is.'

He was surprised. 'Nurse Helga?'

'I want to see you. In the coach house.'

'The coach house?'

'Do you have to repeat everything I say? Come at once. And bring the whip with you.'

'The whip. Oh yes.' His voice sounded both submissive and eager.

She unbuttoned her loden coat until her skirt and boots were in view. When he arrived she was standing at the back of the coach house, beside the truck. 'The whip,' she demanded coldly. He gave it to her with a look of dog-like devotion. She pointed to the bicycle with the whip handle. 'Get that on board and then get in yourself.' He obeyed. 'Now, take your clothes off.' Visibly excited, he did so. 'Down on all fours, facing forward,' she ordered. His buttocks were large and flat, and his penis, red and ugly, dangled between his thighs. She slapped her boot with the whip, making him jump. Then she closed the doors and shot the bolts. The ignition key was hanging from its nail by the telephone as usual.

The gears were similar to those in her Brennabor. She pulled the starter button. After turning over and failing a few times, the engine caught. She put the truck into first gear, stepped on the gas slightly, and engaged the clutch. The truck jerked forward. There was a grinding sound as she changed up into second gear. It was a long time since she had last driven. Just enough light came through the narrow slit left in the headlights, partly obscured to comply with blackout regulations, for her to find the way to the gate. She stopped and hooted impatiently.

Zastrow came out of the porter's lodge looking sleepy, Jule on her leash with him. He opened the gate without looking into the truck. 'Pack of criminals,' he muttered.

She had memorized the map. A driveway led from the gate to the road. You turned right for Lübbenau. The sleet had stopped, but she still drove slowly. Her face was set like stone. She knew that with every revolution of the engine it was pumping deadly gas into the load area. Urban would be coughing, retching, finally breathing stertorously. Convulsions would shake him until he perished miserably, racked by convulsive twitching. The thought filled her with satisfaction.

It took her over half an hour to go the ten kilometres. She wanted to make quite sure. She stopped in the square outside the town hall, empty at this time of night, turned off the engine and jumped out of the driver's cab. She pushed back the bolts. Urban's naked body fell towards her. In his death agony he had been clawing at the doors. His torso hung out of the truck. She took her bicycle out and placed the message she had prepared in advance beside the body:

It took her fifteen minutes to cycle back. When she reached the park wall she put the bicycle over her shoulders and made her way to the small gate by the light of her torch. She opened the gate and pushed the bicycle through it. In the coach house she propped it against the wall.

'All finished?' asked Mato when she joined him in the boat.

'All finished.' Exhausted, she crawled underneath the tarpaulin.

A Gestapo special unit came from Berlin. Their investigations led nowhere. Helga had cut the letters for her message out of the *Spreewaldboten* newspaper and stuck them together. She had taken the sheet of paper from a new school exercise book belonging to the Hejdus girls, the sort you could buy anywhere, and she burned the rest of the exercise book. She had been wearing gloves throughout her nocturnal operations. Moreover, she had been officially missing for weeks, so no one connected her with Urban's death.

'People are furious,' reported Hejdus. He had been in the town. 'They smashed up the gas truck. No one knows who was driving it.' He looked hard at Helga. 'Well, we don't know anything either.'

Special units of the police and the SS combed the entire forest area on foot and in motorboats over the next few days, but the water prevented their dogs from picking up a trail. Helga, Karl, Mato and two other men who had not joined up spent many hours in the hiding place under the house. Finally the search troops were withdrawn. The Spreewald had given away none of those it protected.

Nor did it give them away in the months to come. While squadrons of Allied bombers flew over them in the direction of Berlin, the people on the Kaupe continued their simple way of life. A beautiful spring made up for the last winter of the war. March was warm and sunny, and April as hot as summer. Helga, Mato and Karl had to go down under the house less and less often. The rulers of the Greater German Reich, not so great now, had worse problems than the Sorbs.

Helga and Mato had climbed up to the raised hide at the mouth of the channel, not to keep watch but for one of their secret meetings. Mato was sitting on the narrow bench, leaning back. Helga was astride him, riding them both to a satisfying climax. They made love when the opportunity offered, Mato with a young man's amazed ardour, Helga enjoying herself very much. She was thirty-five, and these physical encounters did her good. The inhabitants of the Kaupe knew about the relationship and tacitly approved.

The others were all sitting in the sun when the two of them came back. A biplane with the red star on its wings flew overhead, purring like a sewing machine. The girls waved up at it. The pilot waved back. 'Well, it'll soon be over now,' said Zastrow. He had given up his porter's job. 'Remains to be seen if the new masters are any better than the old,' he added sceptically.

The new masters arrived on a Sunday. Helga was swimming. She loved those moments in the cool water when she felt weightless and free. In spite of the thunder of the guns, which was getting closer and closer, the war had remained improbable, something which didn't seem to affect her. Now, all at once, it became reality. A shallow, motorized pontoon glided along the waterway and made fast. Six young Red Army soldiers jumped on land, sub-machine guns drawn and ready. One of them had a pockmarked, Mongol face. With a couple of strokes, Helga reached the bank. The soldiers stared at her. They had never seen a woman in a bathing suit before.

One of them shouted and fired a salvo into the blue sky. The others roared something. Two of them seized Helga. She defended herself in silence, but she knew she had no chance.

'Mama, Mama!' Karl came racing up. He was a strong lad of nearly fifteen now, and fearless in his simple innocence. He made for the intruders like a madman, thrust them aside and stationed himself protectively in front of his mother.

'Karl, don't, they'll shoot!' she begged. Her son stood rooted to the spot. One of the six called something out in surprise. He took the pockmarked soldier's arm and pulled him over to Karl. They could all see that the man of Mongolian origin and the mongoloid boy looked like brothers. The men stared in amazement. The soldier hugged Karl and slapped him on the back. The others laughed and applauded. Helga ran into the house, and no one stopped her.

Hejdus had placed himself by the stove with his four women behind him. He was holding a shotgun. 'We'll kill ourselves first,' he growled.

Quickly, Helga flung some clothes on. 'What about your famous Spreewald hospitality?' she cried, running out again. The soldiers were talking to Karl and laughing. Karl took Helga's arm. 'Mama,' he told his new friends. 'My Mama.'

One of them understood. '*Matka.*' He pointed to first mother, then son. '*Sin.*'

Frau Wanda and the three girls had put on their traditional caps and shawls and carried out trays with water, bread and salt on them. They bobbed curtseys, not submissively but with a welcoming smile. The soldiers understood this gesture of hospitality, and took what was offered with thanks. The two Zastrows came hesitantly out of their cottage. After hiding his shotgun, Hejdus joined them.

Then there was real eating and drinking: sausage made with grits, pancakes, millet and cabbage, with sour milk to drink. They all laughed and talked. The Sorbs and Russians were delighted to find words common to both their Slav languages.

Papa Zastrow ventured to put it into words. 'Friends, I think the war is over.'

Helga had never seen her son so happy before. He raced around in high excitement, filling the guests' plates and mugs. Later they danced to Mato's accordion. Karl stumbled awkwardly around with Breda. He couldn't get enough of the fun. Then, in the middle of the dance, he collapsed. Helga was beside him at once. He lay on the ground, breathing heavily, his eyes closed, his pulse barely perceptible.

The men carried him into the house. Helga undressed him, rubbed him with juniper spirit, and covered him up to keep warm. She sat beside the bed and held his hands. She knew this was the end. His heart, underdeveloped as in all mongoloid children, had held out for almost fifteen years. He opened his eyes. 'Mama,' he said thickly.

'You are dying free, my son,' she whispered. 'That's my gift to you.'

Outside, the soldiers started the engine of their pontoon and cast off. The noise of the engine died away. All was quiet in the bedroom. Karl had stopped breathing.

They buried Karl behind the house. The girls wept, but Helga had no tears to shed. The knowledge that she had carried out her task consoled her. She had looked after him and protected him from his first moment of life to his last, had fought for him and defended him, had given him good, happy times. Now that it was all over she couldn't stay in the Spreewald. She returned from Cottbus to Berlin on the roof of a freight train.

The building in Sophie-Charlotte-Strasse was intact, but it was brimming over with people who had been bombed out. Helga kept applying to the Housing Department until they finally let her have a room in her own house. Until then she stayed with her sister in Tempelhof. Monika's small daughter Erika was five. 'She last saw her father in '42 and can't remember him. They say it will be years before the Russians let their prisoners of war go. Young Frau Pillau next door isn't waiting that long. She takes a student to bed from time to time. It must be fun with a really young man, don't you think?'

Helga told her about her times with Mato. 'A dear boy. He insists he's coming to visit me here, but I hope some Spreewald girl will put a stop to that. I really don't like the idea. I have to put my life in order and look for work.'

'Why don't you go back to your old job? Children's nurses are always in demand,' Monika encouraged her.

One day soon after that Helga went to the Charité, which was now in the Soviet-occupied sector. The Western Allies had moved into Berlin a few days earlier and taken over their own sectors of the capital. There were no visible lines of demarcation between West and East, only several large and ugly notices on the major thoroughfares: YOU ARE NOW LEAVING THE BRITISH — FRENCH — AMERICAN — SECTOR OF BERLIN. The Berliners weren't bothered. They went all over their city or out of it, on foraging expeditions or to search for friends and relations who had been bombed out.

'You'd like to come back to us? Good. Just go to the personnel department,' a friendly woman at reception told her.

'Rinke, Helga?' The same man was at the registration desk, except that now he'd removed his Party badge. He brought out a card index. 'Nurse in the children's ward until 1929. Reappointed 1941.' He stopped. 'Just a moment, please.' He disappeared into the room next door. She heard him pick up the phone. '. . . had herself transferred to Klein Moorbach, that euthanasia institute . . . my duty as an anti-Fascist . . .' She couldn't hear any more. She didn't need to. Quietly, she left the office. She had to get out of there! The Western newspapers had reported this kind of thing. The NKVD were looking for alleged Nazi criminals all over the Soviet-occupied zone, throwing them into the camps they had taken over from the real wrong-doers.

'They don't go to the trouble of examining the facts,' she explained to her sister. 'Well, luckily they know me as Helga Rinke and not Helga Lohmann. All the same, no one's getting me back in the East again.'

'Go to the newspapers and tell your story,' Monika suggested.

But Helga wouldn't hear of it. 'That won't bring the children of Klein Moorbach back to life.'

'What are you going to do?'

'Look around here for something.'

Young Frau Pillau next door came to her aid. 'Try the Yanks, Frau Lohmann. They're recruiting Germans to work in all sorts of jobs. Schoolgirl English is good enough. My sister-in-law got a job in the Telefunken canteen, the US intelligence people have set up shop there. I'll ask Marina where you apply tomorrow.'

The place to apply, Helga learned, was the German-American Employment Office in Lichterfelde. She got the address, too. It was in Finckensteinallee. 'Ask for Mr Chalford.'

Mr Chalford was the man in charge of the office. 'How good is your English, Fräulein Loman?'

'Frau Lohmann. My husband fell in the war.' That was close enough to the truth. Death by exploding gun barrel in Döberitz sounded a little banal.

'Can you please say that in English, Frau Loman?'

'My man is dead in the war.' She spoke rather broken English, but it was good enough for Mr Chalford.

'Have you got a profession?' he asked, still in English.

She was surprised to find how well she could understand him. 'I am a sister for children.'

'You mean a children's nurse? Excellent. And do you also know anything about housekeeping? Can you cook?'

'I think so.'

'I believe I have something for you. Colonel Tucker and his family are looking for a housekeeper.' Chalford played with a pencil as he talked. He spoke halting German, with a heavy American accent. 'Mrs Tucker needs help, particularly to take care of her two boys. Their house is in Dahlem. Im Dol – funny kind of street name, don't you think? If Colonel and Mrs Tucker like you, you can have the job.' Helga looked at him with interest. She had never been so close to an American before. Chalford was a friendly man in his thirties with thinning fair hair, a round, rosy face, and pale-blue eyes. He seemed to be a pleasant human being. As a man he left her cold. 'You must have a medical first, of course,' he explained. 'We only want healthy people. And then we'll take a photo for our card index of employees. Where do you live?' Helga gave him her address in Sophie-Charlotte-Strasse. Chalford put the pencil down. 'Good luck, Frau Loman.' He winked encouragingly at her and began to read a file.

The T-Line bus wasn't back in service because of the fuel shortage. The Americans had started a bus line of their own, carrying GIs, US civilians, German employees of the army who held bus passes, and several clever Berlin lads who managed to persuade the naïve German drivers that they were Americans by chewing gum and wearing garish ties.

Helga's journey took her a quarter of an hour, past Truman Hall, named after the new President, which housed the recently set up Post Exchange, as the US Army commissariat was traditionally known. An American could buy stuff in the PX that the Germans didn't even dream of – they had forgotten that such things existed. The engineers had unrolled a stretch of artificial turf outside this unattainable paradise and planted full-grown trees, which were supported by a framework for the first few months. At the same time, Berliners were cutting down the last fir trees in the Grunewald by night as firewood for the coming winter.

'Im Dol' was a quiet street of villas in Dahlem, evidence of the former prosperity of its inhabitants. The Tuckers' house stood at the very back of its plot of land, invisible from the street. Its rightful owner, a reclusive biochemist, had grown deadly bacterial cultures there for the Nazi regime. He was now continuing his work in a Moscow laboratory.

There was a blue Studebaker parked on the drive. A man in Yankee uniform dyed black was raking the lawn between the birch trees. He stopped work when he saw Helga. 'Yes?'

'I'm Frau Lohmann. Colonel and Mrs Tucker are expecting me. It's about the post as housekeeper.'

He looked condescendingly at Helga. 'You'll never get the job, darling,' he said, with offensive familiarity. 'Tucker likes 'em young.'

'Keep your opinion to yourself. And keep your "darling" for your own kind,' Helga snapped back.

'OK. Take a look through the kitchen window there.'

Tucker, in full uniform, was standing at the kitchen table between the naked thighs of a girl sitting on the edge of it. The girl was uttering small, rhythmic cries.

'Don't go away,' the colonel panted when he saw Helga. Obviously he enjoyed it twice as much with an audience. He stowed his prick back in his trousers. 'I suppose you're the housekeeper. Come on in.' The girl slipped off the table and buttoned up her smock. 'That's Rosie the housemaid,' Tucker said. 'Myra and the boys have gone shopping. They'll soon be back. Rosie, show her around the house.'

Rosie was seventeen, a little brunette with bright, brown eyes. 'What am I to do?' she said to Helga, by way of excusing herself. 'If he fires me I'll have to go back to the East as a farm hand. What will you do if he gets fresh with you?'

'Get fired. Does Mrs Tucker know?'

'She looks the other way. In return he lets her drink in peace.'

'Who's that fellow in the garden?'

'Klatt. Gardener, sometimes chauffeur too. Steals like a magpie. Brings the colonel new girls, and worms his way into Mrs Tucker's good graces.'

There was a sudden loud noise outside. Two little boys in baseball kit stormed in. A youngish woman with a cigarette in her mouth followed. Klatt carried her shopping into the kitchen.

'Hi. I'm Myra Tucker. I suppose it's about the job as housekeeper?'

'Helga Lohmann,' Helga introduced herself.

'OK, come on, Helga, let's go into the study. Rosie, see to the twins, will you?' Mrs Tucker went ahead. The panelled study was the room where the former master of the house had worked. 'Like a drink?'

'No thank you, madam.'

'For heaven's sake call me Myra.' Mrs Tucker took a bottle of gin off the cocktail trolley and poured a lavish quantity into a large brandy balloon. 'Dry vermouth,' she said, spraying a little into her glass from an atomizer. She took a long gulp. 'I've given up the olives. You can't get the ready-stoned sort in the PX. I like them stuffed with anchovies. Do you like olives, Helga?'

'I don't know. I've never eaten an olive.'

'Really? Well, never mind. OK, so you're here about the job. No problem. If you can cook and cope with the boys, it's yours.' Mrs Tucker emptied her glass and refilled it. She forgot about the vermouth this time. She laughed briefly. 'Thank goodness, you're too old for the colonel. Do you have any family?'

'My husband has been dead for some time. My son died in May.'

'Oh, I'm so, so sorry.' Myra Tucker looked at her, eyes swimming with tears. It was easy to guess that behind the gin bottle was a woman who sympathized because she'd been so deeply injured herself. 'Can you start tomorrow, please? That will give you and Rosie two days for the preparations. We're throwing a party on Saturday, OK?'

'OK.' Obeying an instinct, Helga carefully took her new employer's glass away from her. 'You don't need that any more, Myra. You have me now.' She took her hand. The American stiffened. A few seconds later she was just a child, seeking shelter in Helga's arms.

Colonel Harold Miles Tucker was a career soldier. He had commanded a battalion in the Airborne Division and fought his way from Normandy to the Elbe with his paratroopers. Service in Berlin was his first peacetime post. He had been assigned to the US city commandant as his adjutant, and it was on the commandant's instructions that he had sent for Myra and the twins. General Abbot expected his subordinates to set an example of family life, particularly to the Germans. It was all part of the 'democratic re-education' of the conquered ordained by the State Department. Since the ban on fraternization had been lifted, contact with them was considered desirable. Helga learned this from Klatt, who admired the crew-cut Tucker, old warhorse and confirmed skirt-chaser.

She and Rosie had prepared platters of cold meats, salads, dishes of fruit and desserts – unknown delights, almost all out of cans. How astonished Karl would be, she thought, and felt a pang of melancholy.

The first guests arrived around eight. Tucker and his wife welcomed them at the front door: strong, healthy army and air force officers. Their wives were conventionally pretty, uttering crows of delight when they saw a

109

girlfriend from the past – that was to say, someone last seen in the hairdresser's that afternoon. US civilian staff in their mock uniforms, a source of amusement to the military, loudly demanded whisky. A few hand-picked Germans were invited.

The city commandant, General Henry C. Abbot, a lean, grey-headed man with a weather-beaten face, came in a plain dark suit. Mrs Abbot was a silver-haired, grandmotherly woman. She asked after the Tucker twins, who were already in bed. The general was a Westpoint-trained army man from an old Boston family. He was an enthusiastic yachtsman, and engaged the mayor of Zehlendorf in conversation about sailing on the Wannsee. He and a couple of British officers had started the sport there again. Dr Struwe listened politely. He had other things on his mind.

Helga was serving at the buffet. 'I'll have some ham and egg salad,' someone asked. Mr Chalford's round, rosy face beamed at her. 'I see you've already settled in here nicely, Frau Lohmann.'

'Yes, sir, and thank you very much for finding me this position.'

'That's my job, Frau Lohmann.' Chalford walked across the room, balancing his plate. He'd seen someone he knew.

Her glance fell on one of the guests, and lingered there. 'Eugen!' she cried in surprise. He didn't hear her. Only when she repeated his name right behind him did he turn.

'Helga, how nice!' he said, arousing an alarming variety of feelings in her.

Professor Eugen Klemm had lost weight. His collar and suit were too big for him now, and his face had the drawn, grey look of thousands of hungry Berliners. 'Have you had anything to eat yet?' It was the first thing that occurred to her.

He shook his head. 'Those who need it most hold back. A question of self-respect, I suppose.'

'Wait here.' She hurried to the buffet and came back with a laden plate. 'Klatt will bring you a beer.'

'Still the considerate young student nurse? I remember one night in the ward when you brought me a cup of strong bouillon at dawn to keep me from collapsing.' There was warmth in his voice. Feelings that she had thought long forgotten broke over her like a wave.

'Excuse me, Eugen.' She went over to the hostess, who was just filling up her glass of orange juice with gin. 'Mrs Abbot asked very nicely about your twins. You ought to have a word with her yourself, Myra. And remember – you don't need that stuff now.' She took the bottle from her hand and gave it to Klatt. Then she offered round Virginia ham rolls, first to the city commandant and Mr Chalford, who were engaged in animated conversation, then to a group of young officers on the terrace. When she turned to look for Eugen Klemm, he had gone.

The last guests left about ten. 'Mrs Tucker stayed sober all evening. How did you do it, Helga?' There was grudging appreciation in the colonel's voice.

'I don't know what you're talking about, sir.'

Tucker beckoned to Rosie, who followed him into the study shrugging her shoulders.

Myra Tucker giggled like a little girl. 'That confused him, didn't it? We must do it more often. Thank you, Helga, you were a great help. You can wash the dishes tomorrow. There's someone waiting for you in the conservatory. Offer him anything you like, and don't let them disturb you. I'm going to bed. Goodnight.'

'Goodnight, Myra.'

Eugen Klemm was sitting in a wicker chair among the potted plants. He looked a little lost. She went over to sit down with him, pleased that he had stayed. 'How did you of all people come to be at this party?'

'I'm working as a junior surgeon at the military hospital, and was landed with the job of removing a wart from the Tempelhof Air Base commander. I suppose they decided I was socially acceptable and worthy of an invitation.'

Helga shook her head. 'You, a junior surgeon? Don't they know who you are?'

'What does it matter? Now, tell me how you've been. What are you doing here?'

'I'm working as housekeeper and nanny for the Tuckers.'

'And before that?'

'I escaped from Klein Moorbach. I'll tell you about it some other time. Karl and I lived in hiding in the Spreewald until the end of the war.' She bent her head. 'Karl's dead now.'

He nodded, distracted. 'So are Renate and the children. Buried under the ruins of our house in Blütenstrasse. A direct hit. I'm living in temporary accommodation, that's to say in the summerhouse.' He stood up and took a couple of steps before going on. 'I've been sitting here for nearly an hour, thinking. I'd like to put a proposition to you.'

'What sort of proposition, Eugen?'

'I want to leave this place, Helga. Make a new start. I'm sixty, I can still do it. My old teacher Professor Levi is eighty and doesn't operate any more. He's made me an offer. I can go and join him as a neurosurgeon at the Philadelphia hospital. He'll make it possible for me and my wife to emigrate.'

'You and your wife? But didn't you say . . . ?'

'Away from here, Helga. Think of it. A new beginning in a new country. No hunger, none of the pressure of the past, no sad memories. A bright future instead. I take it as a sign from fate that we met here this evening. I don't want to go on my own. We could marry in two weeks' time. As good friends – perhaps later as a real married couple if you liked the idea.'

She couldn't utter a word. Understandingly, he placed a hand on her arm. 'Think it over. Come and tell me your answer tomorrow evening. I have to go now. I'm on night duty. They're sending a jeep.' He bent down to her and kissed her on the forehead. 'Goodnight, Helga.'

The jeep sent for him had long ago driven away. The sound of Rosie's squeals came from the study. Helga ignored them. Like a sleepwalker, she fetched her bag from the kitchen and left the house.

A light rain was falling. She took her usual route home, first down Kronprinzallee, which had been renamed a few days before after Clay, the US military governor. The Germans were currying favour. Then she went on along Argentinische Allee, finally turning left past the U-Bahn station and the church.

She was breathing fast, as excited as a child. Suddenly the Atlantic was just a pond. All at once America was close enough to touch. At the same moment, she realized it could just as well have been Madagascar or the Lüneburger Heide, so long as she could be with Eugen. Her love for him hadn't faded in all these years.

The barbed-wire fence of the prohibited zone was unlit at this point. Helga didn't see the figure until it stood before her, arms raised. Goggles shone in the darkness. Metal clinked. A chain came around her neck, cold metal tightened around her throat. Her hands flailed at the empty air.

She breathed stertorously. Greedy fingers felt under her dress, tore her panties off.

Something hard rummaged sharply inside her. An appalling, burning pain tore her vagina. She heard her attacker gasping. She wanted to shout, 'Karl . . . Eugen . . . help me!' but the chain cut off her breath. Then she knew no more.

CHAPTER THREE

INSPECTOR DIETRICH HAD a date to see the chief of police in Alexanderplatz in the morning. Meanwhile, Sergeant Franke was questioning Gerti Krüger, a vivacious Berliner. 'So Frau Rembach was employed with you in the American dry cleaners' shop?'

'Karin, yeah, sure, inspector. Know who she really was?' The witness paused for dramatic effect. 'She never talked about it, not Karin, but I knew. "Hey, I know who you are," I told her. "You're Verena van Bergen." And she said, sounding kind of sad, "That's all in the past." Ever such a nice lady. Not a bit stuck up.'

'Of course.' Franke struck his forehead. 'Verena van Bergen the film star. To think I didn't realize at once! I knew I'd seen her face.'

'So now she's pushing up the daisies. If I could get my hands on that bastard . . .' Gerti forced back her tears.

'Is there anyone you suspect?'

'I wouldn't like to say too much, not me, but that Ziesel is a nasty piece of work.'

Franke pricked up his ears. 'Who's Ziesel?'

'Otto Ziesel, drives the Yanks' garbage truck. Comes for the garbage twice a week. He really hates girls who go with the Yanks. "You two want your cunts burnt out," he said to me and Karin — 'scuse my language, inspector.'

Franke made some notes. 'Thank you, Fräulein Krüger. We'll ask you to come and make an official statement as soon as the inspector's back.'

Gerti Krüger took an old movie magazine out of her shopping bag and put it on the table. 'I brought you that, she's in it. Have a nice lunch, Inspector.'

The brothers came home from school at one o'clock and sat down expectantly at the table. They had to wait, because their father wasn't back from police headquarters until two. 'Talk about an adventure,' said Klaus Dietrich. 'The lines are damaged once you're past Potsdamer Platz. A horse and cart took me on to Alex, where the boss had the nerve to haul me over the coals for being late. And he drives a car with a fuel allowance from the Russians. Then he complained that our investigations were going too slowly.'

But lunch took his mind off his professional troubles. There were real dumplings in real meat broth. Inge had bartered her husband's fur-lined uniform coat with the wife of a Russian officer in Eberswalde for a hundredweight of wheat flour and a piece of tough beef. Klaus Dietrich never wanted to see that coat again. It reminded him of the past too much. How Inge had got the hundredweight sack of flour from the Russian settlement to the rail station and from there to Berlin on the roof of the freight train remained her secret.

She had kept two pounds of flour back for the dumplings and taken the rest to Frau Molch, who lived on Eschershauser Weg and dealt in everything that was in short supply. They agreed on a pair of shoes and a kilo of knitting wool. Ralf could hardly trudge through the snow in sandals next winter, and Grandma would knit two pullovers for the boys.

'With a grating of nutmeg and fried bacon cubes, that's how we used to have our dumplings,' said the district councillor nostalgically.

'What's nutmeg?'

Ralf got no answer, because his grandfather had launched into a convoluted account of yesterday's district council meeting. They had decided to hold de-Nazification tribunals to try former Party members. 'We owe it to our reputation.'

'What reputation?' Klaus Dietrich left the question hanging in the air. He had deep rings under his eyes from sheer exhaustion. The heat was getting to him too; in the shade of the veranda, the thermometer stood at twenty-eight degrees. He dropped a fleeting kiss on his wife's hair and pushed his bicycle through the front garden into the street.

Ben and Ralf went off too. Hajo König was waiting for them on the outskirts of the nearby wood. He was a freckled little lad, in the same class as Ralf. They went through the forest, now stripped bare by illicit tree-felling, and down to Krumme Lanke. The lake lay quiet in the sun. A family of coots left silver ripples behind them as they crossed the water. Where the autumn rains had washed a small, sandy bay out of the bank over many decades, the boys took off their shirts and trousers. They were wearing bathing trunks underneath. Ben wanted to plunge straight into the water. 'Let's go up to the plantation first,' Hajo urged them.

So they made their way through the forestry plantation above the lake, which was fenced. The young trees of what would be mixed woodland in years to come weren't productive enough for firewood thieves, so they had not been harmed, and mingled with brambles, stinging nettles and other weeds to make dense undergrowth. The Forestry Department, its staff decimated by the war, had no one to spare to tidy it up. A clearing lay ahead. The boys ducked. In the hollow before them was a naked young woman on her front, her head thrown back, her thighs spread. She was moving her hips and moaning aloud. The tall grass hid the man underneath her.

Spellbound, the youthful voyeurs stared at her bobbing breasts. Ben thought of Heidi Rödel. Hajo was fingering the front of his bathing trunks. The young woman cried out and collapsed on top of her invisible lover. They waited hopefully, but nothing else happened. After a while the couple got up. The man was quite old, at least forty, Ben guessed. His penis, now flaccid, gleamed wetly in the sun. The young woman squatted down by a bush and had a pee. They quietly went away.

'Usually it's the woman underneath.' Hajo spoke from the experience of earlier observations.

Ralf smirked at his brother. 'So is Heidi Rödel always underneath too? Or aren't you really doing it with her?'

'Of course we're doing it — lots of times,' Ben assured his brother, and then, to be on the safe side, changed the subject. 'Who's going to be first in the water?'

They ran down to the bank. Ralf and Hajo plunged straight in. Ben followed at a more leisurely pace, so as not to be out of breath. He waded in up to his shoulders. Then he took ten deep breaths to enrich his blood with oxygen. He'd read about doing that in the *Neues Universum*. He dived down and swam forward with long strokes, against the flow of the water. He hoped to improve his record for the distance. He kept his eyes open, although he could see barely half a metre ahead in the murky water. With mixed feelings, he thought of the giant catfish said to lurk in these depths. Ehlers the fishmonger's in the shopping street had put a specimen on display a few years ago, a fish over a metre long with whiskery, worm-like filaments and sharp teeth.

He delayed coming up for another couple of seconds, although his lungs were almost bursting. When he couldn't stand it any more he shot up to the surface with two mighty strokes at a diagonal angle, which gave him another metre, and gasped greedily for air. The faces of people on the bank were small, pale specks. He was amazed to realize that he'd swum more than half the width of the lake underwater, at least sixty metres.

'We thought you were drowned,' said his brother. There was admiration in his voice.

'It's all in the breathing technique,' Ben told him.

The couple from the plantation were standing knee-deep in the water. Ben liked the look of the young woman better in her black bathing suit than without it. The man was wearing triangular bathing trunks laced up at the side. He whispered something in her ear. The young woman laughed.

They went back through the Riemeister Fen to catch tadpoles. 'Hey, look at that!' cried Ralf, pointing to the quaking, grassy island ahead of them.

An incendiary bomb, covered with moss, lay among the reeds. The marshy bed of this silted-up arm of the waterway had cushioned its impact and prevented it from going off. Two or three years earlier, after a raid on the city centre, a Lancaster bomber had ditched its remaining load over the Grunewald. Most of the bombs had sunk into the fen. This particular specimen had lasted out the rest of the war near the surface.

Ben pulled their find from the reeds, and carried it from the wobbly island of grass to firm land. The bomb was shaped like a hexagonal stick about six centimetres in diameter and half a metre long. It was made of thermite, as heavy as iron. The upper part had a light aluminium jacket which acted as the control unit. Ben snapped it off. A small, thin lead cross came into view, holding the head of the ignition pin. The cross was supposed to be bent upwards by the force of the impact when the bomb dropped, thus releasing the pin to strike the fuse. It was a simple construction and often failed to work. During the war Ben had quite often let off one of these duds in the sand behind the toboggan run, just to enjoy the firework show.

Before the admiring eyes of both his spectators, he applied the blade of his penknife to the lead cross and bent all four of its shanks up. Then he struck the device on a stone, holding it vertical. There was a plop. Sparks shot out of the holes around the fuse, hissing. Ben held the bomb aloft like a torch. 'Child's play.' He flung it up and away into the air in a high arc. Hajo ran after it. 'Leave it alone,' warned Ben. But the little boy grabbed the end of the thing, which was now burning with a white flame, and held it up with his arm outstretched. 'Like a sparkler,' he shouted enthusiastically.

'Throw it away,' cried Ben.

The detonation came unexpectedly. Hajo's face was suddenly black, and he stared blankly at the place where his hand had just been clutching the burning stick. But there was no stick now, and no hand either. The explosive charge screwed into the improved version of these incendiaries was meant to deter people from throwing them out of the window when they were putting out fires. It had torn the boy's hand off. Hajo collapsed on the ground, his eyes rolling back into his head.

'Oh, shit.' Ben took the belt out of his trousers. 'We must tie it off or he'll bleed to death.' He applied a tourniquet to the unconscious boy's arm with practised expertise; he'd learnt first aid in the *Jungvolk*.

Franke greeted the inspector excitedly when he returned to the office after his lunch break. 'I knew I'd seen her before. Here, look.' The sergeant opened the movie magazine. Klaus Dietrich saw a picture of a beautiful young blonde standing next to a good-looking man. 'Erik de Winter and Verena van Bergen – the new German movie couple,' announced the caption.

Dietrich was surprised. 'The dead woman from the U-Bahn station.'

'She was quite well known.'

'Not to me. I didn't often go to the pictures before the war, and I never got to see the shows in the cinemas at the Front. We were usually fifty kilometres further forward.' Dietrich had served with a Panzer unit.

'First Karin Rembach, now this Helga Lohmann. Both young and pretty,' said Franke, noting the similarities. 'Both blonde with blue eyes. Both killed in the same brutal way . . .'

'. . . both employed by the Yanks,' continued Klaus Dietrich, 'and both murdered after curfew. What does that tell us, Franke?'

'It tells us the murderer is an American, or a German working with

118

the US Army who can be out after curfew. Our witness Krüger suspects a German who drives the Yanks' garbage truck.' Franke told him Gerti's story.

'Try to find out something about this man Ziesel,' Dietrich said. 'Of course it could also be someone out without permission, killing under cover of the general curfew,' he added.

CID Assistant Officer Vollmer put his head round the door. 'Lady called Jutta Weber,' he announced.

The visitor looked pale and exhausted. Klaus Dietrich shook hands with her. 'I'm Inspector Dietrich. You know Herr Franke already. Please sit down, Frau Weber.' He pulled out a chair for his visitor. 'I have a few questions, but it won't take long.'

'Just a moment,' Franke put in. 'First your name, address, date of birth and marital status.' Jutta gave the information he wanted, while the sergeant attacked the antediluvian Erika typewriter, using the one-fingered hunt and peck method. '133 Onkel-Tom-Strasse,' he repeated. 'You live alone there?'

'I share the apartment with a family called König and a Herr Brandenburg, who used to be in the Luftwaffe.'

'And you found the body last night by the fence of the American enclave at about eleven o'clock, is that right?' Dietrich checked.

'Yes, I was going to see some friends.'

'After curfew?' Franke looked up suspiciously.

'I work for the Americans, so I have a pass.'

'Just like the two murdered women,' the sergeant said.

Jutta was horrified. '*Two* women?'

'I'm afraid so. You want to be very careful if you're out alone late at night. But don't worry, we'll soon get our man, and you can help us. We've worked out that you must have found the dead woman quite soon after the crime was committed. Did you notice anything? Did you happen to see anyone?'

'No, I mean, well, yes, there was a man riding a motorbike. He emerged out of nowhere and rode past quite close to me.'

'Was he wearing a leather cap and protective goggles?' Klaus Dietrich waited eagerly for the answer.

'I don't know. His headlight dazzled me.'

'Head-light daz-zled me,' Franke hammered out on the typewriter.

'Which way was he going?'

119

'Towards Onkel Tom. I walked on, and she was just standing there. It was dreadful. Her pale face inside the roll of barbed wire. I didn't recognize her at first. Then I knew who she was.'

The inspector was surprised. 'You knew the dead woman?'

Jutta's eyes filled with tears. 'I used to work in Frau Gerold's bookshop in the shopping street. Helga Lohmann was a customer. She came to our lending library for years with her little boy.' She was weeping quietly.

Klaus Dietrich gave her time. She's as pretty, young, blonde and blue-eyed as the two dead women, he thought suddenly. It was an unsettling idea.

She had become a little calmer. 'Goggles with large lenses?'

'You just said the headlight of the motorbike dazzled you,' Franke objected crossly. Witnesses could be a real pain.

'No, this was a few days ago when I was going home late from work. A pedestrian. I tried to avoid him and fell off my bicycle. As he bent over me I saw the goggles. Then he disappeared, and next moment I heard a motorbike engine start somewhere quite close.'

'Can you remember when this was?'

'Last Wednesday, around eleven o'clock.'

'Not so fast,' groaned Franke as he struggled with the keys.

'Please would you read and sign your statement,' the inspector asked their witness. 'We have your address in case there are any more questions. Thank you, Frau Weber. Try not to take it too much to heart.' He showed her out.

'A serial murderer with a motorbike,' said Franke, narrowing the situation down to a common denominator. 'We Germans had to hand in our cars and motorbikes at the beginning of the war. No one has a motor vehicle today, let alone fuel for it. So the murderer can only be a Yank.'

'Why not one of the French or English occupying forces?' said his boss. 'Or that Dutchman who lives near me? Hendrijk Claasen, big blond fellow. Goes to Nijmegen on his motorbike every two weeks and comes back loaded with black market goods. But he still doesn't have any luck with the women. So my wife says, anyway. Is that suspicious enough for you? On the other hand, how about a Russian coming over to the West on his motorbike by night to commit his crimes here? No, Franke, the murderer isn't necessarily an American. And in any case, who's to say that the murderer and the motorcyclist are one and the same man? What the stationmaster and Frau Weber saw could just as well be a coincidence.'

'Rather too much of a coincidence for me,' muttered the sergeant.

All hell broke loose in the Flora bar in Schöneberg that afternoon. A group of off-duty GIs from the Signal Corps had gone in for a beer and were fooling around with the girls. The Flora was regularly patronized by several GIs from the Transport Division who were also off duty, and claimed prior rights to the Fräuleins. Unfortunately the Signal Corps men were white and the truck drivers black.

When the Military Police arrived, the black contingent was clearly winning, a state of affairs that Sergeant Donovan quickly reversed by bringing his stick down on the heads of the Transport Division men. 'Take those damn niggers in,' he told his men when some semblance of peace had been restored. 'And take in a couple of the whites too.'

'Particularly that one, sergeant,' said a tall black man. He pointed to a white corporal.

'Oh yes? Who's giving the orders around here?' Donovan raised his stick menacingly. The black man rolled down his shirtsleeves. He had three chevrons more than Donovan, who let his stick drop.

'Master Sergeant Roberts,' the black man introduced himself. 'We were all using our fists except for the corporal there, who pulled a knife. One of us was hurt. Well, what about it, sergeant?'

Donovan was seething, but he had no choice. 'Your knife, corporal,' he told the white man, and took charge of it. 'You'll come with us. The injured nigger too.'

The master sergeant kept his temper. 'Black man, coloured man, negro if you like, but we don't care to be called niggers. Particularly by your sort.' Donovan's fist clenched around the grip of his Magnum. Sergeant Roberts, unmoved, put his uniform jacket on. It bore the insignia of the highest war decorations of the US Army. Furious, Donovan got behind the wheel and stepped on the gas. He drove the injured man to the Unter den Eichen military hospital. Fortunately the stab wound was not life-threatening.

The personnel carrier with the men under arrest was already waiting outside Military Police headquarters. 'Send those fighting cocks back to their units,' said Captain Ashburner. 'Their commanding officers can decide what to do with them. The corporal stays here. We'll hand him over to the provost marshal.'

The black master sergeant stood to attention and saluted. 'Your sergeant has requisitioned the knife as evidence, sir. Perhaps you want to put it somewhere safe.'

'Thank you, master sergeant. Put the knife on my desk, Donovan.'

Hesitantly, Donovan produced the knife. 'Let the corporal go, sir,' he asked, when they were alone again. 'I'll make sure he gets a suitable amount of leave docked.'

'The provost marshal will consider whether to lay charges. That will be all, sergeant.'

'Yessir.' Donovan made it clear that he disapproved of his superior officer's decision.

'Get us two coffees, Mike, and sit down.'

'Yes, sir.' Donovan poured two cups of coffee from the Thermos jug.

'Mike, listen, I've been thinking some more about these murdered women. We still can't dismiss the possibility that an American did it. What do you think?'

'I think they were only a couple of German whores. You want one of our brave boys to pay for that?'

'Remember what that German inspector said: the war is over, and murder will be punished again, regardless of who committed it, an American or a German.'

'We had a case in 1944, when we were marching through the Rhineland. One of our boys got a bit too rough with a German girl. Rape and murder, the provost marshal called it. The little tart had opened her legs of her own free will. And you couldn't really blame the GI for putting his hands around her neck in the heat of the moment. Anyway, what we did was, we gave him a minor flesh wound and sent him to the back of the lines as wounded. That gave our colonel time to get him transferred to the Pacific. A practical solution, don't you think, sir?'

'Can I ask you a question in return, Mike? What would you do if the two murdered women were members of our Women's Army Corps and the murderer was a German?'

'Shoot the bastard,' replied Donovan in surprise.

The radio-telephone came on. 'Patrol Three, Miller. We picked up a

Russki in Block Eighteen. Claims he's looking for a man called Kless, something like that. Me and Joe think it's a funny sort of story, captain. What do we do with the guy?'

'Absolutely nothing, Miller, if you want to observe the agreement between the four powers.' Ashburner went off in the jeep. Problems with their Soviet allies were the last thing he needed. The patrol car was standing on the Wannsee bridge, barring the way of an open, white BMW two-seater sports car against which the tall, lean figure of a Russian officer was lounging. He had taken off his cap, revealing wiry fair hair, he was smoking a cigarette with a long cardboard tip, and looking with amusement at Corporal Miller and the driver, Joe, who were waiting a little way off, hands hovering close to their pistol holsters.

Ashburner introduced himself formally. 'Captain Ashburner, United States Army Military Police.'

'Major Berkov, staff officer with City Commandant General Bersarin. Extremely pleased to make your acquaintance, Captain Ashburner.' The Russian spoke an elegant British English that made Ashburner's American accent seem unsophisticated.

The captain quickly ran over all relevant agreements and orders in his mind. They stipulated that members of the armed forces of the four Allies in Berlin had free access at any time to the other Allies' sectors of occupation, so long as they were wearing uniform. 'I hope my men have treated you correctly, Major Berkov. You're looking for a man called Kless?'

'Not Kless, Kleist. I don't think your men entirely understoond me. He committed suicide somewhere in the vicinity, and I'm looking for his grave.'

'A suicide by the name of Kleist. That would be a case for the German police. I'll radio my duty officer and tell him to get in touch with the Germans at once. They can send someone to help you search. Did you know him?'

'Know whom?' Berkov did not understand at first, then it slowly dawned on him. 'Heinrich von Kleist? Oh, no. He and his mistress Henriette Vogel committed suicide here on the banks of the Kleiner Wannsee in November 1811. A German poet from an old aristocratic Prussian family.'

'Well, you certainly caught me out there, major,' murmured Ashburner, with some embarrassment.

'Nonsense, captain. I happen to know about it quite by chance, because I've studied a little German literature,' said Berkov apologetically. Ashburner beckoned to an old man, who showed them the steps leading down to the river bank. 'I'm particularly fond of his plays *The Broken Jug* and *The Prince of Homburg*,' said Berkov, taking some photos of the monument.

'Fabulous car.' Ashburner pointed to the BMW when they were back up in the street again.

'I found it on a country estate, hidden under bales of straw. I'm planning to take it home with me – the spoils of war. Privilege of the victor. Would you like to try it, captain?' The major invitingly opened the low-slung car door.

'That's an offer I can't refuse. Corporal Miller, carry on with your patrol. Joe can drive my jeep back to the station.' Ashburner got in. He indicated a small gold plaque with the letters M.G. on the dashboard. 'Initials of the previous owner?'

'Very possibly.' Berkov turned the sports car and stepped on the gas. Ashburner enjoyed the acceleration. They had both taken their caps off to let the warm air waft around their heads. They glanced at one another and found themselves laughing like little boys. It was a beautiful, late-summer's day. The houses in the western suburbs were hardly damaged at all, and children were playing in the front gardens. Only a few boarded-up windows and traces left by shrapnel on the carriageway were reminders of the war.

'Must have been a good life here once,' said Ashburner.

'Give the Nemzis a few years and they'll be doing better than ever,' Berkov called back.

The picture changed the further they drove into the city. Rubble and ruins lined the streets. People were clearing up everywhere. Chalk and brick dust hung in the air, and the people seemed more depressed and tired than beyond the city centre.

The Russian stopped on a corner. 'My name's Maxim Petrovich. What's yours?'

'John.'

'All right, John, where can I take you?'

'To Uncle Tom. I'll show you the way. I'd like to invite you for a drink, Maxim Petrovich, but I have a date. Another time, maybe?'

'I'd like that.' The major turned, and drove Ashburner back to Uncle Tom at breakneck speed. Jutta was already waiting at the entrance to the prohibited zone. 'What a pretty woman. Congratulations, John,' said Berkov, smiling. Ashburner got out, and his new friend raced away.

Jutta came to meet him. 'Hello, John. Why did you send that dishy man away? He could be dangerous even without a sports car.' She enjoyed teasing him a little.

He took her seriously. 'Major Berkov? I'll invite him along if you'd like to meet him.'

She took his arm. 'Not in the least! It's you I have a date with, remember? I'm ravenously hungry too.'

'I did some shopping.' John Ashburner was glad to be back in safe waters.

They passed the sentry on guard and entered the prohibited zone. Jutta pointed to the tall fence. 'It's terrible, that fence. When I think of that poor woman in the barbed wire . . .'

'It must have been a dreadful shock for you.' She nodded, silently, and he sensed that she would rather not talk about it.

He had laid the table in his living room that morning, with a vase of roses in the centre. He had bribed the gardener of the Harnack House with a packet of cigarettes to plunder one of the flower beds. 'Oh, how lovely,' she said, delighted. 'I last saw roses at my sister's wedding. After that, no one grew anything but potatoes and vegetables. Even in the public squares.'

'I'd like you to take them home.'

'Thank you, John, that's really nice of you.'

'I thought we might cook together.' He handed her an apron and put one on too. Hers bore a picture of a white rabbit with a chef's hat. His had a caricature of a bulldog with a wooden spoon in its mouth. She thought them both rather silly.

The US quartermaster had installed refrigerators in the requisitioned apartments. Ashburner took out a bottle of white wine and filled two glasses. '*Prost*. That's what you say here, isn't it?'

'*Prost*, John.' She took a sip. It was ages since she'd last drunk wine, though Sergeant Panelli sometimes stood her a beer in Club 48. 'What delicious things are we going to have?'

'Shrimp salad, steak with sweetcorn, we'll drink red wine with that, Chianti. Ice cream for dessert. OK?'

'Wonderful. What shall I do?'

'Open the can of shrimp and the jar of mayonnaise, please.'

'Oh, never mind that! If you have eggs, oil, lemons and mustard we can make the mayonnaise ourselves.'

Her own whisk was still hanging in its place in the kitchen cupboard. The ingredients she needed were there too. She put the yolk of an egg into a bowl, mixed it with pepper, salt, a few drops of lemon juice and a little mustard, and added a pinch of sugar. He was watching her attentively; it was an excuse to keep looking at her. She bent over the bowl, and puffed an annoying lock of hair away from her forehead. There was something very touching about the sight. The groove in the nape of her neck, which was bent at a pretty angle, aroused feelings in him that he couldn't really define. Her youthful figure in her light dress made her seem both vulnerable and desirable. At home, Ethel went around in hair curlers and barely visited the kitchen to get herself a Coke from the fridge. The two women were worlds apart.

Jutta slowly trickled oil into the bowl and worked it loosely with the whisk. 'The oil and egg yolk have to be at room temperature, that's the secret of it,' she explained. Before his eyes, she created a wonderful thick, yellow mayonnaise and mixed the shrimp into it. Then she piled it all on lettuce leaves in two dishes.

He heated the canned sweetcorn with a little butter and put it aside. He had bought the grooved, cast-iron grill pan in the PX especially for this evening, along with the aprons. 'It has to be very hot, so the steaks don't braise all the way through but grill fast. Here, let's test it.' He splashed a little water in the pan, and it immediately fizzled out. 'Careful now!' The steaks hissed as they went into the pan. He looked very serious and was concentrating hard on what he was doing, like a little boy with his electric train set. She did not try to fight off the tender feelings arising in her. 'Quarter of a minute each side to seal the steaks. Then two to four minutes each side, depending on the thickness. When the juices show like red pearls, they're *au point*, as the French say.' She could see that he was proud of his expertise.

'Well done, John. That's amazing.' She had found a tube of anchovy paste and was mixing it with butter. 'We can put this on the steaks.'

'We work together pretty well, don't you think?' It was a clumsy declaration of love, and all the better for that. He opened the Chianti and put the bottle on the table.

She took off her apron, and sensed that he was looking at her figure in the light dress, an admiring rather than offensive look. I hope he doesn't think my hips are too broad, she thought. He held her chair for her. She liked his chivalrous gesture, and thanked him with a small smile.

'Tell me about your home,' she asked as they ate. 'I know almost nothing about America.'

'Neither do I really. I know Venice, Illinois. Five thousand inhabitants, two churches, Bill's Bar on Main Street. And the police station house. Green hills and pasture around the town. I grew up on our farm; my brother Jim runs it now. I'm the local sherriff. A peaceful job; not much happens in the country.'

'What about your wife?'

He gave a resigned smile. 'Not much happens with her either. We don't have children. Ethel hated the idea of pregnancy.'

'Jochen wanted a Volkswagen first, and then a son. He never had either. A Polish marksman shot him. He was on the latrine. He didn't even get to die a hero's death.'

'I wasn't in the war itself. They sent me over here afterwards, when they needed police to keep order. Once the fighting stops guys can get stupid ideas into their heads.' He poured more wine. 'You know, I've always wanted just to talk like this – never mind what about. The main thing is to have someone listening.'

'Red check tablecloths and candles in wine bottles, wasn't that how your little German-style restaurant was going to look?'

'You remembered?'

'Of course, I like the idea.'

'Will you have a cognac?' he asked after the meal.

'No, thank you, John. After all that wine it would knock me right out.' She went close to him and raised her face. He hesitated before taking her in his arms and kissing her. He had almost forgotten what it was like. He felt her warm, soft body and breathed in her perfume. It seemed to him that they stood like that for a delicious eternity. Then she moved gently away from him. 'We have plenty of time, don't we?' she said quietly. It was a promise. Elated, he drove her home in the jeep and waited until she had disappeared into the building.

The door to the Königs' room was open. Late as it was, they were drinking schnapps with Brandenburg. Jutta stopped. 'How's your son?' she asked.

'They're doing the second operation tomorrow to pull the skin over the stump.' Pretty Frau König wiped a tear from the corner of her eye.

'Now, now, Ilse. He'll soon get a brand-new hand with all the latest clever inventions. The surgeon says the Americans have made amazing progress in that area.'

'I do hope he'll make a quick recovery. Goodnight.'

Brandenburg followed her into the kitchen. He was slightly tipsy. 'Been brought home in the jeep again? What's the going rate – a packet of cigarettes a trick?' She managed to hit his cheek even in the dark. Her hand connected with a loud slap, and his glasses fell to the floor. He bent down and felt about on the rug for them. When she lit the candle he had them on again. 'Well, congratulations, you have a good aim.' She ignored him, and filled a vase with water for the roses.

In bed, she felt remorse. He hadn't been sober, and he was blind and helpless. She ought not to have hit him. Later, she heard cries of pleasure from his room. Frau König's anxiety about her son was obviously kept well within bounds.

On the way to the bathroom in the morning she met Herr König. 'You mustn't upset the captain,' he told her reproachfully. 'Just think of all the poor man's been through.'

CHAPTER FOUR

BEN AND RALF kept their heads bent at breakfast, but the doomsday blast they were expecting never materialized. Their father's calm approach hurt far more. 'All three of you are to blame,' Klaus Dietrich told them in matter-of-fact tones. 'But Hajo is the one who has to pay for it. All his life. When you two have long forgotten about it, he'll still be going around with one hand. Think about that. Now, off you go to school.'

Relieved, the boys raced off over the veranda. 'Aren't you coming?' Ralf asked. Ben silently shook his head, and went to hide his school bag under the empty potato sacks in the shed. There was time enough for Latin, English and geography tomorrow. The Potsdamer Platz was on his schedule for today.

'You ought to give Ben a little help with his maths. He's having difficulty with logarithms,' Inge told her husband.

'As soon as I get time,' Klaus Dietrich promised her, and glanced at his father-in-law, who was sitting at the breakfast table looking glum.

'We'll have this ghastly ersatz coffee coming out of our ears,' Dr Hellbich complained. But the real reason for his gloom was not the coffee but yesterday's meeting of the Berlin Social Democrat party committee. 'They're seriously thinking of letting former Communists join the SPD, on the grounds that they're anti-Fascists too. Murderers, that's what they are; just as bad as the Nazis, I said, and I successfully opposed the motion. Luckily my friends and I are in the majority. But for how much longer, that's the question? You have to look at it pragmatically, some snotty-nosed youngster told us. The fellow knows nothing about Social Democracy before '33, and he wasn't in the underground movement like us either.'

'You were never in the underground,' Klaus Dietrich pointed out. 'They made you retire early, that's all, complete with your own home and your rose beds.'

Inge signalled to her husband not to continue. She was worried about her father's blood pressure. Hellbich did not explode, but mounted a counter-attack instead. 'So how's your work going? No progress, eh? Or have you caught that serial killer yet? Well, don't let it bother you. Your predecessor before the war wasn't any more successful.'

Dietrich pricked up his ears. 'What do you mean? What happened before the war?'

With an expression of distaste, Hellbich took another sip of the brown brew. 'Oh, it was in '36. The Olympic Games had just begun. I can still see her: Annie, young, pretty, blonde, blue eyes. She was a waitress in Brumm's Bakery and Cake Shop opposite the U-Bahn station. I used to get our break-fast rolls there. Found dead in the front garden one morning. Oddly enough, the newspapers didn't publish the story. It was kept under wraps. I happened to know a police officer, though, and he told me the details. What the murderer did before he strangled her was unspeakable.'

As if electrified, Klaus Dietrich shot to his feet – and fell to the floor with a cry of pain. 'This damn prosthesis,' he groaned.

Inge helped him up. 'Lie down for a little. We'll take the thing off.'

'No time. I must go straight to the station.' But his wife insisted on quarter of an hour's rest for the nerves in his stump to recover a little. Then Dietrich cycled off.

'Franke, we need details.' Dietrich removed the bicycle clips from his trouser legs and put them in the middle drawer of his desk. 'Did the pre-war murderer ride a motorbike? Exactly how did he torture his victim? What was that girl Annie strangled with?'

The sergeant shrugged apologetically. 'Sorry, sir, can't help you. I was with the regular police in Schöneberg before the war. Maybe someone at the station there will know.'

'Then let's go.'

They heated up the Opel. The gears crunched and the transmission howled, but Franke got the vehicle from the CID office to the police station ten minutes' drive away without mishap. Most of the windows in the police station had cardboard filling the panes, but they were wide open in the summer heat. The paving stones in front of the building had been taken up and the space turned into a small potato patch.

Two police officers with grey, hungry faces climbed over the potato plants and set out on afternoon patrol. On orders from the city commandant, their green uniforms had been dyed black, with the result that they were now an ugly, dark and dirty hue, particularly the fabric of their caps. They carried wooden truncheons at their belts. They'd been required to hand in their Parabellum 0.8s with the leather holsters.

'Hey, if it isn't the CID cops,' the man on duty, an old superintendent, greeted the visitors. 'What can we ordinary plods do for you gentlemen?'

'Tell us where to find the pre-war files. Unless someone's been warming his feet with them,' said Franke, going along with the officer's tone.

'It's all there, gents. We lose the odd war now and then, we never lose the files. Herr Ewald will take you down.'

Herr Ewald was a little man with the face of a sparrow, wearing sleeve protectors. 'Got an interesting case?' he asked hopefully as they climbed down the basement steps.

'Depends how you look at it,' growled Franke, looking with distaste at the flooded basement floor. A couple of dead rats were bobbing about in the stinking water. Planks had been laid on bricks between the shelves of files.

'The drains are a total mess. A Russian mortar on the last day of the war,' Ewald apologized. 'What are you looking for?'

'Everything you have on the murder of a woman in 1936. As far as we know, the case was never solved. The victim was found strangled in the front garden of Brumm's Bakery, opposite the Onkel Tom U-Bahn station,' Dietrich told him.

Ewald disappeared among the shelves of files. The planks creaked. Water slopped back and forth in a blocked drain with an unpleasant slurping sound. After a few minutes he reappeared, looking gloomy. 'No murdered woman, case solved or not. Only a manslaughter. The killer confessed. I looked at 1935 and 1937 too, but I didn't find anything.'

'It was in August '36, during the Olympic Games. My father-in-law remembers the exact time. He knew the victim slightly, a young waitress,' Dietrich insisted.

'Could the files have been lost?' asked Franke.

'Nothing gets lost here,' Ewald told him.

'Just take another look, would you?' asked Dietrich patiently. 'It's important.'

Herr Ewald dived in among the shelves again. This time they heard him clicking his tongue and talking to himself under his breath. Fifteen minutes went by before his sparrow-like face appeared. 'I was looking in alphabetical order first, no result, like I said. Now I've been through all the files in chronological order for the whole of 1936. They begin with File 36/1/1/III B, that's year, month, consecutive number, and the Roman three at the end is for theft, and B is for the sub-category pickpocketing.'

'What indicates murder?' Franke interrupted him.

'I A. But like I said, all we had in Zehlendorf in 1936 was a manslaughter, that's I B. There's a gap in August, though. The file with consecutive number 122 is missing, which is odd, because if a file's been lent out there's usually a card index entry in its place, giving the name and department of whoever's borrowed it. And there isn't one here.'

'Can you establish the date of that file?'

Yet again Ewald did a tightrope act across the planks to the shelves. This time he came straight back. 'The files just before and just afterwards were dated the third and the seventh of August respectively, if that's any help.'

The inspector and sergeant were glad to get up the stairs and away from the stench below. Dietrich turned to the man on duty. 'Superintendent, how long have you been at this station?'

'Since '38, inspector. I was in Pankow before that.'

'All the same, it's possible that you can help us. A woman murdered in the Onkel Tom quarter in 1936 – who's likely to have been in charge of the inquiries back then?'

'Wilhelm Schlüter. He was head of the Zehlendorf CID from 1935, ended up as Chief Detective Superintendent. During the war he commanded a Security Police unit in the Ukraine.'

'You don't by any chance know what became of him?'

'You bet I do, inspector. He's in Brandenburg penitentiary. Responsible for mass shootings in Kiev. They say the Russians need him as a witness to cases involving other horrors, or it'd have been a bullet in the back of the neck for him long ago.'

'Brandenburg penitentiary? Franke, we must try to get permission to interview him.'

'What, from the NKVD?' The sergeant gave his superior a pitying glance.

Ben bought a twenty-pfennig ticket at the ticket counter in Onkel Tom. There was nothing on the platform to remind anyone of last week's murder. Passengers were waiting calmly for the train. Ben got into the end carriage and sat down in the empty conductor's seat next to the driver's cab. On the way back this would be the front of the train, manned by the driver and conductor. The rails gleamed in the afternoon sun. Out here in the suburbs the U-Bahn track was carved out of the sand of the Brandenburg Mark, and still above ground. Ben thought of what his father had said about Hajo and his hand, and swore to himself never to forget it. This good resolution lasted all of two stations, as far as Thielplatz. By the time he reached Dahlem Dorf station the torn-off hand was in one of his mental pigeon-holes. Ben had many such pigeon-holes in his head: for school, which he attended as sporadically as possible; for Gert Schlomm, who had taught him to masturbate before he began taking an interest in Heidi Rödel; for Heidi's breasts, which he dreamed of, waking with a stiff penis; for the new GYA youth club, which must surely prove productive; for the Prince of Wales check suit in which he intended to make a conquest of Heidi.

That double-breasted suit accompanied Ben into his dreams; smooth, soft fabric, beautifully tailored, with sharp creases down the trouser legs and broad, slightly sloping shoulders. But best of all were the lapels, which he could see in his mind's eye: they rose elegantly, following the curve of the chest in a gentle arc and complementing the collar at a harmonious angle. After careful consideration of the pros and cons he had decided on a button to close the jacket at waist level and four buttons on the sleeves. He had firmly decided on velvety brown suede shoes, too. They were going to have thick crêpe soles.

After Podbielskiallee, the underground railway lived up to its name and thundered through the tunnel. Bored, Ben looked at the ads in the carriage. He had been familiar with them from his early childhood: the liveried men from the House of Lefèvre delivering carpets; the huntsman from the Pfalz who took salt because Salz rhymed with Pfalz; the green bottles of Staatlich Fachingen water. Just before Nürnberger Strasse, sunlight suddenly shone into the carriage. A bomb had knocked a hole in the roof of the tunnel.

There were crowds of people among the ruins around Potsdamer Platz. Berlin's biggest black market was held here daily. There was nothing you couldn't find being bartered or sold. Gold wedding rings, mink coats and genuine Meissen china changed hands for nylons, coffee, chocolate. American cigarettes, in cartons of ten packets each, fetched a high price. A Leica cost twenty-five cartons of cigarettes. Single packets were more profitable, as Ben knew. The preferred currency was the Allied mark, banknotes which the occupying powers had issued for their troops, although they had soon found their way into the general currency. The old German Reichsmark was hardly worth the paper it was printed on.

Ben was in no hurry. He had to find the right taker. That man in the stained uniform jacket, for instance. Ben sized him up: just back from a POW camp, wouldn't know the current tricks of the trade yet. He walked past close to him, murmuring, 'Yankee fags?'

Then he stopped by a broken lamppost and waited. The man followed him. 'You got some?'

'Lucky Strikes. Three hundred Allimarks.' Ben showed him the packet held in the hollow of his hand. The man reached for it. Ben hung on. 'The money first,' he demanded. 'Allimarks, like I said.'

The man took Ben's wrist and raised the packet to his nose. He sniffed briefly and let Ben's hand fall again. 'Pelikan glue. You don't get rid of that almond smell so easily. Take care you don't get a thrashing, kid.' Ben made off. Next time he'd use UHU. The acetone dispersed at once.

'Got any Yanks?' asked a young girl. In spite of the heat she was wearing a quilted Russian jacket over her thin summer dress, and white socks below bare legs. She was fourteen at the most, but her pale face beneath the red hair reflected the experience of centuries. Ben showed her the packet. 'Over there.' The girl went ahead, into a ruined building. Ben followed, but stayed on his guard in case she had a boyfriend lurking there.

Weeds grew in the yard of the ruin. A rat scuttled away among chunks of rubble. The girl stopped, turned, and raised her skirt. The pubic hair on her little mount of Venus was bright red in the sun. 'Want to fuck? Or shall I give you a blow job? You can have ten minutes for four Yankee fags.' Ben silently shook his head.

Outside the ruins of the Wertheim department store a thin woman was hanging about in a threadbare but once elegant tailored suit, her bony cheeks slightly rouged. Her eyes greedily devoured the packet Ben showed her.

'Three hundred and fifty Allimarks,' he said, opening negotiations.

'Too much.'

'Three hundred.'

She opened her handbag, took out a couple of notes and offered the to him with nicotine-stained fingers. 'I'll give you two hundred and fifty.' She spoke educated, standard German and was obviously repelled by the bargaining.

'Two hundred and fifty, OK.' Ben took the money, gave her the packet and made his getaway. On the steps down to the U-Bahn he looked round. The woman had torn the packet open. Its contents fluttered to the ground. Disappointed, she picked up one of the snippets of paper and read the New Testament words. She laughed soundlessly. Her laughter turned to a dry cough.

Ben had found an old gentlemen's magazine in his grandparents' attic, with a picture of a man with a moustache in the English style and a firm jaw wearing an immaculate, Prince of Wales check, double-breasted suit. He kept the picture in his hiding place behind one of the rafters, along with a notebook with a black oilcloth cover where he recorded the sums he had made from his fake packets of Chesterfield, Lucky Strike and Philip Morris cigarettes. He always took the money straight to Heidi's father, Rödel the master tailor in Ithweg. Today's two hundred and fifty marks were another step on his way to becoming an arbiter of elegance. The trouble was, he couldn't let himself be seen in Potsdamer Platz too often, so the instalments were mounting up slowly. As things stood at present, he wouldn't get the shoes and suit for less than fifteen thousand marks, so Ben was trying to think of other sources of income.

Perhaps he could make something out of Mr Brubaker. Mr Brubaker was an American, and for that very reason, in Ben's opinion, rather nutty. Ben had known him since he'd found him hopelessly lost, and showed him the way to the Harnack House. Where he came from, Clarence P. Brubaker was what they called a 'nice guy'. He was no great intellectual luminary, but his father owned the *Hackensack Herald*, which supported the Democrats and thus the new President Harry S. Truman. The newspaper proprietor sometimes played piano duets with Truman.

Brubaker senior had pulled strings to ensure that his son and heir was spared the dangers of service in the armed forces. Instead, Clarence became a war reporter, which sounded more adventurous than it was. Daddy took care that his offspring was assigned to Allied headquarters, which like most headquarters in the military history of modern times was situated well behind the lines, so that while the generals waged war, the war itself would not disturb them.

Clarence P. Brubaker arrived in Berlin with the American army of occupation, intending to file reports from the post-war front line. A cousin on his mother's side was something quite high up in the military government. On his say-so, Brubaker was quartered in a requisitioned villa behind US headquarters and thus outside the prohibited zone. Accommodation of this quality was usually reserved for high-ranking officers with families.

The house was well furnished and in the past had belonged to one Dr Isaak, who discreetly helped the ladies of Berlin society out of certain difficulties and sent them steep bills for his services. An 'Aryan' colleague called Krüger made sure that Isaak was sent to a camp when Hitler came to power, and took over his villa and his practice for peanuts. He sent the wives of high-up Nazi functionaries equally hefty bills until his racket was finally busted. He too had been providing ladies with abortions.

The two doctors met again in Buchenwald. They both survived the war, and were liberated by American troops. Isaak emigrated to Palestine, where he was hanged by the British as an active member of the underground Hagannah movement. Krüger, as a victim of the Nazis, received a good sum of money in compensation and became a respected member of Dr Adenauer's Christian Democrat party.

Neither Ben nor Mr Brubaker knew about the intertwined fates of the two doctors, nor would they have cared. Ben wanted his suit. Brubaker wanted Nazis.

'Nazis,' said Brubaker. 'I want to meet Nazis. Do you know any?'

'What for?' asked Ben cautiously.

'I won't give anyone away. I just want a first-hand story. I'll pay well.'

'How well?' Ben asked, sucking one of the Cokes he had taken from his host's fridge through a straw.

Brubaker did not answer because someone was knocking at the kitchen door. He opened it. 'Hello, Curt, come on in.'

Ben looked at the newcomer with interest. Another American who might turn out to be profitable. He'd have to test the ground first, of course. The man had thin fair hair, a round, rosy face, and pale-blue eyes. His uniform showed that he was a US civilian.

'This is Ben,' Brubaker introduced him. 'Say hello to Mr Chalford, Ben.'

'Hi.' Ben went on sucking with concentration.

Curtis Chalford lived in the villa next door. 'Could I borrow some coffee? I was too late for the PX.'

'Sure. Would you like a drink, Curt?' Brubaker offered politely.

'No thanks, Clarence. Goodbye, my boy.' Chalford left with a couple of sachets of Nescafé.

'Would you like a coffee too?' Ben shook his head. He was perfectly happy with his Coke. 'I'll make you a sandwich.' Mr Brubaker might not be very bright, but he was a kind-hearted soul.

'OK,' Ben generously agreed. 'So what will you pay?'

'A couple of cartons of cigarettes for a genuine Nazi with a story to tell.'

'All right, I'll keep my ears open,' promised Ben. He was wondering feverishly how he could come up with a Nazi in these lousy times, when everyone was so keen never to have been one.

Little Hajo König came to his aid. He had been discharged from hospital now, and the bandaged stump of his right arm lay in a sling. His greatest grief was that he couldn't go swimming. The wound hadn't healed well enough yet. 'But they send me to school,' he said gloomily.

Before his accident, Hajo had made a discovery in the loft above the false ceiling at home. 'A dagger of honour with the eagle and swastika, a brown uniform and a whole lot of other stuff.' The uniform and its accessories had belonged to Tietge, the Nazi local group leader, who'd taken his own life.

Ben did some very quick thinking. He must have this valuable find. 'It's strictly forbidden, you know,' he told the younger boy. 'If they find that stuff at your place you'll all end up in jail.' He let this sword of Damocles hover in the air for a little while before making his generous offer: 'I'll get rid of it all for you for ten Yankee cigarette ends.'

'Suppose they catch you, though?'

'Oh, well, you know my old man's with the cops.'

One Sunday in September the König parents went to visit relations. Jutta Weber was working at the Club as usual. Herr Brandenburg was out too. It seemed like the perfect opportunity. 'I only found six,' Hajo apologized, holding out the cigarette ends on the flat of his hand. 'I'll get you the rest next week.'

Ben put the cigarette ends carelessly in his trouser pocket. 'Wait for me at your place.' He ran home and fetched an empty potato sack from the shed at the end of the garden.

Hajo let him in. 'Up there.' He pointed to the loft, which was above the bathroom door. They carried the kitchen table into the corridor and put a chair on it. Ben climbed up, and wriggled into the loft on his stomach.

'Oh wow!' he murmured, catching sight of these treasures of the Thousand-Year Reich. 'Can you hold the sack open?' he asked out loud. Hajo managed it with his teeth and his unharmed left hand. One by one the dagger, uniform garments, Party insignia, a cap, and a Party booklet with a once-coveted low membership number went into the potato sack. 'That could get you at least two years in jail,' Ben prophesied darkly.

'Just get rid of it,' begged the little boy. 'I'll find you the rest of the cigarette ends next week, I promise.'

Ben hid the sack with his booty in the garden shed, having first removed a round swastika badge with a gilt edge. He took this to Mr Brubaker, who was brooding over a news story.

'Look, this belongs to a Nazi. He'll sell it for a carton of Yank fags because he can't wear it right now, he says.'

Brubaker took a carton of Camels from a cupboard. 'Where is the man? Can I talk to him?'

'He doesn't want to see anyone, he's afraid they'll put him behind bars because he was the Führer's right-hand man.'

'Hitler's right-hand man?' Clarence P. Brubaker was delighted.

'Or maybe his left-hand man, I'm not quite sure.'

'Tell him I'm prepared to meet him secretly. No one will hear about it.'

'I'll see what I can do,' Ben promised, and he put the carton of Camels under his shirt and left. Suddenly he was in a great hurry.

Meanwhile, Brubaker opened his Remington portable and, with a blissful expression on his face, began hammering out his story on the typewriter: 'Hitler's right-hand man goes underground in Berlin . . .' The folks back home would tear the *Hackensack Herald* from each other's hands. His colleagues on other papers would be green with envy. But that was only the beginning of a path that would lead inevitably to the Pulitzer Prize. Daddy would be proud of him.

On his way home, Ben thought of the fairy-tale of the donkey spewing gold at both ends. The animal was visibly assuming the features of Clarence P. Brubaker.

*

Captain Ashburner braked sharply outside the terraced house in Riemeister Strasse and unfolded his long legs from the jeep. He walked through the front garden and pressed the bell, to no avail; the power was off again. He knocked on the door. Inge Dietrich opened it.

'John Ashburner,' he introduced himself.

'I know your name. I'm Inge Dietrich.'

'How do you do, ma'am? Is the inspector in?'

'He's just come home. Please come in, Mr Ashburner.'

'Thank you, ma'am.' The captain took of his cap and put it, very correctly, under his left arm.

'My husband is on the veranda. Just go through the living room.'

Klaus Dietrich was wearing shorts and a polo shirt, resting in a deckchair and looking relaxed. He had taken off his troublesome prosthesis and put his leg up. He glanced up from his newspaper in surprise. 'Captain Ashburner?'

Ashburner, taken aback, glanced at the amputated limb. 'I didn't know about that.'

'Oh, just ignore it. I do.' The inspector hauled himself up by the table with practised ease.

'I went to your office, but you'd left. I apologize for disturbing you at home, but that's all I'm planning to apologize for.'

'What's the matter, Captain?'

'A phone call from the city commandant's office, that's what's the matter,' Ashburner said angrily. 'Asking why I am preventing you from questioning Private Dennis Morgan and why, furthermore, I am withholding an item of evidence from you.'

'Well, aren't you?'

Ashburner took the scrap of olive-green fabric from his pocket and handed it to the inspector. 'I've had this examined. It's certainly from an officer's trench coat. However, such coats are traded on the black market, so it could have been worn by a German. You can question Private Morgan in my office any time. Are you happy now?'

'Not until we've caught the murderer. I'm sorry I had to turn to the commandant's office. Your Sergeant Donovan was blocking all our attempts to investigate, and we couldn't reach you. Captain, this case may be taking an unexpected turn. I need a permit to visit the Brandenburg penitentiary. The NKVD is holding former CID Chief Superintendent Wilhelm Schlüter there, for mass executions in Ukraine. I want to question him about the murder of a woman in Berlin before the war. There could be parallels.'

Ashburner made a couple of notes. Inge Dietrich joined them. 'You're welcome to stay and eat with us, Mr Ashburner.'

'Potato soup à la Uncle Tom,' said Dr Hellbich sarcastically, appearing behind her. 'You grate a couple of raw potatoes into boiling water, add salt and a pinch of spice if available, and there you are. Guaranteed to be an entirely new experience for our overseas guest. Do you by any chance have a cigarette?'

Dietrich was embarrassed. 'My father-in-law – Captain Ashburner,' he introduced them.

'Pleased to meet you. I'm sorry, sir, I don't smoke. Thank you for the invitation, ma'am, but I have a dinner date.' Ashburner turned to Dietrich. 'With an acquaintance from the Soviet commandant's HQ, who may be able to help us.'

'I'll show you out.' Dietrich hopped to the door on one leg; it didn't seem to bother him at all. Ashburner stopped for a moment in the living room, looking at the framed photograph on the sideboard. It showed a laughing Klaus Dietrich with the epaulettes of a colonel. The Knight's Cross with oak leaves stood out brightly from the black uniform of the Panzer troops.

'And I didn't know that either,' said Ashburner, impressed, as he swung himself up into his jeep.

*

Ashburner quickly fetched the statements and photographs relating to the two murder cases from his office and put them in the jeep. Major Berkov had surprised him by phoning. 'Do you know the "Seagull" in Luisenstrasse?

Through the Brandenburg Gate, left into Neue Wilhelmstrasse and across the Spree.'

'I don't know it, but I'll find it,' Ashburner promised.

'Shall we say eight?'

'Eight it is.' Ashburner was pleased that Berkov had called. He liked the cultivated Russian, so different from his earlier assumptions about their Red allies. He drove from Uncle Tom through the Grunewald to Halensee and the Kurfürstendamm, which was in the British sector. The tower of the Kaiser Wilhelm Memorial Church with its top broken off rose into the sky creating a bizarre spectacle. Tauentzienstrasse was full of rubble and ruins too. There were people clearing up everywhere. Women with grey faces under grey headscarves were knocking the remains of mortar off bricks. Elderly men passed them from hand to hand, conveying them to horse-drawn carts or trucks running on wood gas. It was amazing, what these half-starved Germans were doing.

He thought of the inspector and his family. Their life must be damn hard. On the other hand, hadn't the Germans brought it on themselves? Who had begun that crazy war, and who had lost it? Or were the Dietrichs just victims? Wouldn't it have been the same for him and Ethel and everyone else in Venice if Hitler had won the war? The idea of watching Ethel grating raw potatoes into boiling water at the stove amused him. He decided to tell her the story sometime, just to see her reaction. He braked sharply as he came to a shell crater overgrown with weeds in the middle of the street and drove around it.

He went along the overpass and then left towards Potsdamer Platz, where the Soviet-occupied sector of the city began, past the bustling black market in the square to the ruins of the German Reichstag, which he gathered had been a kind of parliament, and through the Brandenburg Gate. A red flag with the hammer and sickle was flying above it. Chunks of plaster crunched under his tyres as he stopped in Luisenstrasse.

The Berlin Artists' Club had been housed in what was once Prince Bülow's town palace. Soviet cultural officers had named it after Chekhov's *The Seagull*, an image of which adorned the curtain of the Moscow artists' theatre. But Berlin's artists came less for the culture than because, thanks to the artistically minded Russians, there was plenty to eat here, and no disapproving waiter snipping bits off your ration cards.

Maxim Petrovich Berkov was waiting for his guest at a table half-hidden behind pot plants. 'Good evening, John. How are you?'

'I'm always feeling fine after working hours.'

'And your beautiful girlfriend?'

Ashburner grinned. 'I'm not sure if it was the white BMW or its driver that impressed her most.'

'I'd be happy to take the lady for a drive.'

'I'd sooner you didn't. The glorious Red Army has made enough conquests. Maxim Petrovich, can we talk freely here?'

The major reached into the small bay tree behind him, and after a little groping about produced a small microphone from among the leaves. He broke the fine feed line with a jerk. 'A loose contact. Such sloppy work,' he remarked dryly.

The waiter brought the menu, and Berkov ordered a bottle of Crimean champagne. 'Yes, major,' said the waiter, and clicked his heels.

'Hasn't been properly re-educated yet,' remarked Berkov, amused. 'Usually the Germans adapt very quickly. Take Russian Eggs, for instance, that savoury little starter – they've renamed it Soviet Eggs. I can recommend it, by the way. And how about saddle of venison to follow? My boss's contribution to the cultural life of Berlin. General Bersarin doesn't just enjoy racing around the city on his looted Harley Davidson, he goes hunting in Göring's old preserves. He decides when the season ends. Oh, by the way, do you remember our first meeting?'

'You were looking for the grave of that man Kleist.'

'I've been reading up on the subject. She wasn't his mistress – Henriette was a romantic girl who made a suicide pact with the poet.'

Ashburner was glad to see the waiter bringing the champagne and their starters. It meant he didn't have to say anything on a subject where he was out of his depth. 'What's your sport?' he asked, changing the subject to be on the safe side.

'We played tennis at the Frunse military academy. Marshal Tukhachevsky was keen to make his young officers gentlemen in the Western model. Stalin had him executed. An irreplaceable loss to the Red Army.'

'You're very outspoken, Maxim Petrovich.'

'Ah, well, the microphone installed by our comrades from the Kommissariat just happens to be out of order.'

'What Kommissariat is that?'

'The *Narodnyi Kommissariat Vnutrennikh Del*, probably better known to you as the NKVD. The People's Commissariat of Internal Affairs.'

'That brings me to my request. I need your help. My German colleague, Inspector Dietrich, is investigating the murders of two women. He wants to compare them with a similar pre-war murder case, which means questioning a former CID officer called Wilhelm Schlüter, at present an inmate of the Brandenburg penitentiary. To do that he needs a visitor's permit from the NKVD.'

'Two murders?'

'Of two pretty, blonde young women.' Ashburner handed him the records of the investigations and the photographs of the dead women. Berkov instantly recognized Karin. His face turned stony.

'Is something the matter?' asked John Ashburner. Berkov heard him as if from a great distance.

'No, no, it's nothing.' He hid his face behind the notes, but he wasn't reading them. He was thinking of those few weeks of passion with her, hearing her warm voice: 'Come here, Maxim Petrovich.' He felt her soft body again, breathed in her pleasantly sharp perfume. He would have liked to groan out loud, but he said only, 'I believe I can help your German colleague. I play chess with Colonel Nekrassov of the NKVD. I'll let the colonel win; that will put him in a good mood.'

Master Sergeant Washington Roberts was waiting behind the shops. A narrow access for delivery trucks led there from Wilskistrasse. This was also where the big, zinc garbage bins stood. Their lids refused to close, they were so full of garbage from the requisitioned shops and apartments. Chocolate bars that had just been broken into, half-empty cans of baked beans, luncheon meat, condensed milk — the Americans threw away scraps that would have fed a hungry family for days. It all went to the American garbage dump and, by order of the chief army doctor, had quicklime tipped over it before the bulldozers ploughed it in. Even the rats couldn't dig for it.

Gerti Krüger waved to her brown skinned boyfriend from the back door. He waved back, with a broad grin. They would eat and dance at Club 48, and later go back to her place to make love. Her landlady was happy to close both eyes in return for a packet of Lucky Strikes.

Gerti was looking forward to the evening, and she wasn't going to let even Ziesel the garbage truck driver spoil it for her. Ziesel came in just before the dry cleaners' closed, to collect the empty chemicals containers. Sergeant Chang had lined them up ready.

'Get a move on, do, we're about to close.'

'Oh, so the lady can't wait to see what her black stallion's going to stick into her.'

'My Washington at least has something to offer a woman. Unlike you, you feeble wimp. Can't even get your little finger up!'

'When we get to have a say in things again, you'll be the first we shave bald, you Yankee whore.'

Gerti laughed out loud. 'You're too stupid even to shave a head. You see to your garbage bins, they're brimming over.'

'Cunt. Yankee tart,' muttered Ziesel as he went out. 'Good evening, sergeant,' he ingratiatingly greeted the American.

Washington Roberts watched Ziesel lift several empty bins off the truck and heave the full ones up on it. The sergeant's eyes widened. A slender white hand was hanging out from under the lid of one of the containers.

The black Packard limousine drove down Unter den Eichen with its blue light flashing, a corporal from the Women's Army Corps at the wheel. The US city commandant was in a hurry. He sat in the back with his face set like stone, trying to digest the news that had reached him a quarter of an hour earlier.

The sentry at the entrance to the military hospital saluted. The limousine stopped outside the main building. A captain of the US Medical Corps was waiting for the general. 'May I lead the way, sir?'

'Please, doctor.' General Henry C. Abbot followed the doctor down a narrow flight of steps. The bright neon lights of the mortuary met them.

Several uniformed men were gathered around an autopsy table in the background. Colonel Tucker moved away from the group. 'I hope it was right to let you know, sir.'

'Of course. Don't talk nonsense.'

'This is Captain John Ashburner of the Military Police, sir,' Tucker introduced the man. Ashburner saluted. Abbot offered his hand. Tucker indicated the head of the German–American Employment Office. 'And you know Mr Chalford.'

The general nodded. 'Hello, Curtis.'

Curtis S. Chalford passed one hand awkwardly over his thin fair hair. His rosy face with its pale-blue eyes was distressed. He was clearly at a loss. He cleared his throat. 'They called me because they could tell at once that she was a German employed by the army. Of course I immediately knew who she was. I'm very sorry, general.'

The city commandant bent over the marble slab. They were all silent. The dead woman had been covered up to her chin with a white sheet. Her regular features, surrounded by blonde hair, looked calm and grave. Captain Ashburner broke the silence. 'General Abbot, I have to ask you formally: Did you know this woman?'

Henry C. Abbot silently bowed his head. It was both confirmation and a last goodbye.

HENRIETTE

'DETTA!' SHIMMERING SUNLIGHT filters through the branches of the old trees, falling like a cap of invisibility on the blonde hair of the girl in the grass. 'Detta!' The girl ducks down even further into the long grass. 'Time to get changed, Detta!' Get changed? Why? What's wrong with her tartan blouse and jodhpurs?

'Detta!' The voice is dangerously close. The girl picks up one of last year's fir cones and flings it into the bushes in a high arc. The sound will lure Adelheid the wrong way. Detta doesn't want to get changed. Getting changed will mean a bath, nothing wrong with that, but a bath will inevitably be followed by hair brushing, quick and hard, and the stupid frilly dress that makes her look like a twelve-year-old even though she's fourteen.

Anyway, why all this fuss? Just because visitors are coming from Potsdam? 'Important visitors,' as Adelheid puts it, pursing her lips elegantly. Detta carefully peers above the grass. The governess has turned her back. A good opportunity to disappear among the rhododendrons – three strides will do it – and run to the stables. If she saddles Henry quickly enough she can be off long before Adelheid appears.

Oh, how stupid: Adelheid is already standing by the horsebox, patting Henry. There's no getting past her. Or is there? Hans-Georg suddenly appears and starts talking to the governess, leads her away from the stable. Her brother is sixteen, but his smooth, dark head of hair makes him seem older. How good he looks. He turns briefly, gives her a conspiratorial grin, and leads Adelheid a little further away. Detta quietly opens the door of the box. No time to saddle the horse. She quickly gets the snaffle on Henry and mounts him bareback. Duck her head at the door, dig her heels in outside, and off they gallop. No, not along the gravel drive, Hans-Georg and Adelheid are walking there, but straight ahead into the trees.

The gate at the end of the park is child's play for Henry, they've jumped it dozens of times, but you can easily lose your seat without a saddle, particularly when Henry jams on the brakes instead of jumping. Detta sails solo over the bars, rolls over as she comes down, and finds herself sitting in the meadow, surprised. Henry turns and trots briskly home. 'You beast!' she hisses after him, and sets off on the long walk back, slightly dazed and with a triangular tear in her jodhpurs over her left thigh.

A red-striped marquee has been put up behind the house. It's crowded with people. Detta hopes to get past, but Bensing has seen her. Bensing, clad not as usual in shirtsleeves and an apron but in dark-blue livery with gilt buttons, takes a deep breath, thrusts out his chest and trumpets: 'Henriette Sophie Charlotte, Baroness von Aichborn.'

Father is suddenly beside her. As Bensing is announcing the next guest, he steers her through the throng towards a slender gentleman in tweed. 'Imperial Highness, may I present my daughter Henriette?'

Detta bobs a half-curtsey. Adelheid has practised it with her, and has taught her that a full curtsey is due only to the Kaiser; the Crown Prince gets a half-curtsey, even if he isn't really a Crown Prince any more and nor, in the tenth year of the Weimar Republic, is the Kaiser a Kaiser.

'My dear Aichborn, what a splendid young lady.' An appraising glance at the firm, girlish thigh showing through the tear. His Imperial Highness likes them young.

'A little riding accident. I hope your Highness will excuse us.' Mother removes Detta from the danger zone. 'You'll be confined to your room for a week,' she says sternly. 'Hans-Georg will bring you your meals.'

'Yes, Mother.' The fourteen-year-old smiles to herself. That won't be so bad, not if Hans-Georg can visit her.

The gong summons the family to breakfast: bacon and eggs, kidneys, grilled sausages, tomatoes and toast. This is 'English morning' at Schloss Aichborn. Miss Imogen Thistlethwaite, the English governess from Somerset, makes the two younger siblings sit down at the table. 'Fritz, sit still. Viktoria, put your hands on your lap and straighten your back.'

'Ah, *Bratwürstchen*,' says the Baron with pleasure when he sees the sausages.

'Speak English, darling,' his wife reminds him.

'I bet none of you know what *Haferbrei* is in English,' Hans-Georg challenges the company. Detta looks affectionately at her big brother. He looks fabulous. He's a senior officer cadet, and home on leave. Now that Germany has a proper army again, not just a ridiculous force of a hundred thousand men by kind permission of the *entente*, he has a whole career laid out ahead of him. Of course he will join the traditional Aichborn regiment, the Ninth Cavalry in Potsdam, known popularly as the '*von Neun*' because so many of its blue-blooded members' names contain the aristocratic *von*.

'*Haferbrei* is porridge.' Detta's reply comes quick as lightning. She is twenty, and has been speaking fluent English since she was six.

'What are you going to do this morning?' her father asks.

'I plan to show the girls how to shoot,' Hans-Georg announces.

'The girls' are Detta and the girl with the black, bobbed hair just coming downstairs in culottes and a shirt with two top buttons undone – which is two too many. She is yawning. 'What an unholy hour – when all good people are still in their beds,' Miriam complains, casting Hans-Georg a glance that Detta doesn't like at all. The extremely chic Miriam Goldberg is heiress to the banking house of Goldberg & Cie. She arrived yesterday in her sensational white BMW sports convertible. Hans-Georg has invited her to Aichborn for the weekend. 'I ought really to be in Biarritz. Grandfather has rented the Braganzas' villa. He's negotiating with the Portuguese there – he's planning to move the bank to Lisbon, and the family's supposed to go too. Totally crazy, what would I do in Lisbon? When the Berlin season's about to begin any moment! Lilian Harvey is giving a phenomenal cocktail party on the Pfaueninsel, and the Bülows are planning a ball at the Adlon. I mean, are we going to miss all that just because of this new Reich Chancellor? The man doesn't even speak proper German, and he has no sex appeal at all,' she says, nonchalantly dropping the latest fashionable term into the conversation and sipping her tea. Another glance at Hans-Georg, who returns it with a smile.

What on earth, Detta wonders crossly, does he see in that snake in the grass? 'Let's go shooting,' she says out loud, although she is not particularly fond of the sport. However, she would be happy to go fishing, hoe weeds, cycle or catch butterflies with her brother, just for the sake of his company.

Bensing bends down behind the wall of the nursery garden and puts a clay pigeon in the sling. 'Pull!' calls Detta in her clear voice. The little disc rises in the blue August sky. Detta raises her gun and pulls the trigger. A loud bang. Her target falls into the nearby meadow, intact. The shot comes down on the greenhouse in a fine shower of lead pellets. 'Oh, shit.' Detta lowers the shotgun in disappointment.

'Your turn, Miriam.' Hans-Georg stations himself behind her. Miriam leans back, pressing close to him. Like a cat with a tom, thinks Detta scornfully, and traces Miriam's shot into the void with satisfaction. Impatiently, she snatches the gun from her hand.

'You have to settle the butt into your shoulder, Detta,' says her brother, looking lovingly at Miriam. 'Look straight along the barrel. Follow the course of disk, swing with it, take a step forward and press the trigger as you move. Ready, Bensing?'

Bensing is ready. Detta waits. 'Pull!' A swinging movement, a bang, the clay disk shatters into a cloud of white. Again. 'Pull!' Swing, bang, a hit. Now she has the knack of it. Her brother is beaming.

Miriam is pouting flirtatiously. 'Come on, Georgie, never mind this silly old shooting.'

'Georgie', indeed! Detta reloads, throws Miriam the gun. 'Here, you do it.' Miriam jumps back in alarm. The gun falls to the ground. Hans-Georg picks it up. 'Bensing, pull!' He shoots a double. Detta tries, but she hits only one of the two flying disks. 'You lower the gun after the first shot, then you take aim again,' her brother tells her. He knows all about these things, he's a soldier after all. 'Pull!' She hits both clay pigeons. Hans-Georg is pleased with her. The gong goes for lunch in the house.

'Well, how was it?' asks the Baron.

'Boring.' Miriam helps herself to a tiny chicken wing and half a stick of celery. Detta tucks in heartily.

'Detta has a real gift for it,' Hans-Georg praises her.

'Maria Inocencia is arriving the day after tomorrow,' Mother tells them. 'I'd like everyone who can to speak Spanish to her, even if you may not be as fluent as in English.' Maria Inocencia is a cousin from Madrid.

'I wonder if she can shoot?' Detta tries it out loud in Spanish. '*Me pregunto si María Inocencia es buena tiradora.*'

'*No seas tonta. Una mujer española no tocaría nunca un arma,*' Mother tells her in elegant Castilian. 'A Spanish woman doesn't touch a weapon.' The Baroness was born an Alvarez de Toledo.

There is more shooting after lunch, this time with a rifle and a telescopic sight. Hans-Georg has put up the target by the cowsheds; the heap of dung behind it will catch the bullets. 'Point the gun, take aim, breathe out, pull the trigger slowly, rather as if you were squeezing a sponge, or you'll swerve to one side.' Detta follows her brother's instructions and aims at the centre of the target, using the cross-hairs. Slowly, she pulls the trigger. The recoil hurts. A three. Not a good start. When she finally hits the twelve her shoulder is hurting like hell, but she doesn't let anyone see, if only because of Miriam, who is watching with a bored expression.

'Well done, Detta!' Hans-Georg is genuinely proud of his sister. 'We'll go hunting together this autumn.'

Detta beams. 'Shall we go for a ride later? Miriam can have Senator. He won't try anything on with her.'

'Another time, my dear,' Miriam says. 'Coming, Georgie?' The two of them disappear into the park.

I suppose they just can't wait, thinks Detta with venom.

The sound of an engine catches her attention. An aeroplane is skimming low over the trees and comes down like a hawk on the lawn behind the house. A daring landing. The pilot climbs out of the open plane and comes towards Detta, taking off his flying cap and goggles. A brown, masculine face smiles at her.

'Thomas Glaser,' he introduces himself. 'And you must be Hans-Georg's sister Detta.' Suddenly Detta's heart is thudding, and there is a rather pleasant tingling inside her. 'Where's your brother, then?'

'Somewhere in the park with his new flame.' Funny, but the thought of Miriam suddenly doesn't bother her. 'Do you always come calling by plane?'

He grins. 'Not on the Kurfürstendamm. The overhead tram cables would get in the way. Have you ever flown?'

'Not yet.'

'We'll take a little trip tomorrow.' He doesn't ask if she wants to, this astonishing man, he just decides. She imagines flying through the air, pressing close to him in alarm, an unrealistic thought since the two open seats in the Klemm 25 are arranged one behind the other, but it's nice all the same. Even the hope of a ride with Hans-Georg pales in comparison.

They have all changed for the evening. The Baron wears a starched shirt-front with a wing collar under his dinner jacket. Hans-Georg looks fantastic in his white uniform jacket, but Detta has eyes only for her airman. He appears at the top of the stairs, looking round for help. 'Could someone please tie my bow tie for me?'

'Come down, Herr Glaser, and I'll do it,' calls Detta eagerly.

'If you call me Herr Glaser again I shall use Henriette for you,' he threatens her, smiling. 'I'm Tom to my friends.'

The Harsteins from the neighbouring estate have come to dinner, the local clergyman Pastor Wunsig and his wife, the veterinarian and his wife. And a certain Herr Fanselow, the district farmers' leader. 'A kind of Party agricultural official,' the Baron surmises. 'He could help us finance the new stud farm. That would be a good contribution to National Socialism – or in this case local Socialism.' The Baron is prepared to move with the times.

Wearing boots to dinner? Detta doesn't take to Fanselow at all.

It turns out that the man used to be a shoe salesman at Leiser's in Berlin. The Party has given him his lucrative position as a functionary in the country because of his record as a 'meritorious old campaigner', someone who backed the National Socialists from their early days. He hasn't the faintest idea about farming or stock breeding, but he lards his conversation with jargon about 'blood and the soil', 'sound Reich husbandry' and 'iron ploughshares'. Detta thinks it all rather silly.

'Have you seen the plans for our stud farm yet?' Father steers the conversation straight to the subject on his mind. 'A project intended to benefit all the farms in the area. With your Party's support it could be up and running in half the time.'

Fanselow dismisses the idea. 'Later, Baron. First we must cleanse the new Germany of Jewish bloodsuckers and parasites. Take our own district here. Two Jewish doctors, a Jewish dentist, a Jewish notary. And the architect of the stud farm you're planning is called Grünspan. They'll all have to go.'

'Oh, and will our friend here have to go too? Or when you were introduced did you conveniently overlook the fact that Fräulein Miriam's surname is Goldberg?' Hans-Georg asks sharply.

Bensing brings in a platter of crayfish. 'We mustn't let the last month without an R in it go by uncelebrated,' says the Baroness, smiling as she changes the subject. 'Will you do the honours, Pastor?'

Wunsig says grace, his voice loud and clear. All but Fanselow bend their heads. 'I suppose,' Detta challenges him, 'that as a Local Socialist you don't believe in God?'

'National Socialist,' Fanselow corrects her, and announces grandly: 'I believe in the German spirit as it manifests itself at this historic time and place.'

'My plaice had an awful lot of bones in it last Friday,' says Detta innocently, earning herself an amused look from the airman and a glance of annoyance from the champion of good Reich husbandry, who is waiting for someone else to tackle the crayfish first. He's never eaten them before, Detta realizes.

'Do you like crayfish, Herr Fanselow?' Detta pushes her plate aside and spreads her napkin on the table in front of her with a business-like air. She holds her soup spoon in her left hand. With her right hand, she picks up a crayfish by driving her fork into its soft part. Fanselow does the same. She ceremoniously transfers the shellfish from the platter to her spoon. Fanselow follows her example. Then she puts down her fork and takes the crayfish from her spoon with the serving tongs. She drops it from chest height to her napkin.

'Here, Herr Fanselow.' She politely hands him the serving tongs. The others are watching this performance, spellbound. Miriam is grinning to herself. Detta carefully folds all four corners of her napkin over the crayfish and brings her fist down on it a couple of times. Fanselow copies her. Detta unfolds the corners of the napkin. 'Delicious,' she murmurs. Fanselow opens his own napkin and looks rather doubtfully at the smashed crayfish inside. Then he begins poking about in the ruins with his fork.

Detta tips her work of destruction off the napkin and into the dish standing ready for the shells, lifts a couple of fresh crayfish to her plate with the tongs, and skilfully takes them apart with her fingers, one by one. 'Enjoying your crayfish?' she asks her neighbour with a sweet smile.

'That was very naughty of you,' her mother reprimands her after dinner, when the gentlemen have adjourned to the library for cognac and cigars.

'The man's a commoner and an anti-Semitist,' Detta says, her tongue tripping over the word.

'Well, yes, he is certainly an anti-Semite,' her mother corrects her. 'Heaven knows what he and his kind have in store for us. All the same, he is our guest.'

Miriam has brought some gramophone records from Berlin. Jack Hylton and His Orchestra. 'They play on the "Eden" roof garden. Fabulous, really fabulous.'

'Negro music,' grumbles Fanselow. 'Anything so alien to our race should be banned.'

Miriam dances exuberantly with Hans-Georg. She knows the latest steps of the shimmy. Detta isn't at all jealous of her any more. After all, she has her airman now. In high spirits, she tries out the wild contortions of the dance with him. But best of all is resting in his arms as they dance a slow foxtrot. She's never been so close to a man before. Except for Hans-Georg, but of course that's quite different.

'Wednesday, 1 August '34. Fabulous airman lands here. He's a friend of Hans-Georg, his name is Thomas Glaser but he asked me to call him Tom. A few guests to dinner. A Herr Fanselow, no idea how to eat crayfish. If he'd been nice I'd have shown him, tactfully, how to do it. But he was a horrible man and said nasty things about Herr Grünspan, and how all the Jews would have to go. I suppose he meant Miriam too. Hans-Georg put him in his place, and I made him look a fool over the crayfish. Well, he deserved it.

Thursday, 2 Aug. '34. I borrow Vati's driving cap and his big owl goggles. Everyone's gathered on the lawn behind the house. The estate workers and their families are gaping at the aeroplane. Tom shows Hans-Georg how you start the propeller turning. I climb up on the left wing and squeeze into the front seat. Tom gets in behind me. I hope he can see well enough.

The engine coughs wearily a couple of times, but then thinks better of it and starts. We bump across the lawn, the trees are coming closer uncomfortably fast. Then they're below us. We're flying!!!

Aichborn quickly gets smaller. People wave. I turn round. Tom smiles at me. Life's so wonderful! The engine roars. Suddenly the ground is above me, and so is my stomach. I discover later that it's called looping the loop.

153

Phew – my stomach and the ground are back in their proper places. I take a deep breath. After a quarter of an hour we drop straight down, it's like being in a lift. Tom catches his aircraft up just above the ground and brings it down safely on the lawn. Everyone applauds. I climb out and try jumping elegantly off the wing, but my knees are soft as butter. Luckily Hans-Georg catches me.

Another adventure in the afternoon. Miriam lets me drive her fabulous car. Jeschke taught me to drive a tractor a couple of years ago, and it's not so very different, except that the roadster is considerably faster and has good brakes, which are useful when a haycart unexpectedly crosses the road. People around here aren't expecting fast, white sports cars, only Dr Kluge's old Opel . . .'

The diary entry was a year in the past, but Detta was re-reading it, as she had so often before . . .

'Thomas asks, don't I ever come to Berlin? I know why. He can't live without me. He flies off after tea. I take refuge in my room. I feel like a widow. Or worse.

Reich President Hindenburg died today. Vati says without him that man Hitler will go right off the rails. I don't care. I'm not interested in politics. All I want is to go to Berlin – and Tom! Aichborn is really nice, but nothing goes on here except country life.

Vati says Berlin is out of the question. Mother would like me to wait until I've come of age. A whole year. How am I going to bear it without Thomas . . . ?'

Detta closed the diary and put it in her shoulder bag. Her cases were packed. Bensing was waiting downstairs with the Maybach to drive her to the railway station. Liselotte, the estate manager's daughter, was going to exercise the horses daily, which took a weight off Detta's mind.

She would stay with Miriam at first. Hans-Georg had fixed that. Berlin, here I come, she thought, meaning Tom Glaser. She could hardly wait to see him again. She had written to him quite often, but he hadn't answered. He probably wasn't much of a letter-writer. And then he was sitting his exam to be a commercial pilot. That would be taking all his time. Flight Captain

Glaser didn't sound bad, she thought, imagining his delight and surprise when she turned up. She hadn't told him she was coming to Berlin.

Miriam Goldberg lived in the new Westend area of the city. The banking heiress owned the top floor of a modern building in Gumbinner Allee. Many streets here had East-Prussian names. Before Detta's astonished eyes, wide glass doors opened on to a big roof garden with a swimming pool, an extraordinary luxury even for this fashionable part of Berlin in the year 1935. 'You can swim naked up here, no one can see,' her hostess told her. Detta blushed; she would never have dared think of such a thing. 'Come on, I'll show you your quarters.' Her 'quarters' were a modern little sitting room with a bedroom next to it and a black-tiled bathroom. Detta couldn't help thinking of the zinc bathtub and roaring stove in the bathroom at Aichborn.

Miriam pointed to Detta's modest suitcases. 'You don't seem to have brought much to wear. Never mind, we'll have a glass of bubbly and then go to Horn's. Horn's have the most fashionable things.'

'Thanks, but I don't have that much money. Mother says I should go to Brenninkmeyer's if I need anything.'

'Oh, we won't need money at Horn's. They send the bills to Herr Schott. He's Grandfather's authorized signatory. He's always complaining I spend too much, but he has strict orders to settle it all, right up to the last minute.' Miriam disappeared. Detta was already picturing herself in an elegant dress. Tom would be so surprised to see how the girl of last year had blossomed. She could hardly wait.

'What do you mean, the last minute?' she called through the open kitchen door.

'Grandfather's finally moving the bank to Portugal. The family's left already. I'm following soon. A man from the Ministry of Economic Affairs is taking over this apartment. So it'll be goodbye Horn, Braun and all the other divine fashion houses. Heaven knows what kind of shops they have in Lisbon.' A loud pop. Miriam emerged from the kitchen with an opened bottle of Taittinger and two glasses.

Detta pointed to a silver-framed photograph. It showed Lieutenant Hans-Georg von Aichborn on horseback. 'And he has to be away in Trakehnen just now,' she lamented.

'He'll be back next week,' Miriam consoled her.

155

'You and Hans-Georg – do you see each other often?'

Miriam poured the champagne. 'Cheers, little one. Not quite so often now he's insisting he wants to marry me.'

'Don't you want to marry him, then?'

'The regimental adjutant came to see me the other day. Major Count von Stuckwitz. Your brother would have to resign his commission if we married. The major told me so straight out.'

'What nonsense,' said Detta, shaking her head. 'Little Prince Ratibor married a Fräulein Schulz. His friends formed a guard of honour with their drawn swords outside the church. Snobbery is a thing of the past.' She sipped her champagne. It tickled her nose.

Miriam gave her a thin smile. 'A Fräulein Schulz is more acceptable these days than a Fräulein Goldberg.'

'What do you mean? You're beautiful, rich, well educated, amazingly chic and you can outshine anyone, not just at the regimental ball either.'

'Thanks for the compliment. But Jews are undesirable as wives for officers in the new German army. Don't be shocked, my dear, Georgie and I have no end of fun in bed. He confuses that with love, so he thinks he has to make our affair legitimate at the altar. If he were there beside the Tejo he'd be longing for Potsdam and the '*von Neun*' regiment, and in the end he'd blame me. Anyway, I've no intention of playing the mother and housewife. Cheers.' Miriam drained her glass in a single draught. 'Come on, let's go and plunder Horn's,' she cried, apparently without a care in the world. But Detta sensed the depth of her hurt.

They raced along Heerstrasse in the open BMW, in the direction of the city. A long convoy of trucks came towards them. 'Building materials for the Olympic stadium,' Miriam explained. 'Next year's games are to outshine any that have gone before. Georgie and his friend Stubbendorf are already training their horses like mad for the three-day eventing.'

The atmosphere at Horn's was muted. Elegant, cool ladies were having the latest models shown to them. Young salesgirls hurried silently to and fro. The *directrice* was with a stout customer, recommending a loosely draped ensemble. 'Paris is showing fluid lines this season.'

'It looks all baggy,' the customer objected.

'I'll be happy to show you something close-fitting. If you'd just excuse me for a moment, madam?' Smiling, the *directrice* walked towards the two young visitors. 'Fräulein Goldberg, how kind of you to honour us like this!'

'Frau Mohr, my friend Henriette von Aichborn urgently needs something to wear.'

'Of course, ladies. What did you have in mind, Fräulein von Aichborn?'

'Something really chic for the afternoon that could go on into the evening,' Detta said hastily. She wanted all her weapons ready to hand in case her airman asked her out to dinner.

'We can't always find the time we need to change, can we?' said Frau Mohr.

'Where, may I ask, is my dress?' The stout customer was shooting poisonous glances at Miriam. 'Fancy keeping a person waiting on account of a Jewish tramp!'

'Did you hear what she said, Miriam?' Detta was outraged.

The *directrice* shrugged, and said quietly, 'We're getting a new type of customer these days. Her husband is some kind of big noise in the Party.'

'I do understand your impatience, my dear People's Comrade,' Miriam said to the woman, sweet as sugar. 'But perhaps the trainee is having difficulty finding something in your amazing size.'

Frau Mohr discreetly separated the combatants. 'Perhaps you young ladies would like to go into the small salon? Giselle has a figure like Fräulein von Aichborn's. She'll show you a selection.'

'Why didn't you biff the woman?' asked Detta furiously. 'She deserved it.'

'On no account let anyone provoke you, that's what Grandfather has always told us. Oh, Giselle, there you are! No, not yellow polka dots for my friend. Could you show us something in a plain colour? When are you seeing your airman?'

'When we leave here. He doesn't know I'm coming. I want to surprise him. I do hope he'll be at home.'

'Wouldn't it be better to warn him first?'

'Why?'

Miriam did not answer, but called, 'Yes, the blue silk is perfect. Giselle, please help Fräulein von Aichborn into it.'

Hat, handbag and shoes completed the picture of an elegant young lady. Elated, the two of them left the fashion house after Miriam had tried on an ocelot fur. 'No, bad for Herr Schott's blood pressure and too warm for Lisbon,' she decided. 'Where does your airman live?'

Detta consulted her little notebook. 'In Nestorstrasse. Could you drop me just outside the door?'

'A surprise. I know.' Stepping on the gas, Miriam drove down the Kurfürstendamm to the corner of Nestorstrasse. 'Bring him along this evening. It's my farewell party.'

'A farewell party? Why?'

In reply, Miriam made an irritated gesture that embraced the entire Kurfürstendamm, its elegant pedestrians and luxurious shops. 'Good luck with your airman, my dear.' The car roared away.

Detta went into the building. As the lift carried her up she checked herself in the mirror to make sure the seams of her stockings were straight, smoothed down her new dress, and tipped her hat slightly to one side. Hm, not bad. But suppose he wasn't at home?

He was, and he looked even better than a year ago. What a man, she rejoiced! It took him a moment to recognize her. 'Detta, how nice. I had no idea you were in Berlin. Do come in. You're really grown-up now.' He closed the door behind her.

The living room was furnished in the modern style. There were photographs of aircraft hanging on the walls, and a propeller dangling over the kitchen doorway.

'Sit down. Ulli will be here in a moment. She'll be so pleased to meet you.'

'Ulli?' A dreadful foreboding came over her.

'Ulrike Spielhagen. Girl Friday to the director of Lufthansa, my new boss. We're getting married next week. I'll make some tea.'

Detta was paralysed. 'You must come to our wedding,' she heard him say from the kitchen. 'Do you like Leibnitz biscuits? I'm afraid that's all I have. The fact is, I'm hardly ever at home. Our chief pilot is instructing me on the JU 52 at the moment. It's a three-engined plane. I'm going to be second pilot on the Trömso run to start with.' He brought a tray with a teapot and cups. 'Will you be mother, as the English say?'

She poured the tea. Inside, she had turned to ice. She couldn't think, was incapable of reacting, just stood listlessly outside herself and listened with detachment to Fräulein Henriette von Aichborn making polite conversation. 'Lapsang Souchong, my favourite tea. I love that smoky aroma.'

'How are your parents?'

'Fine, thank you. They offered Mother the chair of the Countrywomen's

Association, but it would have meant joining the Party, and she's not keen on that. Father is fully occupied with the new stud farm.'

'Would you like to have dinner with us? They have fresh mussels at Schlichter's.'

'Thank you, but no; I have another engagement. I'm afraid I'll have to leave. Please give my regards to your fiancée, although I haven't met her. My congratulations to you both.'

She ran like the wind to nearby Kurfürstendamm. Only there did her inner paralysis give way. 'Taxi! Taxi!' She shouted, so loudly that people turned in surprise. A cab drew up. 'What's the panic, little lady?' asked the moustached driver good-humouredly. 'To Gumbinner Allee, please.' She dropped into the back seat and closed her eyes. Over. It was all over. Tom Glaser didn't love her. As the cab rattled along through the dense afternoon traffic, she wanted just one thing: to die. She hoped she could find some sleeping tablets in Miriam's apartment. Or should she make a noose from the cord of her dressing gown? Or of course she could equally well open the door of the cab and throw herself in front of the next tram. Jumping from the radio tower they were just passing was another possibility. Then again, she could cut her wrists, preferably in the bath. There were five and a half litres of blood contained in the human body; she'd read that somewhere.

Looking in the rear-view mirror, she straightened her hat. She didn't particularly like it. She'd take it back tomorrow and choose another, perhaps the little red one with the veil, or the black cap with the silver feather. As they turned into Gumbinner Allee, she had settled on a straw picture hat as top of her list, because of the fascinating shadow that its broad brim cast. If she raised her head slowly and bent an enigmatic glance on the next table Ulrike, sitting beside Tom, would certainly ask who that mysterious woman was. Detta imagined the scene in every detail, and decided that by comparison any kind of death, however dramatic, had a drawback: you wouldn't be able to enjoy other people's reactions.

Miriam was dog-paddling about in the water, a bottle of champagne on the side of the pool. She waved. 'Get yourself a glass and come on in.' Detta stripped her clothes off. Until an hour ago she would never, ever have shown herself naked. She jumped into the pool, poured a glass of champagne, emptied it at a single draught and then drank another. 'He's found someone else,' her friend remarked dryly. 'What did you expect? Berlin is full of pretty girls, and your airman is a desirable man. Luckily there are plenty more of them, as you'll find out this evening. As I told you, I've invited a few people round. My very special farewell performance.' There was a determined set to her mouth. Detta was about to fill her glass for the third time, but Miriam took it from her hand. 'That's enough. Go and lie down so you'll be feeling fresh later. Here, have my dressing gown and I'll use the towel.'

The door to the guest lavatory was open. A plumber in blue overalls was installing a new lavatory bowl. He misunderstood Detta's appearance. 'Another five minutes, then you can use it,' he told her.

In the cool twilight of her room she sobbed quietly on the bed. She thought of her first meeting with Thomas Glaser: his bold landing in Aichborn, dancing with him after dinner, the flight in his open aeroplane next morning. She stopped crying when she realized, with surprise, that he had given her no reason, in word or deed, to entertain hopes of any kind. She had imagined the whole thing.

Around seven a delivery van from Kempinski brought platters of cold food and a couple of dozen bottles of champagne, which were cooling on blocks of ice in a zinc tub. Miriam's American Frigidaire wasn't large enough for them. Detta thought of the ice cellar in Aichborn. In winter people sawed thick chunks of ice off the frozen pond; packed in straw, they would last for months in the cellar, and were used to cool drinks for the annual summer estate party. Father insisted on continuing this age-old tradition.

'Are you expecting many people?'

'Everyone who wants to say goodbye to me. But I'm much more interested in seeing who *doesn't* come.'

'Do you really have to leave?'

Miriam laughed bitterly. 'Oh, no, my dear. We're going entirely of our own free will. Come along, find yourself something long and close-fitting from the wardrobe. Your new silk dress is really more suitable for the afternoon.'

The first guests arrived at eight. Miriam introduced Detta to them. 'Hella and Gottfried Siebert. We play mixed doubles at the Red and White Club, if anyone is mad enough to partner me.'

'Nice to meet you.' Detta shook hands with the young couple.

'Gottfried is head of programmes at Radio Berlin,' Miriam told her friend.

'Director of Transmissions for Reich Radio,' Siebert corrected her. 'A few things have changed.'

'The station signal is the same. "*Üb' immer Treu und Redlichkeit*", isn't it? "Be true and honest evermore,"' Miriam replied, with obvious irony.

'Laugh if you like, but you won't stop the new times coming.'

'The new times won't stop us going either. The family's already left, and I'm following in a few hours' time.'

'Those who think as we do have nothing to fear,' said Hella Siebert, with conviction.

Detta scrutinized the couple curiously. The Sieberts were in their late twenties, and looked very athletic and healthy. They both wore the Party badge, and were looking challengingly around, as if rather on the defensive. Yet otherwise they seemed perfectly normal. She couldn't make them out.

'Hello, Rolf.' Miriam waved to a stout man in his thirties. 'Rolf Lamprecht cuts people's stomachs up,' she said, introduced him to Detta. 'He's promised me the smallest scar in the world if he ever has to take my appendix out. Rolf, darling, I thought you were bringing the Froweins with you?'

'Paul and Marianne send apologies. Hay fever.'

'Poor things. Billie, Fritz, give a paw. This is my friend Henriette von Aichborn, but you can call her Detta. Sybille and Friedrich von Coberg are a genuine princely couple, I'd have you know.'

'Only to impress the customers. We have a small art gallery in Charlottenburg,' said Prince Coberg apologetically.

'*Ah, Madame et Monsieur Montfort, quel plaisir. C'est mon amie Mademoiselle von Aichborn. Elle reste chez moi.* Detta, the Montforts import the very best wines from Burgundy.'

'And it's not easy with these new restrictions on foreign exchange.' Monsieur Montfort spoke in faultless German.

'German folk drink German wine!' cried a smart young man, raising his hand in a mock Hitler salute.

'Behave yourself, Egon,' Miriam told him. 'Detta, this is Egon Jeschke, reporter for *Berliner Zeitung*, even livelier when he writes than when he's talking nonsense. All Berlin enjoys his stories.'

Egon Jeschke made a face. 'With the exception of Dr Otto Dietrich, the new Reich press chief. I wondered in an article whether his legs are as beautiful as the pins of his famous niece in Hollywood, and was told I could leave out Jewish jokes like that in future. I think I'll play safe and switch to the sports section. They don't expect you to be funny there.'

More guests arrived, to be vivaciously greeted by Miriam and lavishly plied with champagne. Detta wandered around, watching them and picking up scraps of their conversation. 'That man Hitler ought to have been made Transport Minister instead of Reich Chancellor. He's mainly interested in building motorways.' The speaker had dark hair and slender artist's hands, and was talking to the Cobergs. Detta joined them.

'This is Detta von Aichborn,' the Prince introduced her. 'And this is Dr Felix Gerhard.'

'A doctor of medicine?'

'No, a D.Phil. I'm a composer. I write film scores for the UfA studios.'

'For as long as they'll let him,' Friedrich von Coberg remarked. 'Heaven knows what those Nazis have against our Jewish friends. How are the theatre, the movies, the cabaret to survive without Reinhardt, Holländer, Spolianski, Lang, Weill and all the rest?'

Dr Gerhard gave a thin smile. 'The last Jew in our family was called Schmuel Gelbfisz. He was my grandfather. He wore a caftan and ringlets, and the Tsar's Cossacks killed him. After that my father fled with us to Posen in the German Empire. He had the whole family baptized, and our name's been Gerhard ever since. My father rose to the rank of artillery captain in the war and won the Iron Cross. I studied in Breslau and took my doctorate in Berlin. I'm a good German, a good taxpayer, and a good friend of the actress Emmy Sonnemann, who's engaged to Göring, prime minister of Prussia. General Göring takes a lively interest in cultural life, and Emmy's going to introduce me to him.'

Dr Gerhard paused, and added cautiously, 'Anyway, film scores will be needed outside Germany too. I've written to my friend Lubitsch in America, just in case.'

'Detta, darling, you absolutely must meet David Floyd-Orr.' Miriam had a lanky, youngish man in tow. 'David, this is Detta von Aichborn,' she told him, speaking English. Detta fell into the same language.

'How do you do, Mr Floyd-Orr?' she said, shaking hands.

'David's something at the British Embassy,' Miriam informed her, before moving on.

'How do you do, Miss von Aichborn? I'm third secretary, to be precise. Which leaves me with a lot of time to explore this marvellous town.' The Englishman had unruly red hair and a few freckles under his grey-green eyes. He was casually elegant, and unusually clad for the Berlin of 1935, in a pair of pale-grey flannels and a double-breasted blazer, with a button pulling it in slightly at the waist. A German tailor would have ironed out that effect without mercy. 'Perhaps you could show me around?' he suggested, looking at her with admiration.

'I'd be happy to, but you probably know Berlin much better than I do. I'm only just up from the country.'

'A country girl, how wonderful!'

'A rustic is more like it.'

'Would you have lunch with me tomorrow?'

'Oh no, Mr Floyd-Orr, that's too sudden for me. I mean, I don't even know you.'

'And if you refuse my invitation you won't get to know me. What a pity that would be. You'd regret it.'

'You're not at all conceited, by any chance?'

'Not in the least. Just convinced of my inner worth, which generally reveals itself to good effect over lunch in charming company. So how about it?'

'The answer is still no — this time.'

'What about next time?'

Miriam interrupted them. 'Herr Karch, what an honour!' She hurried to meet a gentleman with a small silver pin sparkling on his dark suit. 'Come in and I'll introduce you to some people. Let's start with my friend here: Under-Secretary Aribert Karch — Baroness Henriette von Aichborn.'

A slight click of the heels, a damp kiss of her hand, while Detta looked down at a short parting, straight as a matchstick, and when the man had straightened up into a pair of grey eyes behind rimless glasses. Miriam nodded at them and disappeared. The Englishman had gone away. Oh dear, I've put him off me, thought Detta. She pointed at two little silver lightning flashes on Karch's lapels. 'Are you with the electricity works?'

'I belong to the Circle of Friends of the Reichsführer SS,' he informed her, looking important.

'A Circle of Friends, how nice. I expect you do all sorts of things together. Do you go for expeditions? Or maybe you go to the pictures together?' Karch was struggling for words. Detta saved him the trouble. 'I don't really want to know the details. Come along, Herr Karch, let's find something to drink. Do you like champagne? And I've heard that the smoked Rhine salmon is excellent.'

'After you, Baroness.' Karch followed her to the buffet. He pointed to a very good-looking, youngish man in a light-coloured suit. 'Isn't that Erik de Winter the film actor?'

'It could be. Everyone meets at Miriam's.'

'But luckily the Goldbergs and their like are not the majority. Germans like you and me predominate, Baroness.' Karch put a salmon roll in his mouth and dabbed his lips with a pure-white handkerchief, which he had taken from his breast pocket. After using it he tucked it into his left sleeve. All this was done with rather too much nonchalance, in the same way that he held the foot of his champagne glass between thumb and forefinger rather than clutching it by the stem.

'It would be a great pleasure if I could invite you here again in a few weeks' time.'

'Oh, now I know who you are. You're from the Ministry of Economic Affairs, and you're taking over Miriam's apartment.'

'I shall be giving a reception when I move in.' Karch cleared his throat. 'Exclusively for German guests. I am planning to have a string quartet playing German music, and I shall serve German sparkling wine and a few choice tidbits.'

'German caviar, perhaps?' Detta couldn't help saying, and earned herself a suspicious look from the under-secretary. She watched Miriam, who was tossing back glass after glass of champagne, with concern.

Hella Siebert came back from the guests' lavatory looking distraught. She began speaking to her husband in great agitation, but Detta couldn't hear what she was saying. Miriam, swaying, climbed on a chair. 'My dear friends!' she cried at the top of her voice. They all looked up at her. 'I want to say goodbye to you, dear friends. I am leaving in an hour's time. And I owe some among you special thanks. The Sieberts, for instance. Gottfried and Hella, thank you so much for all the efforts you've been making recently to have me thrown out of the Red and White, because someone like me is not welcome as a club member now. But for me they'd never have accepted a couple of little social climbers like you.' Gottfried Siebert went red in the face. His wife began to sob.

Miriam was sobering up with every word. 'And many thanks to Paul and Marianne Frowein, who unfortunately are not with us this evening. They have hay fever, poor things. Remarkable at this time of year, don't you agree? When they wanted a loan to buy their own house and asked me to put in a good word with Grandfather, they were always dropping in here.'

'Stop it, Miriam,' Rolf Lamprecht warned her.

'Not yet. First I must also thank Herr Aribert Karch. A remarkable man, Herr Karch. Promoted within a single year from a little nobody in the filing room of the Ministry of Economic Affairs to under-secretary in the same ministry. I'd like to see anyone equal that. Such unappetizing blobs of fat swim to the top of the brown soup these days.' Karch went pale. 'He considerately arranged for the Goldbergs to leave, the under-secretary did. And he was so generous too. Imagine, the family can take a tenth of what they own with them. The remaining ninety per cent goes to those brown-clad upstarts. The under-secretary calls it an emigration tax. If they didn't go, the family would be taken into protective custody. Only to protect parasites like us from the righteous anger of the German people, of course. Not that he personally has anything against us. But it's a good opportunity to get his hands on my apartment for peanuts, isn't it, Herr Karch?' She flung her glass on the floor at his feet. Furious, Karch stormed out.

Miriam jumped down from the chair. 'Listen!' she cried, laughing. 'Just a word to everyone who hasn't been to the guest lavatory yet. Yes, Gottfried, what your wife saw is correct: I had it designed by an artist for my farewell party. A talented painter on porcelain has immortalized the Führer's portrait in the lavatory bowl, so anyone who feels like it can shit on him. It's a pleasure I shall certainly allow myself before I leave.'

Incredulous silence, contained laughter, horrified whispers. The range of reactions was wide. Monsieur Montfort found it difficult to suppress a grin. Dr Gerhard, his face unmoved, looked at the floor. Egon Jeschke smiled and murmured, 'Miriam, you're fantastic, girl!'

Miriam took his glass from his hand. 'Your good health, Egon, my friend. Your very good health, all my true friends!' She emptied it in a single draught. 'And as for the rest of you, you unpleasant little crooks who have been sponging on me for years, enjoying the delightful feeling of belonging to society – to hell with you!'

David Floyd-Orr was the only one now standing by the buffet, concentrating on choosing delicacies and carefully piling them on his plate. 'As a diplomat he can't take sides. He has to exercise restraint,' said Friedrich von Coberg, quietly drawing Detta aside. 'Listen, Karch has phoned the Gestapo. Our friend must get out of here at once.'

Miriam was about to pour herself another glass of champagne, but Detta steered her into the bedroom. 'Quick, get changed. There's no time to lose. Karch has alerted the Gestapo.'

Without haste, Miriam stepped out of her cocktail dress as if she hadn't heard what Detta said. Clad in her silk camiknickers, she opened the wardrobe that ran all the way along the wall and inspected its contents with a critical eye. 'The green tweed suit from Scotland, maybe? Or Coco Chanel's travelling ensemble would look pretty. What do you think? Maybe I should wear the pale-grey flannel dress with the black turban? That would suit my white car, don't you think?'

'Give it to me.' Detta took the turban, put it on and stuffed her fair hair under it.

'Oh, that really suits you. You can have it. I'll wear Madame Schiaparelli's sporty felt hat.'

'You go into my room, take my raincoat and beret, and keep calm,' Detta told her. Tyres squealed outside. 'I hope the Prince can hold them off long enough. I'll come and see you in Lisbon sometime. Goodbye, Miriam.'

The garage door flew open. The white BMW, its hood down, roared up the ramp to the street in first gear, racing past a black limousine. The man at the wheel of the black car watched it go, startled, and then hooted his horn hard. Men in leather coats rushed out of the building and piled into the car. 'Go on, follow her!' one of them panted. The sports car was lurching round the corner well ahead of them. It turned into Heerstrasse. 'She drives like the devil,' said the driver in annoyance.

Detta pushed the turban back from her forehead as it threatened to slip down over her eyes. She stepped on the gas. The car jolted forward and shot down the street, going she didn't know where, except that she was heading out of town. A sign saying 'Frankfurt/Oder 130 Kilometres' made up her mind. The road went straight ahead. The Mercedes in her rear-view mirror looked smaller. Why not let him catch up a bit, she thought, grinning. The poor driver's going to such trouble. The black limousine behind her grew until it was large enough for Detta's liking. She stepped on the gas, and her pursuers shrank again. She repeated this game several times, beginning to enjoy herself. Then, unexpectedly, a level crossing barrier came down. Detta trod on the brake as hard as she could. The BMW stopped just centimetres from the barrier as the Warsaw express thundered past.

Next moment four men in leather coats surrounded the car. Detta beamed at them. 'Phew! I only just made it in time.'

'Gestapo,' the leader of the men barked.

'Pleased to meet you, Herr Gestapo.' She offered him her hand. 'And I'm Detta von Aichborn.'

'Never mind the silly jokes. *Geheime Staatspolizei*. Can you prove your identity?'

'As it happens, I have my passport with me. I'm going to Poland. A flying visit to the Potockys. Prince Potocky is my godfather.' She pulled the black turban off her head, revealing her blonde hair.

'Baroness von Aichborn, Henriette Sophie Charlotte,' one of the men read out loud from her passport. 'Is this your vehicle?'

'No, a friend lent me the car. She thought she'd take the train to Vienna instead. The papers are in the glove compartment. Want to see them?'

'Come on, back to Berlin. Perhaps we can pick her up at the station,' said the leader.

The black limousine turned and disappeared in a cloud of dust. Detta watched it go. 'Led you a nice dance,' she told herself with satisfaction, patting the little gold plaque with M.G., Miriam's initials, on the dashboard.

The call from Copenhagen came in the afternoon. It was Miriam, bright and cheerful as if nothing had happened. 'Hello, darling, I got here safely.'

'Oh, my God, Miriam, I'm so glad.'

'It was a great idea of yours, drawing the pack off with the car and sending them in the direction of Vienna. My passport is up to date, so there were no problems at the Danish border.'

'Promise me to stay there and rest for a few days. Copenhagen is said to be very beautiful.'

'Very beautiful and very *petit bourgeois*. I miss Berlin already. I'm going to take the next ship to England and then fly from London to Paris. Listen, darling. I want you to keep the car. Put it somewhere safe. I'll write to your family notary, and Dr Rossitter will make out the deed of gift. Have fun at the wheel, and don't drive straight into the nearest tree. Stay in my apartment as long as they'll let you. I'll call from Lisbon in a few weeks' time. Bye now.'

Detta didn't stay in Miriam's apartment. It would have felt like treachery. She put the roadster in the garage building in Kantstrasse, and took a room at the Pension Wolke in Windscheidstrasse. She stayed in her room all the next day and the following night. She didn't want to see anyone after all that had happened. On Sunday she felt better.

'You poor thing, you must be half-starved,' said Frau Wolke, welcoming her to the lunch table. Detta got to know the handful of long-term guests in the boarding house; Herr Köhler, a genteel, reserved man who was head clerk in a nearby attorney's office, wore a monocle and tried to put on aristocratic airs; friendly Vera Vogel, secretary to an insurance company director; elderly Fräulein Dr Burmester, who taught at the French School. And Marlene Kaschke, a tall young blonde with long legs and rather too much *décolleté*, who seemed to Detta to have a curiously hunted look. She said she was looking for a job.

Albert Wolke had been blinded by poison gas at Ypres, and now sat by the radio listening to marching music interrupted by enthusiastic news bulletins: German troops had entered the Saarland. 'The Saar is German again!' announced the newsreader triumphantly.

'Yup, and it'll be the Rhineland next, and then Alsace. That Hitler won't ever be satisfied. And nobody's going to stop him, either,' Wolke grumbled. 'Weren't our fingers burnt bad enough last time?' But no one was interested in his comments.

'Like to come to the pictures?' Marlene Kaschke asked. 'I'm thinking of applying for an usherette's job at the UfA Palace, and I fancy seeing the new Willy Fritsch movie.'

'That's nice of you, but I'm expecting a visitor.' Detta had sent Hans-Georg a postcard with her address on it, asking him to call on Sunday. She went to her room and leafed through the *Berliner Illustrierte*, but its photo-reports from all over the world didn't interest her. She kept thinking of Tom

168

Glaser's smiling, manly face, and how she'd never again be as close to him as when they had danced that slow foxtrot at Aichborn. It's going to take you time to get over that, she thought in her sober Prussian way.

Frau Wolke came to her room about four. 'Gentleman to see you,' she announced, rather suspiciously. 'Young man in uniform. Kindly leave your door open.'

Hans-Georg stormed in, beaming. 'Detta, at last!'

She hugged him and gave him a big kiss on the cheek. 'My brother, Lieutenant Hans-Georg von Aichborn; Frau Wolke, my landlady,' she introduced them.

Frau Wolke melted when he kissed her hand. 'Well, in that case of course you can close the door. I'll bring you coffee and home-made cake.' She wafted away.

'Come on, sit down. How was Trakehnen?'

'Stubbendorf and I tried out some promising young horses. There's a four-year-old mare I particularly like. She moves beautifully . . .' He talked enthusiastically about the studs in East Prussia and his excursions in the area, but Detta saw the sorrow in his eyes.

'You miss her a lot, don't you?'

'More than anything in the world,' he confessed. 'Detta, what am I going to do?'

It hurt, but she made herself speak firmly. 'You've trained to be a soldier and nothing else. You don't know a word of Portuguese. What would you do in Lisbon? Live off your wife, a prince consort with nothing but an aristocratic title and some social graces?'

He tried a smile. 'You sound so grown up, little sister.'

'Well, I *have* grown up these last few days, because now I know that girlish dreams have nothing to do with reality. The reality is that Tom Glaser's getting married next week. Silly fool that I am, I've been obsessed with him. Reality is fat ladies buying dresses in Horn's, insulting other people and getting away with it, and greedy under-secretaries rising to the top of the social order under the new regime.' She told her brother about the events of the last few days. 'Miriam told it to them straight when she said goodbye, she was wonderful.'

'I shall wait for her. There are enough sensible people in the government to restrain the few extremists. The Chancellor can't really want to have half the world against him, particularly now that he's as good as finished liberating Germany from the Treaty of Versailles. You wait, Miriam and her family will soon be back, unharmed.'

He really believes it, thought Detta in amazement.

Frau Wolke brought coffee and marble cake. 'A lovely day,' she said, trying to make conversation, but when brother and sister reacted politely but in monosyllables she quickly beat a retreat.

'What are you going to do?' Hans-Georg asked.

'Go to Thomas Glaser's wedding. As a form of aversion therapy, so to speak. And look for work and a place to live. I phoned Father, and he knows someone in the Foreign Ministry. I'm to go for an interview there. And as for my free time — well, it's not far to Potsdam. I'll come over as often as you like.'

'I know Stubbendorf will be happy to lend you a horse. We can go riding together.'

She carried his hand to her cheek. 'You're still my favourite man,' she said affectionately.

The 'someone' in the Foreign Ministry was not only a member of the Baron's old student fraternity but also Reich Foreign Minister. Herr von Neurath had a kindly, paternal manner, but not much time. 'I'm sure one more young lady here in the FM can't hurt. Your English is perfect and your Spanish very good, I hear. You can lend Arvid von Troll a hand on the Western Europe desk. My personnel adviser will see to the formalities. You must come and have dinner with us one day soon. My wife will be delighted.'

An elderly secretary inspected Detta with reserve, and indicated that Herr von Troll was in Geneva at the moment. 'You can meet him next week. Although we really don't have any vacancies,' she added sharply.

'Excellent, that'll give me time to look for an apartment,' said Detta cheerfully. She was determined to make the best of everything.

In Wilhelmstrasse a man waved to her from the other side of the road. It was David Floyd-Orr. He launched himself into the traffic with death-defying daring, and steered his loose-limbed way over the road. His red head was shining in the sun. 'Miss von Aichborn, how nice to see you.'

'Likewise, Mr Floyd-Orr. Are you out on diplomatic business?'

'I'm visiting shoe shops, to be honest. I'm looking for a pair of white canvas deck shoes, which in my size seems to be downright impossible.'

Detta glanced down at his feet. 'Bensing goes to Wertheim once every two years. He doesn't come to Berlin more often than that.'

'Bensing?'

'He runs the whole place at home. You'd probably call him a butler. His shoe size is positively illegal.' Her hand flew to her mouth. 'Oh, forgive me! That was tactless!'

He laughed. 'So where is this shoe shop?'

'You've been in this city longer than me and you don't know Wertheim?'

'Luckily not, I think, because now I depend on you to help me, and a helpless man is usually halfway to winning his lady, or so says my friend Jack, who knows a lot about women. At least, he's on his third marriage.'

'Dear me, a Bluebeard!'

'No, only an American.'

SA men were standing outside the Wertheim department store on Potsdamer Platz with sandwich boards that read: 'Germans, Don't Buy from Jews!' But no one seemed to be taking any notice; the big revolving doors were in constant motion. The people of Berlin were not going to let themselves be told what do so easily.

Inside, Detta and the Englishman stared up at the glass dome, beneath which an aircraft hung from steel cables. 'It once belonged to a famous airman called Udet,' Detta explained to her protégé, and asked a salesman the way to shoe department, where they found the right size in no time.

'Shall we have a coffee?' he suggested.

'Yes, let's.' They went up to the store café, where there was a pleasant smell of chocolate and whipped cream, and smart waitresses in lace caps were serving the customers. 'So you're a sailor,' she remarked.

'Because of the shoes? Oh no. My colleague Nigel Hawksworth was unexpectedly transferred to Shanghai, and he's lent me his motorboat. It's moored by the Stössensee bridge, and has two cabins to the fore. If you bring a girlfriend you can safely accept my invitation to a weekend on the water. I like fresh night air, so I sleep on deck anyway.'

Detta put on a show of reserve. 'I'll ask Marion if she'd like to come. Can I phone you, Mr Floyd-Orr?'

He gave her his card. 'If you can bring yourself to say David, it would save you a lot of time.'

'I'm Detta, then.'

He took her to the U-Bahn, and she caught the Kaiserdamm train. It wasn't far from there to the Pension Wolke. Her heart rose at the thought of a weekend on the water. The only problem was – she didn't know any Marion.

Detta had told the family at home her present address, and it was passed on to Dr Theodor Rossitter the notary, who wrote asking her to visit his office in Unter den Linden. She had known him from her earliest childhood; he came to Aichborn every year for the shooting.

She took the bus to the Brandenburg Gate. The guard was being changed, with drums and pipes, at the Neue Wache Memorial. A captain on horseback accepted the report of the officer leading the parade, a dashing young lieutenant. Detta mingled with the spectators enjoying the colourful show. 'Not like those spruced-up SS fellows outside the Reich Chancellery,' someone said. 'This is something else!'

'Never you mind that Adolf,' said the man's neighbour. 'They've got their own doormen outside the Adlon too.'

Detta went down Unter den Linden, past the Café Kranzler. The notary's office was in an old building not far from Friedrichstrasse, and had a dusty but solid appearance. The affairs of the landed gentry of Prussia had been handled here for over two hundred years.

'Fräulein Henriette,' Dr Rossitter welcomed her in his old-fashioned way, always rather stiff. 'On behalf of Fräulein Miriam Goldberg, I have prepared the deed of gift of a motor vehicle to you. Please sign here. My clerk will see to registration in your name.'

'Thank you, Dr Rossitter.'

He gave her a melancholy smile. 'I do wish you'd call me Uncle Theo, as you used to.'

'Thank you, then, Uncle Theo.'

'And there's a second reason why I asked you to come to see me. Your father has written to me. He wants you to have your grandmother's legacy at your disposal now. You are of age, and old enough to manage your money.'

'Is it an awful lot?' she asked, rather scared.

'You will be sent a precise account. Mainly it consists of papers, securities and landed property which your family's bank is managing for you.

There is also a savings account for you to use as you wish. Ewald will give you the documents proving your ownership of the account, which will enable you to withdraw money or make transfers in any of the bank's branches. For instance, I have in mind your new car, which will mean a certain amount of expense for you, and we mustn't forget your rent, since I'm sure you will soon be moving into your own apartment.'

'I have a job at the Foreign Ministry. I'll be earning a real salary,' said Detta proudly.

'Congratulations. A very suitable post for a young lady.' Dr Rossitter escorted her out. 'If you need help or advice, I'm at your service any time. Don't forget that; like any other big city, Berlin can be a dangerous place.'

'Many thanks, Uncle Theo. I'll take care of myself.' Elated, Detta ran down the steps and went straight into the bookshop next door to buy a map of the city. Then she took the white roadster out of the garage. She couldn't wait to explore the capital at the wheel.

Admiring and envious glances followed the young blonde in the open sports car. Women at the wheel were almost as rare a sight as the stylish BMW 319 itself. 'You want a personal invitation, Fräulein?' inquired the police officer directing traffic outside the Kaiser Wilhelm Memorial Church. Although he had signalled to her for the second time, Detta had remained at the road junction without moving – she had suddenly thought of Marlene Kaschke. Just the right chaperone for her weekend with the freckled Englishman. She smiled an apology at the policeman and stepped on the gas.

Detta met her new boss on Tuesday. Arvid von Troll had caught the night express from Geneva. He was in his mid-thirties, with a thin, well-shaped face and a scar on his left cheek which, Detta discovered, was the result not of a duel but a motor accident. The diplomat was an enthusiastic cross-country driver.

'Do you go in for any sports, Fräulein von Aichborn?'

'Only if you count riding as a sport. Exercising a dozen horses every day isn't all fun. Our estate manager's daughter is doing it for me now. If they're always out at pasture, the dear creatures fall into bad habits.'

But Herr von Troll wasn't really interested in that. 'We're just preparing for the Minister's visit to England. The official part is all in the clear, but then there's the invitation to a weekend at Chequers. Can you think of a

173

good present for him to take the master of the house and Mrs Macdonald?'

'When do you need my suggestions by?'

'By the day before yesterday.' Troll turned to the stack of files on his desk.

Frau Wilhelmi the secretary showed Detta her little office on the other side of the corridor. The only furniture was a desk, chair and filing cabinet. Two floors below was the yard, with official cars parked in it. The secretary pointed to an electric bell above the door. 'When that rings you go straight in to Herr von Troll. You'll find paper and pencils in the cabinet there.'

She turned to leave. Detta stopped her. 'I need the latest edition of *Who's Who*, the big Muret-Sanders dictionary, a typewriter and most important of all, a telephone. I'd like the reference books and the typewriter at once, please, and the telephone by this afternoon.'

'There's a telephone kiosk down on the ground floor.'

Detta ignored this declaration of hostilities. She pointed to the socket in the skirting board. 'I see there's a connection here already. The caretaker can install the phone after the lunch break. That will give him enough time to inform the switchboard. He can bring a table and chair for the typewriter at the same time; I'd like to keep my desk free for other work.' The secretary was about to object, but Detta cut her off, saying coolly, 'That will be all for the time being. Thank you, Frau Wilhelmi.' The secretary lowered her gaze. Detta had won.

That afternoon an Olympia was standing in all its glory on a typewriter table which had been brought to stand in the window, carbon paper and copy paper within easy reach beside it, the reference books were on the filing cabinet, and the telephone cord was coiling its way to the socket. Detta picked up the receiver. The switchboard answered at once. 'Extension 124 here. Please connect me with Aichborn in the Uckermark. The number is Wrietzow 0–3.' She hung up.

A few minutes later her phone rang. Bensing was at the other end. 'Fräulein Detta?' he cried in excitement, recognizing her voice. 'How are you?'

'Fine, thank you. Listen, this is a business call, so we must keep it short. Would you go up to my room? I left my red address book there. Bring it down to the phone. There's a number I need. I'll hang up now and call again in a few moments.' Five minutes later she had the number she wanted. She set to work.

The office closed at six. Detta took the U-Bahn home. She had left the BMW in the garage; it didn't seem suitable for her to be cruising around in a sports car when she was a very junior member of the Foreign Ministry staff.

The usual evening tedium set in after supper at the Pension Wolke. Herr Köhler was studying the *Almanach de Gotha*, his monocle glinting; Vera Vogel was reading *Die Dame* magazine. Dr Burmester was correcting her pupils' homework with a red pen. Marlene Kaschke wasn't there. Detta knocked at the door of her room. The young woman was lying on her bed in her dressing gown, painting her toenails. Detta had never seen anyone do that before. She came straight to the point. 'Are you doing anything on Saturday and Sunday?'

Marlene Kaschke was not, and was absolutely delighted. 'A motorboat on the Havel? You bet I'll come. And I've just bought a fabulous sky-blue Bleyle too!' Detta learned that a Bleyle was a bathing suit in the latest style, with a little skirt and low-cut back. 'You can get them in all colours at Leineweber's. You ought to buy yourself one too,' Marlene Kashke advised her. She had no objection at all to being an old friend of Detta's called Marion for the weekend.

'I'll be delighted to meet your friend Marion,' said David Floyd-Orr happily over the phone. 'Saturday at nine in the morning at the Stössensee bridge, then. Just go down the steps to the moorings, you can't miss me.'

Detta hung up. She had no idea how she was going to keep that date. They worked until one o'clock on Saturdays at the FM.

Detta went in to her boss at eight in the morning. Arvid von Troll was busy unpacking the contents of a shabby attaché case on to his desk. 'This thing was already in use under Privy Councillor Holstein. Well, what do you suggest as presents?'

'For Mrs Macdonald I'd recommend a classic vase from the state porcelain manufactory. And you could get the prime minister a *netsuke*.'

'A what?'

'They're thumbnail-sized Japanese figures in many different shapes, often carved from exotic woods. As far back as the fifteenth century, the Japanese were using them as toggles to fasten their tobacco pouches to their belts.'

'Well, I'm sure Prime Minister Macdonald will be glad he can finally fasten his tobacco pouch to his belt,' said Arvid von Troll sarcastically. 'What's the meaning of all this nonsense, Fräulein von Aichborn?'

'It's not nonsense, Herr von Troll,' replied Detta calmly. 'Ramsay Macdonald is very knowledgeable about Japanese art. His collection of woodcuts is famous.'

'So why a thumbnail-sized Japanese carving?'

'A *netsuke* lies comfortably in the hand and makes you feel good when you touch it. Its exotic wood gives off a strangely stimulating perfume.'

'And you think someone getting one of these things as a present will want to handle and smell it?'

'Before long the prime minister won't be able to see his woodcuts any more because his eyesight is deteriorating. But he'll still have his senses of touch and smell. And he'll soon be retiring.'

'Deteriorating eyesight? Retiring? What on earth are you talking about?'

'I had to know what kind of person Mr Macdonald is so I could suggest a really personal present for him.'

'And I suppose you read all this in your coffee grounds at breakfast?'

'Good heavens, no. I telephoned the ambassador in London.'

'You telephoned our ambassador without permission?' Troll asked, stunned.

'Oh, not our ambassador. I phoned Uncle Juan. My mother's brother is the Spanish ambassador to the Court of St James,' said Detta, mollifying him. 'He's usually very well informed.'

Arvid von Troll cleared his throat. 'Well, I must apologize for my tone, Fräulein von Aichborn. We'll take your advice about the present.' He hesitated. 'I suppose your uncle Juan doesn't happen to know who will be Ramsay Macdonald's successor?'

'I asked him that too,' Detta was happy to tell him. 'Stanley Baldwin, he says.'

'Herr von Neurath will be impressed,' Troll said, with obvious satisfaction. 'You can ask a favour in return.'

'May I have the whole of Saturday off?'

'You may,' Herr von Troll generously agreed.

She rose early on Saturday to pack her raffia bag, containing toiletries, towel, new Bleyle and her Agfa box camera. A blouse, bright wrapover skirt, matching shorts and sandals completed her ensemble. Detta was armed for the encounter.

She knocked on Marlene Kaschke's door at seven-thirty. 'It'll be no use knocking, Fräulein von Aichborn,' Frau Wolke told her. 'Some man she knew fetched her yesterday. Even paid her rent. Would you like an egg for breakfast?'

Detta did not reply. She was feverishly trying to come up with a solution to the problem that had so unexpectedly arisen. But there was no solution without someone to play gooseberry. Goodbye, weekend on the water, she thought furiously.

They were far from prudish at home in Aichborn. At the age of six, Detta had helped the head groom take mares to the stallion. Her mother had used the example of Lina, a kitchen-maid impregnated by a seasonal worker who had long since moved on, to explain that even if you weren't married you could find yourself in circumstances that were far from desirable, since a child needs a father and a woman needs a husband. It all depended on doing things in the right order, she said, so it made sense to get your man to the altar before having fun with him. Because it was indeed fun, the Baroness happily concluded her explanation, and you could have fun more often and for longer with a husband – where, for instance, was Lina's seasonal worker now?

The practical Detta thought all this sounded very plausible, although she would have liked to know more about the fun. At the next opportunity she asked Lina, who told her in a whisper how you went about it and why it was so nice.

From then on Detta looked at the village boys in a completely different way, and the idea of 'having fun' crept into her longing dreams. To make sure they remained dreams, her mother sent Adelheid with her as a chaperone when Bensing drove her to dancing classes in the nearby town, or when one of the young gentlemen from the neighbouring estates accompanied her to a summer ball. Detta saw nothing wrong in that. It wasn't a matter of morality but of etiquette, just as everyone knew you didn't eat fish with a knife.

Although she had come of age, and there was no one to keep an eye on her in the cosmopolitan city of Berlin where anything went so long as you enjoyed, it would never have entered her head to break the rules of etiquette.

But now everything was different. Very well then, I'll eat my fish with a knife, she thought daringly, and took the BMW out of the Kantstrasse garage.

She parked the car by the Stössensee bridge and, in high spirits, ran down the countless steps carved out of the steep slope. David Floyd-Orr's shock of red hair was visible from far away. He was wearing a white polo shirt with immaculate, white linen trousers, and instead of a belt he had knotted a Winchester old school tie around them.

'Good morning, Detta. How nice of you to come.'

'Hello, David, thank you for asking me.' That was enough to satisfy English good manners. 'My friend Marion is so sorry, she can't come. She's not feeling well.' She looked out at the Stössensee, which despite its name was not really a lake, but a bay just off the river, bordered by old trees. Landing stages ran out on all sides, like wooden fingers pointing at the water. Yachts, motorboats and rowing boats rocked at their moorings. 'It's really lovely here.'

'I practically live here in the summer. This way, please.' They walked over sun-warmed planks to a motorboat. Its name, *Bertie*, stood in shiny letters on the prow. The Union Jack above it made a pleasant change from the swastika flags flown by the other vessels. David helped her on board. Everything here was brass and mahogany.

'There's an awful lot to clean,' said the ever-practical Detta.

'Not this weekend, though. Down here.' Three steps led down to the cabin that reached all the way to the bows. The seats by the two long sides could be pulled out to make comfortable beds. A wall cupboard contained the tiny galley with its spirit stove. David pointed to the zinc-plated refrigerator. 'We're just waiting for the man to bring ice to keep our drinks cold, then we can start. I thought we'd go past Potsdam up to Brandenburg, and then go a little further into the Havelland tomorrow. We'll be back here tomorrow evening, if that's all right by you?'

It was all right by Detta. The slight smell of marshy water, oil and gasoline, the gentle rocking of the water, the tinny sound of a gramophone playing on the boat next to David's — it was all new and fascinating.

The man with the ice delivered his load, stowed it below decks with a clatter, and wished them a nice weekend. David undid the rope and pushed off from the landing stage. Puttering, the engine started and took the boat at a leisurely pace under the Stössensee bridge and into the Havel, which opened out before them.

Down in the cabin Detta found a white, peaked cap with an anchor on it, and put it on at a rakish angle over her left ear. She had taken off her wrapover skirt and was now sitting on the cabin roof in shorts, with her knees drawn up. She looked over the gleaming, silvery water where white sails bobbed, slender canoes cut their way through the water, and now and then a motorboat left its wake behind. She felt free and at ease, the way she usually felt only in the saddle.

Gradually they gathered speed. David stood at the wheel, concentrating as though he were steering *Bertie* close to a cliff. It was a little while before Detta realized that he was desperately trying not to stare at her bare legs and, to her amusement, was not entirely succeeding.

'If you'll take the wheel I could fix our drinks. Just keep going straight ahead. And if an iceberg appears, please avoid it.'

She couldn't help laughing, for he said this totally straight-faced. The last man to make her laugh had been Tom Glaser back in Aichborn. How long ago that seemed. She felt a tiny pang, and then it went away. David disappeared below deck and after a few minutes brought up two tall, misty glasses clinking with ice.

'I hope you like Pimm's Number One?'

'Tell me what's in it first.'

'Well, originally only Mr James Pimm knew that. He was an apothecary in London around 1840, and he invented this gin-based drink at his customers' request. The herbs and spices added to flavour it are still the secret of his heirs. Lady Phipps made the lemonade to top it up – she's the wife of our ambassador Sir Eric – in an attempt to keep the younger members of the embassy staff away from the demon drink. And the cucumber strips, with a slice of orange and another of lemon, are my personal ingredients.'

'Tastes good,' she pronounced.

'All the same, we'd better stick to just one glass, what with the sun and the aforesaid demon.'

Detta chuckled.

'Did I say something funny?'

'No. It's just . . .' She couldn't help coming out with it. 'It's just that I

179

really don't need a chaperone with you.' David went red – and even redder when, soon afterwards, Detta appeared on deck in her sky-blue Bleyle.

They passed the Wannsee. Potsdam and then Geltow went by, and they cast anchor in a bay near Werder. Detta, standing very straight, went to the bows. She felt more self-conscious about her figure than ever before. I hope he doesn't think my thighs are too thin, she worried. At home, swimming in the Aich with the village boys and girls, such a thought would never have occurred to her. For safety's sake, she avoided his gaze by jumping into the water. David came in after her. She dived, and surfaced again a little further on. He swam after her with long strokes. She went down again, and then came up behind him. She repeated this game several times – it was fun to tease him a little. Then she dived down right under the boat and kept close to its side.

'Detta? Detta!' His calls became more urgent. She thought of Tom Glaser. Would he have worried about her? 'So there you are.' A pair of strong arms came around her. For a second she felt his firm body. 'Oh, I thought . . . .' Awkwardly, he let go of her. 'You were just leading me on!'

'Me? How do you mean?' she said, feigning innocence, and pulled herself up on board. She lay on deck in the sunlight, dozing and dreaming of Thomas Glaser. He was holding her hand, and she returned its gentle pressure. But it was David's hand; he quickly withdrew it from hers when she opened her eyes. How shy he is, she thought, captivated.

Thomas Glaser's wedding was very much an aeronautical affair. After the service, the bridal couple walked out under a triumphal arch of crossed propellers, and a colleague of the newly appointed Flight Captain Glaser flew his biplane low over the tower of Pastor Niemöller's Old Dahlem parish church. The director of Lufthansa had generously paid in advance the fine that this stunt would incur. The bride, now Ulrike Glaser, was a friendly brunette of twenty-five. 'What a good choice, Tom,' said Detta in deliberately tomboyish tones.

'Glad you think so,' Glaser thanked her.

'Here's to friendship,' Ulli declared at the wedding breakfast, raising a glass to her.

'To friendship.' Detta pulled herself together. No one else guessed what was going on inside her, except for Hans-Georg, who simply knew her too well. 'You may not think so, but the right man for you will come along, you just have to believe it,' he consoled her. That was exactly the trigger for the tears she could have done without. 'Make my excuses to everyone,' she managed to tell him.

She started the BMW, engaged first gear with a crunch, and jerkily drove off. She swerved in front of a bus as she turned into the Kurfürstendamm and almost knocked a cyclist down at Halensee S-Bahn station. She noticed none of it. She wasn't sitting at the wheel of her roadster but in Tom Glaser's plane. The slipstream tugged at her hair as he took the Klemm up to loop the loop. Her stomach heaved. A horrible need to retch overcame her. She braked with a screech and threw up on the pavement. Luckily there was no one nearby, and traffic was thin at this time of the evening.

There was a small family bar opposite. She ordered a coffee and quickly went to the Ladies. Vigorous gargling rid her mouth of the sour taste of stomach acid. She plunged her face in cold water, and was glad to find a clean hand towel by the basin. *'Contenance, ma petite,'* she could hear her mother saying. That had been when Detta, aged twelve, bungled a dressage trial at the local gymkhana and was taking Henry back to the stables, in floods of tears. She smoothed her hair and her dress; she had lost her hat on the way here. As she entered the café again she was very much the cool Prussian aristocrat again on the outside, friendly but reserved, perfectly poised. Inside, she was telling herself dryly: so much for your aversion therapy, my dear. You need stronger medicine.

Making up her mind, she got behind the wheel and stepped on the gas. Twilight was falling as she ran down the countless steps from the Stössensee bridge to the landing stages. The warm light of an oil lamp shone in *Bertie's* cabin. David Floyd-Orr was lying full-length, reading, old-fashioned half-moon glasses on his nose. He looked up. 'Oh, hello,' he said, showing no surprise.

'Hello to you too.' Detta was frantically wondering how, when you were a completely inexperienced girl, you went about seducing a man for thera-peutic reasons without making a fool of yourself.

She was woken by the cry of a coot. The diffuse light of early morning came in through the portholes. The sleeper beside her was lying on his side, hands folded under his cheek, snoring quietly. So this was the man she would never in her life have imagined as a lover, a lanky Englishman of twenty-eight with red hair and freckles. But as everyone knows and as Bensing used to say, things never turn out just as you expect, and all things considered it had really been very good.

They had laughed a lot, particularly when David confessed that he had enjoyed this kind of experience only once before, with his nanny Ruth when he was sixteen. Nannies, Detta learned, were an English institution, and though they officially cared for children only up to school age they generally remained in the family, quite often provided adolescents with practical enlightenment, and later looked after their former charges' progeny too. Even a repeat performance of that practical instruction wasn't out of the question.

She suppressed a smile as she thought of the earnest, focused expression which he had worn as he set about the natural but difficult task of penetration – difficult because he was guided less by passion than by his anxiety not to hurt her. In the end it was she who braced herself against his body and took him right into her, so that the pain was kept within bounds and soon gave way to a promising tingling sensation. It did not lead to orgasm, but gave some idea of the pleasures of which her mother had once spoken, and which the kitchen-maid Lina, giggling, had so rapturously described.

She softly rose to her feet and climbed the few steps to the deck. Morning mist lay over the sleeping boats around them. Without a sound, she slipped into the cool water which washed around her naked body. She swam far out, dived down on returning the last few metres to the boat, and hauled herself up by the side. David, looking the other way, was holding a towel ready for her. She wrapped herself in it. 'Good morning, darling.' She gave him a wet kiss.

He was reserve itself. 'I hope you slept well? Breakfast's almost ready.' He climbed down. There was an aroma of fresh coffee and fried eggs. 'The bacon's from Hefter. I'm afraid they didn't have any Danish,' he stiffly apologized. 'And afterwards I thought we could take a little round trip to the Tegeler See. Before Nigel Hawksworth went away he told me the Lake Pavilion there serves a good lunch. Poor fellow, he's having to eat Chinese food now. Although there are supposed to be a number of outstanding European restaurants in Shanghai.' He spoke with his face turned to the spirit stove, and in a great hurry, as if afraid she might interrupt him. 'Would you like an orange juice first?'

She let the towel drop. 'David, look at me.' He turned round. 'You talk too much, darling,' she said, in a deep, cooing undertone that was new even to herself. His Adam's apple, bobbing up and down, betrayed the fact that he was swallowing hard. She stood on tiptoe and kissed him. As she did so, she took his hand down to her sex.

It was an unforgettable encounter for them both. Amazed as children, they explored their bodies, giving themselves up to this wonderful game. Ever afterwards, the smell of burnt bacon would always bring back the memory of her first delicious orgasm.

'You must forgive my silly behaviour,' he said, apologizing for his awkwardness. 'We English are permanently embarrassed.' It was a concept that she found difficult to translate into German.

When they reached the dessert course in the Lake Pavilion, his face assumed his expression of grave concentration again. 'Would you marry me?' he asked over red summer fruit purée with vanilla sauce.

'I don't know,' she said truthfully. 'But I'll think about it.'

Frau von Aichborn had come to Berlin for the Olympic Games. A year earlier, she had offered to look after the wives of the Spanish team. But there was no Spanish team. The Civil War was raging on the Iberian peninsula.

Lieutenant Hans-Georg von Aichborn had not qualified for the three-day eventing. His mother and sister consoled him for his disappointment. 'I can't go to Spain with the Condor Legion either,' he complained. 'My commanding officer won't let us. Prussian officers are not mercenaries, he says.'

'Well, he's right,' said Detta. 'Imagine how easily something could happen to you there. I don't even like to think of it,' she added quietly, looking at her brother with affection. 'Anyway, what does the war in Spain have to do with us?'

'More than you think,' said the Baroness gravely. She was watching her daughter closely, and summed up her observations in the laconic inquiry: 'When are you going to introduce him to us?'

Detta was surprised. 'How did you guess?'

The Baroness smiled. 'I'm your mother.'

'When he's back from England,' Detta promised.

'Does he have a name?'

'David Floyd-Orr. He's third secretary at the British Embassy.'

They had been together for nearly a year and saw each other almost daily, either at his place in Tiergartenstrasse or Detta's small apartment on Steubenplatz, where she had moved in January. She had recovered from her obsession with Tom Glaser, and had no regrets. She loved David, his dry English manner, his occasional 'embarrassment' and the lanky, youthful appearance that belied his twenty-nine years.

They explored Berlin together. They drank lager at the Plumpe, as the people of Berlin called the Fountain of Health; they visited Museum Island; they watched the annual firework show 'Treptow in Flames'; and they drank sticky lemon liqueur at 'Goldelse's'. The proprietress as a blonde child had modelled for Zille, the illustrator and photographer. Detta hadn't been able to entice David up the Radio Tower, known affectionately to Berliners as their *langer Lulatsch*, the term for a tall beanpole of a man. 'I get vertigo if I so much as climb on a kitchen stool,' he confessed.

'He is the heir of the eighth Earl of Bexford, which makes him Viscount Floyd-Orr,' the Baroness wrote to her daughter. She had looked the family up in *Debrett's Peerage*.

'David hasn't said anything to me about that,' Detta replied. 'He wants me to accept him as he is.'

'Invite him to Aichborn,' her mother wrote. 'If he can stand the shock of meeting the family he'll probably be up to dealing with you too.'

In the summer of '38 Detta was a guest at Bexford Hall, and won the hearts of David's parents and the rest of his family. 'A Prussian wife with an impeccable background,' said the delighted Lord Bexford. 'You couldn't have done better for yourself, my boy.'

At the house party held in Detta's honour, the earl expressed his admiration for her countrymen. 'Fine people, these Germans. Particularly their Reich Chancellor. Amazing, the way the man is creating order out of chaos.' The other guests, all members of the establishment, seemed equally impressed by Herr Hitler. Only the Duchess of Newcastle had reservations. 'The man isn't married, and apparently he speaks terrible German. So Queen Mary says, anyway. She heard him on the radio.'

There had been changes in Berlin. Arvid von Troll introduced Detta to the new Foreign Minister. Joachim von Ribbentrop had previously been ambassador to London. 'Minor gentry from the Rhineland,' remarked her secretary disparagingly. Detta laughed. 'Frau Wilhelmi, you're a snob.'

'He's good-looking and polite,' Detta told David over supper. 'We talked about horses a little. He used to be a hussar officer.' They were eating potato salad and meatballs, which she bought ready made from the butcher and put in the pan; she was no great cook. David had fetched a siphon of light Bötzow beer from the bar on the corner.

'My boss Sir Nevile Henderson calls him a social climber,' he said, shrugging his shoulders. 'Could I have some more potato salad, please?' He liked the hearty Berlin fare.

Detta put some on his plate. 'Herr von Troll thinks it's time we fixed a date for the wedding.' She waited to hear his reaction.

'Why?' he asked, teasing her a little. 'Is Herr von Troll hoping for an invitation?'

'He told me that as a Foreign Ministry staff member I have to apply for permission to marry a foreigner, and it could take a little time.'

David nodded. 'My people see it the same way. I'm a diplomat in the service of his Britannic Majesty and I want to marry a German girl.'

'Your king is as German as I am. I'm sure he'll have no objection.'

But Detta had to wait. 'The Foreign Office wants to be clear about Great Britain's future relations with the German Reich before it will agree to our marriage,' David patiently explained. The usually down-to-earth Detta was too much in love to wonder what their wedding had to do with international politics, of which she only very occasionally took any notice – although she began to take notice in March 1939.

'Goodness, can we actually do that?' she cried in surprise when German troops marched into Prague.

'We have written a protest note to the government of the German Reich asking the same question,' David told her.

'And?'

'Your ambassador, like his colleague in Paris, simply refused to accept the note.'

A week later, when the German Wehrmacht occupied the Memelland, the Western powers expressed no more protests. The shocked Lithuanian government gave up the territory without opposition, and it was incorporated into the province of East Prussia.

'The Memel was always German and still is,' was the reaction of

Lieutenant Hans-Georg von Aichborn to the well-executed manoeuvre in which his own regiment had taken part. 'Now we'll get West Prussia back from the Poles, and Alsace from France,' he added briskly. 'And then we can finally consider the shameful Treaty of Versailles null and void.'

'I only hope it can be done without bloodshed,' said Detta anxiously.

'They won't dare attack us.' There was a combative look in her brother's eyes, but he was probably right. The Western powers had long ago lost their bite, and in whose interest, for heaven's sake, could it be to fire the first shot?

David was not so sure. 'I'm afraid we're drifting towards war,' he said, when London and Paris declared guarantees of support for Poland.

'Then we shall be on different sides,' said Detta, sounding concerned.

'Only until your side surrender,' replied David. 'And then you can marry the victor.'

'Don't be so arrogant,' she snapped at him, and he left the apartment in a huff.

Next morning he sent flowers and tried several times to get in touch with her. But the pride of the Aichborns held out. She refused to speak to him for a week and then, when she called his apartment on Wednesday to make her peace with him, there was no reply. 'Mr Floyd-Orr has been temporarily recalled to London,' they told her on Thursday morning at the British Embassy. There was an atmosphere of imminent departure about the place.

On Friday 1 September, German troops marched into Poland. Two days later, Great Britain and France declared war on the German Reich. The Foreign Ministry was very busy that Sunday. Rumours were flying rife.

'The Führer has offered to reinstate the Duke of Windsor on the British throne. As Edward VIII, he'll make peace with us at once and see that we get our colonies back,' Frau Wilhelmi the secretary had heard.

'Oh yes? And Frau Göring will take tea with Queen Wallis,' Arvid von Troll finished the absurd story. But not even that could cheer Detta. Pale and withdrawn, she got through her work and thought of David. Would she ever see him again?

The four-engined Focke-Wolf quietly pursued its course at a height of six thousand metres. Detta looked out of the window at the snow-covered peaks of the Pyrenees. They had taken off from Berlin-Tempelhof a few hours earlier, and would reach Barcelona at eight in the evening. The war was a year old, France had been defeated, fighting was in progress on all fronts, and special bulletins preceded by fanfares flooded in. First Lieutenant Hans-Georg von Aichborn was in Saumur with his regiment, performing dressage exercises on the black horses of the French cavalry school. 'I'd rather be at the Front somewhere, there's no firing here except by a few French partisans when they're not drinking pastis,' he wrote, much to Detta's relief. 'We'll be home by Christmas,' he optimistically concluded.

Her boss at the Foreign Ministry did not share that opinion. 'We should expect a long confrontation, and we mustn't neglect our neutral friends,' Arvid von Troll told her. 'Who knows when we'll need them, and what for? You speak excellent Spanish, you have family in Spain on your mother's side, and we want you to go to our diplomatic mission in Barcelona as vice-consul. Consul-General Dr Kessler is already expecting you.'

Away from Berlin and her memories of those wonderful times with David. Another country, another language, new friends – perhaps that would help her to come to terms with the past. Detta agreed to go.

They were shaken by turbulence above the mountains, and dropped height suddenly a couple of times. A few faces turned green. Detta didn't notice. She was imagining herself lying in David's arms. A pleasant feeling overcame her, driving away the reality of this senseless war which had torn them apart, heaven knew for how long, and which meant that David was now her 'enemy'. What an absurd idea.

A hand was laid on her shoulder. She jumped. 'Welcome aboard.' It was Thomas Glaser.

'Tom, how reassuring to find you flying us.'

'My first officer is at the controls just now. How are you, Detta?'

'Fine. I'm really looking forward to taking up my new appointment in Barcelona. Your uniform suits you, Flight Captain. What's Ulli doing these days?'

'She's busy with the twins and our house in Mahlow.'

'And meanwhile you're flying all over the place?'

'Not all over the place, I'm afraid, in view of the international situation. Many destinations are barred to us. The Americans, for instance, won't let Lufthansa land anywhere, on the flimsiest of grounds.'

'You mean you wanted to fly to America?' asked Detta, incredulous.

'We did fly there, without landing, just to show the Yankees,' he said proudly. 'Non-stop Berlin – New York – Berlin. Thirteen thousand kilometres in forty-four hours, thirty-one minutes. That certainly surprised them. Their Pan-American Airline can only make it as far as the Azores, with a tail wind at that. Will you excuse me, please? I have to go back to the cockpit. Shall we eat together sometime soon? I'm in Barcelona twice a week.'

'I'd like that, Tom. Call me at the consulate.'

After landing, he waved to her from the pilot's cockpit, as if to confirm the arrangement. She waved back, glad to think that she would have a friend in this foreign country.

*

Consul-General Dr Heinrich Kessler was a cultivated man in his sixties who had been consular representative of the German Reich in the time of the last king of Spain. 'Alfonso XIII was a real gentlemen, well educated, and with a sharp wit when he didn't like something,' he said approvingly.

'Uncle Rex,' said Detta, apparently inconsequentially.

Her new boss was baffled. 'What do you mean?'

'We called him Uncle Rex, because no one was supposed to know who he was when he came to Aichborn with Uncle Juan for the shooting,' Detta explained. 'He was a very bad loser when we played ludo. My brother Hans-Georg and I sometimes cheated just to get him into a rage. He would swear in Spanish like a *vaquero* then. It was very funny to hear him.'

'Well, Arvid von Troll didn't exaggerate when he described you. You could always be relied on for a surprise, he wrote. As for your quarters – your predecessor Jagold has had his call-up papers sent express, so he'll be off to join the colours next week. You could take over his apartment.'

'That would certainly make life simpler. When do I start work, Dr Kessler?'

'In a day or so will do. There's nothing urgent going on in the passport department, for which you'll be responsible as vice-consul. Who's applying for a visa to visit Germany these days? Ah, there you are, Jagold.'

A youngish man had come in. He had dark-blond hair that curled at his temples and the nape of his neck. Detta thought him rather dandified with his brown and white shoes, cream linen suit, and dark-blue shirt, which he wore with a lemon-yellow cravat that matched the carnation in his buttonhole.

'Axel Jagold – Henriette von Aichborn,' the consul-general introduced them.

'My charming colleague and successor!' The vice-consul kissed her hand. 'If our boss doesn't object I'll show you my apartment, and then we can have lunch together. After that I'll take you to the hotel for your siesta, and in the afternoon you'll meet the rest of the team here.'

'Do that, Jagold,' Kessler agreed. He turned to Detta. 'My wife and I would be glad if you'd come to supper with us. I'll send Pedro with the car for you at eight.'

'That's very kind of your wife and you. Thank you so much, Dr Kessler.' She followed Jagold out. Blazing heat hit them in the street, and even the breeze through the open taxi window didn't provide relief.

Jagold's apartment on the Ronda Sant Antoni was a pleasant temperature. 'The architects of Barcelona gave their Art Noveau buildings remarkably thick walls,' her host explained. 'May I offer you an iced tea?' He took a glass pitcher out of the refrigerator and filled two tall glasses, garnishing them with sprigs of fresh mint.

Detta looked around. The living room was in the Moorish style. There was a photo propped on the sideboard, showing a bare-chested, athletic young man. She could see half-packed suitcases through the open bedroom door.

Jagold noticed her glance. 'I've booked a passage to Spanish Morocco. My friend has gone ahead.' He pointed to the photograph. 'Gunnar is Swedish. We plan to go on to Angola and open a restaurant in São Paolo de Loanda. The Portuguese don't particularly mind where you come from or who you are, just so long as you bribe the right people.'

'Dr Kessler said you'd received your call-up papers and had to fly home.'

'To go to war? I'm not crazy. Well, imagine, suppose the enemy were to shoot at me!' He laughed a little too shrilly for her liking.

She understood, and everything in her Prussian soul rebelled. 'My father's too old for armed service, and it grieves him,' she said icily. 'My brother is in France with his regiment. Two of my uncles and three of my cousins reported for duty on the first day. One of them fell in Poland. We don't shirk our duty in my family, and nor, which is lucky for you, Herr Jagold, do we denounce anyone.'

'Do you like the apartment? I can let you have the furnishings very cheap,' he said, trying to change the subject. 'The rent isn't very high, and the owner of the building is a friendly soul. I'm sure you'll feel comfortable here, my dear Henriette.'

'Baroness von Aichborn to you,' she told him sharply, and left. Outside she took a deep breath, and in spite of the heat marched off, full of energy.

Military men were in the majority on the streets and squares. There were police officers everywhere. The Civil War had been over for a year now, and General Franco was holding on to what he had won with a grip of iron. The people of Barcelona ignored him. The dictator was Spanish, while they were proud Catalans.

She had calmed down by the time she reached the Plaça de Catalunya. A taxi took her to her hotel near the cathedral, and she showered and changed. Then she chose a table for lunch in a small niche behind some potted palms, where she wouldn't be disturbed. She studied the menu over a glass of chilled rosé.

'The grilled *gambas* with fresh figs are said to be particularly good today.' David Floyd-Orr stood before her, smiling. She was about to leap up and embrace him. 'No, don't,' he said quietly.

'David . . .' She couldn't say any more.

He sat down. 'We're just good friends. Public displays of emotion would only attract attention. The entire foreign colony comes to this hotel. The Front runs right through the restaurant: Axis powers on the left, representatives of the *entente* on the right. The neutrals go now to the left, now to the right, as the mood takes them. You see everything and everyone here. Don't forget, we're on different sides.'

'Not us, darling, our countries.' She could have shouted out loud for joy, but she pulled herself together, saying casually, 'Grilled prawns with fresh figs sound good, and they'll be a first for me. We don't have those at home even in peacetime. David, what are you doing here?'

'I'll tell you later.'

In his suite, they fell on each other like two people dying of thirst. Later, lying side by side as the shutters kept out the blazing afternoon sun, blissfully exhausted, they talked.

'I was sent here at my own request. The alternative was Rio, but naturally I wanted to be near you. I'm vice-consul here, just like you, running the press department.'

She ought to have asked him how he knew that she was the German vice-consul in Barcelona, but the aftermath of their stormy love-making was like a state of pleasant intoxication, clouding her ability to think clearly. She looked at her watch. 'Oh heavens, I should have been back at the consulate ages ago.'

'You're not the only one. Shall we see each other this evening?'

'I don't know, David. You said yourself that we have to be careful.'

'We'll find a solution, far away from this bloody war,' he promised.

The solution was offered by a romantic painter's studio that they found on one of their walks down by the old fishing harbour. Its tenant, a fiery young artist, had gone to banned Republican meetings and amused himself by caricaturing the new Fascist masters. He escaped the garrotte because his sister was mistress of the military commandant of Barcelona. But she couldn't get him spared the stone quarry, so the studio was to rent. A notice on the door of the building had drawn the lovers' attention to it.

Detta was enchanted by the view of the picturesque harbour, and immediately went down to buy fish – fresh giltheads – from a cutter that had just come in. Cool red Rioja from the harbour bar completed their simple meal. For dessert they made love again. They hadn't seen each other for a whole year.

'How are your parents?' he asked as she decked the studio with flowers.

'Thanks for asking. Mother's packing parcels of smoked sausage and cigarettes for all our friends and relations in uniform.'

'And the lieutenant-general?'

Yet again, Detta should have been on the alert. David knew her father as a country gentleman; how had he learned that Papa had been recalled to service and promoted? The Baron had ended the Great War as a colonel commanding his regiment. But she was too deeply in love to pick up such nuances.

'Father is putting in petition after petition to High Command to be transferred to the troops, but he's getting nowhere,' she informed him, and went on rearranging the furniture. The young artist's narrow couch had been replaced by a large double bed. 'Our first apartment of our own,' she said happily.

'Your apartment, darling. No one must know about me,' David warned her. 'Don't forget we're at war.'

'We'll leave the war outside,' said Detta firmly. She took mischievous pleasure in inventing a Spanish lover called Carlos, who soon became a familiar name in the consulate, thanks to the talkative driver, Pedro. When Pedro came to her apartment to fetch urgent files, she would call into the next room, 'Carlos, darling, put the wine to chill!' A few telephone conversations with Carlos, which she interrupted when someone looked into her office, completed the little deception. Soon the whole consulate knew about 'Don Carlos' and her love nest down by the harbour.

David grinned. 'Mine's called Conchita. A fiery creature with black eyes who leaves me no time for the club and playing cricket. Most of them have swallowed it. There's only little Jenny from the Coding Department, who keeps batting her eyelashes when she crosses my path – and she crosses my path remarkably often.'

Detta laughed. 'Don't make me jealous.' But she mounted a counter-attack just in case. On their next evening together she was wearing her wonderfully sinful Parisian underwear, bought from Madame Solange on the Rambla, when she let him in. But he failed to notice her seductive appearance.

'What's the matter, David?'

He was frowning. 'Your Luftwaffe – it's bombing London day and night. They say that's a certain sign of the landings soon to come. Detta, you must help me. When does Sealion start?'

'Sealion?'

'The code name for the German invasion of the British Isles. Our nanny Ruth is of Jewish descent, and if the rumours are true my parents want to send her to Canada in good time. You're flying home next week, aren't you? Just ask your father.'

'Ask him to tell me a military secret? You can't be serious, David.'

'Oh, come on!' he said casually. 'I expect even the Berlin sparrows are chirping it from the rooftops. But never mind, forget it.' He drew her close. His lips passed over her cheeks, his damp tongue licked her ear, sending a thousand volts thrilling through her body and making her weak at the knees. She cried out loud as he made love to her on the raffia mat under the big window.

A man called Gleim came to see Detta in her office. She had seen him in the building several times, but he was not a member of the consulate staff. His Panama hat and bamboo cane gave him the look of a Cuban tobacco planter. He came straight to the point. 'Fräulein von Aichborn, it's come to our knowledge that you are meeting the Englishman David Floyd-Orr. We know that this is a private relationship dating back to before the war, and no one holds it against you.'

She did not let her surprise show. 'How am I supposed to take that?'

'Your friend wasn't posted to Barcelona just by chance, as he let you think. His meeting you was even less of a coincidence. Captain Floyd-Orr is a member of the British Intelligence Service.'

Everything went round in circles. All of a sudden, the fact that David knew about her appointment as vice-consul and Papa's military rank made terrible, logical sense. He had been sent to get information out of her, and she, poor unsuspecting lamb, was so in love that she hadn't suspected.

She remained calm. 'Thank you for telling me, Herr Gleim.'

'Lieutenant-Colonel Gleim, Counter-Intelligence, if I may. Have you and your friend discussed any subject that might be of significance to the other side? In all innocence, obviously.'

'No. But Captain Floyd-Orr made a harmless excuse for taking an interest in the date of Sealion. He wants me to ask my father about it when I'm in Berlin next week.'

The lieutenant-colonel nodded, pleased. 'Excellent. You will take your friend the information he wants.'

'I'm not a traitor, and I won't even pretend to be. Please don't count on me to do it.'

Her visitor stood up. 'Well, it's a pity if you won't help us, but I understand your motives. I will just ask for one thing – your silence.'

Detta retained her aristocratic Prussian poise. 'As I have said already, I am not a traitor. Goodbye, Herr Gleim.' The lieutenant-colonel left the room. When he had closed the door, she collapsed in sobs.

'I'm afraid Carlos isn't an invention after all,' she told David that evening.

'Nor is Conchita.'

'Goodbye, David.'

'This damned war will destroy us all,' he said in a flat voice, and left.

Detta suppressed all thoughts of David, immersing herself in work. She turned the entire filing system of her passport department upside down and set about reorganizing it, a job as unnecessary as it was boring. In her free time she tried her hand at a translation of Calderón's *The Lady Phantom* and went to Frau Kessler's bridge parties. Tom Glaser called regularly when he was in Barcelona, and they went out to eat together. She went to Madrid to visit Uncle Juan and the rest of the Alvarez de Toledo family, who wanted to marry her off to a Spanish grandee. The young man concerned told her tearfully about his love for the gardener at his palace. *Lady Chatterley* in reverse, thought Detta.

Miriam came on a flying visit from Lisbon. She had grown a little plumper, was married to an American banker and had two children. 'We're flying home next week. Do come to America with us. Bill can fix it for you. He has good connections with the State Department.'

'Not homesick for the Kurfürstendamm any more?' Detta couldn't help asking.

'You must be joking,' said Miriam.

Detta spent her annual vacation at home as usual. So much had changed at Aichborn. All men 'able to bear arms' were fighting at the Fronts, which were falling back. Their wives did almost all the work at home. Townsfolk who had fled from the air raids populated the estate, and ladies in high heels made their way through the muck, laying themselves open to mockery and derision. Frau von Aichborn had difficulty keeping the peace. In addition, the foreign labourers had to be protected from Fanselow, the district farmers' leader, who particularly liked harassing the Poles when he was at Aichborn.

Today he had his sights set on the Polish groom. Jurek was just harnessing up 'Loschek', as he affectionately called the old horse that pulled the muck cart. 'Get a move on, you damn Polack.' Fanselow snatched the whip from its place on the cart.

Detta came between them, holding out the basket full of eggs she had just been collecting. 'Oh, please, Herr Fanselow, would you take these to my mother in the kitchen? Thanks, that's very kind of you.' Surprised, Fanselow put the whip down and took the basket. Jurek's brown eyes looked gratefully at Detta.

The Baron was sceptical and silent when he came home from his desk job at Army High Command one February day in 1943. The truth about what had been described as the heroism of the German Army in its defeat at Stalingrad had filtered through. 'No one's going to get us out of this mess now,' was one of his few observations, which were made grimmer by their scarcity.

Hans-Georg, on leave from Paris, was more talkative. 'There's no doubt of it, Hitler must go,' he told his sister as they rode in the snow-covered park together. 'Only a government formed from the best conservative forces in the country can bring us an honourable peace. The Allies have already agreed not to exploit any confrontation within Germany for their own military ends.'

'The man will never go voluntarily,' said Detta.

'A bullet at close quarters will solve that problem,' said the newly appointed cavalry captain with conviction. 'Luckily, some comrades who have access to him are willing to risk all. Oh, Detta, I wish I was among those select few.'

She heard the enthusiasm and determination in his voice, and felt glad he was not. Thank goodness he's not in the firing line in Paris, she thought with relief, spurring her horse on.

Detta received the message in April 1945. Someone had pushed it under the door of her apartment by the harbour. Captain David Floyd-Orr, serving with his special unit, had fallen to his death on the steep coast of Normandy three years earlier. She did some arithmetic. He must have volunteered for this suicide mission just after they parted. She could hear him saying, 'I get vertigo even standing on a kitchen stool.'

You fool, she thought, you dear, dear fool. A wave of tenderness swept over her.

Her boss had work for her that morning, which took her mind off things. The consul-general pointed to an elegant crocodile case bearing the initials F.M. 'Sent to us by the Foreign Ministry. Its owner died a few days ago in an air raid on Berlin: Fernando Mendez, a Spanish diplomat. He and the case were dug out of the ruins of a house on the banks of the Lietzensee, where he'd been spending the night with his girlfriend. Among the few items retrieved was a letter from his parents in Barcelona. Hand it all over to Señor and Señora Mendez, and express condolences from the government of the German Reich,' Dr Kessler told his vice-consul.

So now the case stood open on Detta's desk, and she set about making a list of its contents; she would be asking for a receipt in line with regulations. Blue and white striped silk pyjamas, washing and shaving things, the dead man's diplomatic pass, a half-full travel flask of cognac, his parents' letter, and a bar of Sarotti bitter chocolate which had been broken into. She discreetly disposed of a packet of condoms and picked up the phone to arrange her visit. The cleaning lady answered: Señor and Señora Mendez were at their daughter's house in the country.

Detta put the case away in the filing cabinet and turned to some papers. Shaking her head, she read an application from one Federico Vargas for a visa to Germany. This lively little man had already visited her office several times. He was keen to get to Cologne and make business contacts for the future. 'Eau-de-Cologne always sold well here before the war,' he had assured her.

'Rejected!' she wrote right across the application, adding, with more than a touch of sarcasm: 'We recommend the applicant to turn to the British Consulate, now responsible for Cologne and the surrounding area.' She couldn't help smiling. David would have liked that. Then grief got the upper hand again.

She was grateful when Tom Glaser invited her out to dinner that evening. The flight captain was in Barcelona for two days. He was waiting for a spare part for the plane to come from Madrid. 'Is it bad?' he asked with sympathy. She was silently weeping, and he didn't try to comfort her. He had something even worse to tell her. 'Do I get a coffee?' he asked at her front door.

'Another time, Tom. I'm very tired.'

'I have news of Hans-Georg,' he said quietly.

Detta was electrified. She let Tom in. It was months since she had heard anything about her brother. After the failed assassination attempt on Hitler, he had disappeared without trace. 'A secret special mission to the Eastern Front,' was the story spread by the family, although they knew better.

'He joined the Wehrmacht's successful *putsch* against the SS in Paris, and after that operation was abandoned he went underground at first, with the help of the French Resistance,' Glaser told her. 'I know that from an Air France colleague who's in the Resistance too. But he soon looked like being discovered, and he reached Germany with a transport of wounded men.

Somehow or other he made his way home. Even the Gestapo didn't think he'd be crazy enough to hide at Aichborn. That's been his good luck so far. But they've been there twice already looking for him. Detta, it's no use pretending, he's in a hopeless situation. It's only a question of time before they capture him and kill him.'

'Can you get a message to him?'

'I can phone your parents from Berlin. They'll understand me, even if the message is coded. What shall I say?'

'Tell them I'll get Hans-Georg out.'

'You're crazy,' exclaimed the flight captain.

Detta's mouth was set in determination. 'Very likely.'

Dr Kessler had never addressed her by her first name before, nor had he ever spoken to her so frankly. 'Henriette, you can't leave. Germany is in rubble and ashes. The end is just a question of weeks now. Friends in the government have promised that even after we've lost our consular privileges we won't be expelled. It's simple for you. Your family in Madrid is very influential, they'll protect you. You are young, you have plenty of time ahead of you. Everything will get back to normal at home some time.'

'I'm still applying for short-term leave, Consul-General,' said Detta firmly. 'I have to go to Berlin. I'll be back in a few days' time,' she added optimistically.

The Mercedes with the pennant of the German Reich and the CC plate of the *Corps Consulaire* took Vice-Consul Henriette von Aichborn to Prat de Llobregat airport on the outskirts of Barcelona. The driver carried her bag to Departures. 'You'll be back, won't you, Doña Henrietta?'

'Yes, of course, Pedro. This is just a little business trip.' She took her bag from him and showed her diplomatic pass at check-in. The official gallantly opened the barrier for her.

The four-engined Junkers 290, numbered D-AITR, was waiting on the runway. Detta looked up at the cockpit. Tom Glaser was busy making preparations for take-off. Things had changed since her last flight. No one had cleaned the cabin. The seats were sagging and their covers worn. Instead of a steward, a man with a stubbly haircut and ill-tempered expression received them on board, introduced himself as Flight Engineer Bichler and handed out parachutes. 'Instructions for use are on your seats. Enjoy your flight.' It sounded derisive.

Detta sat by the front left-hand window. Tom had told her you felt turbulence least there. Slowly the engines roared into life. The heavy commercial plane rolled slowly forward and swayed into position for take-off, quivering with the force of a thousand horsepower. The four large three-winged propellers cut through the air and hauled the giant plane forward. At rapidly increasing speed it shot down the runway, pressing the passengers back in their seats. The airfield sank away below them. DLH-Flight K22 was on course for Berlin.

A year ago the plane had been well staffed, and champagne had been handed round. Now there was no on-board service; you got a sip of water at the most. She counted six passengers. They were a Swedish couple going on to Stockholm from Berlin, a Siemens representative flying home, a major in the Spanish 'Blue Division' who wanted to go to the Front, and an elderly German husband and wife from Valencia whose daughter was expecting her first baby in Frankfurt an der Oder. 'Going to Frankfurt an der Oder? You think you'll make it before the Russians get there?' scoffed the Siemens rep, launching into a lengthy assessment of the situation which interested no one.

Detta closed her eyes, because the talkative Siemens rep looked as if he intended to sit down beside her. She had to think, she had to go over her plan, checking for weak spots. Her brother's life and hers depended on it. Of course the plan was total madness, yet at the same time, it seemed to be wildly simple. So simple that nothing could go wrong.

She would take a train from Berlin to Aichborn. She would wrap Hans-Georg's head in bandages and take him back to Barcelona by Lufthansa, disguised as Fernando Mendez, the Spanish embassy secretary who had been injured in an air raid. She had made out an official order for her mission on the consulate's letterhead and with the consulate's official seal. She had the dead Mendez's diplomatic pass with her. It would stand up to any amount of checking. His injury would make it impossible for the supposed embassy secretary to speak, so her brother's German accent couldn't give him away to Spanish passengers on the flight. No, nothing could go wrong if they both kept calm. Oh God, don't let them find him before I can get him out, she prayed silently. For that was the one real danger: that the

Gestapo would turn Aichborn upside down, or someone would denounce Hans-Georg.

'Chocolate?' Tom Glaser brought her out of her thoughts. As always, he was wearing immaculate Lufthansa uniform.

'Oh, hello, Tom. Yes please. I'll take it with me as iron rations. How do things look?'

He had been in Berlin yesterday. 'Bleak. The city is at its last gasp. Everything's bombed or burnt out. No one knows exactly how far off the Russians are. Some people hope the Americans will arrive first.' He lowered his voice. 'I could phone. But I do suggest you hurry.'

'When do you fly back to Barcelona?'

'In two days' time.'

'That will be enough for me to carry out my consular task. I've booked two seats for the return flight.' The flight captain nodded. He had understood.

'Contact with the enemy, captain!' shouted the stubble-headed Bavarian from the cockpit in agitation. Glaser hurried forward. Confusion and alarm spread through the cabin.

'Have a nice day,' said the Siemens rep, getting his parachute ready.

A dot appeared in the blue sky, quickly getting larger. She could see a slender, two-engined aircraft with English markings making straight for them. Flashes shot from its wings, from the mouths of the aircraft cannon. The enemy dived under them, turned and prepared to attack again, but Captain Glaser wasn't waiting. He dived and dropped almost vertically. Passengers and baggage were tossed about the cabin.

Detta braced herself in her seat. Her stomach rebelled as they raced towards the earth. A few metres above ground the pilot brought the plane up. They raced ahead, flying very low, with trees and farmhouses sometimes not under but beside them. She guessed that the pursuer was behind them. Mortal terror came over her. This is the end, she thought. But the JU 290 gained height and went into a sharp curve. Below them a mushroom of black smoke rose in the air. The enemy pilot had shown less skill than Tom Glaser in flying at low-altitude.

'An RAF Mosquito,' said the Siemens rep, quickly recovering his loquacity. 'Must be the first case of an unarmed commercial plane winning a victory in the air. A *tour de force* on our pilot's part. The man deserves an order.'

Four hours later, towns and villages loomed below them. The radio officer had to rely on vague information received from the Reich transmitter in Berlin. Lacking better navigational aids, he took the plane past the dying capital and behind the Russian Front, where luckily they were ignored. They turned and flew back from the east to ruined Tempelhof airport without further incident. The plane came down with a loud crash and bumped over the cracked runway.

It was 20 April 1945. In the bunker beneath the Reich Chancellery, the lord of all this horror was celebrating his final birthday.

'Welcome home!' said the Siemens rep, with a loud laugh.

Stettin rail station was swarming with military men. Military policemen with shiny breastplates were checking the papers of all the soldiers, privates and officers alike. They led a young corporal away weeping. 'Tried to desert, that's what he did,' Detta heard a passer-by say. 'They'll hang him now for sure.'

A passenger train was waiting at a distance, beside the unroofed part of the platform. It was terribly overcrowded. People crammed into the toilets. She found a place to stand in the corridor. The journey lasted for ever, because the train was diverted into sidings several times to allow troop transports past. Jurek was waiting at Wrietzow with the horse and cart. '*Wilcome, Freilein.*' The Polish groom helped her up with pleasure and admiration in his eyes.

Her mother was preparing rutabagas in the kitchen with Lina. 'Oh, you should have stayed in Spain,' she said, sounding concerned.

'You know I had to come.' Detta hugged her. 'How are you, Mama?'

'With potatoes, marjoram and bacon this will make a perfectly acceptable one-pot meal for all of us,' said the Baroness, evading the question. 'Your father's in the library.'

The Baron was sitting by the fire. He had grown old. 'I'm finished, they've retired me because of my heart. Detta, child, how good to see you. It will cheer your mother up. She takes refuge in her duties, or what she considers her duties. She doesn't show it, but she misses our two little ones a great deal.' Fritz and Viktoria, now thirteen and fifteen, were studying in Munich.

Detta was hardly listening. 'Where is he?' she asked impatiently.

The door flew open and her brother strode in. He whirled her around, beside himself with delight. 'Sister dear, at last.' He was pale and had lost weight, his breeches and thick pullover were too large for him, but he was as lively and enthusiastic as ever.

'This is the time to bring out the last of my Armagnac.' As if by magic, their father produced a bottle from behind the works of Detlev von Liliencron and poured them glasses.

'Cheers, Father, Detta — here's to our future!' cried Hans-Georg confidently.

'To your future,' the master of Aichborn corrected him. 'My time is over. There's nothing left for me now. The old values are all gone.'

'There'll be new values and a new, free Reich, peaceful and respected by the whole world.' Hans-Georg sounded as though he were trying to persuade himself.

'But first we must get you out of the old Reich,' Detta soberly interrupted. She rang the bell by the fireplace. Bensing appeared. In honour of the day he had put on his shiny black jacket, which didn't really go with his gumboots. 'The Maybach, Bensing?'

'With your BMW in the old barn, hidden under straw and old junk. Both cars have full tanks. I check on them regularly.'

'Take the D plate off my roadster and paint a C beside it. Then screw it on the Maybach. CD stands for *Corps Diplomatique*. And take that little throw over the back of the sofa, the one I embroidered with Mother's family coat of arms in the Spanish colours, and fasten it on the radiator as a pennant. Polish up the car and iron your chauffeur's uniform. We're off on Wednesday morning. My brother's a Spanish diplomat, and our flight to Barcelona leaves from Tempelhof at two in the afternoon.'

'I'll get to work immediately, Fräulein Detta.' Bensing went away with measured tread.

'Barcelona?' asked her brother incredulously.

'Tom Glaser will fly us out.' She explained her plan.

'I hope to God it works,' murmured the Baron, shaking his head.

A hunting horn sounded from somewhere above. 'We have a lookout posted on the tower.' Hans-Georg was suddenly in a hurry. She watched from the tall window as he sprinted across the yard and disappeared down the hatch into the potato cellar. Bensing chugged up with the tractor and dumped a load of muck over the entrance.

Fanselow climbed out of his car in his brown Party uniform and stalked up to the entrance of the *schloss*. The Baron wrinkled his nose. 'He often comes to pay what he calls a friendly visit, to see how I am. I think he's trying to hedge his bets.'

'I'll go and see the horses.' Detta had no desire to meet the man.

Tom Glaser's call reached her at lunchtime. The night before, an incendiary bomb had destroyed his JU 290, which had been tanked up for the return flight. 'There isn't a spare plane. The whole of Lufthansa is grounded.'

And that, in an instant, was the end of Detta's bold plan. But she did not let her disappointment show. 'Oh well,' she told her brother. 'A few more days among the potatoes won't kill you. The BBC is saying the Russians have crossed the Oder at Frankfurt. And that's at most eighty kilometres from here.'

The hunting horn on the tower sounded early in the morning. Hans-Georg disappeared into his hiding place. Bensing pushed the muck over the hatch. Two jeeps drew up outside the *schloss* and eight Red Army soldiers jumped out, pointing their Kalashnikovs menacingly. A limousine stopped in the entrance. An officer stepped out, followed by Fanselow. The district farmers' leader was wearing a cloth cap and a red band round the arm of his jacket.

The master of Aichborn, standing very straight, appeared in the entrance. 'There's the Fascist general!' cried Fanselow.

'General yes, Fascist no,' snapped the Baron. Detta went to his side.

'And that's the daughter! A Fascist cow.' Fanselow's voice rose and broke.

Detta calmly approached him. 'No crayfish today, Fanselow, just potato soup. You can slurp it up from the tip of the spoon, I expect that's more your style.' Fanselow went red in the face. Detta turned to the Russian and spoke French to him. '*Je suis* Henriette von Aichborn. What will happen to my father? He's old and sick.'

'Major Rubakhov, NKVD,' the officer introduced himself in perfect German. 'My orders are to arrest Lieutenant-General Heinrich von Aichborn as a war criminal.'

Aichborn indicated his cardigan. 'I suppose I can change first.' He did not wait for the answer.

'Make a break for it, would you?' Fanselow grabbed the Baron's sleeve.

'Don't do that,' the Russian officer told him, and turned to look at the family pictures in the hall.

'I am a war criminal too.' The Baroness appeared at the top of the staircase in her hat and coat.

The major shrugged. 'As you like.' The Baron came and stood beside her. The general's stripes on his breeches shone red, and the blue enamel of the Prussian order *Pour le Mérite* gleamed on his collar. He kissed his wife's hand with old-fashioned courtesy and gave her his arm. With inimitable dignity the two of them walked downstairs. Bensing helped his master into his coat. The major held the door of the car open, Heinrich and Maria von Aichborn got in, and the limousine started.

'We'll be back,' Fanselow spat, jumping into the jeep. Bensing shook his fist at him, tears of rage in his eyes.

'I'm sure they'll be back soon.' Detta put a comforting arm round his shoulders. Suddenly it dawned on her. 'The war's over, Bensing. We're free,' she said in amazement.

'Yes, Fräulein Detta.' Bensing walked away, his steps weary.

'Hans-Georg, we're free!' She ran across the yard and picked up the pitchfork. 'Free! Free! Free!' she shouted, exultant. The muck flew in all directions, and the hatch swung open. Like a phoenix, her brother came up into the light. The morning sunlight coloured his thin face gold. Detta fell on his neck, and danced exuberantly across the yard with him. 'No more Gestapo, no more fear.' She kissed him lovingly. Then her euphoria evaporated. 'The Russians have taken Father away,' she said. 'Fanselow must have denounced him. Mother went with him.'

'Father's done nothing wrong. They'll soon set him free,' Hans-Georg soothed her.

A military vehicle roared into the yard, followed by two motorbikes with sidecars. Six SS men in long rubber coats pointed their sub-machine guns at everyone present.

An SS lieutenant got out of the vehicle. 'Sturmführer Keil, Special Commando Unit. 'He gave Hans-Georg a cold look. 'Who are you? Your papers!' he barked.

'Five minutes ago I was Cavalry Captain Baron von Aichborn. Now I'm just a farmer. The Russians have been here. The war's over – for you too, Herr Keil.'

'We decide when the war is over. Hang the traitor,' ordered the Sturmführer.

Two men seized Hans-Georg. A third took a piece of cord out of his coat pocket and tied his hands behind his back. The driver brought a milking stool and calf's halter out of the cowshed. They dragged Hans-Georg, who was resisting in vain, under the light fitting outside the coach house. It all seemed horribly routine.

'Please wait,' Detta heard her voice as if from very far away. 'I'll get his papers.'

'I'll give you one minute,' the SS executioner called after her. She crossed the yard like a sleepwalker.

At the gun-room window she came to herself again. She saw them lift Hans-Georg on the stool and put the noose around his neck. One of the SS men was raising his leg to kick the stool away. She felt the smooth shaft of the rifle against her cheek, she had her brother's forehead in the cross-hairs of the telescopic sight. 'Breathe out, pull the trigger slowly, rather as if you were squeezing a sponge, or you'll swerve to one side,' she heard him say.

I love you, she thought. The sound of the shot drowned out her stifled cry.

A Russian airman, flying low, had put the SS unit to flight. Silence lay over Aichborn. The spring sun warmed the silent people. The Polish workers took off their caps and crossed themselves. Women wept as they looked at the body.

They carried him into the house and laid him on the big ash table where game was skinned and cut up in the hunting season. Detta washed his naked body with slow, caressing movements. Lina helped her to dress the dead man in his uniform. They had to cut his riding boots open at the back to get them on. Then they laid him on a bed of ivy in the Aichborn chapel. Bensing would have made the coffin by evening.

Torchlight illuminated the graves behind the chapel where the Aichborns had been laid to rest for the last four hundred years, except for those who had fallen in battle far away. The night was cold and starlit. Pastor Wunsig spoke of the peace in the land that Detta's brother would not see now, and the eternal peace that he had found. Detta stood heavily veiled by the grave-side, as tradition demanded. In the kitchen she took her veil off. She offered the pastor grog to warm him up, and told an amusing story about herself and Hans-Georg as children. Aichborn women never showed their feelings, and Detta had no feelings any more. Everything inside her was empty.

She registered what went on around her in the next few hours: the arrival of the red hordes under a fat little captain who watched what his soldiers were doing with approval and had the youngest girls brought to him; the screams of the raped women and beaten men; the senseless slaughter of horses and cattle. She registered it but did not really take it in. She and Lina made huge pans of soup in the kitchen for the victors, and that preserved her from the worst for the moment, but she cherished no illusions about the future.

As she was carrying a soup pan out to the men round their fire, Jurek grabbed her. He had been drinking with the soldiers. 'Come here, German whore!' he bellowed, dragging Detta away from the fire into the dark. His breath smelled of vodka. He let go of her behind the stables. 'You scream so they think I kill you,' he whispered.

Detta screamed until her throat hurt.

'I saddled Loschek. Get away quick, right?'

He had tied a blanket on the old horse's back with a girth. He helped her up. The night was cold and starry once again. She orientated herself by the Great Bear. Berlin, here I come, she thought. I'm repeating myself, she realized bitterly.

The Berlin city commandant looked up from his desk. 'Good morning, Curt.'

'Good morning, sir.' Curtis S. Chalford indicated his companion. 'Sir, this is Henriette von Aichborn.'

The general shook hands with Detta. 'Glad to meet you, Miss von Aichborn. I am Henry Abbot. We're all here to find out whether you'd like to become my German liaison.' Abbot was a lean, grey-haired man with a weathered face. He had the clipped, dry accent typical of New England aristocracy. Detta liked him at once, and the feeling seemed to be reciprocated.

'That's entirely up to you, General Abbot. But why don't we give it a try?' she said.

'A trial period, excellent,' Chalford agreed. Detta had gone to see him at the German–American Employment Office, and he had suggested her for the post – the applicant spoke fluent English, was a real lady, and had that certain something that you couldn't learn but were born with.

Detta would have taken almost any job. She wanted just one thing – to immerse herself in work and to forget it all; her wild flight from Aichborn, first on horseback and then on foot, after hungry, homeless people had killed the old nag. She had hidden from the marauding liberators in the undergrowth or in barns by day, taking remote paths through the woods and fields by night, then spent the following weeks with the Glasers in Mahlow on the outskirts of Berlin – the fact that a woman Red Army major was billeted on them meant that they escaped the worst. News came from the faithful Bensing, by roundabout ways, that her mother had been released, but her father was in the NKVD camp at Buchenwald.

After the Western Allies had entered the capital, Detta ventured to the Steubenplatz, which was in the British sector. Her apartment was occupied. A family who had survived the trek from East Prussia had been quartered there. She was able to retrieve a few things from her wardrobe, though where she would take them she didn't know.

At the Housing Department, where she stood in line for hours on end, someone spoke to her. 'It's Fräulein von Aichborn, isn't it?' The woman wore a once elegant, foal-skin coat and a headscarf. 'Elisabeth Mohr. You visited us once at Horn's fashion house on the Kurfürstendamm, with Fräulein Goldberg. It must have been in about 1935.'

'Frau Mohr, yes, I remember.'

Frau Mohr had to give up a room in her apartment. 'I'd rather find a tenant for myself than have someone billeted on me.' So Detta and her few things found a place to live in Waltraudstrasse on the Fischtal park, and had the benefit of Frau Mohr's good advice, too. 'If you speak any English, you could try getting work with the Yanks. They pay in Allimarks, but most important of all, they give you something to eat.'

And now she was in the process of taking up one of the most important posts open to a German at this time: advising the US city commandant and liaising between him and the people of Berlin. But she felt no pleasure or satisfaction. She felt empty and alone.

The arrival of her mother was an unexpected gleam of light. The Baroness had made her way to Berlin on foot and on the roofs of overcrowded freight trains. Fanselow and his Red friends were ravaging Aichborn. They had looted the *schloss* and expropriated the land.

The Baroness smiled painfully. 'Bensing had to go through a session of self-criticism as a "minion of the Junkers". He insisted on staying. Someone must be at Aichborn when Father comes home, he says. Oh, Detta, I have so little hope. I hear that conditions in the camp at Buchenwald are even worse under our new masters than before.'

From then on mother and daughter shared the same bed. Frau von Aichborn was not a refugee and had no right to accommodation in Berlin. She lived like a shadow, spending her days reading or going for long walks in the Fischtal. 'A pretty park,' she said. 'Did you know that the name Fischtal has nothing to do with fish? The farmers of Zehlendorf used to call the pastures there the "Viehstall", the "cowshed". A man out walking told me that.'

She revived when she was allowed to start teaching a Spanish course at a new adult education centre. And she was finally allotted a room too, in the basement of a villa in Katharinenstrasse, quite close to Detta. A photograph on the chest of drawers showed the Baron in gumboots inspecting a breeding bull. Both the Baron and the bull looked happy.

The way to work wasn't far: over the Waltraudbrücke to Argentinische Allee and then to Oskar-Helene-Heim U-Bahn station. Opposite stood the buildings of what had been the Luftgaukommando, which the Americans had made their Berlin headquarters, and by virtue of their liking for absurd acronyms called OMGUS, 'Office of the Military Government of the United States'. The sandstone façades of the Third Reich were intact and the same as ever. The smell of Nescafé and Virginia cigarettes in the polished corridors was new.

Detta went that way every day, and every day the blind man met her. He was a youngish man, small, with dark glasses and a white stick, wearing a uniform mended in several places and bearing the outline of a Luftwaffe eagle that had been removed from its breast. She supposed he lived somewhere nearby.

She felt sorry for him. But it would have gone no further – she was in no mood to make new acquaintances – if he hadn't almost walked into the path of a car one morning. She grabbed his sleeve and held him back. He was alarmed, then understood and thanked her. 'I know you, I know your footsteps. We meet here every morning, don't we? I'm taking my daily constitutional, so as not to get old before my time.'

'Come on.' Detta took his arm and led him across the street. 'Have a good morning,' she wished him on the other side. He walked away, his footsteps sure. He obviously knew every paving stone.

Her new daily routine began as she showed her pass to the guard at the entrance. Lieutenant Anny Randolph, personal assistant to the city commandant, was waiting for her in the outer office with a black coffee. It had taken a little while for Detta to get used to it; the Americans boiled their coffee instead of brewing it. 'Hi, Detta, how are you this morning?'

'Thanks, Anny, swell,' said Detta, imitating the lively New Yorker's speech. 'What's on?'

'The boss wants to see you. The people wanting a newspaper licence have an appointment at eleven.'

A normal working day began. Colonel Tucker, adjutant to the city commandant, looked in briefly, but there was nothing for him. Mr Gold, the inscrutable representative of the State Department, who apparently didn't speak a word of German although he came from Frankfurt am Main, brought the city commandant an envelope with 'Confidential' stamped on it, and Anny Randolph gave him a receipt. Herr Bongarts did his weekly round with his little bottle and brush, disinfecting the four hundred phones in OMGUS. The Americans feared germs even more than Communism.

Henry Abbot rose courteously when Detta entered his office, and pointed to one of the armchairs. 'Do sit down, Henriette.'

'Thank you, sir. It's about the licence to publish a new Berlin newspaper, isn't it?'

'My press officer Major Landon has checked up on the applicants. He has no reservations about them, but I'd like you to see them both. I rely a great deal on your understanding of human nature.'

'Only a bit of common sense, General,' said Detta.

The German visitors were punctual. Detta introduced them to the general. Hermann Lüttge was a printer and had the necessary machinery. He didn't say much, but his partner talked enough for two. 'I shall look after the publishing side. I've had years of organizational experience in the Ministry of Economic Affairs, entirely apolitical, as you can see from my files. My school friend Leo Wolf will be editor-in-chief and put the editorial team together. He was in a concentration camp,' he concluded on a triumphant note.

Detta interpreted. Henry Abbot listened attentively. 'Does having been in a concentration camp automatically qualify you for the post of editor-in-chief?'

'Oh, please, commandant! The man is Jewish, of course. They're the cleverest folk you can find. Apropos of which, I would just like to say that I helped many of my Jewish fellow countrymen. I can prove it.'

The Goldbergs, for instance, thought Detta. She had recognized former Under-Secretary Aribert Karch at once. He obviously didn't know what to make of her. 'For a moment I thought we'd met before,' he said when they were back in the outer office.

'You thought correctly, Herr Karch. At Miriam Goldberg's farewell party in Gumbinner Allee. You were generously helping her and her family to get out of the country at the time. I'll write to her in America. I'm sure she'll support your application for a licence. By the way, do you still belong to the Circle of Friends of the Reichsführer SS?'

Karch winced as if he had toothache. 'We all had to move with the times.'

'And some of us moved further than others.'

'I don't understand a word of this,' said the printer.

'It does you credit, Herr Lüttge. Goodbye, gentlemen.'

'Herr Karch has withdrawn his application,' she told the general.

'Couldn't he have done so a little earlier?' growled Henry Abbot, annoyed.

'He needed a little coaching.'

The blind man moved away from the street light on the corner of Waltraudstrasse and fell into step with Detta. 'I heard you coming a long way off. How are you this morning? I've been thinking of you all night. You are beautiful. A real lady. I can tell from your voice. I once knew many beautiful women. None of them have any time for me today. But you're different.'

Detta bristled. The fact that she had kept him from an accident yesterday gave him no right to take liberties. 'Excuse me. I'm in a hurry.'

She walked faster, but he was not to be shaken off. His stick kept time with her footsteps. It somehow sounded threatening. 'You work for the Americans, don't you? You'll be showing them what German punctuality is like. Unfortunately none of that concerns me now, out of service as I am. Who'd be interested in whether I arrived late or indeed at all?'

The guard would stop him following her in. She wasn't in the mood for this chatter. He took her silence as interest. 'Not so long ago it was different. The ground crew welcomed me back with a bottle of bubbly for every victory in the air. I got the Knight's Cross after the twenty-fifth.'

Thank goodness, the guard. 'I'm afraid you can't come any further. Goodbye.'

'Brandenburg, Captain Jürgen Brandenburg, Richthofen Fighter Squadron,' he called after her.

The city commandant was in unusually high spirits. 'Guess what, Henriette, I found a completely intact, seaworthy yacht in the Wannsee wharf. All mahogany and teak. A fine boat. The old boat builder there says it will take him a month to strip the *Astra* down. He'll do it for a few cartons of cigarettes. And then Colonel Hastings of Transport Command will take her to Bremerhaven for me, and we'll ship her home. Six weeks in the shipyard and she'll be like new.'

'What about the owner?'

'Some German.'

Detta was indignant. 'I am "some German" too, General Abbot. Unfortunately I don't have anything you can take away from me and ship home. If you'd excuse me . . .'

'One moment, Henriette.'

He's going to fire me, she thought.

'The owner of the yacht is called Erpenborg, a stamp dealer. A nice old fellow who doesn't sail any more. We agreed that I'd send the estimated value in dollars to his sister's account in Rio. She'll use it for her children there.'

'Will you accept my apology, sir?'

'Only if you'll come to dinner with us this evening. We have a surprise for you. Lucy likes you very much. So do I.' Embarrassed, he looked at the floor. Then he was the correct West Point officer again. 'Well, now to work. What do we have?'

The Evangelical Bishop of Berlin had a request. Curtis S. Chalford put his rosy face round the door. He had a proposal for regulating the working hours of German employees of the army. The city commandant saw a group of district council members from Schöneberg. Then it was lunchtime.

Detta could have gone to eat lunch in the Harnack House. She had a special permit, making her the only German woman there. But it went against her deep-rooted Prussian principles to accept favours from the victor. She saw her own dilemma clearly: on the one hand, she was grateful to the liberators who had freed her from the yoke of the oppressor; on the other, she still saw them as the enemy.

There was a stretch of woodland behind Truman Hall. The pine trees here were young, and so far had escaped the attentions of the black-market woodcutters. Soon they would be uprooted and a housing estate would be built on the sandy site; there had been plans before the war to erect one for the growing population of Berlin, and now it was to be built for the Americans. She sat down on the warm ground, which was cushioned with pine needles, and closed her eyes. Ever since Henry Abbot had mentioned the yacht and the Wannsee she had been thinking about David and the motorboat *Bertie*. It was ten years ago, yet those ten years seemed an eternity. She imagined his freckled face over her, grave and concentrated, concerned rather than passionate, as he tried to penetrate her without hurting her. She couldn't help laughing, and it did her good.

'You're in a cheerful mood, ma'am.' A voice interrupted her memories. The blind man was standing in front of her. 'May I?' He sat down close to her. 'Captain Jürgen Brandenburg, as I said before. Twenty-eight victories in the air, until the rear gunner of a B-17 got me. A blow on the head. Everything suddenly blurred around me. I've no idea how I got my plane down. Everything was black after that. Until today.'

Dislike arose in her. She wanted nothing to do with this man. 'I'm very sorry, but I can't help you.'

'Only a year ago I'd have invited you to Horcher's or the Adlon. The waiters bowed there, and all the pretty ladies couldn't say yes quick enough.'

She rose to her feet. 'Please don't try to meet me again.' She forced herself not to run but walk calmly. There was no reason to panic. The OMGUS entrance was barely a hundred metres away. Yet she still had that oppressive feeling, even when she had passed the guard.

Frau Mohr inspected Detta's simple black dress and her blonde hair, smoothed back and worn in a chignon. There were no hairdressers open yet. She pointed to her shoes. 'Those casuals won't do at all. Try my black pumps.' The smoky-grey nylons were a present from Anny Randolph, and set off Detta's long, slender legs to perfection. 'Quite a few gentlemen will be turning to look,' said her landlady happily.

'Thank you, Frau Mohr.' Detta put the pumps in her shoebag and got back into her old casuals. She had a half-hour's walk ahead, but that didn't bother her. It was a warm, dry evening.

The American city commandant's residence was a solid old villa in Pacelliallee, which had once belonged to a member of the Rothschild family. Two curving flights of steps led up to the veranda. A maid in a cap and starched apron let Detta in. An orderly in a white mess jacket appeared and led the visitor to the big salon. Lucy Abbot came to greet her in rustling blue organza. 'Henriette, my dear, how are you? It's almost a month since we saw each other — that mustn't happen again, you must promise me. Harry, introduce our guest.'

General Henry C. Abbot was wearing a claret-coloured dinner jacket and looked very handsome. He introduced them one by one: 'Brigadier and Mrs Anthony Thompson — Baroness Henriette von Aichborn.' Then came a French air force colonel with his wife and daughter; a Russian husband and wife, both in major's uniform; a German orchestral conductor with his wife; several administrative officials with their ladies; and a man in a grey suit. 'This is Andrew Hurst, your neighbour at table. We flew him in from Washington especially for you,' joked the host.

'Are you the surprise, Mr Hurst?'

'Well, yes, you could say so.'

The orderly carried in a tray of drinks. Detta took a glass of white wine. 'And have you come straight from Washington?'

'The Department of Justice has asked me to prepare the case against a number of German war criminals who are to be tried at Nuremberg.'

Detta was about to say something, but Hurst, smiling, raised a hand. 'I know the problems of such an enterprise: many people will see it as the justice of the victors, but Stalin insists on it, and as his allies we have to go along with him. I wouldn't have broached the subject this evening if it wasn't connected with some good news that I have for you. We are calling Lieutenant-General Heinrich von Aichborn, formerly a head of department in the German Army High Command, to give evidence to the Allied tribunal. Our Soviet allies therefore had to release him from their camp and transfer him to us. He is a free man, and will be our guest until the end of the trials.'

Detta could have flung her arms around him, but she controlled herself. 'Oh, thank you, Mr Hurst, that's the best news I've heard in ages. I must go and tell my mother at once.'

'After dinner, my dear,' Lucy Abbot intervened. 'Tell her that my husband has arranged a flight to Nuremberg for her. Your parents and the other witnesses will be staying in a comfortable guest house.'

There was game soup and chicken fricassee, cheese and dessert, and white and red wine to drink. Andrew Hurst was an amusing conversationalist with a dry, Anglo-Saxon wit. Detta forced herself to talk cheerfully too, hiding her impatience. After dinner, however, she couldn't bear it any more.

'Off you go, my dear. Give your mother our regards.' Lucy Abbot discreetly saw her out so as not to disturb the party.

The night air had cooled a little. The scent of flowers drifted from the gardens. Detta didn't notice it. She hurried on to the Thielplatz and then down Ihnestrasse. Hedges cast back the echo of her swift footsteps. Less than ten minutes now, and her mother would hear the wonderful news.

On the corner of Garystrasse her feet went on strike. The pumps were too tight. She had entirely forgotten the comfortable casuals in her shoebag. She leaned against a garbage bin on the pavement to change her shoes.

She became aware of her pursuer only when she felt his breath on the back of her neck. 'What's the idea?' she cried, reacting angrily, and tried to turn round. A chain was thrown around her neck. Panting, her attacker pulled at her dress. She fought back with hands and feet, but the metal cut deeper and deeper into her throat, until she was merely flailing her arms helplessly. A burning pain tore her vagina. She retched, struggled in vain for air, had no strength to fight any more, knew that this was the end.

Her last thought was: how banal.

CHAPTER FIVE

EARLY IN THE evening brakes screeched to a halt in Riemeister Strasse. Surprised, Inge Dietrich opened the front door. A Military Police corporal lifted a large carton off the back seat of his jeep and carried it past her into the living room, where he put it down on the table. 'From Captain Ashburner, with his best regards.' The corporal saluted caually and raced off again. Inge opened the carton and stared, speechless, at the treasures that spilled out.

'Wow, I don't believe it!' Ralf fished out one of the olive-green cans. 'Pineapple in syrup', the label read. 'OK, so I know what an apple is, syrup too,' he mused. The English and German words were similar enough. 'But what about this "pine", then?'

His mother took her father's old encyclopaedia out of the bookcase. 'Pine,' she read, finding the entry on pine trees. 'Apples on pine trees?'

A glimmer of enlightenment dawned on Ralf's angelic face. 'Sure. Pine-cones in syrup. The things those Yanks will eat!'

Dr Hellbich appeared, and with delight picked a carton of Camels out of the cornucopia. Moments later a spicy cloud of Turkish tobacco hung in the living-room. 'SPAM,' his baffled wife read from a rectangular can. 'Is it something to eat, do you think?' The district councillor drew on his cigarette with pleasure, and did not reply.

'I'll fetch the can opener,' an unusually helpful Ralf told his grand-mother.

'You don't need it for this one.' Ben had just come home. He broke off the little key that was welded to the lid of the can. Then he cleverly threaded the little flap on the side of the can into the slit in the tiny instrument and began turning the key. Before the astonished eyes of all present, a thin strip of metal unwound from the can. Ben rolled it around the key until he could lift the lid off. A solid pink mass of meat appeared. 'Spam,' he informed them casually. 'Short for spiced ham.' He knew about it from Mr Brubaker, who had made him a sandwich with this delicacy, adding pale yellow Heinz salad dressing, which oozed out of the sandwich to right and left at each bite.

Ralf stuck his finger in the can. His mother slapped his hand. 'Everyone will get a slice for supper.' She took the open carton, which now contained only nine packets of cigarettes, away from the disgruntled district councillor. 'I can get fifteen litres of cooking oil and two sides of bacon for this. It may even stretch to a few eggs too.'

Meanwhile, the others were puzzling over a can of peanut butter. Dr Hellbich translated 'pea' and 'nut' into German literally, marvelling. 'Heaven knows how they make butter out of peas and nuts. Must be some kind of substitute, like our chestnut coffee,' he said.

'Here comes Papa. Wow, will he ever be surprised!' Ralf said happily. His father propped his bicycle on the veranda and took off his cycle clips.

Inge was beaming. 'Darling, look at all these lovely things Mr Ashburner's sent us.'

'Pine-cones in syrup. Butter made from peas and nuts,' muttered Hellbich. 'These Americans really are barbarians.'

Klaus Dietrich just walked past his family in silence and climbed the stairs with a heavy tread. Inge anxiously watched his progress. 'Don't any of you dare open a can. We have to plan how best to use all these good things,' she warned them, before following her husband upstairs.

The inspector was lying on their bed, staring at the ceiling. Inge sat down beside him and took his hand. 'Klaus, what's the matter? Do you want to talk about it?'

'It just goes on and on,' he said softly.

She knew what he meant at once. 'Another murder? Oh, my God, poor woman.'

'Which poor woman?' he asked. 'The daughter he killed, or the mother when I had to tell her that her daughter had been murdered and dumped in a garbage bin?'

'I'm sure you broke the news as gently as possible.'

He laughed bitterly. 'Imagine – *she* was concerned about *me*. It must be very hard on me too, she said, would I be all right?'

'It is hard on you, darling, I can see it is. Sleep for a little. I'll bring you up something to eat later. I saw a bottle of Mosel among Mr Ashburner's presents. We'll open that too.'

'I have to get him before he kills again,' muttered Dietrich. Then, exhausted, he fell asleep.

Herr Rödel's tailor's workshop was on the veranda of the house on Ithweg which he, his wife and Heidi shared with two other families. Only four window panes had survived the pressure waves of the bombing, the splinters raining down from anti-aircraft shelling and the Red Army's salvoes of machine-gun fire. The other fifty-six were covered with cardboard or celluloid that had originally been made for the windows of Wehrmacht military vehicles. Rödel had bartered several reels of sewing silk for this material; he needed plenty of light to work by.

'How I'm going to manage in winter is a mystery to me. You can't heat this place — no use sticking a hot stovepipe through the cardboard.'

'There's a piece of tin lying in our garden at home. You can have that,' Ben offered. 'If you cut a hole in it you could stick the stovepipe through.' Ben was dropping in more and more often. It gave him a sense of getting closer to his suit. He watched with interest as Rödel took apart a threadbare overcoat brought in by a customer to be turned.

'You wash the parts in cold water so the colour doesn't run. Then you iron them dry and put them together again inside out, and there's your new coat. Luckily I still have some horsehair and padding.'

'I hope you have some for my double-breasted suit too.' Ben could already see himself in that perfect suit, turn-ups of the trousers exactly five centimetres high, just brushing his suede shoes so that there was no more than the suggestion of a fold above them. He stroked the length of fabric in the cupboard, full of the pride of possession. It was the best pre-war wool, firm and soft, the classic, grey-brown pattern with a red thread woven into it. 'The English call it Prince of Wales check, don't they? I read that in a gentlemen's magazine.'

'Fingers off, young man. Business first.'

Ben took Mr Brubaker's carton of Camels out from under his shirt and put it on the tailor's table. 'That's three thousand Allimarks, right?'

'Two fifty.' Rödel noted it down with his tailor's chalk on the suiting, which already bore notes of previous instalments paid. 'You still need a lot of credit. Better hurry up, my boy. Herr Kraschinski next door is thinking of selling his watch to buy his son a suit for his wedding day.'

Ben was indignant. 'You can't do that, Herr Rödel. I've already paid you seven thousand, nine hundred marks.'

The tailor looked at him over the top of his glasses. 'I'll be happy to make you a top-quality suit, but I can't wait much longer. My wife needs shoes. And she's found a source of poultry and winter potatoes. That costs money. Yes, and we want a little real coffee for Christmas too.'

'Christmas is in December. This is August,' Ben reminded him. 'You'll get the rest really soon, I promise.'

But there was a long and arduous way to go between making that promise and keeping it. Although there were definite possibilities at the GYA in Bruckstrasse. Where there were Yanks, he knew from experience, there were good pickings to be had.

The Zehlendorf GYA Club was housed in a big villa. The Signal Corps colonel in charge had detailed a sergeant who knew a little German to be club leader. Sergeant Allen was a young sports teacher from Philadelphia who was able to arouse enthusiasm in his young charges, and he had immediately set up a baseball team. Ben hung around the club and kept his eyes open. You just had to have patience.

His patience was rewarded a few days later when an army delivery truck brought several cartons. Ben read the labels with growing interest. 'Mars Bars, 250' one of them said. Another, according to its label, contained 300 Sunshine Marshmallows, and a third 500 Hershey Bars, chocolate and hazelnut flavour.

These riches came from the Catholic garrison chaplain, Major Baker, who had generous donations from home at his disposal. Baker was a regular guest at the club. 'He says he'll start handing out some of the stuff from those cartons next week,' said one club member. 'Only after his Bible class, of course.' The man of God was a realist.

Under Sergeant Allen's supervision, Herr Appel took the cartons off the delivery truck. Herr Appel, who looked after the building, was a grey-headed man with a short parting in his hair and bulging eyes. Like all German employees of the Americans, he wore a dyed army uniform. He had been caretaker of a boys' school until it was demolished by Russian rocket-launchers. Appel didn't speak a word of English, not that anyone noticed, since he hardly spoke at all. He became talkative only on the subject of his allotment; he was chairman of the South-West Allotment Gardeners' association.

Ben helped Herr Appel to carry the cartons. Sergeant Allen locked them in the old storeroom in the cellar. There was no way of getting at them for the moment. But he couldn't let those treasures lie there untouched, or Major Baker really would end up distributing the goodies to his flock. Ben began giving the situation his undivided attention. The black-market rate for chocolate was rising.

'That villain's name is Franz!' a voice proclaimed in the big basement room of the clubhouse one afternoon. The drama group was rehearsing Schiller's *The Robbers*. Ben was sitting on a bench, yawning. He'd rather have a good Western any day. Heidi Rödel was holding a Reclam edition of the play. She didn't know the part of Amalia by heart yet, but she had mastered a toss of the head, not planned by the director, which sent her hair tumbling around her shoulders. It did not, however, have the desired effect. Ben's eyes were fixed not on her silky hair but on the door to the storeroom. The loot down there was very tempting.

Getting at it was the problem. The key was in the pencil tray on the office desk, and either Sergeant Allen or his deputy Corporal Kauwe, a small Hawaiian with a shining moon-face, always sat behind the desk. All through the third and fourth acts, Ben was thinking hard. But no solution occurred to him.

'The man can yet be helped,' announced Gert Schlomm, the director, probably the first to play the robber-hero, Karl Moor, in short lederhosen, as the rehearsal came to an end. The words sounded like a prophecy.

Heidi came up to the edge of the stage. 'How did I do?' She pulled her skirt up to her tanned thighs, jumped off the improvised platform, twisted her left ankle as she landed on her wedge heel in front of Ben and, with a little cry, grasped his shoulders for balance. Her body felt warm and soft, and gave off a pleasantly astringent perfume.

'You were OK.' He helped her to sit on the bench.

She rubbed her ankle. 'I must go home now. Will you take me, Gert? I can hardly walk.'

'I'm busy. Ben can take you,' said the great actor from up on the stage.

Ben looked at the seventeen-year-old's hairy thighs with distaste. What on earth, he thought scornfully, does she see in him? 'Aren't you in the model-making group?' he asked Heidi.

She was still rubbing her ankle. 'Yes, we're making a doll's house for the local kindergarten, with Corporal Kauwe. Want to come along?'

'No thanks, not my thing. Could you take a little break from building your doll's house?'

'What for?'

'To make a board with hooks for keys on it. I'll have a word with the painting group, they can paint flowers and varnish the whole thing. It's for Sergeant Allen's birthday next week, it would look good in his office. We can screw it to the door as a surprise.'

'Could be done.' Heidi hobbled a step or two. 'So will you take me home?'

This was his great opportunity to be alone with her. But since it came by permission of his rival, indeed almost by command of his rival, Ben couldn't take it. 'No time,' he said briefly.

'Please yourself,' she snapped, and stopped hobbling.

Sergeant Allen thanked them for the lovely present. Corporal Kauwe grunted cheerfully and hung all the keys on the hooks, including, as Ben noted with satisfaction, the key to the cellar storeroom. The office door folded outwards. If you opened it just far enough then the inside of it, to which the board with hooks was screwed, was out of sight of anyone sitting at the desk. Ben had come up with the solution to his problem.

Now he had to find the right moment. It came when Sergeant Allen was training the baseball team in the garden and Corporal Kauwe was on the telephone in the office. Ben flung the door wide and reached quickly for the key while the Hawaiian was conversing in a guttural voice with a fellow countryman, his gaze directed on the far-away Pacific Ocean.

'Oh, sorry, I'll come back later.' Ben slammed the door and raced downstairs. There was no one in the cellar; the drama group wouldn't be rehearsing until later. He opened the storeroom, picked up a carton labelled 'Mars Bars', hid it under the stage in the main basement area, locked the storeroom door again and went up.

Corporal Kauwe was just finishing his conversation as Ben opened the office door for the second time, and slipped the key back on its hook. 'OK, what do you want?' Ben asked if he could see the latest *Saturday Evening Post*, thanked the corporal and went off with the magazine. He sat in the hall and leafed through it for a little while, just for the sake of appearances, before going down again.

He pulled the carton out from under the stage, heaved it up on his shoulders, and peered through the little window in the cellar door. The baseball team had finished training. Concealed by shrubs and bushes, Ben climbed the fence to the neighbouring plot of land, and then made his way through a gap in the hedge and into the street. No one took any notice of him. Everyone was carrying something somewhere these days, whether home or to barter it. Ben was going to Frau Molch's to dispose of his goods.

The cartoon was rather heavy. Two hundred and fifty Mars Bars with that dense, sweet, sticky filling were bound to weigh a lot. Most important of all, they weighed a few thousand marks. The coveted suit, that emblem of elegant masculinity and the key to the favours of the woman he adored, was coming closer. As he shifted the carton to his other shoulder, Ben was already toying with the idea of a second raid on the cellar. Life, complete with the made-to-measure clothing suitable for a man of the world, was expensive.

Frau Molch was an energetic little woman who ran a bar at the toboggan run in winter. But it was summer, and in any case, there were no drinks available to serve at the bar. She had set herself up on the black market when she exchanged her dead husband's clothes for other articles after he fell at the Front. Soon her apartment on Eschershauser Weg was a positive warehouse.

Sacks of yellow peas, cans of condensed milk built into pyramids, shoes for ladies, gentlemen and children, candles, bicycles, powdered milk, coffee beans, cigarettes, Swiss watches – there was almost nothing in the way of desirable goods that you couldn't get from Frau Molch. She was an institution in the Onkel Tom quarter. Anyone who wanted a smoked sausage and a cup of coffee more than they wanted to hang on to a wedding ring or a camera, and didn't fancy going all the way to the Potsdamer Platz, visited her instead.

Ben let the carton slide off his shoulder on to the living-room table, where it landed between a packet of biscuits and a pair of binoculars. 'Two hundred and fifty Mars Bars,' he said, in a businesslike voice. 'Three thousand Allimarks, OK?'

'Not worth more than a thousand eight hundred,' said Frau Molch.

'Ten marks each. That makes two-five,' Ben countered.

'Two thousand,' Frau Molch offered. She would sell them for three times that amount. 'Open it up.'

The carton was sealed in a makeshift way with a strip of sticky tape. Ben hadn't noticed that before. He tore back the tape and unfolded the four sides of the lid. Before them, neatly packaged in dozens, lay six hundred yellow pencils. Major Baker had used the empty carton to hold his well-meaning gift. 'To give the kids something to write with,' the chaplain had explained to Sergeant Allen with a kindly smile. The carton of Sunshine Marshmallows held erasers, and the label on the Hershey hazelnut and chocolate bars concealed stacks of virgin notepads.

Frau Molch was annoyed. 'You think you can take me for a ride?'

Ben was shattered. 'I didn't know. Honest.' He pulled himself together. Business was business. 'How about two hundred marks? People can really do with pencils, specially pretty yellow ones like these.'

'Fifty, and now clear out.'

Ben pocketed the fifty Allimarks, designed to imitate an American dollar bill, and went away. 'Bloody awful outfit,' he muttered, meaning the US Army in general and its youth clubs in particular. Places where they promised you Mars bars and gave yellow pencils.

*

Klaus Dietrich had passed a restless night. It was partly due to the bottle of wine he had shared with Inge; he wasn't used to it. But most of all, his gloomy thoughts of the dead women and their murderer had tormented him in his dreams, and still pursued him now that he was awake. A terrible premonition of other appalling deeds accompanied him on his way to work, making him aware of his helplessness. He had made no progress yet, he wasn't a step further on.

'We know some more about that garbage-truck driver,' said Franke, saluting the inspector. 'Seems like Otto Ziesel has a pathological hatred of German women who sleep with Yanks.'

Dietrich was unconvinced. 'So pathological that he brutally murders three women and gets himself caught disposing of the last?'

'It wouldn't be the first time in the history of criminal investigation that the murderer has pretended to "find" his victim.'

'A bit far-fetched, don't you think, Franke?'

'The suspect has previous convictions, inspector. His files have survived. There was a preliminary inquiry brought against him during the war, for rape. It was set aside. The woman was Jewish so it was decided she couldn't be believed. Ziesel was the driver for some Nazi big cheese. Another reason to dismiss the case.'

'Where is the man?'

'I've told him to come here at ten. There's one thing this third case indicates a lot more clearly than the first two, inspector. The killer's working for the Yanks.' There was a touch of irony in Franke's tone. 'No ordinary German criminal has a pass that allows him to kill in the prohibited zone and then stuff his victim into an American garbage bin.'

Tyres squealed outside. Sergeant Donovan strode through the open door like a fighting bull and straight into Inspector Dietrich's office. 'My captain wants you,' he barked. 'Let's go.'

'Good morning, sergeant. Sorry, I'm busy. I have to question a man at ten. Tell your captain I'll be happy to look in this afternoon.'

'I said let's go!' Donovan shouted. 'Now!' He laid his hand threateningly on the grip of his Magnum. Did this damn German still not realize who'd won the war?

'Stop this nonsense, sergeant,' said Dietrich calmly. 'I'll come as soon as I have time.'

The sergeant went red in the face. He drew his gun and pointed it at the German. 'Come on, you goddam Kraut.'

Klaus Dietrich stepped forward. A chop to Donovan's forearm with the side of his hand, quick as lightning, and the Magnum clattered to the floor. Dietrich picked it up, took the magazine out and emptied it with his thumb. The cartridges tumbled out on the floor too. He handed the weapon back to Donovan, who made for him. Dietrich dodged his charge. 'I was in a judo club before the war. I may not be fully back on form, but I can deal with bad manners.' Boiling with rage, Donovan put the gun back in its holster. Sergeant Franke hid his grin behind a file. 'Come on, then, sergeant, we don't want to keep your captain waiting,' Dietrich told him. 'Franke, hang on to this man Ziesel until I get back.'

But Otto Ziesel was in Captain Ashburner's office, and stared challengingly at Dietrich as the inspector walked in.

Ashburner took his feet off his desk. 'Hello, inspector. I wanted you to be present at this interview in case I'm accused of blocking your inquiries again. Bring us coffee, Donovan, and sit down.' Donovan poured two cups from the thermos jug, put one in front of the captain and took the other himself. 'Coffee for everyone, sergeant,' Ashburner told him. Donovan sulkily obeyed.

'So you found the body, Herr Ziesel?' Ashburner's tone was polite.

'Not directly, captain. It was that black sergeant who saw the arm hanging out of the garbage can.'

Dietrich joined in. 'The container you had just loaded up at the back of the shopping street.'

Ziesel shook his head. 'Not there, no. It was on the corner of Ihnestrasse and Garystrasse, that bin was. There's a whole lot of Yanks live there. It was damn heavy when I put it on the truck. Now I know why.'

Dietrich turned to Ashburner. 'So the murder didn't take place in the Onkel Tom prohibited zone.'

'And just about any Kraut could have done it,' said Donovan, triumphant.

'Or any Yank,' Ziesel snarled.

'Don't push your luck,' Dietrich warned him. 'You should go carefully. We have statements about you. Your vicious outbursts against German girls who make friends with American soldiers are very incriminating.'

'Yankee whores, sure, I said that. So? It don't mean I'm going to touch one of 'em.'

'What about Lea Finkelstein? Didn't you touch her? We have the 1944 file on that investigation, Herr Ziesel. It doesn't show you in a very good light.' Klaus Dietrich explained to the captain what he was talking about.

'OK, let's put him in the cells for now. Take him downstairs, Donovan.' The sergeant twisted Ziesel's arm behind his back and steered him to the cellar steps. 'Happy, inspector?'

'With interim custody, yes. With Donovan's brutal manner, no. You should straighten him out a bit.'

'We're dealing with a serial killer.'

'That's not proven. But I'll keep it in mind.'

'You'll have plenty of time to do that on the train.' Ashburner gave the inspector a red slip of paper bearing several official stamps. 'Your visiting permit for Brandenburg penitentiary. My friend Maxim Petrovich Berkov let an NKVD colonel win a game of chess. Good luck.'

'Thanks, captain. And thank you for your gifts. You gave six hungry Germans a glimpse of a long-forgotten paradise. Very gracious of you.'

'A simple thank you would have been fine,' replied Ashburner, irritated. Then he thought of Jutta, and his expression softened. They were going to meet this evening.

Jutta was waiting at the gate of the prohibited zone at seven. John Ashburner jumped out of the jeep and mimed a chauffeur opening the door of a limousine for her. 'Where to, madam?' he inquired in what he thought a very British accent.

'The Ritz, John,' she said, playing along. They drove through the gate and turned right at the corner into Wilskistrasse. He opened the apartment door and let her in first. She turned and stood close to him, her lips parted. Putting her arms around his neck, she drew his face down to hers and kissed him with an intensity he had never known before. His reaction was spontaneous, and embarrassed him. Jutta felt his penis harden through her thin dress, and went damp herself. Later, she thought, and the deliberate postponement excited her.

'A whiskey?' he asked, covering his embarrassment.

'Too strong for me. I'd rather have a glass of wine. Do you have anything to nibble with it? Or I'll be falling over.'

'A few crackers, some peanuts.' He put the packets on the table, opened a bottle of white wine and poured himself a whiskey. 'How wonderful to relax with a glass of bourbon,' he murmured contentedly, stretching his legs out. She liked the fact that he let himself relax in her company. It created a sense of intimacy between them, the kind felt by young lovers and settled couples. 'How about going to the movies?' he suggested.

'Oh, lovely, what's on?'

'No idea.'

The Onkel Tom cinema was part of the requisitioned area around the

U-Bahn station nearby. Germans were allowed in only if they were with American soldiers. There was an aura of Pepsi Cola and Wrigley's Spearmint chewing gum in the air.

The usherette went ahead of them down the central aisle, a grotesque lilac bow in her long blonde hair. She indicated a row of seats. Ashburner thanked her with a smile that did not escape Jutta. A silent duel developed between the two women. 'You like him, don't you, but he's mine, understand?' – 'OK, I'm not planning to take him away from you.' – 'You'd better not even think of it.'

They watched a movie featuring Gary Cooper, Rita Hayworth and a mail coach. Gary Cooper said 'Yep' and 'Is that so, ma'am?', Rita Hayworth showed as much of her beautiful legs as the prudish US censor allowed, and there was gunfire from the mail coach. Bags of popcorn rustled. While the fiery Rita clicked her castanets for the laid-back Gary, John Ashburner hesitantly felt for Jutta's hand, but his fingers landed on her thigh. He was about to withdraw them in alarm, but Jutta gently held them where they were. She enjoyed his touch, anticipating what was to come, and found she could hardly wait for the end of the film.

At last the hero, nobly giving up the heroine, strode away into the sunset behind the corral. The curtain closed, the lights came up. Everyone flocked out. Jutta took John's arm.

'How about dinner at the Harnack House?' he suggested.

'Oh, no thank you, John, I've eaten too much popcorn. I need fresh air now.'

'Let's drive down to the lake, then.' She squealed with pleasure as they bumped through the wood, over sticks and stones. He only just missed a shell crater before the way led so fast down the steep slope to the moonlit Krumme Lanke that it took your breath away. It was nothing to the jeep, which had seen service in a dozen theatres of war.

'That was terrific.' She put her arms around his neck. 'Come into the water.' She jumped out of the jeep and stripped off. Ashburner turned off the headlights. Slowly, she waded into the water up to her knees and then turned. She wanted him to see her.

The moonlight caressed her body. She bent forward, scooped up water and threw it over her breasts. It ran down over her belly and hung like a glittering network in her blonde bush. Her body was singing with excitement.

Hesitantly, he took his uniform off and followed her in. They embraced, kissed and sank into the shallow water that had retained the warmth of the sun, unerringly finding their way to each other. Under his thrusting movements she rose, rejoicing, to an unstoppable orgasm. Pleasure carried them both away, and if Ashburner had been capable of thinking at all he might have compared this passionate love-making, with amazement, to the lukewarm encounters of his marriage.

They remained intertwined until desire took hold of them again. Jutta rolled him over so that she could sit on top of him. Delighted, he enjoyed the way she passionately rode him, uttering rhythmical cries. Another couple were making love noisily on the bank nearby. It did not inhibit but stimulated them – accomplices in love.

He took her home and kissed her lovingly. 'See you tomorrow.' A sense of happiness, something she hadn't known for a long time, came over her.

The report came over the jeep radio as Ashburner was parking it outside his apartment. 'Shit,' was his first reaction. Then he shouted into the microphone, 'I'm on my way!'

Number 198, a yellow apartment building, was the only ruin in Argentinische Allee. A stray British bomb had torn it apart from top to bottom. Moonlight illuminated the ghostly scene, assisted by the headlights of Sergeant Donovan's jeep.

Ashburner made his way through the neighbours who had ventured out into the street, ignoring the curfew. A woman dangled from the steel bars that had emerged from the concrete as it burst apart and now protruded, bizarrely twisted, from the third floor. She was swinging back and forth like a doll, hanging over the abyss below from the belt of her dressing gown. Three German police officers in black-dyed uniforms and two military policemen were crawling on all fours towards the edge of the floor. They got a rope under her arms. One of them lay flat on his stomach and cut the belt. Carefully, they lowered her lifeless body, and it landed at Ashburner's feet. The dressing gown fell open. The blue-black indentations around her neck and her bloodstained sex told their own terrible tale.

'Brutally abused and strangled with a chain like the others,' said Donovan, his voice strained. 'What do you think, captain?'

'I think this rules out Otto Ziesel as the murderer. You can let him go, sergeant.' Ashburner cast another glance at the dead woman. Strands of her long blonde hair were sticking to her pale cheeks. A few hours ago, in the cinema, it had been prettily arranged and adorned with a grotesque lilac bow.

The back of the property bordered on a strip of woodland that had been plundered for firewood. It had been named Sprungschanzenweg by the town planning department, although the old ski jump for which it was named had long ago been converted into the Onkel Toms Hütte toboggan run. Young people zoomed down it on their sleighs in winter. At this time of year, the ground was covered with dry pine needles on which the motorbike tyres left no trace. Its rider knew every inch of the way, even in the dark. He pushed the bike into the garage through the narrow door. Old mattresses and broken furniture barred the way to the front of the garage. Even the Red Army men looting immediately after the war hadn't got this far.

'Is that you, son?' asked a voice on the other side of the piled lumber.

'Yes, Mother.'

'Was she blonde again?'

He didn't reply. He had found the satisfaction he couldn't get in any other way. Now he was calm and relaxed, and he didn't want to talk about it. In silence, he put away his gauntlets, goggles and leather cap.

'They'll find you this time.'

He pulled the torn eiderdown over the bike. 'They won't find me, because I don't exist. Goodnight, Mother.'

He left the garage the same way he had come. In Argentinische Allee he joined the gaping crowd outside Number 198. Two ambulance men carried the dead woman past him on a stretcher. Someone had closed her eyes. Her face wore a peaceful expression which unsettled him. He thought of her distorted face and the rattle in her throat that had brought him to climax.

'I have her found, captain,' said a man beside him, in broken English. He had a dachshund on a lead. 'Her name is Marlene Kaschke.'

CHAPTER SIX

THE TRAIN MOVED slowly through the summer landscape of the Brandenburg Mark, where the ugly scars of war had disappeared under the green of the meadows and the yellow of ripening grain. A burnt-out signalman's hut at Krielow reminded passengers of the recent past – as did the stench of the cattle trucks which not so long ago had been taking prisoners to camps, and had been only superficially cleaned since. Anyone who couldn't find room inside stood out on the footboards. Singing and accordion music drifted back from the single passenger car at the front. Some Red Army soldiers were on their way to their unit at Rathenow.

Klaus Dietrich had managed to find himself a place on the roof next to an elderly man with a rucksack and a briefcase, who moved rather pointedly away from him. 'Did I get too close to you?' the inspector could not refrain from saying.

'Not me, it's my eggs. They'd be an irreplaceable loss if they were cracked.'

It turned out that Dietrich's companion looked after the aviary in the Berlin Zoo. 'Two parrot eggs, a number of other rare eggs from Amazonian birds, all in protective packing in my son's sandwich boxes. I'm hoping to get them to safe keeping with the help of a colleague at Leipzig Zoo. Everything's wrecked at our place. How about you? Off on a foraging expedition?'

'A business trip.' Dietrich closed his eyes and turned his face up to the sun. He didn't feel like a lengthy conversation.

Outside Brandenburg station, the twisted tracks of sidings stuck up into the air like steel snakes. Broken glass glittered everywhere in the gravel. The train stopped a little way outside the station itself, and the passengers had to make their way across the tracks to the platform. They helped each other up. The barrier at the end had been repaired, and a railwayman in a dusty blue uniform was collecting tickets. Two men, in hats and leather coats in spite of the heat, were inspecting the arrivals through narrowed eyes, and checking the papers of male passengers.

Dietrich was not spared. 'Got a pass.' It was a command, not a question. The inspector showed his ID and the much-stamped red pass. The man waved to his colleague. They took Dietrich's arms and led him out of the station. Several sympathetic glances accompanied him, but most people looked the other way. They didn't want anything to do with men in hats and leather coats, not now any more than in the past.

A black Tatra limousine was waiting outside. The men squeezed in to right and left of Dietrich on the back seat. They stank of *machorka* and vodka. A third man, wearing a Mao cap, was at the wheel. After driving for twenty minutes they passed several Russian guards and barbed-wire barriers. A tall gate opened, the car rolled through and stopped. They were in the yard of the Brandenburg penitentiary. The gate closed behind them with a booming echo. Will I ever get out of here? Dietrich wondered with mixed feelings.

A red-brick building. Another guard, with a sub-machine gun. Inside, they went down some stairs and along a corridor with a concrete floor. One of Dietrich's companions opened an iron door. The other pushed him into the bare room, which was illuminated by a single bright light. A fat Russian woman in NCO's uniform sat behind a desk.

'Name?' she barked at him.

'Klaus Dietrich. Inspector in the Criminal Investigation Department in Berlin. I have a visiting permit.' He handed her the red paper.

She put it down on the desk in front of her. 'Undress,' she ordered. Dietrich froze. 'Didn't you hear?' His two guards had positioned themselves by the door, arms folded, obviously ready to help. He knew he had no choice. He had entered the lion's den of his own accord, and now it would be unwise to provoke the lion. With studied indifference, he took his clothes off. He kept on his prosthesis, with its shoe and sock. It was his only support; there was nothing else to hold on to.

The Russian woman rose and waddled towards him. She walked slowly all round him, looking him up and down. Then, just as slowly, she waddled back to her desk. She brought a stamp down on the red paper and gave it to him. 'Get dressed,' she ordered, without giving him another glance. Then he understood: the whole thing was routine; every visitor had to go through it.

He fastened his last trouser button. 'Pleased to have met you,' he said wryly. She took him at his word, and a broad smile appeared on her round face.

An officer with NKVD tags on his collar was waiting for him in a large office on the first floor. 'Lieutenant-Colonel Korsakov,' he introduced himself. 'CID Inspector Dietrich, am I right?' He spoke excellent German. 'A vodka?'

'Thank you very much, *Tovarich* Lieutenant-Colonel.' After his treatment in the cellar, this reception was reassuring.

Korsakov filled two glasses, and they tossed them back standing up. 'Now, please sit down. Tell me, how is he?'

'You'll have to tell me who you mean first.'

'Why, Gennat, of course. Detective Superintendent Ernst Gennat. Fatso Gennat, that's what your bunch used to call him. A great police officer. Inventor of the flying squad for murder cases. We adopted that idea ourselves, it was very successful.' It turned out that Korsakov was a detective superintendent with the Moscow CID, and an admirer of its Berlin counterpart.

'He retired quite a while ago. I think to somewhere in the Rhineland,' Dietrich improvised. 'I'm afraid I don't know any more details.'

'Well, give him my regards if he ever comes to Berlin. Another vodka?'

'No, thank you. You know why I'm here, and I'll need a clear head for that.'

'Chief Superintendent Schlüter. Another Berlin CID man. Pity about him. He's waiting next door.' Korsakov opened the door to the next room. 'Please go in. Knock when you've finished.'

The room was empty except for a chair and table, and a stout wooden armchair in front of it. Straps on the arms and legs of this chair left no one in any doubt of the methods of interrogation employed here. The man at the barred window wore a mended drill suit which was the same dirty grey as his thin face.

'I'm Wilhelm Schlüter. Don't suppose you want to shake hands with me.'

'Klaus Dietrich. Acting head of the Zehlendorf CID. I'm not your judge.' The inspector offered his hand.

Schlüter gratefully took it. 'My successor, are you? What do you want from me, Herr Dietrich?'

'Your help. It's about the murder of a woman back in 1936. You were leading the inquiries at the time, and the files have disappeared. I'd be very glad to know all the details.'

'Why?'

'Three women have been tortured and murdered on our patch.'

'Ah. Vaginally abused with a sharp object, strangled with a chain. All of them fair-haired and blue-eyed.'

Klaus Dietrich swallowed. 'How do you know?'

Schlüter was pacing up and down. Finally he stopped right in front of Dietrich. 'It wasn't just one murder. There were six of them, between 1936 and 1939.'

'Six?' Dietrich was appalled.

'What the FBI calls a serial killer. At the time I read everything I could about similar cases in the USA, to get more information. That series of murders in Milwaukee, for instance. The murderer tied his victims to a tree and throttled them with his bare hands before raping them. Eighteen red-haired girls and women.'

'Six murders at Onkel Toms Hütte, all following the same pattern?'

'Only the first was made public. When the second woman was killed, it was clear we were dealing with the same murderer, and that he was fixated on a certain type. The following cases confirmed it. Himmler commandeered the files and put his own people in charge. He ordered secrecy. A manic sex murderer didn't fit the picture of the healthy German nation. He forbade us to say anything more about it.'

'And you obeyed his orders?'

'I went on working on the case on my own initiative. It was a challenge to any true investigator, and those Bavarian amateurs in the Gestapo weren't getting anywhere.'

'The murders were all similar?'

'Particularly in the way the murderer played cat and mouse with me. He knew I was after him, and he accepted the challenge.' Schlüter laughed soundlessly. 'Case number three. Gerlinde Unger. Probationary teacher at the Zinnowald School. That was in the winter of '38. He buried her in a sandbox at the Onkel Tom U-Bahn station, leaving her face showing. She looked like a Madonna. I found her after he left a clue in my car, a bag of sand. Gritting sand for the roads was mixed with red salt at the time, so I knew where to look.'

'But you still didn't catch him.'

'I was hot on his heels. I hoped the tools he used would lead me to him. But the murders suddenly stopped at the beginning of the war.'

'Because the murderer was called up,' said Dietrich, excited. 'He was away right through the war. Now he's back, and killing again.'

Schlüter stopped pacing, and pointed to the sturdy chair with its leather straps. 'They've stopped torturing me. They've got all I know out of me.'

'What advice would you give me, Herr Schlüter?'

'Carry on where I left off. Look for the tools he uses, like I said.'

'The chain?'

Schlüter did not reply. He was gazing into the distance. 'They'll shoot me soon now. A bullet in the back of the neck at close quarters. It's quick. My men and I did it thousands of times in the Ukraine. Goodbye. I wish you and our country a better future than the one we thought we must murder for.'

Klaus Dietrich hammered on the door. Lieutenant-Colonel Korsakov let him out. 'A serial killer, how interesting. I wish I could work with you in Berlin.' He had listened to the entire conversation.

Six hours in the sidings at Potsdam because of endless Russian military transports and two laborious inspections by Saxon railway police officers made the journey back to Berlin as bad as the journey out. They passed through Zehlendorf West station at snail's pace, which meant that Klaus Dietrich was able to jump out on the platform and land unharmed. From there it was only a few paces to the police station.

'Another woman murdered, inspector.' Franke received him with this depressing news. 'And we're not a step further forward.'

Dietrich's reaction was matter-of-fact and professional. 'What do we know?'

'The murder was committed around ten yesterday evening, at 198 Argentinische Allee. The victim lived there. Name of Marlene Kaschke. Same type: blonde, blue eyes, worked for the Americans. Usherette in the Onkel Tom cinema. Strangled with a chain like the others. And the autopsy findings match the others too.'

'I'd like to see the scene of the crime. Is the car heated up? We can leave in five minutes.' Klaus Dietrich went to the men's room, where he pulled his trouser leg up above his knee. Groaning, he took off his prosthesis, then hopped over to the wash basin, ran it full and dipped in his reddened stump. The cold water felt wonderful. He dried the scar tissue with his handkerchief and sprinkled powder in the hollow depression at the top of the artificial leg. He always carried a small can of it with him.

The car was ready. Franke stepped on the accelerator, making the Opel cough indignantly. 'The toggle chain,' Dietrich reflected out loud. 'What does that tell us?'

'Nothing much,' said Franke, shrugging. 'You can get a thing like that in any pet shop, if they've opened again. It's what they call a throttle collar, meant for large dogs. If Fido pulls on the leash too hard it tightens round his neck. No, sir, we won't get far that way.'

Ten minutes later they were standing in front of the wrecked façade of Number 198. 'She was hanging from the third floor up there,' the sergeant told him. 'A tenant in the building found her, man named Mühlberger. As far as we can tell, the murderer pushed the dead woman over the edge. The belt of her dressing-gown got caught in those twisted steel bars, that's what stopped her falling.'

'Or else he was deliberately putting her on show up there,' said the inspector. 'He has a sense of the macabre. Think of the dead girl inside the roll of barbed wire, and that other poor woman in the garbage container.'

They climbed up to the third floor in the intact part of the building. 'Our colleagues have sealed off the apartment.' Franke tore away the official seal, which still bore the eagle and swastika.

A pot of geraniums, used glasses, plates and an empty bottle of champagne stood on the table in the bedroom. Three candles burnt down to their stubs were a reminder of yesterday evening's power cut. Klaus Dietrich looked at the poorly executed picture of a rutting stag in an autumnal landscape that was hanging over the chest of drawers, shaking his head. An order lay on it, under the picture. 'Cross of the French Légion d'Honneur. I wonder what junk dealer she got that from?'

Franke helped himself to a single prune wrapped in bacon which lay on one of the plates, and followed it up with a few peanuts. 'She had a visitor.' He pointed to the rumpled bedclothes.

'Her murderer?' The inspector opened the door to what had once been the living room. Less than a couple of paces lay between him and the drop to the street. 'Let's find out if the other tenants know anything.'

Franke knocked on the door of the second-floor apartment with a name-plate saying 'Mühlberger'. A man in a casual jacket opened it. A black dachshund was yapping between his check slippers. ' CID, Sergeant Franke. This is Inspector Dietrich.'

'You're lucky to find me home. I'm off work sick. I work for the Yanks.'

'We'd like to ask you a few questions, Herr Mühlberger.'

'Sure. I mean, I found her.'

'Can you tell us when that was?'

'Around ten-fifteen. That's when I take Lehmann here walkies. Only a step or so outside the house because of the bloody curfew. Lehmann likes to do his business on that sandy strip where they're going to build the second carriageway some time. As I was standing there, I could see something pale dangling level with the third floor.'

Franke was sceptical. 'In spite of the dark?'

'I have a strong torch and a few batteries. I was works security guard for Leuna during the war. Only been back a few weeks.'

'And you heard a motorcycle start up nearby, I expect,' said Dietrich casually.

'That's right. It moved away pretty quick. An NSU 300. I'd know that chugging exhaust in my sleep. Had a bike like that myself once. Hey, how'd you know, inspector?'

'A guess. Go on, Herr Mühlberger.'

'Well, so I shone the beam of the torch up and saw her hanging there. Very sad, sure, but no great loss. Cheap little tart, she was.'

A woman in a headscarf and apron was coming up the stairs. 'That's what he says because she wouldn't have anything to do with him. Bräuer, first floor,' she introduced herself. 'She was a good girl, she was, just wanted to be left alone. Who knows what she'd been through.'

'Did she have many men visitors?' asked Franke.

Frau Bräuer shook her head. 'Hardly at all.'

'Except the bloke that did her in,' Mühlberger said. 'Fellow with a dimple in his chin.'

Inspector Dietrich pricked up his ears. 'You saw him?'

'You bet your life. Just before ten, it was. Come on in, gents. Not you, Frau Bräuer.' Frau Bräuer moved away with an injured air. The police officers followed Mühlberger into his apartment, as Lehmann growled with hostility. 'Where was I? Yes, right, so just before ten I hear someone coming down from the third floor. I open my door. After all, you want to know who's hanging around the place in these difficult times. Had a candle in his hand. Probably helped himself to it up there so's not to fall down the stairs. I saw the dimple in his chin quite clearly.'

The sergeant was not satisfied. 'Can you describe him in more detail?'

'Had a dyed uniform jacket on.'

'A German one?'

'Nope, it wasn't German.'

Franke took a framed photograph off the sideboard. It showed a younger Mühlberger astride a motorcycle, his booted feet braced in the sand to left and right of it. He was wearing gauntlets, and had pushed his protective goggles high up on his leather helmet, just like his companion. Both their faces were stained with dust.

'My mate Kalkfurth and me,' said Mühlberger proudly. 'After a cross-country in the Grunewald before the war. We were in the NSKK, the National Socialist Motorcycle Corps. We did some pretty good cross-country runs in those days. It wasn't all bad back then.'

The sergeant put the photo back in its place. 'What happened to your mate?'

'Kurt? Killed during the march into Poland, right at the start of the war.'

'This man in the dyed uniform jacket with the dimple in his chin – would you recognize him?' Dietrich returned to the subject.

'Should think so.'

'Thank you, Herr Mühlberger. We'll ask you to come to the police station and make a formal statement.'

'That's OK, inspector. I guess you'll get him soon.'

'I guess so,' replied Franke, giving him a sharp look.

'Chief Superintendent Schlüter knows of six more murders before the war which match ours to a T,' Dietrich said when they were back in the car.

'You mean this Marlene Kaschke is the tenth?' asked the detective sergeant, incredulous.

235

'Looks like it, Franke. According to Schlüter, the murders stopped when the war began.'

'And now the war's over they're happening again. That suggests a man back from the army, sir.'

'It does, doesn't it? Someone who lived here before the war, and knows his way around the Onkel Toms Hütte quarter very well.'

'Mühlberger. He was away all through the war, he's only been back a couple of weeks. He could have hidden his motorbike somewhere. And he has a job with the Americans, too.'

Dietrich shook his head. 'That doesn't necessarily make him the murderer. But he's our only witness. I know from Captain Ashburner that there's a card index of all the Germans employed by the Yanks, with their photos. We'll look through it with Mühlberger. Who knows, this man with the dimple in his chin may be there.'

*

A heap of something was smouldering in the garden behind the terraced house. Ben looked at it with dire foreboding.

'Looks as if someone didn't know what to do with all his old Nazi junk and dumped it in our shed,' said his grandfather, confirming his fears. 'A complete Party uniform with all the bits and bobs. Take the poker, boy, and keep pushing the stuff into the flames.' Dr Hellbich went back to the house.

Ben poked about among the remnants, downcast. There was no hope of saving anything but the dagger of honour. He smuggled that upstairs under his shirt, and freshened up the steel blade and leather sheath with Sidol and shoe polish. Then he polished the swastika on the hilt with an old sock.

The gullible Clarence P. Brubaker was in transports of delight. 'A truly historic artefact!'

'The Führer himself gave it to him.'

'I just must meet him,' the hopeful aspirant to the Pulitzer Prize urged.

'The Führer?'

'The man with the dagger. Hitler's right-hand man, didn't you say? When can I meet him?'

'He wants five cartons of Chesterfields for his dagger.'

Brubaker agreed at once. 'Five cartons of Chesterfields, OK. You take them to him and tell him he'll get another ten from me in person. He can pick the time and the place. That's a fair offer, right?'

'I'll tell him. But I can't promise anything. He's very cautious.'

Mr Brubaker found an army bag made of olive-green sacking, which comfortably held the five cartons of cigarettes along with a pack of a hundred pieces of chewing gum as a reward for Ben. This payment for such a sensational underground story seemed well worth it to Hackensack's star reporter. 'You can keep the bag,' he said.

'You don't have an empty potato sack, do you?'

'I don't think so, but look around in the cellar if you like.' Brubaker had long since given up wondering about the peculiar things that Germans wanted.

There was no potato sack in the cellar, just a mountain of dirty washing going mouldy. A horde of Red Army soldiers had dragged the building's washerwoman away from her boiler and into the garden, where thirty men raped her before the thirty-first killed her. That had been four months earlier. Ben pulled a large pillowcase out of the heap and took it upstairs with him. Only a fool would carry an olive-green bag, easily identifiable as the property of the US Army.

'Don't forget to mention the ten cartons of Chesterfields,' Brubaker told him.

Ben boldly followed this up. 'Fifteen would be better.'

'Fifteen it is.'

Satisfied, Ben fetched himself a bottle of Coke from the fridge, put the pillowcase with the bag inside it over his shoulder, and marched straight off to Rödel the master tailor, who noted down credit for five cartons of Chesterfields on the suiting with his tailor's chalk. He added credit of a few hundred marks for the bag, chewing gum and pillowcase too.

On the way to the GYA Club, Ben did his sums. If he could get twenty cartons of cigarettes out of Brubaker instead of fifteen, he would be certain of his suit and his shoes. But the great reporter wouldn't pay up until he could shake the hand of Hitler's right-hand man, and this was going to be a difficult feat to bring off, even for the ingenious Ben. 'I'll think of something,' the German Reich's latter-day beneficiary told himself.

The drama group was rehearsing. '*We lead a life of liberty*,' bawled Schiller's robbers down in the cellar, '*we lead a life of joy . . .*' Meanwhile, behind the improvised stage, Herr Appel was taking a mouse out of a trap and tipping it into the garbage. Ben watched with interest as Appel removed the chewing gum from his mouth and stuck it on the little board as bait, then set the trap again .

Heidi Rödel sat down beside him. 'What did you think of the song?'

'Not much different from what we sang in the *Jungvolk*.' Only a few months earlier, he and the other members of his troop had sung 'Flames arise!' Or as his grandfather Hellbich called it under his breath, 'Song of the Young Brown Fire-Raisers'. That had been the full extent of Hellbich's public opposition to the regime.

Heidi moved close enough for their knees to touch. 'We're going skinny-dipping when it gets dark. Want to come?'

On weekend expeditions with the *Jungvolk* they had held swimming races naked, comparing penis size with their neighbours as they lay in the sun and thinking nothing much of it. But plunging into the water at night with a naked Heidi was something else. Ben suddenly had a feeling like climbing the bars in gymnastics. Confused, he went upstairs, dropped into an armchair and reached for the latest issue of the American soldiers' paper, *Stars and Stripes*.

Herr Appel made his laborious way up the stairs. He unwrapped a new piece of chewing gum from its silver paper, stuck out his tongue and applied the gum to it. With his bulging eyes, he reminded Ben of a chameleon he'd seen in the reptile house at the zoo. Except that Herr Appel drew in his tongue with its prey rather more slowly.

'*We lead a life of liberty, we lead a life of joy . . .*' sang the chorus down in the cellar for the umpteenth time.

'Not bad, that Goethe,' said Appel appreciatively, chewing.

Ben didn't bother to put him right. He picked up the newspaper and read the headline: 'WEREWOLVES GETTING ACTIVE'. An over-eager correspondent had written about an alleged conspiracy of former members of the Hitler Youth, which he claimed had organized itself into a secret league called The Werewolves, whose aim was to oppose the occupying power. In his mind's eye, Ben saw the solution to his problem begin to emerge, if only in vague outline for the time being.

Inspector Dietrich was waiting in the outer office of the German–American Employment Office. The German secretary was painting her fingernails.

'Would you like a coffee, inspector? And a sandwich to go with it? I'll have one brought over from the canteen. We have plenty of everything here.'

'That's very kind of you, but I don't want to go in to see your boss with my mouth full.'

'Tell you what, I'll pack one up for you to take away,' she whispered in conspiratorial tones. 'My name's Gertrud Olsen.'

'Extremely nice of you, Frau Olsen.'

'I'm looking for a man, see? Well, a girl will try anything. Even sandwiches. Are you married, inspector?'

'Yes, these last fifteen years. We have two sons.'

'We'd been married just a year, Horst and I. He was a military airman, went on reconnaissance flights for the artillery. They shot him down at Smolensk. I lost our baby when the news came. I mean, it's not that I'll ever forget Horst. Only when you're on your own you feel kind of claustrophobic. Come and see me some time. Irmgardstrasse 12a.'

'That's very close to me. We live with my parents-in-law in Riemeister Strasse. As I said, I'm married.'

'The nice men always are.' She took a mirror out of her handbag and retouched her lips. Dietrich thought the colour of the lipstick was rather too bright. 'Present from the boss. It's what he prefers,' she said apologetically.

'What's your boss like?'

'Mr Chalford? I don't think he likes Germans much. Otherwise he's OK. A bit impatient sometimes, maybe. But then again, he often brings me a little something from the PX.'

Chalford arrived about five o'clock. He had been in a meeting with the city commandant. 'Come into my office, inspector. Captain Ashburner said you were coming. Let's see what we can do for you.' Dietrich looked at the American with curiosity. Chalford was round and well nourished, a messenger from a world where everything was all right. 'Terrible, all these murders.' The smooth, pink face with the pale-blue eyes was distressed. 'OK, inspector, let's come straight to the point.'

'What do you know about the dead woman?'

'We don't as a rule give information to Germans. But Captain Ashburner has asked me to help you, so I'll make an exception.'

'How good of you.'

Curtis S. Chalford stroked back his thin fair hair, looking a little uncertain. Was this German making fun of him? 'What would you like to know, inspector?' he asked.

'Who was she?'

Chalford picked an entry out of a card index. 'Marlene Kaschke, aged thirty-three. No sexual diseases. I gave her a job as an usherette in the Uncle Tom cinema three weeks ago. She lived at 198 Argentinische Allee.'

'The house where she was murdered,' the inspector told him. 'Is anything known about her past?'

'She said she'd been working as a farmhand.'

'Can you give us any more detailed information?'

'That's all I know. Are you on anyone's trail yet?'

'The murderer is presumably a German employee of the US Army and knows his way around Onkel Toms Hütte. You probably gave him a job yourself.'

'The Uncle Tom Killer,' said Chalford in his broad American accent. 'Why the hell does he kill in Uncle Tom?'

'We're assuming that he has a hideout somewhere there.' Dietrich came out with his request. 'Captain Ashburner says you have a card index containing photographs of employees. We have a witness who claims to have seen the murderer. I'd be very grateful if you would let him take a look at the pictures of all the Germans employed by the army.' Chalford's face twisted. He obviously didn't like this at all. Perhaps it upset his routine. 'It really would be a great help to us, sir,' the inspector said with great courtesy. Chalford was playing impatiently with a pencil. 'We'll fit in with your engagements, of course.'

Chalford put the pencil down. 'All right, inspector. Come tomorrow, and Gertrud will show you the card index. Time to go home, Gertrud!'

'Yes, Mr Chalford,' said the secretary from the next room.

Franke was waiting downstairs in the Opel. 'How did it go, sir?'

'Chalford is a pompous ass. Probably a low-grade office worker at home, but he puts on airs here. It doesn't matter to us, just so long as we can see his card index. Let Mühlberger know.'

Curtis S. Chalford took the army bus from his office in Lichterfelde to the OMGUS headquarters in Clayallee, as he did every evening. From there he had only a couple of minutes to walk home. He was living in a requisitioned villa in Gelfertstrasse, assigned to him because of his position.

He was looking forward to his evening. The reason was a plump woman with dark curly hair, a pretty, full face, and the beginnings of a double chin. Renate Schlegel was twenty-eight, and the maternal type.

She had come to the German-American Employment Office to look for work. She spoke passable English. Chalford invited her to lunch. Over chicken and rice he made her an offer: she could live with him as his housekeeper and look after him. He offered her three cartons of cigarettes over and above her official wages, and of course good food, as well as those little items from the PX that a woman likes to have.

Renate Schlegel was on her own. Her husband had fallen at Narvik, at the very beginning of the war. After that she had two affairs, one with a bank manager who was too old to fight in the war and died of a heart attack in the shelter during an air raid, the other with a Swiss businessman who hurried home before the Russians arrived. The American seemed to be a quiet, undemanding man. Renate agreed.

Chalford rang the bell. He had keys, but he liked it her to open the door to him, neat in a flowered overall, a wooden spoon in her hand, the mixing bowl close to her big, soft bosom. 'There are pancakes for dessert,' she told him, beaming, and went back to the kitchen.

The dining room, the big sitting room and the master of the house's study were on the ground floor of the villa. Chalford worked in the study for half an hour every evening. He would sit at the desk in front of the cupboard where he kept his papers, bending over exercise books from which he took notes. 'A correspondence course in bookkeeping,' he told her. 'My job here in Germany is only for the short term. I have to think of the future.' She admired his ambition and industry,

Today, as usual, he spent half an hour in the study before closing the cupboard and going upstairs to the bathroom. Ten minutes later he reappeared in a comfortable casual jacket. 'What's for supper?' he inquired good-naturedly.

'Pork chops in breadcrumbs, with young carrots and roast potatoes.' She brought him a beer.

He looked at her with pleasure, and that was where his interest in her ended. He wanted only her comfortable presence. She wondered if he had a family. A photograph of a young brunette and two little girls suggested that he did, but he never mentioned them. She hoped he would stay a good long time. She liked their arrangement.

'Do they know any more about that new murder?' she asked. 'It's the fourth victim, isn't it?'

He drank from the bottle. 'They're calling him the Uncle Tom killer. I heard that from a German inspector who visited the office today. They don't have any good leads yet.'

'Well, I hope they catch the brute soon.' She went to put the pork chops in the pan. Soon a promising aroma wafted out of the kitchen.

He waited in the shelter of the decorative shrubs outside Club 48 in the morning. He had to see her, had to imagine over and over again how he would possess her as soon as he had the opportunity. He had buttoned the officer's trench coat with the big tear over the left-hand pocket up to his chin, turning his collar up against the rain. From a distance he could just as well have been an American as a German, except that a Yank would have thrown the trench coat away or given it to a German long ago because it was torn.

She was punctual, as she was every morning. She got off her bicycle, pushing up her raincoat and dress in the process so that her knee and part of her thigh were visible. She untied her headscarf and shook out her long blonde hair. He swallowed in excitement.

It stopped raining. The sun broke through, promising a hot day. He hurried off as if hunted, as if he could escape his own thoughts. But they wouldn't let him go. Even work did not distract him.

When it was dark he took the motorcycle out of its hiding place. Restlessly, he rode through the night, going the same way as usual, but she must have stopped work early today. Women were so unreliable. Disappointed, he put the bike back in the garage.

John Ashburner opened the door when Jutta rang. 'You're early,' he said, pleased.

'By popular request Sergeant Varady is cooking a genuine Szegedin goulash, so my culinary skills weren't called for and I was allowed to go.'

He was still in his basketball gear. They had formed an army side and an OMGUS side, and turned the gymnasium of a school in Dahlem into a basketball arena. The captain's height made him a very welcome member of his team.

They hugged and kissed, and for a moment it seemed they might go straight to bed. Then he turned away and poured himself a bourbon.

'What's the matter, John?'

'Nothing. Or rather, nothing but trouble. Colonel Tucker was in my office today, expressing the city commandant's displeasure in no uncertain terms. The general wants us to work more closely with the Germans to make sure more women aren't murdered. The public are getting uneasy. On the other hand, he doesn't want the Military Police to intervene directly in German affairs. So I have to confine myself to an advisory role.'

'My poor darling. You're between a rock and a hard place.'

'You could say that.' Ashburner sipped his whiskey. 'Sorry, would you like one?'

'I'll make myself a coffee.' She plugged the electric kettle in.

'And by the way, I've written two letters back home to Venice. One to Tony Mancetti, who wants to sell his pasta bar. With my discharge bonus and a loan from the local bank, I could buy it. The red check tablecloths can stay if you like. The other letter was to Ethel. I've told her I want a divorce. She can keep what we've accumulated these last ten years – the house, the life insurance, the Ford and so on. What do you think?'

She put her arms around his neck. 'I think you ought to consider all this very carefully. Because you'll never get rid of me again.'

'If you like, I'll find out whether we can get married in Berlin. Then we could ask your family, and a few friends. Klaus Dietrich and his wife, for instance.'

'And that good-looking Russian with the white sports car?' she teased him.

'Maxim Petrovich? Why not? What about your parents? You must introduce me to them.'

'Father will be delighted. Mother will burst into tears. Both for the same reason: because I'm going to America. I'll fix a time for us to go and see them next week.'

He pulled her close. 'Will you stay tonight, or shall I drive you home?'

'Would you take me home, please? I have to digest all this.' She picked up her shoulder bag. 'That murderer – will you catch him soon?'

'He's very clever. He could even be taunting us. Inspector Dietrich thinks it was no coincidence that his latest victim was found hanging from the third floor.'

'Who was she?'

'Marlene Kaschke, one of the usherettes at the Uncle Tom cinema. Do you remember – those girls with the funny bows in their hair? She obviously knew her murderer. He was visiting her at her home after curfew.'

'Poor thing,' said Jutta, her voice filled with pity.

MARLENE

FRIDAY WAS PAY day. Lene could tell from the strength of the alcohol on her father's breath whether he'd drunk more than half his wages on the way home. More than half meant she'd have to go and see Herr Pohl at the front of the building. He had a skull shaved bald, he smelled strongly of cologne, and he would watch calmly as the fourteen-year-old undressed. Sometimes he fingered her first, sometimes he sat her straight astride his prick, which luckily wasn't very large. Then Herr Pohl would begin snorting, clutching her tight.

Not that it hurt. Lene got the painful part behind her at the age of eight, the first time she was told, 'You go off to Herr Pohl now and ask him to wait for the rent. And don't make a fuss about it.' No, it didn't hurt now, it was just damp and cold in Herr Pohl's basement apartment, summer and winter alike, and Lene shivered, waiting for the moment when the caretaker would finally be finished and she could get dressed.

'And tell your Dad he's got to pay next week, see? Otherwise it's eviction for you lot,' Pohl told the girl as she left.

'Eviction', that dreaded word, loomed over the back yards of Berlin-Moabit like the black smoke from the AEG and Borsig chimneys. For the Kaschkes, father, mother, Marlene and her two little brothers, the bleak picture of a family turned out on the street with their few sticks of furniture and no idea where to go was a familiar sight. Egon Kaschke was on good terms with his foreman at Siemens and had overtime now and then, earning a little extra. That saved them from the worst, usually at the very last moment.

Lene climbed back into the daylight that filtered grudgingly into the four back yards of the five-storey tenement at 17 Rübenstrasse. The yards were evil-smelling playgrounds for rickety children and stout rats. A football goal

245

had been marked out in the second yard, and at the age of six Marlene had dived for balls there like a boy. She kept them out most of the time.

Each yard measured twenty-eight square metres, laid down in the building regulations of 1874 as the minimum size for horse-drawn fire engines to turn. Now, in 1926, the Berlin firefighting service had long since been motorized, and a start had been made on building pleasant housing estates for workers in Britz and Zehlendorf. But these were not available for the likes of the Kaschkes.

Alfred Neubert was leaning against the wall in the passageway between the third and fourth back yards. He wore a suit, collar and tie, which in itself amounted to a challenge to this wretched environment. He nodded to her. 'Hello, Lene, how's things?'

'You back, are you?' It was a long time since she'd seen Fredie, but she recognized him at once, in spite of his stylish moustache. Fredie was nineteen, dark and good-looking, and at the age of thirteen had realized that there was only one way out of Rübenstrasse. He had embarked on his career in the urinals of Alexanderplatz, and continued it in the Tiergarten, where he would go behind the bushes with real gentlemen. The second porter at the Bristol Hotel finally recruited him as a pageboy. The head porter rented out the hotel pageboys to male guests.

A rich Englishman took a fancy to the pretty boy. His mentor travelled the world with him for two years, and then left him for a handsome Moroccan boy in Mogador, abandoning him without a penny. Walking by night and day, Fredie followed the couple to Marrakesh. There he beat up the pederast in cold blood and took his travel funds, all of two hundred pounds sterling. Lord Trevelyan sent to London for more money rather than going to the authorities.

Once back in Berlin, the thief paid his loot, over four thousand Reichsmarks, into a dozen different savings accounts. Besides the money, he had acquired a knowledge of English and French, good manners, and a deep and abiding hatred of men like Lord Trevelyan.

'Just dropped in to see my mother.' Fredie had shaken off the accent of Rübenstrasse and now spoke the Prussian-tinged German of the Berlin upper classes. 'What about you? Still being nice to Pohl?'

'Got anything against it?' Lene spoke in the Berlin working-class dialect that had once been natural to Fredie too.

'Against your being such a fool?' Fredie dug his thumb and forefinger into his waistcoat pocket and brought out a silver one-mark coin. To Lene it was a fortune. 'Here, that's your bus fare. Take the bus from Turmstrasse to Kantstrasse. You get out there and turn right. Weimarerstrasse is on the first corner. Turn right into it. Number 28, back of the building, third floor left, name of Wilke. Ring three times and I'll open the door. Got it?'

'I'm not daft.'

'Come on Tuesday afternoon.' She didn't ask what he wanted her to come for, so overwhelmed was she by this invitation into a different world.

She didn't break into the money, although she was tempted by the thought of riding on the bus for the very first time in her life, preferably on the top deck. Even climbing the spiral stairs to get up there would have been an adventure. But she remained steadfast. She set off on foot at two on Tuesday. She had put on the white lace scarf that Grandmother Mine had left her, the most precious thing she possessed.

She would have walked the long distance faster but for the shop windows, which held displays that were increasingly lavish with every step she went further west. A milliner was showing the most extravagant creations. In Rübenstrasse, such a display would have set off angry pro-tests. Marlene counted thirty different models of ladies' shoes in the window next to the milliner's. She compared them ruefully with her shapeless, old-fashioned button boots. They had belonged to her mother's sister Auntie Rosa, who died of tuberculosis.

She couldn't tear herself away from the display in a butcher's shop. A mountain of ground beef lay on a silver platter, its red appetizingly speckled with white fat, and garnished with onion rings inside which little mounds of plump capers nestled, seasoned with ground pepper and salt crystals. A round loaf of rye bread and a bottle of brown Bötzow lager completed this handsome still life. An enticing message in black writing on a celluloid tag stuck into the meat read '30 pfennigs a portion'. Lene tightened her grip firmly around her one-mark coin.

The window of Hefter's contained a lavish platter of sliced meats, surrounded by cans of other delicacies. Next to it, rich and yellow, lay a sphere of butter; you could tell it was freshly made from the pattern left by the butter pats. Lene knew only the unpleasant-smelling margarine brought from the corner shop where thin, blue, skimmed milk dripped from a tap.

Her mother gave this milk to her younger son. Her breasts had dried up when she was suckling Lene.

Outside the cinema on one street corner, colourful posters and glossy stills from movies lured customers in. The film now showing was called *The Sheikh*, starring Rudolph Valentino, who looked unbelievably handsome. Two usherettes were chatting outside the door. Lene gazed in wonder at their red uniforms trimmed with gold braid. She'd like to be an usherette too. You could see the movies for free all the time, she thought.

At four o'clock she turned into Kantstrasse, and then right into Weimarerstrasse at the next corner. Number 28 was a four-storey building with an ornate façade and pot plants in the tall bay windows. The entrance hall was all marble and crystal, the brass of the folding grille over the lift gleamed. The back of the building wasn't so grand, but compared to Number 17 Rübenstrasse it was dreamy.

She rang the doorbell on the third floor beside the nameplate saying 'Wilke' three times. Fredie opened the door. He was wearing a long, silk dressing gown and smoking a Turkish cigarette in an almost equally long holder. 'Oh wow, you're pretty posh these days!' Lene couldn't help exclaiming.

'Come in.' His room was at the very back of the building. 'Here, sit down.' He pushed a chair in her direction. A Black Forest gâteau covered with chocolate stood on the table. Whipped cream was piled above the rim of the dish beside it. 'Help yourself.' Fredie poured sweet wine into small glasses. She drank too fast and it went down the wrong way.

He watched with amusement as she devoured huge mouthfuls of gâteau and heaped spoonfuls of cream. After the third helping he took her plate away. 'Otherwise you'll be throwing up on me in bed,' he said in a matter-of-fact tone. 'You can have more afterwards. Now, get undressed and wash.' There was a washstand in a niche and a longish, curved sort of basin beside it. 'What's that for?' Fredie poured warm water into the basin from a jug. 'That's for underneath you,' he told her. 'But not just yet.'

Five minutes later she climbed into bed with him. It seemed to her a perfectly fair arrangement, after he had given her so much cake and whipped cream, and the promise of more to come. All she ever got from Herr Pohl was a little longer to pay the rent. Fredie pulled the covers off and looked her up and down.

'You're very pretty,' he said, pleased, as his fingers slipped over her skin. A wonderful feeling went through her as the tip of his tongue made the tiny bud of her clitoris burst into flower. Little sighs rose in the air, culminating in a cry of delight.

That afternoon, young as she was, she experienced what most women didn't even venture to dream of. 'That was nice!' she said breathlessly as she tucked into more Black Forest gâteau and whipped cream.

So for the first time in all those years, Lene rebelled when she was told, 'You go off to Herr Pohl now.'

'Go yourself!' she snapped at her mother, and ran down to the yard, where she kicked the garbage bins. Suddenly everything was different. Until now, the squalor had been hidden by the veil of familiarity. Now it showed its ugly, mocking face. She realized that she had to get out of there before it was too late.

When her mother set off for the Welfare Office with the little ones that afternoon, to beg for an extra loaf of bread, Lene tied her few possessions up in a cloth. She stuck the box containing Grandmother Mine's lace scarf under her arm. This time she marched right on without giving the shop windows a glance. She had to get out, that was her only thought.

Fredie took a long time before to open the door. He was unshaven and bleary-eyed. 'What d'you want?' He yawned. 'Well, come on in.' His room was untidy. A half-eaten slice of bread, on a plate smeared with egg yolk, lay on the table.

She looked at him critically. 'Hey, you don't look so good.'

'I went to bed late,' he said, which was far from the truth. He had gone to bed rather early, and the bed in question had belonged to the widow Deister in Neukölln. Fredie now specialized in mature ladies whom he approached in the Resi dance hall, where the pneumatic message service and telephones at the tables made chatting them up easier. The ladies often invited him home and showed their appreciation of his services. The number of his grateful clients was growing. 'Well, what do you want?' he repeated impatiently.

'I ran away.'

He pointed to her bundle. 'Yes, I can see you ran away. Now what?'

'Now I'm going to be an usherette and work in the flicks.'

Fredie went out of the apartment without a word, and came back via the kitchen with a jug of hot water. 'I told Frau Wilke you're my sister, so you can stay.' He disappeared behind the curtain. Lene heard water splashing and gurgling sounds. He reappeared with his wet hair combed, wiping the last traces of shaving foam from his face. Standing in front of the wardrobe mirror, he put on his collar and carefully arranged his tie. Next came his waistcoat, jacket, and pale felt hat.

'You look really smart now. So?'

'So we're going to get you something to wear yourself.' They took the tram to Tauentzienstrasse, where Fredie withdrew money from one of his savings accounts. In the big Kaufhaus des Westens department store Lene happily tried on a dozen off-the-peg dresses, and chose one with a flowery pattern. Rayon stockings and medium-heeled strap shoes completed the ensemble, although Fredie wouldn't let her put on the fashionable cloche hat until the store hairdresser had set her blonde hair in the latest style and helped with her make-up.

'No one would know you,' said Fredie, satisfied. 'Your parents won't believe their eyes.'

'You're not getting me back there,' she told him.

'You'll hold your tongue and do as I say. I know what's good for you, OK?'

'OK,' she reluctantly conceded.

Egon and Anna Kaschke were speechless when they saw their daughter. Fredie made good use of their astonishment. 'I found Marlene a job as nursemaid with Dr and Frau Schlüter. She'll get ten marks wages.' He took a five-mark piece out of his waistcoat pocket and threw it on the table, where it clinked. 'Here's a first instalment. Marlene will give you the same every week because she can't go to see Pohl any more. I'll drop the money in every Friday.'

Lene was bowled over. No one had ever called her Marlene before. She wanted to say something, wanted to promise her mother and father that she'd be sure to come home when she had time off. Fredie urged her, 'Hurry up, girl, your employers are waiting.'

'I thought you were taking me to those people with the kids?' Lene said in surprise when they arrived back in Fredie's room.

'Look, Frau Wilke is asking five marks more a week because you're staying with me. Then there's five for your mother and father, so they won't make any trouble . . .'

'That comes to ten a week. There won't be any left over.'

'You're quick. Listen, darling. There's a man I know, he feels lonesome, he'd love to meet a nice girl. He'd be happy with just an hour, and he says he wouldn't be mean. So I take you to him, you're nice to him, and we're thirty marks better off.'

Lene was no fool. 'You want me to go to bed with some guy I never met before in my life? Not likely!'

'Then put your old clothes on and get out.' He flung them at her. 'You're not so choosy when it comes to Pohl.'

'I'm not a tart!' she defended herself for the last time.

He drew her close. 'Nobody says you are,' he whispered in her ear. 'You're a sweet little thing.' His lips moved down her throat as his hand wandered between her thighs.

She pushed him away in order to take her dress off. 'So it won't get creased.' She was a practical girl.

She cried out with pleasure under his thrusts, and experienced another firework display of heavenly orgasms. Soon she'd be craving it like an addict, but she didn't know that yet. She cuddled up to him as the sensations died away. 'It's lovely with you,' she murmured drowsily.

'You'll help us get that dough, won't you, darling?' he whispered in her ear.

She didn't answer, but moved slightly away from him. Narrowing her eyes, she thought hard for a minute or so. Then she sat up abruptly. 'Right, then. So where's this bloke who's a friend of yours live?'

'Herr Hildebrand — Fräulein Kaschke,' Fredie introduced them at the door, and made himself scarce. Herr Hildebrand was a coal merchant. 'Wholesale,' he liked to emphasize.

His men delivered fuel from the warehouse beneath the arches of the S-Bahn station to the entire west of the capital. The central heating systems of the blocks where the gentry lived in their grand apartments devoured coke by the ton. Hildebrand was forty, neatly dressed, with sparse hair. He hid his shyness behind a stiffly waxed moustache and a punctilious, genteel manner.

'Delighted to meet you, Fräulein Kaschke, do come right in.' Hildebrand ushered her into the drawing room, where they sat on hard chairs in silence. 'May I offer you some refreshment?' he finally managed to say.

'Ooh, yes,' Lene graciously agreed, and was given a seltzer water with lemon, which she sucked up noisily through a straw.

'A fine day,' said Hildebrand, trying to keep the conversation going. Lene replied with a nod as she went on sucking through the straw with rapt concentration, wondering how he would broach the subject. 'Such a nice day for sunbathing,' Hildebrand continued. 'Would you like to see?'

'See the sun?' Lene was puzzled.

'My balcony.' Hildebrand opened the glass doors. 'South-facing, Fräulein Kaschke. And not overlooked at all.'

Lene went out. A half-lowered awning, a sun lounger, both of them in red-striped fabric . . . gradually it dawned on her. Herr Hildebrand fancied doing it in the open air. 'Then I guess I'll undress and sunbathe,' she announced, and lay down. Herr Hildebrand's eyes followed her, delighted. 'Suppose you undressed too, then we could both sunbathe,' she encouraged him.

Herr Hildebrand withdrew and came back in a dressing gown. Lene spluttered. He had protected his Wilhelm the Second moustache against immoderate outbursts of passion with a broad tape to hold it in place. 'Come here, darling,' she called from the lounger, spreading her thighs.

Herr Hildebrand reached his goal with deliberate, measured movements. The whole business was not unpleasant to her, but she felt nothing at all. He wrapped the dressing gown around his arms, legs and torso and hurried off to get dressed. Lene made herself respectable too.

'With your permission, a little present, Fräulein Kaschke, in the hope that I shall see you again soon.' Hildebrand indicated the small table in the sitting room. Four ten-mark notes lay beside the empty lemonade glass. She put them in her bag, stuffing one down so deep that it wouldn't come to light even when she counted them out for Fredie, who was waiting downstairs.

'Thirty marks, not bad for a start.' Fredie was pleased. 'One of the tens is for you, one for me, the rest for our payments. What will you do with your money?'

Lene was quick at sums. 'Save nine-seventy, buy thirty-pfennigs worth of ground beef with the rest.'

'A little more Beluga, my dear?' Eulenfels dipped the silver spoon into the crystal bowl and piled gleaming grey caviar on Marlene's plate.

'Thank you, Ferdinand.' The downy fair hair on her bare arms shimmered seductively in the candlelight. Eighteen-year-old Marlene smiled at him. She knew the effect she had on men.

'Do you know, they're making a talkie of Dr Mann's novel! That raises an interesting question of copyright, since the movie is based on a book. I shall have to discuss it with our legal experts. The actors will speak and sing just like actors on stage. By the way, the leading lady is called Marlene, like you.'

Ferdinand Eulenfels liked delivering little monologues on subjects related to his profession as a publisher. He owned the most important newspapers and magazines of Berlin, but his real love was books. His authors included several great names and many lesser ones. Eulenfels had invented the idea of the 'One-Mark Book', and was very successful in selling works of light entertainment.

Marlene looked out of the window. Moonlight glittered on the snow-laden trees. The publisher's hunting lodge lay an hour's drive east of Berlin. Eulenfels used it for discreet rendezvous. She had stumbled into his arms at the press ball at the Esplanade, spilling a little champagne on his starched shirt-front, a scene cleverly staged by Fredie. His mature widows were a thing of the past; he now devoted himself entirely to promoting his protégée. He had taught her to speak educated German and eat properly with a knife and fork. Marlene was a good pupil, and lapsed into the language of Rübenstrasse only when she was upset or taken by surprise. French and English were on her educational programme too, and her pretty, youthful looks did the rest.

She quickly understood what was wanted by her clients, rich men in the prime of life who paid generously for the satisfaction of their usually modest desires. Fredie used those desires to finance their apartment in the new Westend district and good clothes for both of them. 'You don't get anywhere without white tie and tails these days,' he had said.

'You mean actors can really speak and sing on screen?' Marlene asked Eulenfels in amazement.

'Yes, indeed. Although I don't really know what the point of it is.' Eulenfels poured more champagne.

'Let's drink this next door.' She picked up her glass and went into the bedroom. When he joined her she had taken off her dress and was standing in her diaphanous lingerie.

'Enchanting.' He kissed her hand. She emptied her glass in a single draught and flung it recklessly into the flickering flames on the hearth. He kissed her shoulder, and she began to breathe heavily. That excited him, something she'd known ever since they first had sex. The rest was routine. She let him do as he liked and uttered little sobs and cries, giving the sixty-year-old man the impression that he was an overpoweringly wonderful lover. It was all over after ten minutes.

As she was leaving he gave her a paperback with a red cover. 'Vicki Baum's latest novel. Do tell me what you think of it.' He escorted her through the snow to the high-built, chestnut-brown Mercedes. The driving seat of the old-fashioned car was exposed to the elements. The chauffeur closed the passenger door and got behind the wheel. Marlene, looking through the glass pane from the comfortable warmth of the back, saw the heavy fabric of his coat, the turned-up collar, the gloves and earmuffs under the peaked cap as they drove through the winter night to Berlin. On the way she opened the book, and a hundred-mark note fell out.

'You must be absolutely frozen. Come in with me and get warm,' she said to the chauffeur when they had reached the apartment.

'That's very kind of you, miss, but it's getting late.'

'Oh, come on.' She switched on the light. Fredie would be at some gentlemen's club or other, hunting for potential clients. He always took photographs of his supposed ex-fiancée with him. She let her Persian lamb coat drop. Fredie had hired it from the Jewish furrier on Spittelmarkt. 'Take your coat off and I'll make you a hot grog.' When she came back with the steaming glasses, he was waiting bareheaded in his grey chauffeur's uniform and shiny black leather gaiters. He was of medium height, with a friendly, round, boyish face, a dimpled chin, and carefully combed, nut-brown hair. He was twenty-eight, she learned later.

Hesitantly, he sat down and blew on the hot drink 'You're very kind. Some of your sort are really stuck-up.' He reddened. 'Sorry, didn't mean it that way.'

'Oh, nonsense!' she said, lapsing into her old Rübenstrasse accent. 'It's no secret what I do. What's your name?'

It was Franz Giese, and he came from Breslau. He grinned. 'Same as most real Berliners.'

'I really wanted to be a cinema usherette,' she said apologetically, explaining herself. 'But as so often happens . . .' Giese nodded understandingly.

Keys clinked. Fredie appeared in a dinner jacket, the inevitable cigarette holder clamped between his teeth. He took in the scene at a glance. 'May I ask what this idyll is in aid of?'

'I brought him up for a moment to get warm.'

'Out.' Fredie jerked his thumb at the door. Franz Giese picked up his coat and cap in silence.

'You could have let him finish his grog,' Marlene complained.

Fredie came close to her. His face expressionless, he rammed his fist into her stomach, making her gasp for air. She writhed under the blow and collapsed into a chair, weeping soundlessly. It wasn't so much the pain – that soon died down – it was her sense of being utterly alone.

Crooking his forefinger, he raised her chin. 'I pick the guests you entertain, understand? How about the money?' She gave him the hundred-mark note from Eulenfels. He took a small notebook out of his pocket and entered the sum. 'Thirty for expenses, thirty-five for me, thirty-five for you.' He conscientiously kept accounts, although she never got to see her money. 'I'm managing it for you,' he replied when she asked about it.

'There's a Herr von Malsen coming to tea tomorrow. I hinted that you're a member of the impoverished aristocracy and very demanding. We can expect a couple of hundred.'

All she wanted was to creep away and forget it all: Fredie, the men, everything about life in the fashionable Westend that was no better than the squalor of Rübenstrasse, just less honest. A thought suddenly went through her mind – Franz Giese is different.

Fredie smiled wryly. Then he pulled her down on the couch. She had no power to resist him. She tried to think of something to put her off, but there was no holding back the orgasm. Contemptuously, Fredie walked away from her.

Herr von Malsen was a wiry man, owner of a landed estate in West Pomerania, who politely asked her to keep her stockings on. Herr

Nussbaum was an asthmatic liqueurs distiller from Köpenick who wanted to be called dirty names. Dr Bernheimer was a Potsdam lawyer who liked to be called Sonja as he was being laced into a corset. She fulfilled all their little wishes, and was generously rewarded.

There was a foreigner among her clients too. She had met him over tea in the Adlon. That trick had proved its worth a couple of times before. Fredie took her into the hotel lounge, then had a pageboy call him and hurried away. Marlene liked the atmosphere. Well-dressed men and women. English voices in the background. Snatches of conversation in French. A German gentleman asking the waiter for the London *Times*. A Swedish woman ordering cigarettes. Two Spaniards greeting each other effusively. Really elegant and international here, she thought, looking at it through Rübenstrasse eyes.

'My brother had to leave unexpectedly on business, and I don't have any money on me,' she told the waiter, loud enough for a solitary gentleman at the next table to hear her. The gentleman was an American, and immediately offered to pay the trifling sum. Marlene smiled in embarrassment. 'How can I thank you, sir?'

'By having a drink with me.' After that he invited her to dinner and champagne in his suite. 'I'm sure you won't mind staying a little longer?' He pushed a hundred-dollar note under her glass.

She laughed. 'How did you know what I do?'

'I saw your companion disappear into one of the telephone cabins, and he was called away straight afterwards. It wasn't difficult to guess the rest — which suits me down to the ground. I'm new to Berlin, and the only woman I've met so far is the cleaning lady at my office.'

His name was Frank Saunders, and he was a correspondent for the *New York Herald Tribune*. 'He spoke quite good German. Which was, not least, what got me the job here. Darn interesting city, your Berlin. Especially in the present situation. Do you think this Herr Hitler will win the election?'

'Can't you ask me something easier?'

'You're not interested in politics?'

'Not a bit. You?'

'Only professionally. Privately, what I love is beautiful women and horse racing, like most of us men from Kentucky. I like to lay a few bets. How do you feel about coming to Hoppegarten with me?'

'Maybe . . .'

He was thirty, and had a boxer's nose. 'Lowered my guard for a split second during the university championships at Yale. That was my reward.'

Frank Saunders was a sportsman, good figure, nice smelling. He was uninhibited in bed and put his mind to what he was doing. 'It's real fun with you,' he said appreciatively. 'I'm moving into my new apartment next week. Will you visit me?' He wrote the address down for her.

From then on they met regularly. Marlene liked the uncomplicated American. Fredie liked the flow of dollars. He even allowed her to go to the races with Saunders. She bought herself an elegant afternoon dress and an extravagant hat, and was delighted by all the beautiful people surrounding them and her good-looking companion in his grey flannels.

They played a little game which excited them both. 'That man in the bowler hat there is a client of mine too. Guess what he does to me?' And she whispered an erotic fantasy in his ear. Another time it was a bony baroness with special tastes. After her, two stylish young cavalry lieutenants. 'Just imagine what those two want me to do . . .'

After the races, back in his apartment, they released their pent-up excitement. It was like a spring storm. He was the first client with whom she felt anything at all, and the first man she liked talking to afterwards.

Then there was Dr Friedhelm Noack, always clad in a black jacket, dove-grey waistcoat and striped trousers, his hair meticulously parted, wearing a silver tie. Noack was a senior civil servant in the Prussian Interior Ministry, but liked to be addressed as Major. 'So he made it all the way to paymaster in the war, but never mind, let's not dash his illusions.' Fredie always knew how to deal with people.

Dr Noack came every Thursday. He would drop into an armchair, groaning, and she would kneel in front of him and unbutton him. It was always quite hard work, but eventually he would come, and then leave looking satisfied. This would have been pure routine if she hadn't been required to service him for free, on Fredie's instructions. 'We don't take money from a friend of the Party,' Fredie had told her. Marlene had not the faintest idea which Party Dr Noack had befriended.

Fredie didn't beat her any more; he had understood the nature of his power over her. He fixed her appointments, and she kept them. Her bank account was growing, at least on paper. He generously allowed her more money for her parents, which she sent them by special messenger.

At around three in the morning one Sunday, Wilhelm Kuhle, unemployed, turned on the gas tap in his one-room apartment in Rübenstrasse, because Pohl and two strong assistants were going to evict him in a few hours' time. He died according to plan, but Marlene's parents and two little brothers would have liked to live a little longer. Gas fumes had passed through the cracks of the partition wall between the apartments.

The funeral was on the last Monday in January 1933. Fredie had anticipated that the newspapers would send reporters, because of all the publicity given to the tragedy, so he had Marlene dress in some old clothes he'd bought from a second-hand dealer. That way she wouldn't be conspicuous, and wouldn't have to answer any questions. On the Monday evening she wore silk stockings and pearls. Herr Eulenfels had invited her to his hunting lodge.

Franz Giese came to fetch her. He was waiting with his cap on by the door of the new Pullman limousine. His leather gaiters gleamed. Marlene shook hands. 'Hi, how's things?'

'Oh, not too bad. Can't complain.' He got behind the wheel.

She pushed the glass partition aside. 'Well, at least you're not exposed to the elements now.' He swallowed, as if he wanted to say something. 'Anything wrong?' she encouraged him.

'Don't know.' He started the car.

'Oh, come on. We've known each other long enough.'

'You mustn't be angry.'

'How could anyone be angry with you, Herr Giese?'

He seemed to be concentrating hard on the road ahead. Then he came out with it. 'I've got an apartment in Schöneberg. All nice and neat. Would you visit me there some time? I'll pay. Just like Herr Eulenfels.'

'But I'm extremely expensive. Can't do it under a hundred and fifty,' she said, lapsing into her old Berlin accent as she tried to put him off.

He pulled over and stopped the car. Face grave, he counted sixteen notes out of his wallet. He handed the banknotes to her in the back of the car. 'A hundred and fifty marks. And ten extra for the taxi. What about Sunday evening? Here's my address.' He gave her a piece of paper.

Fredie was never home before one on a Sunday. 'Comradeship evening,' he told her. Marlene had no idea what that meant.

'Sunday evening. Yes, all right.' She put the money and the piece of paper in her handbag.

At Nollendorffplatz he turned round. 'It'll take us a bit longer today. They closed off Unter den Linden and the Government area for the torchlight procession. It's for the new Reich Chancellor.'

Marlene wasn't interested in Reich Chancellors. She looked at Giese's back, the stiff white collar, the grey cloth of the chauffeur's uniform, on which the neon signs cast patches of coloured light as they passed by. She saw his face in the mirror. No different from the others after all, she thought.

After midnight she was another two hundred marks richer. She had drunk a little too much of Eulenfels's 1926 Ruinart Père & Fils, and on the way home sang a selection from the Comedian Harmonists.

Fredie went through her handbag as usual. 'Three hundred and sixty? Did something special for Herr Eulenfels, did you?' She was too tipsy to answer.

At nine in the morning she went out to buy breakfast rolls. There was a lively discussion going on at the baker's. 'The man's right. He's not letting those foreigners intimidate him. You wait and see, he'll soon see off that disgraceful Treaty of Versailles.' Korff, a retired teacher who lived next door, looked triumphantly around the room.

'Yes, and you just wait – Herr Hitler will soon be locking up everyone whose nose he doesn't care for, like mine,' said the man next to him, Louis Silberstein, flautist in the philharmonic. 'You can read all about it in his ghastly tome *Mein Kampf*. I'm moving to Weingartner at the Vienna Opera. Small white loaf, please.'

'He wants to send Hindenburg into well-earned retirement and bring the Kaiser back,' said the baker's wife knowledgeably. 'Well, we'll be getting the right people to lead us at last.'

'You mean those aristocratic idiots with their *von und zu* titles?' mocked Anita Kolbe, a sculptress who lived in Westendallee. 'Heads like wood all the way through. It comes from all those family trees.'

'Four white rolls, please,' Marlene interrupted the artist.

Back at the apartment, a young man and an older man, both in coat and hat, were waiting for her. 'Superintendent Eggebrecht and Officer Meiser,' the older man introduced them.

'These gentlemen are from the Vice Squad,' Fredie explained with derision. He was in his dressing gown, drying his hair, and appeared more annoyed than anxious. There seemed to be no immediate danger.

The superintendent cleared his throat. 'You are Marlene Kaschke, the tenant of this apartment?'

'And you are a lout!' Marlene retorted. 'Kindly take your hat off. What do you want?'

Eggebrecht actually did take his hat off. 'Another tenant in this building has laid a complaint against you for your immoral way of life.'

'And you believe such nonsense? Well, I'm going to make breakfast. Would you like a cup of coffee?'

She made for the kitchen, but Meiser roughly grabbed her wrist. 'You'll stay in here and answer our questions.'

She placed a sharply pointed heel on his left foot and turned it slowly back and forth. Meiser screamed. 'Behave yourself, you boor,' she said defiantly. Furious, the officer took let go of her.

'Leave it out, Meiser,' said the superintendent, calming him.

'And just who are you?' Meiser jabbed Fredie in the ribs with two fingers at each word.

'Alfred Neubert, Fräulein Kaschke's fiancé. You have no right to burst in here like this. Or do you have a search warrant?'

'Don't get fresh with me, kid.' Meiser jabbed him in the ribs again.

The superintendent remained courteous. 'Fräulein Kaschke, witnesses have noticed a great many gentlemen visiting you.'

'Oh yes? And what sort of witnesses might those be?'

'A man named Ebel on the third floor,' Meiser told her. 'A bookkeeper with an excellent reputation. He has no reason to lie.'

'And moreover, you are often collected from this building by luxury automobiles or taxis,' Superintendent Eggebrecht continued. 'To visit clients, I assume.'

'You assume quite correctly,' said Fredie, his voice calm. 'As a secretary with a good knowledge of foreign languages, my fiancée naturally works outside her home now and then.'

'This pimp's trying to pull a fast one on us!' cried Meiser.

'I can refer you to the Prussian Interior Ministry,' said Fredie coldly. 'As a senior civil servant in that ministry, Dr Noack does not, of course, have to

260

give information to a snotty-nosed little cop like you. But he will be happy to confirm to the superintendent here that the ministry commissions Fräulein Kaschke to translate documents for them and also recommends her to international clients. These clients then either visit Fräulein Kaschke here or ask her to go to their own offices or hotels.' Fredie reached for the telephone.

The superintendent made a deprecating gesture. 'Oh, there's no need, Herr Neubert. Please excuse us, Fräulein Kaschke. Come on, Meiser.' The officers left.

Marlene hugged Fredie. 'Wow, that was great! You really showed them. But suppose they come back?'

'Just leave that to me.' Fredie dialled a number. 'Neubert here. Please put me through to Dr Noack. Hello? Good morning, Major. Yes, a great victory for us all, isn't it? And now I expect there'll be some mopping-up operations. Of characters like a man called Meiser in the Vice Squad, for example. He actually dared to question whether you had been recommending my fiancée Fräulein Kaschke as a secretary with foreign language skills. The man's a Social Democrat or worse. It's possible that his superior officer Superintendent Eggebrecht may be in touch with you, and perhaps you should let him know just what his subordinates are like. Heil Hitler, Major.' Pleased with himself, Fredie hung up.

Marlene giggled. 'Heil *who*?'

Fredie grinned. 'Heil Hitler. That's how the new Reich Chancellor likes to be addressed. He's an Austrian, he's a bit crazy. But I joined his bunch to be on the safe side. Noack's been in it longer than me. You have to back the right horse.'

She pressed close to him. 'Hey, I really fancy you today.'

'Come on, then,' he said graciously.

On Wednesday Ebel, a cross-grained bachelor, was attacked and beaten up by a troop of Brownshirts on his way home. He died on his way to Westend Hospital. Marlene heard nothing about the incident.

There was a healthy smell of soft soap in the hall of the building. The sound of children's voices drifted from of a ground-floor apartment. Marlene climbed the stairs. 'Giese' she read in ornate black lettering on an oval white enamel nameplate on the second floor. She pressed the bell beside it.

Franz Giese opened the door at once. He was wearing a dark suit with a pale-grey tie, attire he had probably copied from Herr Eulenfels. 'Goodness, you do look smart!' Embarrassed, he looked down at the floor. 'May I come in?' Tulips glowed brightly on the round dining table in the living room, a luxury at this time of year. The dining chairs had dark-red, velour upholstery. There was a bottle of wine on the walnut sideboard, and above it hung a gilt-framed picture of a rutting stag in an autumnal woodland landscape. Lace covers adorned the velour sofa, and a potted plant – an African hemp – stood on the window sill. It was all neat and nice. He doesn't often use this room, she thought.

Franz Giese opened the bottle. 'A glass of Piesporter to welcome you? It's really nice of you to come.'

Just in time she stopped herself saying, well, you paid enough for it. 'You have a pretty place here, really comfortable.' She tried to imagine his bedroom. Probably dark oak with a slight musty smell about the pillows. She'd find out soon enough, that was what she was here for. She wondered when he'd get down to business. Some of her clients were keen to get going at once, others needed a long build up. With hopeless cases she took the initiative herself.

They sat down. 'Cheers.' He raised his glass, put it down without drinking, turned it back and forth. This looked like a sticky start.

'Your health, Herr Giese. So you come from Breslau?'

'With a little detour by way of France. I was there at the end of that unholy mess. They sent the regiment straight on to Berlin. We were supposed to put down the rebels.' He spoke calmly and thoughtfully. 'Most of us refused to shoot at our countrymen. The commanding officer was furious, shouted stuff about refusing to obey orders and called us deserters. "What His Majesty can do, we can do as well," I told him to his face, and I was off before he got his breath back. Well, I stayed in Berlin. I was a mechanic in a workshop for big trucks, I'd learnt about them in the army. Then I was a delivery driver for the Tietz department store, and now I'm chauffeur to Herr Eulenfels. Our local union found me the job. I'd better tell you I'm a Socialist.'

'What, a real Red?'

'Not exactly. We Reform Socialists don't want to take stuff away from someone just because he owns more than we do. We want our sort to be better off, without making anyone else worse off for it.' He took plates, cutlery and paper napkins out of the sideboard. 'I hope you like pork chops.' Marlene was taken aback. She had not been expecting an invitation to supper.

'With green peas. You can get them in a can. I'm no great cook. Back in a minute. Drink all you like, there's another bottle.' He disappeared. She heard pans clattering and meat sizzling in the kitchen.

The boiled potatoes had been roughly cut up into irregular chunks. Marlene chuckled. 'I see peeling potatoes isn't your strong point.'

'There's no woman about the house.'

For dessert he brought out a cake on which the confectioner had piped *Marlene* in white icing. He waited with bated breath for her reaction.

'But it's not my birthday until June,' she protested.

'Never mind. Coffee and a kirsch with it?'

She glanced surreptitiously at the time. Something really had to happen soon if she was going to be home when she planned. 'No coffee, thank you. And we can drink the kirsch in the bedroom.'

It took Franz Giese a moment to understand. 'You thought I'd invited you because I wanted to . . .'

Her Rübenstrasse accent broke through as she said robustly, 'Well, that wasn't such a daft idea, was it? Not when you gave me a hundred and fifty, plus an extra tenner for the taxi!'

'I never thought of anything like that. I just wanted to see you. I like you very much. I hope that when you know me better . . . Fräulein Marlene, my intentions are honourable, if you know what I mean.'

'Oh, come on, just call me Lene.' She was touched. She swallowed a couple of times, because she didn't find it easy to dash his hopes. 'I have someone already, Herr Giese.'

Face grave, he devoted his attention to his piece of gâteau. 'I've been thinking about a little haulage business. Starting with a three-wheeled van, they have a surprisingly big load area. Later we could expand, get a three-axled truck, employ a driver. Not a great future, but I'd make a decent living.'

'I'm from Rübenstrasse. Know it?'

'In Moabit. Not a very nice area.'

'Not nice at all. The children there are born with bones like rubber because no one eats enough fruit and vegetables. If you don't get out of it as fast as you can you're finished.' She reverted to her educated German accent. 'It was Fredie who got me out of Rübenstrasse. We've waded through a lot of muck together, but the outlook's good. Fredie knows the right people. He has a great career ahead of him, and I want to be part of it.'

'Will he marry you?'

'Does marriage matter?' She knew just how much it mattered to her.

'I want you to be my wife.'

She shed a few tears. Then she had to laugh because he couldn't get his handkerchief out of his breast pocket for her; he had folded it and fixed it in place with a safety pin. Instead, she blew her nose vigorously on her paper napkin.

'It doesn't make any difference,' he said firmly. 'I want to marry you.'

'. . . I hereby declare you man and wife; allow me to be the first to congratulate you.' The registrar shook hands with the newly married couple. Bright, June sunlight streamed through the tall windows of the panelled room, falling on Grandmother Mine's lace scarf, which Marlene had draped over her blonde hair. She buried her face in her fragrant bridal bouquet.

She reached for the bridegroom's hand. She still couldn't believe it: his almost casual question three weeks ago, her hesitant answer, the proposal. Everything would be different now – no, much better – oh, come on, it would be really good!

Fredie looked fabulous in his light, summer suit. He had been different recently, really nice and pleasant. He'd been bringing her flowers and little presents and taking her out.

'If I may ask for your signatures?' The registrar was waiting at the desk under the portrait of the Reich President. Fredie signed with a flourish. She wrote slowly in her girlish hand: 'Marlene Neubert, née Kaschke'. Like a dream, only much better.

The two witnesses signed next: Dr Friedhelm Noack, who'd been promoted within a few months from his civil service post to a new body, where he was head of his own department, and his secretary, Frau Hermine Anders. In honour of the day, Noack had a carnation in his buttonhole and was in jovial mood. He kissed Marlene's cheek. 'I hope the bride will remain kindly disposed towards me.' She knew what that meant. He had made the arrangements for their wedding breakfast at Horcher's in Lutherstrasse, just why Marlene was not sure. 'To your health, children.' He raised a glass to them.

'Thank you very much, Obersturmbannführer!' said Fredie, addressing his mentor by this new title. It denoted a rank more or less corresponding to lieutenant-colonel.

'Much work lies ahead of us. The Führer needs everyone to be at his place. Or hers – you too, my dear Frau Marlene.' The turtle soup grew cold as Noack embarked on a long discursion on the new Germany. What a load of guff, Marlene thought.

Dr Noack was one of the founders of the new Secret State Police, the *Geheime Staatspolizei*, soon to be abbreviated to the Gestapo. He had appointed Fredie to his staff, in a special operations department. That meant salary group IIIc, and came with the rank of an SS Hauptsturmführer, roughly equivalent to a captain. Marlene remained unimpressed. 'Just so long as the cash is OK.'

It obviously was, for how else could they have afforded their new home, a house on the Kleiner Wannsee with a big kitchen, a tiled bathroom, and a garden running down to the water? She had clapped her hands with delight. 'Oh, just look! What lucky people lived here before us?'

'Jewish riff-raff. But they're gone now, like your Eulenfels.' Eulenfels had been obliged to sell his publishing empire for a fraction of its value, and had moved to London with what was left.

'A cultivated man, Herr Eulenfels. He was very nice to me,' she defended her former client.

Marlene let herself down cautiously from the landing stage into the water. It came up to her shoulders if she dared to stand on the bottom rung of the ladder. She couldn't swim, but she loved the summer warmth of the Kleiner Wannsee. She squealed with glee as the wake of a motorboat racing by lifted her up off her feet. Then she climbed back to the landing stage. Time to make lunch. Fredie came home from the office early on a Saturday. She felt free and happy in her new surroundings, light years away from the squalor of Rübenstrasse and the demands of paying clients. Now she just had her husband and her own home to think of. She even entertained the idea of a baby. She'd talk to Fredie.

At one o'clock an open-topped, silver-grey Horch bearing the SS badge stopped outside the house. It was the official car of Obersturmbannführer Dr Noack, who was in his black uniform today. Fredie preferred a white, raw silk suit. Because of those special operations, he could wear what he chose.

'Enchanting.' Noack's eyes lingered on her figure. She hadn't been expecting a visitor, and was wearing only an apron over her bathing suit. She took the bathing suit off in the bedroom, slipped quickly into a light-weight summer dress, and then laid a third place. They ate in the garden, under an old birch tree. There were stuffed peppers with rice, and a light Mosel to drink. Marlene had acquired some culinary skills. She took her housewifely duties seriously.

Over coffee, Dr Noack got down to business. 'As I'm sure you have guessed, I didn't come just for lunch, for which thank you very much, by the way, it was excellent. Your husband has asked me to explain what we expect of you.'

An uneasy feeling came over her.

Noack took two spoonfuls of sugar and stirred his coffee in a leisurely manner. 'It's about the Communist leader Eddie Talberg. A dangerous enemy of the German people. There's a warrant out for his arrest. He got wind of it and has gone underground. One man certainly knows where Talberg is hiding: his friend the writer Dr Erwin Kastner, one of those intellectuals tainted by Jewish influence who foul their own nests, although we've spared them until now. Kastner goes to the Romanesque Café every afternoon. You will make his acquaintance there and find out from him where Talberg is hiding. Much depends on your success, not least the career of your husband. He will give you the details.' Noack rose to his feet and went into the house.

'Fredie, what's all this about?'

'It won't be difficult for you to get to know Kastner in the Romanesque, I'm sure.'

'Fine. So I get to know this Dr Kastner, apparently by chance. Then what? Am I supposed to ask, "Oh, and just by the way, where's your friend Talberg hiding?"'

'They all talk in bed.'

It took her a few seconds to realize what he was asking. 'I won't do it,' she said firmly.

'You'll do what I want you to do.' He forced her back against the trunk of the old birch tree. Noack was watching from the study window. Fredie pushed her thin dress up to her hips. She was naked under it. He raised her left knee and took her violently, standing. She screamed like an animal. When he had finished, he twisted her arm brutally behind her back and led her into the house. Noack was sitting on the couch. Fredie forced her to her knees in front of him. 'Go on, do it,' he ordered.

Afterwards she went into the bathroom to gargle and shower. Fredie handed her a towel. 'It's not that bad, girl.' He patted her bottom as if to mollify her. 'Noack can do us no end of good if you play along, so don't make such a fuss about it.'

'Why did you marry me?' she asked, painfully.

'A long-standing fiancée with lots of different gentlemen friends no longer suits our sound and healthy German national mood. With these new bigwigs in charge you have to look moral to the outside world.'

She dressed in a light pullover, wide-legged, pale-grey flannel trousers and sandals. She looked at herself in the mirror, a pretty young married woman, fashionably dressed, with an ambitious husband and a home in a prime location. That was how any observer who didn't know better would see her. 'And you're nothing but a tart,' she spat at her reflection in the glass.

Fredie was in a deckchair on the terrace, reading the *Lokalanzeiger*. 'Fabulous!' he cried. 'There's a million and a half motorcars in the country now. Every forty-second German owns one. What do you think of a nice convertible?'

'What do you think of the S-Bahn?' She brought him down to earth. 'You could take it into town and get me some of this Erwin Kastner's books. From now on I'm one of his greatest fans.'

'Astonishing what a bit of exercise against a birch tree will do,' he mocked her.

'One of these days I'll murder you, Fredie,' she replied equably.

Marlene had been reading a great deal lately She indiscriminately consumed everything written by Stefan Zweig, Hedwig Courths-Mahler, Theodor Fontane, Thea von Harbou and many more. The former owners of the house had left their library behind. She spent two days and half a night reading

267

Erwin Kastner's *The Family Visit*, *The Peep-Show* and *The Giraffe's Guide*. They were satirical commentaries on modern life. Marlene sensed rather than understood that the author was knocking holes in grandiose façades.

On Tuesday she went into town, very much the chic Berliner, tall and slim, her blonde hair fashionably set. She noted admiring looks from men, and expertly parried several attempts to approach her. At Stiller's she bought a pair of shoes, and in the Wertheim department store some artificial silk stockings. At Aschingers she allowed herself a couple of sausages for lunch, and in the afternoon she went into the Romanesque Café near the Kaiser Wilhelm Memorial Church.

There was a picture of the author on the dust jacket of one of his books, and she recognized him at once. Erwin Kastner was a dapper little man with wavy grey hair. There was nothing Bohemian about him; he looked more like a kindly public-school teacher in his neatly pressed suit. He was sitting at a little marble table with a dozen well-sharpened pencils in front of him, and a pad of lined writing paper which he was covering with spindly handwriting. Marlene watched him from the next table. Now and then he raised his head, as if searching in the distance for the next part of his story.

She waved to the waiter and gave him a book. 'Would you take that over to Dr Kastner, please?' The waiter did as she asked, and put *The Family Visit* in front of the writer, murmuring a few words and discreetly indicating Marlene. She had slipped a note inside the book: *'My name is Marlene Neubert. I specially like the character of Arnold Wagenfeldt. Could I ask you to sign this for me?'*

Kastner wrote a few words in the book and handed it back to the waiter. *'For Marlene Neubert, from Arnold Wagenfeldt, who doesn't appear in this book,'* she read. She had mixed up Erwin Kastner's *Family Visit* with *The Giraffe's Guide*.

This time he returned her glance. He had an amused expression on his face. She shrugged apologetically, and paid her bill. A man with neatly parted fair hair put down the newspaper holder containing the *Vossischer Zeitung* and followed her. She had noticed him before on the S-Bahn, on her way into town.

'I made contact with Kastner at the Romanesque,' she told Fredie that evening. 'But you know that already.'

'*For Marlene Neubert, my enchanting young reader, from Erwin Kastner, September 1933*,' was the inscription in the copy of *The Giraffe's Guide* that the waiter took over to Marlene's table next afternoon, asking, 'Dr Kastner would like to know if he can offer you a cup of tea.'

The writer rose courteously. He came up to Marlene's shoulders. 'This is very nice of you. Do sit down. Do you come here often?'

'Yesterday was the first time. I wanted to meet you.'

'Well, now you have. A China tea?'

'I'd rather have a coffee.'

'And why did you want to meet me?'

'Let's simply say that I like mature men.'

'Just like that?'

'I'll tell you tomorrow if you'll invite me round to your place. There are too many eavesdroppers here.'

'Will my collection of first editions do as an excuse? I live on Bayerischer Platz. At four o'clock?' He gave her his card.

That evening Marlene handed the card to Fredie. 'He's invited me to his place tomorrow.'

'Make yourself out to be an ardent Young Communist who wants to help her idol Talberg.'

'Kastner's no fool.'

'You'll soon get him where you want him, with your abilities in bed.'

'Don't you mind it when I sleep with other men?'

'No, why should I?' was his surprised answer.

Erwin Kastner made coffee in a kind of double glass balloon over a spirit flame. Marlene watched, fascinated, as the water rose in the device and the dark-brown brew flowed down again. 'A bachelor needs these little house-hold gadgets,' her host told her, rather apologetically.

She pointed to the book-lined walls around them. 'Have you read all those?'

'Most of them. Do you take sugar?'

'Yes please. And how many books have you written?'

'Just under a dozen.'

'Is writing fun?'

'Hellish hard work. I avoid it as soon as I come up with a good excuse.

Sharpening pencils, for instance. I can spend a whole morning sharpening pencils and never get a line down on paper. Wonderful!'

She scrutinized him, not sure whether he was being serious. 'What are you writing at the moment?'

'A children's book. I'm forbidden to write for adults now. I could always go to Austria. I'm told there are some very fine coffee houses in Vienna. But I'm attached to the Romanesque and this apartment of mine.'

'A real children's book?'

'It's called *Lucie the Snake*, about an anaconda who escapes from the zoo. A class of schoolchildren protect her from the keepers' search parties.'

'The way you're protecting your friend?'

'What friend?' he asked warily.

'Eddie Talberg the Communist leader. The *Geheime Staatspolizei* want to know where he's hiding.'

'You are either very clever or very stupid, my dear.'

'Neither. I just don't want to send anyone to his doom, least of all myself.'

'Well, you can tell your masters that Talberg has been in Warsaw for a week, on his way to Moscow.'

'Spoilsport!' she complained, smiling.

'How do you mean?'

'I wasn't supposed to worm that information out of you over a cup of coffee, I was meant to do it in bed.'

He kissed her hand. 'Then you've been spared a disappointment, and I have acquired a charming fan. May I ask why you are working for our new masters?'

'No, you may not!' she said firmly. 'Anyway, I must go now.'

Dr Noack praised her. He had come to supper. 'Good work, even if Talberg has eluded us. You ought to give your wife her reward for that, Hauptsturmführer.'

Fredie took Marlene on the carpet. Then he forced her between Noack's knees. She did what was expected of her.

It was a June morning, and Fredie was getting dressed: pale-grey worsted trousers, white shirt, blue cotton tie. Marlene handed him his lightweight, cream linen jacket. No one would have suspected that this elegant apparition in his mid-twenties was a member of the Gestapo.

'Would you like scrambled eggs or fried?'

'Scrambled, please. And a buttered roll.'

'The coffee's ready. Eggs coming in a minute. I'll just fetch the papers in.' All was well with the world today. The property beside the water, the pretty, roomy house, breakfast with her husband – it was sunny pictures like these that made her think there could be such a thing as good fortune and happiness.

The newspapers were sticking out of the letterbox on the garden fence: the *Völkischer Beobachter*, the official and thus unreadable organ of the Party, and the *Morgenpost*, which so far had retained its comfortable everyday character, apart from a few dutiful political pieces.

Fredie was on the phone. 'Yes, Obersturmbannführer. The Hotel Bristol, room 221. I can guarantee that the operation will be conducted swiftly and smoothly. I'll report back to you personally. Over.'

'Would you like to have breakfast in the garden?'

'My uniform. Come along, get a move on.' He flung off his jacket, tore the tie from his neck, took off his trousers. She helped him into the black breeches made by Benedict, and put the hooks into the tongues of the smart riding boots from Mahlmeister's so that he could pull them on over his calves. Fredie hated uniform, but as it couldn't always be avoided it might at least be tailor-made.

'Fredie, what's up?'

He put on his belt and shoulder strap, took the 7.65 Mauser out of the desk drawer and put it in its holster. 'Get that black dress and white apron on,' he ordered. 'Don't forget the lace cap. And hurry.' She had last worn that costume for a guest who liked to have a housemaid tickle him with a feather duster. Was Fredie taking her to a client with similar tastes? But why the uniform and the pistols? Anxiety took hold of her.

As she straightened the seams of her stockings, he was getting the Ford out of the garage. The car had belonged to a Communist Reichstag deputy who had been beaten to death while in 'protective custody'.

They entered the Bristol through a side door. Fredie raced to the back stairs. He knew every corner of this building from his days as a hotel pageboy. A room-service waiter was wheeling his trolley past on the second floor. Fredie stopped him. 'I'll take that.'

'It's the breakfast for Room 230.'

'It's the breakfast for Room 221 now.'

'But you can't just . . .'

Fredie took out his pistol and loaded it. 'Give me your key to Room 221.' White as a sheet, the man took the key off his bunch. 'And now get out.' The waiter rushed away, panic-stricken.

Fredie wheeled the trolley over to Marlene. He lowered his voice. 'Knock on the door of 221, open it and say: "Chambermaid with your breakfast, sir."' He gave her the key. 'Then you push the trolley in and get over to one side straight away. Go on.' She obeyed, although she guessed that something terrible was going to happen.

'Chambermaid with your breakfast, sir.' She heard her own voice as if from far away. She pushed the trolley into the room. Brown uniform garments lay strewn around the floor. There were two men in the bed, a pretty, fair boy and an older, dark-haired man. The older man put on his glasses. 'You haven't forgotten the orange juice, I hope?'

Suddenly Fredie was standing at the foot of the bed. 'Get out of there!' he snarled at the boy, who obeyed, trembling. Fredie raised the pistol. He saw the terrified face of the man in the bed. To him, it was the smooth, self-satisfied countenance of Trevelyan the pederast. The shots echoed agonizingly in Marlene's ears. The man jerked this way and that, as Fredie emptied the magazine into him in cold blood. The bed was drenched and red.

The naked boy stood in a corner, weeping. 'Put your clothes on and get out,' said Fredie, in a gentle voice. 'Come on, Lene.'

'SA Chief of Staff Röhm personally arrested by the Führer. Seven more treacherous SA leaders arrested at perverted orgies in Bad Wiesensee and Berlin and summarily shot,' announced the evening edition of the paper. Fredie let it fall to the floor and reached for the cognac bottle, in high good humour. 'They'll promote Noack, and he'll be grateful.'

Standartenführer Dr Noack took his time to demonstrate his gratitude. He had many new jobs to be done. When summoned, Fredie would put his 7.65 Mauser in his toilet bag, often staying away for days. Marlene asked no questions, because she didn't want to hear the answers.

Instead she took refuge in her dream. She was floating weightlessly through a truly beautiful cinema, showing members of the audience to their seats. She wore a scarlet uniform with gold braid. Ahead of her she carried a tray of vanilla ices on sticks, and she could lick as many as she wanted. All the people around her were really nice.

She would wake to find herself back in the cold light of reality. Reality meant strangers, to whom Fredie handed her over for his and his boss's purposes whenever it suited. Reality meant Fredie's sexual attacks on her. Her body was greedy for them, while her mind despised them.

The only bright spots were her carefree hours with Frank Saunders. But even he would remind her of reality by unthinkingly handing her the fee in public instead of discreetly putting it in her bag.

Frank Saunders lived in Tiergartenstrasse. On her way to him this Tuesday Marlene went through the park as usual. She heard shouting and laughing behind the bushes. A boy of about ten was tied to a tree, weeping, with a crowd of adolescents prancing around him. They had pulled his trousers and underpants down. 'Jew-boy, Jew-boy!' they sang in time to their prancing, and spat on his circumcised penis.

At the Neuer See she had passed a policeman on his beat, and now she ran back to fetch him. He didn't seem to be in a hurry. 'Do something!' she cried, with the terrible scene fresh in her mind.

'But he wouldn't lift a finger,' Marlene told Saunders indignantly. 'Luckily a young park keeper came along. He grabbed the ringleader and gave him a good shaking. And what do you think the young lout shouted? "We'll get all you Jew-lovers!" I untied the little boy and comforted him as best I could. You ought to write about that sort of thing in your American newspaper. No one's allowed to in ours.'

Saunders was not much impressed. 'No one at home would be interested. And we don't want to harm good relations with our German hosts by writing up some story about silly boys.'

'How bad does it have to get before you all wake up out there?'

'The world is wide awake, sweetheart. It admires your wonderful economic upturn. There is anti-Semitism everywhere, always has been. At least the Nazis admit it.' He drew her close. 'And right now I can think of something much nicer to occupy our minds.'

'That's what you're paying for,' she said dryly.

Ton français n'est pas mal,' Fredie remarked one evening. He had come home late from a meeting at the office.

'Remember how you drummed it into me? I could polish it up a bit, don't you think?'

'You'll soon have an opportunity to do just that. The opportunity is called André Favarel and he speaks hardly any German. He's taking up his post as French military attaché next month. Dr Noack thinks we ought to get him on our side in good time.'

'You want me to go to bed with him.'

'Not exactly. You'll meet Favarel at the Five O'Clock in Eden. He fancies young blonde women with a certain touch.'

'What kind of certain touch?'

'According to our information, Colonel Favarel has a liking for stern treatment. We've hired the Blue Salon at Kitty's. It's wired for hidden cameras. Think something up.'

'You want to blackmail him with photographs.'

'Reichsführer Himmler would like us to stay just ahead of the Wehrmacht's intelligence service.'

'So I'm to play the dominatrix in Kitty Schmidt's whorehouse.'

'You said it.'

She felt hurt and humiliated, and summoned up the very last of her self-respect. 'Well, I won't, understand? And you can tell your friend Noack so too.'

He undid his fly. 'Then we'll have to make the lady a little more willing.' She did not defend herself; it would have been no use. He took her as ruthlessly as ever. The dreaded orgasm came. Afterwards she lay there breathing hard, the victim of her own addiction. He casually did up his trousers. 'Well, darling, have we thought better of it?'

She called on all her strength. 'Not if you stand on your head. I just won't go along with a thing like that.'

Then he beat her, cold as ice, systematically, until she was a whimpering heap. She dragged herself into the bathroom. A swollen, bloodstained horror mask looked back at her from the mirror. 'You'll be as good as new by the time Favarel arrives,' he told her.

The swelling went down, the wounds healed. Her black eye lasted longer, and her injuries gave her time to think, not that she needed it. The will to survive that she had developed in Rübenstrasse told her it was time. Time to go, she thought, just as she had when she set out from Moabit to the smarter area of Berlin.

She packed her things one Monday, folding her most precious possession, Grandmother Mine's white lace scarf, and putting it at the top of her suitcase. Fredie wouldn't be home before seven. That gave her the advance on him she needed. She got a Reich Railways timetable, and put a cross beside a connection from Berlin to Hanover and on to Essen, laying a false trail to be on the safe side. She didn't think Fredie would weep many tears over her, though. He'd just train some other girl. On the other hand, she mustn't underestimate his possessive instincts. He had spent a good deal on her, and he might not be ready simply to wave goodbye to his investment.

She had kept the old passport that gave her name as Marlene Kaschke, a memento of a short trip to Austria. Fredie had found some old Archduke in Baden near Vienna, totally gaga, but he paid well. She'd had to dress up as a schoolgirl and sit on His Royal-and-Imperial Highness's lap.

She had long ago found out where Fredie kept a supply of cash: in the lavatory cistern, packed in oilskin. She took far less than the considerable amount due to her after all these years.

She was briefly tempted to turn to Frank Saunders for help, but quickly rejected the idea. Frank was a paying customer. Paying customers, however nice they might be, wanted a short-term playmate with no strings attached, not someone's runaway wife.

There was a note stuck in the passport. She took it out and read the firm, slightly clumsy handwriting. It was the address that Franz Giese had written down for her back in the past. She had entirely forgotten it, but now it was like a sign from Fate. Of course, Giese would help her. She was about to put the note back where she had found it when the telephone rang. It was Anita, an acquaintance: would she like to go to the movies? 'Sorry, I can't today. See you soon!' Marlene hung up and put the passport in her handbag. The note dropped to the floor.

She took the S-Bahn to Schöneberg. It wasn't far from the station. The entrance hall of the building still smelled of soft soap. She pressed the doorbell on the second floor. It was a little while before he opened the door. 'Fräulein Lene?' he asked, surprised. 'Come in.' He was wearing braces and a collarless, striped, blue wool shirt. His friendly, boyish face had grown thinner, but it was as calm and full of good sense as ever. A man you could rely on, Marlene's instincts told her.

He spoke slowly and deliberately. That hadn't changed either. 'It's pure chance you found me in. I'm just getting the papers ready for my next trip with the truck. They check up on me quite often, my rival Meier sees to that. He's a fanatical Party member, grudges a former Socialist like me the least little thing. Well, never mind that. I'm not interested in politics these days. How are you, Fräulein Lene?'

'Frau Marlene Neubert. I married Fredie. He still makes me go with other men, and he beats me. Herr Giese, I have to get away.'

'Franz to you, Fräulein Lene. Let me make us a coffee. The truck can wait.'

Everything in the living room was as it had been on her first visit: the round dining table, the chairs with their dark-red, velour upholstery, the rutting stag in his gilt frame, the lace covers on the plush sofa, the pot plant in the window.

He had put on a collar and tie, and now carried a tray with the coffee pot, cups, and a tin of biscuits to the table. 'So you've started up your haulage business.'

'With a three-wheeled Tempo. As a one-man outfit I couldn't afford more. You want to get away from him?'

'Can I stay here? I mean just for the time being, until I find somewhere else. I'm sure we'd get on all right. And I owe you a hundred and fifty marks,' she said boldly.

He lowered his gaze. 'I don't like to hear you say such things. And I don't want you to stay either. Not the way you mean. I want everything to be right and proper between us. If you want me at all, then I'll wait, if you don't mind.'

'You're the nicest man I know.'

He cleared his throat, embarrassed. 'A lady I know keeps a boarding house in Charlottenburg. I'll give you a note to take her. What are you planning to do?'

'Be an usherette, I hope.' She laughed. 'I always wanted to be something in the movies.'

The Pension Wolke was in Windscheidstrasse, on the first floor of an apartment building, and looked neat and tidy. In addition, it was a good base for job-seeking at the cinemas of western Berlin.

Frau Wolke introduced Marlene to the other lodgers, beginning with the girl in the room next to hers, who was about her own age and another blonde. Otherwise they were different in almost every way. Henriette von Aichborn wore simple, practical clothes and not a trace of make-up, and had a friendly if slightly distant way of addressing people.

Not like a posh aristocrat with a von in her name at all. Marlene soon took to her. 'Like to come to the pictures?' she asked. 'I'm thinking of applying for an usherette's job at the UfA Palace, and I'd like to see the new film with Willy Fritsch.'

'That's very kind of you, but I'm expecting a visitor.'

'If you'd make do with me . . . ?' Herr Köhler adjusted his monocle. He had the room across the passage, and Marlene did not care for his manner. She was a good judge of men.

'No, thank you,' she politely turned him down.

On Monday she applied to the *Marmor Haus* cinema and the UfA Film Theatre, on Tuesday to the Astor and the Kurbel. No one needed an usherette. She considered her situation over a cup of coffee on the terrace of the Café Schilling. Perhaps it would be better to leave Berlin. Even if Fredie wasn't looking for her, she might still run into him. Involuntarily, she turned round. There was only an old gentleman reading the paper behind her.

She postponed her decision. Berlin was still Berlin, everywhere else was the provinces. But the real reason for her hesitation was called Franz Giese. Better a modest future than none, she thought. And Frau Giese doesn't sound so bad. She pushed aside the thought of facing Fredie and asking him for a divorce. 'It will all work out,' she comforted herself.

She had seen a pair of white sandals that she couldn't resist in the window of the Salamander shoe store. That evening she lay on her bed in her dressing gown, painting her toenails. She had cotton wool between her toes. 'Come in,' she called cheerfully, when someone knocked.

It was Fräulein von Aichborn. 'I hope I'm not disturbing you?' She looked at Marlene's artwork with interest. Obviously she hadn't seen it done before.

'Looks good with bare legs. Bright red is just the thing for blondes. Like to try?'

'Another time I'd love to.' Her fellow lodger came straight to the point. 'A friend of mine has invited me to spend the weekend on the Havel in his motorboat. I'd like to take a friend along to play gooseberry. Would you care to come?'

Marlene Kaschke was absolutely delighted. 'A motorboat on the Havel? You bet I'll come. And I've just bought a fabulous sky-blue Bleyle too! The latest style, with a little skirt and a low-cut back. You can get them in all colours at Leineweber's.'

'Your name is Marion, if you don't mind, and you're an old friend of mine. You must call me Detta.'

'If that's all, you're welcome.'

'See you Saturday, then. I'll get my convertible out of the garage, and knock on your door at seven-thirty.'

'Us two lovelies in an open car? This gets better and better.' Marlene went on painting her nails.

She tried further afield on Friday. There were some cinemas in Steglitz and Zehlendorf. The Onkel Tom cinema was last on her list. 'One of our girls got married. We're looking for a replacement,' the manager told her. 'But it's Herr Star, the owner, who makes the decisions. Come back on Monday.' He let her watch the documentary, the newsreel and a film with Hans Albers for free. On the way home she bought some fruit and took a couple of magazines up to her room with her. Her landlady knocked on her door at around nine. 'Visitor for you, Fräulein Kaschke.'

It was Fredie. 'I'll help you pack,' he offered with a winning smile. 'Thank you very much, Frau Wolke.' He closed the door.

Marlene tried to stay calm. 'How did you get here?'

'I found the note with your Herr Giese's address under the table. Rather incautious of you, my love. Herr Giese was not very forthcoming at first and wouldn't tell me where to find you. He was more talkative down in the chat room. Hurry up, will you?'

'I'm not coming with you. Even if you kill me.'

'Who said anything about killing you? I need a wife who is alive, and plays her part willingly and convincingly. My career depends on it.'

'I couldn't care less about your career.'

'Or your Herr Giese either?'

'What's going to happen to Franz?'

'Very soon nothing will ever happen to him again, if you don't play along. We've taken him in. As I said before, he was willing to give us the information after a while.'

'Where is he?'

'In Prinz-Albrecht-Strasse. Want to see him?' She nodded in silence. He closed her suitcase. Down below, a black limousine was waiting with an SS man at the wheel and a man in a leather coat in the front beside him. Fredie helped her into the car and put the suitcase in.

She saw Franz Giese through a peephole in the cellar door. Her heart constricted. They had tied him to a post. His shirt was in tatters, his face disfigured by blows. The SS man in front of him raised a hissing blowtorch.

'Franz . . .' Her voice was toneless.

'That Socialist would confess to being Stalin's father-in-law if we wanted. They all talk in the chat room. So how about it?'

'Let him go. I'll stay with you.'

'Very sensible, my dear.' Fredie opened the door a crack and called, 'Take him home. The case is closed.' The SS man untied Giese and helped him into his jacket.

On the way home Fredie was kindness itself. 'I've put champagne on ice. And we have a few delicate little canapés to go with it. I'm so glad you're coming back to me.' It was grotesque.

'So what are we celebrating?' she asked without interest.

'I'll tell you when we get home.'

Three-quarters of an hour later they had reached the Kleiner Wannsee. The men saluted. 'Good evening, ma'am. Heil Hitler, Herr Obersturmbannführer.'

'Do I congratulate you on yet another promotion?'

Fredie poured champagne. 'Among other things. Cheers.' Elated, he raised his glass. 'They've appointed Noack head of the Berlin Gestapo. He's shown himself grateful for certain operations I've carried out for him. I'm being made commandant of Blumenau. Orders from on high: the commandant must be happily married.'

'Happily married,' she repeated, remembering Franz Giese's clumsy declaration of love. She would never see him again, and then they would leave him in peace. His injured face would heal. It would smile for another woman some day. The haulage business would flourish. There'd be children. 'Back to the same old round,' she said sadly.

'What do you mean?'

'I mean I'll go along with you. You'll be satisfied. And if anything should happen to Franz Giese I'll make such a shocking scandal that your career will be ruined.'

'You know something? I actually believe you.'

Marlene sipped from her glass. 'Blumenau, did you say? Never heard of it.'

The Mercedes drove through the tall gates. Bronze swastikas were worked into the wrought-iron grille of the gate, and beds of begonias in lines that could have been drawn with a ruler bordered the drive. They drew up on the white gravel outside the house, which had a red, twin-gabled roof and welcoming green shutters. Over the door, picked out in marguerite daisies, were the words: WELCOME TO BLUMENAU.

Fredie helped Marlene out of the car. He was wearing his new dove-grey uniform with the insignia of an SS Security Service Obersturmbannführer. A girl in a striped dress and apron was waiting on the steps, holding a bunch of tulips. She had spiky black hair and kept her eyes lowered.

'This is your housemaid Jana,' Fredie introduced her. 'If you need more domestic staff, let me know. I don't want the housekeeping to be a burden on you.'

He had been acting in a very civilized way these last few days. It was probably to do with his new post. If only this goes on, she thought hopefully. Jana held the flowers out to her. 'Thank you, how nice.' She took the bouquet. 'I'm sure you know where we can find a vase.' She used the polite *Sie* pronoun to address the girl.

'Jana is nineteen and used to being called *du*,' her husband corrected her. 'I have to go for a meeting in the office building now. It's over there.' He pointed to the tall, impenetrable yew hedge and a grey, corrugated-iron roof just above it. 'Jana will show you the house. We are expecting a few of my staff to dinner this evening. Don't worry, the girl can cook.' He moved quickly away over the crunching gravel.

'Shall we go in, Jana?' The driver had put her cases in the yellow-tiled hall. 'Show me the kitchen first.'

'Yes, Frau Obersturmbannführer.' Jana stumbled over the pronunciation of the long title.

'You just forget about all that!' Marlene told her firmly. 'I'm Frau Neubert, right?'

'Yes, Frau Ober . . . Frau Neubert.'

'Good. Now for the kitchen.'

'Yes, Frau Neubert.'

Blue and white tiles on the floor and walls, a black, cast-iron coal-burning stove with shiny brass fittings, a large fridge made of white wood and lined with zinc. It had a nickel-plated tap at the front to drain off the melted ice water. A pantry beside the cellar steps.

The dining room next to it and the living room contained the familiar, pale-wood furniture from the Kleiner Wannsee house. Upstairs there were three bedrooms and two bathrooms. From up here you had a view of old fruit trees and a neatly raked lawn. A wall covered with climbing roses divided the garden from the road. It was a spacious and idyllic property.

'I think I shall like this place. Have you been here long, Jana?'

'One year five months.'

'And before that?'

'Everywhere.' Jana couldn't be induced to say more.

Marlene's neighbour at table was a thin man in his mid-thirties with dark hair and, despite careful shaving, a trace of five o'clock shadow. 'Our medicine man, Sturmbannführer Dr Alwin Engel,' Fredie had introduced him. Marlene found him interesting, because he talked about literature. He had read Erwin Kastner, which gave her an opportunity to show off her own knowledge. 'His children's books are little masterpieces. More for adults really, don't you agree?'

Engel didn't seem to have heard her. He was watching Jana as she brought in the starter: smoked herring fillets on lettuce, with grated horseradish. He took hold of the girl's chin and turned her face to him as she served him. 'What pretty black eyes you have,' he said, smiling. Jana vanished into the kitchen. 'Purely professional interest,' he said apologetically.

Marlene was understanding. 'Jana is a pretty girl, though not very communicative, I'm afraid. I asked where she'd been before, and couldn't get anything out of her except "Everywhere".'

Engel smiled. 'Well, of course Jana has been everywhere, up hill and down dale with her people in their caravan. My dear lady, the girl's a gypsy, didn't you know?' Jana served the main course. Engel raised a piece of meat from the platter with his fork and examined it critically from all sides. 'I do hope you haven't palmed us off with roast hedgehog.' Everyone laughed.

'No, Herr Sturmbannführer.'

'This is roast duck from our own farm. Like the vegetables and the cream for the sauce. We are self-sufficient here, Dr Engel,' a tall woman of around forty answered him. She had penetrating blue eyes and heavy fair hair worn in a chignon, and she alone hadn't joined in the merriment.

Marlene had noted down the names of the guests on her napkin, so she knew that this woman, seated opposite her, was Gertrud Werner. Frau Werner had high cheekbones and regular features, very much in line with the new Germanic ideal of womanhood. She was wearing a long, dark-blue velvet dress with a white collar fastened high at the neck, and her healthy complexion showed that she spent a good deal of time out of doors. She had glanced disapprovingly at her hostess's fashionable make-up and modish Berlin outfit. Marlene instinctively disliked the woman, but she didn't show it. 'You really must show me round, dear Frau Werner. Perhaps I can even help a little on the farm?' she asked, feigning interest.

'My women do that themselves,' said Gertrud Werner coolly.

'Now, don't be stern with our city girl, Frau Hauptsturmführerin,' said Dr Noack, smoothing things over. So Frau Werner held SS rank in her own right. Noack had arrived only a few minutes earlier from Berlin, with a large bouquet of tea roses for Marlene and a bottle of cognac for Fredie.

'I'd be happy to show you round, Frau Neubert,' the guest to her right offered.

Marlene consulted her napkin. 'That's very kind of you, Herr Schäfer.'

'Nothing here works without Oberscharführer Schäfer. He's our real boss,' announced Fredie good-humouredly, eliciting an awkward grin from the heavy-set man with bristly grey hair.

'Don't let his better half hear that,' the young man next to Frau Werner joked.

'Untersturmführer Siebert runs our laboratory,' Fredie told his wife. Marlene's head was swimming with all these elaborate ranks and titles; the napkin was no help there. 'Siebert is a bachelor and very popular with the girls.'

'How interesting.'

'That I'm a bachelor or that I run the laboratory?' Siebert winked at her.

'As a happily married woman, I mean the latter. What delicious things do you brew up in your witches' kitchen, Herr Siebert?'

'We're doing research work.'

The telephone rang. Fredie picked it up and listened briefly. 'Doctor, it's Raab. His circulation is going crazy.'

Engel leaped to his feet. 'I'll see to him at once.'

'Don't let anything go wrong,' Noack told him. 'Reichsführer Himmler takes a personal interest in him.'

The doctor returned during the dessert course. 'His circulation has stabilized. Would you excuse me, ladies and gentleman? I have to be up quite early tomorrow.'

'Time we all went our separate ways,' Noack said. 'Thank you very much, dear Frau Marlene, a delicious meal. It deserves a special reward.' She knew what he meant.

Fredie and Noack were waiting for her in the drawing room. Fredie seized her and took her on the floor, while Noack watched avidly. Then Fredie forced her down between his mentor's knees.

Years earlier, just once, she had said it out loud. Now she repeated it over and over in her mind. One of these days I'll kill you, Fredie.

Her husband had already left by the time Marlene woke. She took a bath and dressed. Jana was waiting for her in the kitchen with steaming white coffee and fresh croissants. The sun filtered through the leaves of the fruit trees, casting bright patterns on the table. The world was all right again.

'Sit down, have a coffee with me. Would you like a croissant?' The girl shook her head vigorously, making her short black hair fly. 'Oh well, if you don't want to . . . You've been here eighteen months, you said? Wouldn't you rather be with your family?'

That silent shake of the head again, a gesture that might mean no, or denote fear or incomprehension. Marlene couldn't make the girl out. Perhaps gypsies just reacted differently from normal people. Although gypsies were really normal people too — only a little *different* from normal people.

'Is there a basket around?' She shook off these complicated thoughts. 'We'll go and ask Frau Werner for some vegetables. I'm sure you'll know where we can find her.'

Jana found a large basket in the larder. They went from the kitchen to the garden, and crossed the forecourt to the yew hedge. A green tunnel led through it to a corrugated iron door at the far end. Jana pulled the bell beside the door. It clanged, and a flap in the door was raised. 'Open up for the Frau Commandant.' Jana obviously enjoyed giving an order.

The guard let the flap drop into place and opened the door. 'Sorry, Frau Obersturmbannführer, didn't recognize you.'

'Look, I don't want to be called Frau Commandant or Frau Obersturmbannführer. I'm Marlene Neubert. Would you please repeat that?'

'Certainly, Frau Neubert.' The guard went a few steps with them.

She pointed to the low, wooden building at the end of a well-tended gravel path. 'Is that where my husband works?'

'Yes, Frau Neubert, that's the office building.'

Jana bent over the rose bed at the entrance and smelled a flower. 'Pretty roses.'

'You like roses?'

'Yes, I like them very much.'

Marlene turned a few leaves over. 'Greenfly. The bushes need spraying. Soap solution would do it.' She'd learned that from the woman next door to them at the Kleiner Wannsee house.

'I'll tell the trustee.' The guard went back to his post.

'We'll visit my husband later – let's go and find those vegetables. Come on, Jana.' The gravel crunched under their feet. 'Are your parents around here somewhere?'

Jana put the basket down. 'Mama over in women's camp. Papa at fence, wanted talk Mama a little, like used to. Frau Hauptsturmführerin see. Call Oberscharführer. Oberscharführer come with big stick.'

'What, that nice Herr Schäfer? He surely didn't . . . ?'

'Did,' was the laconic answer.

'I expect he lost his temper for a moment. As far as I know the supervisory staff aren't allowed to use violence. Your father should complain.'

'Oberscharführer hit Papa with big stick till Papa dead,' was the matter-of-fact reply.

Marlene felt paralysed. It took her a long, long time to react. 'It must have been an accident. I'm sure Herr Schäfer didn't mean to hit so hard,' she said, trying to retrieve her view of the world as it ought to be. 'What about your mother?'

'Mama seven days in cellar with rats. When she come out, three toes gone.'

'Three toes?' Marlene was horrified.

'First you not want sleep. Then you must sleep. Rats wait till you sleep.' The gypsy girl picked the basket up again. Marlene followed her – and froze. Ahead of her, a tall barbed-wire fence clawed its way up to the sky. The wooden watchtowers at its four corners seemed to have been borrowed from a chess set for giants. A guard with a dog was on duty at the gate. Huts of a dirty grey hue lay beyond it, in rows of five. Not even weeds grew on the perfectly straight clinker paths between them.

Before they arrived, Fredie had explained to her, 'Blumenau is where they put people who don't belong in our society. Jews, homosexuals, Communists, gypsies and so on. Those who really want to prove their worth can do it by working. As camp commandant I'm responsible for discipline and order.'

An eerie silence lay over this bleak wilderness. 'But of course, the people are all working.' She was relieved to have found an explanation for the deathly silence. She nodded to the guard. The dog growled as they passed him.

'You strong, you work, you eat.' Jana pointed to a row of neat dark green wooden buildings in the background, obviously the workers' quarters. She pushed open the door to one of the grey huts in front of them. A stench of excrement and urine met them. When her eyes were used to the dim light, she made out long rows of wooden bunks stacked four high. On them cowered skeletons with skin stretched over them, wearing striped rags. Heads shaved bald were raised, with difficulty. Eyes lying deep in their sockets stared expressionlessly at her. 'No work, no eat. Only get thin soup.' Jana spoke like a tourist guide, her voice devoid of emotion.

Marlene felt only a dull emptiness. In the last five minutes she had seen more horrors than in her entire life. The squalor of Rübenstrasse was a sunny memory by comparison, the repulsive desires of men who paid for sex a harmless bit of fun. 'I'll speak to my husband. I'm sure he doesn't know anything about this.'

Jana pointed ahead. 'Farm there.' The striped backs and headscarves of

285

a hundred women weeding rose in hunched outline above the endlessly long vegetable beds. Women overseers supervised the work.

Hauptsturmführerin Werner stood tall and slender between the beds, her cap pulled down over her forehead. She was wearing boots with her uniform coat, and carried a riding crop. In a terrible way she was beautiful, and well aware of it. Marlene went towards her. 'Good morning, Frau Werner.'

Jana muttered something that sounded like 'Good morning.' She was evidently frightened.

Marlene offered her hand. Frau Werner ignored it. 'I came to ask you for some vegetables. A few carrots and sugar peas, and two lettuces, if you wouldn't mind.'

Frau Werner turned to the gypsy girl. 'Have you forgotten how to address me in your new position?' she hissed.

Marlene leaped to Jana's defence. 'She did say good morning.'

'Come here. How do you address me?'

Jana took a step forward, assumed a wooden military stance, took a deep breath and shouted, her voice breaking, 'Prisoner 304476. Heil Hitler, Frau Hauptsturmführerin.'

There was the ugly sound of a blow. A bloody weal crossed Jana's cheek from her left ear to her chin. Frau Werner lowered her riding crop. 'To help you remember how to speak to your superiors.'

Marlene was beside herself. 'You monster! My husband will see that you pay for this!'

Gertrud Werner looked her coldly up and down, and kicked the prisoner crouching closest to her in the ribs with the toe of her boot. 'A basket of carrots, sugar peas and two lettuces for the Frau Commandant. Free delivery to the big house,' she added mockingly.

'Come along, Jana. Dr Engel will see to you.' The red cross on the white background showed Marlene the way. The infirmary building was all sterile white tiles. Surgical instruments glittered in little glass-fronted cupboards. A swing door led to the next room, obviously the operating theatre, from which a smell of disinfectant wafted.

Jana screamed as the doctor dabbed alcohol on her would. When that dreadful woman hit her she didn't utter a sound, Marlene thought in surprise.

'Fancy hitting out like that – terrible!' she said to the doctor, venting her outrage.

'Very unpleasant, admittedly. Camp life gets on all our nerves. To be honest, I'd rather be at the Front. We're marching west now after our blitzkrieg on Poland.'

Dr Engel pulled down the girl's lower lids down. 'Fascinating, these black gypsy eyes.' He stuck a large plaster over her cheek. 'The wound will heal in a couple of days.'

'The people shut up in those grey huts are starving. They get nothing but thin soup.'

Engel took a test tube from its holder and held it up to the light. 'The commandant is responsible for the camp. My place is here with my scientific work.'

'We won't trouble you any longer, doctor.'

'Oh, you're not troubling me. Do visit me whenever you like.' Engel patted Jana's unharmed cheek.

A young woman prisoner was waiting for them in the kitchen with the basket of vegetables. She whispered something in Jana's ear and then ran away full tilt. 'Sema gypsy too.' Jana began shelling the peas into a pan.

'A good-looking man, Dr Engel. I think he likes you.' Marlene picked up a handful of pods and helped to shell them.

'It's nine o'clock,' she told her husband when he came home late from the camp that evening.

'No end of administrative stuff. Sorry, darling, I should have let you know. Or you could have called. The field telephone in the kitchen connects directly to my office. You only have to lift the receiver. So take care cleaning – a temporary connection like that isn't very stable.'

'I'll remember that. Come and eat.' She was determined to talk to him about conditions in the camp and Hauptsturmführerin Werner after supper, but he nipped her story in the bud. 'By no means is everything here just as it should be. Getting the place under control is a considerable task, but I shall do it. And I want you backing me up, right?' Marlene understood. He didn't wish to be bothered with complaints.

'Thank you, Jana, go to bed now,' she dismissed the girl. 'We'll wash the dishes tomorrow. Goodnight.'

'Heil Hitler, Herr Commandant. Heil Hitler, Frau Neubert.'

'Nice girl.'

'A prisoner like the others, don't forget that.' Fredie poured himself a cognac and leaned back comfortably in his armchair. 'Not bad, this house, eh?'

'As long as the hedge is high enough,' she couldn't help saying.

When she went to lock the door of the house, she heard quiet weeping outside. Jana was sitting on the steps, her head between her knees. 'Hello, child, what's the matter? Don't you want to go to bed?'

The girl raised her tear-stained face. 'Sema say Frau Hauptsturm-führerin very angry. She wait for Jana with whip.'

'I'll go with you. She won't dare do it again if I'm there.'

Agonized black eyes looked up at her. 'When Frau Neubert gone, Frau Hauptsturmführerin more angry. Then Jana have to go in with rats.'

'Come along.' She drew the girl back into the house and took her upstairs. Fredie had already gone to bed. There were a couple of mattresses in the attic. 'This will have to do for tonight. Tomorrow we'll see.'

As usual, Fredie was in a good temper at breakfast. He gave his permission for Jana to move into the house. Marlene was delighted. She cycled into the village and bought flowered linen curtains and bedlinen. They found some sticks of furniture in the attic, and she and Jana painted them pale blue. Together they refurbished the little attic bedroom.

In the afternoon she picked up the field telephone to ask Fredie if he wanted to come over for a cup of coffee. Surprised, she heard both his voice and a stranger's. He was speaking to his head office in Berlin. She hung up again at once. There was probably some problem in the temporary line, which went out of the kitchen window and then wound its way from tree to tree and over the yew hedge to the office building. She'd mention it to him.

Jana brought her an old nickel-plated alarm clock that she had found in a chest. The thing rattled fit to wake the dead. 'Well, you won't oversleep and be late for work,' Marlene teased her.

'Jana not sleep. Jana like work for Frau Neubert.' The girl flung her arms round Marlene's neck and kissed her cheek.

'Oh, what nonsense,' said Marlene, moved. 'Tell you what, I'll ask my husband if you can cycle into the village to fetch the breakfast croissants from the baker's. Can you ride a bike?'

'Not know.'

'Never mind, child, I'll teach you.'

Jana squealed when Marlene put her on the bicycle. They both had a lot of fun, and Marlene forgot all about the telephone.

You couldn't forget about the camp. It was omnipresent. When the wind blew from there towards the house, Marlene could smell it. It smelled of hunger, latrines and mortal fear, of the sweat of its inmates and the black shoe polish the slaves used to clean their masters' belts and boots.

She avoided the camp, but the camp came to her every day, when a female prisoner brought the vegetables. Then she saw not the basket of lettuce and carrots but the army of women's bent backs among the endless vegetable beds.

Fredie banned Jana's expeditions to the village, so Marlene herself cycled to Blumenau once a week to do the shopping. Conversation in the grocer's shop died away when she came in. There was suspicion, fear and hostility in the air. She felt like crying out, 'I can't help it! None of this is anything to do with me!' She didn't, offering a friendly greeting instead. Today, Friday 14 June 1940, the radio drowned out her voice. The German Army had occupied Paris.

She bought bread and butter; their rations were generous, and there was a special allocation of coffee and chocolate from looted stocks. The British had abandoned all their supplies of food in their headlong flight to the Atlantic coast.

Outside the shop, someone asked her quietly, 'Can I speak to you?' The woman was about fifty, simply dressed, holding her small handbag close to her breast. In her other hand she carried a brown paper shopping bag. She looked careworn and sick. You could only guess at the beauty that had once been hers.

'Speak to me? Why?'

'You're the commandant's wife. My name is Mascha Raab. My husband is in your camp.'

'Raab?' Marlene remembered the name. 'He had something the matter with his circulation. Dr Engel treated him.'

'He's a diabetic. They take good care of him so that he'll last a long time. Pure philanthropy.' There was no mistaking the irony in her voice.

'You are very incautious, Frau Raab. Don't forget, I'm Obersturm-bannführer Neubert's wife.'

Mascha Raab lowered her handbag. A yellow Star of David with the word JEW on it came into view. 'People like me are perceptive. It's a matter of survival. I sense that I have nothing to fear from you.'

'But suppose your feelings deceive you?'

'Then you can have me imprisoned or killed. That's all. Forgive me, I didn't mean to alarm you. They won't do anything to deprive Georg of hope.' She raised her shopping bag. The neck of a bottle stuck out of it. 'A 1934 Chablis. Very dry, suitable for diabetics. A luxury – Jews aren't allowed such things. But the wine merchant knows us from the old days. Georg loves French wines, and today is our thirtieth wedding anniversary. Would you give him the bottle?'

'I'll ask my husband to let you have a visitor's permit as a special case.'

'No, just take Georg the bottle. Lie to him for me – say I'm looking young and healthy, tell him I'm confident that he'll soon be back with me. My train leaves in ten minutes. You're a good woman, I know you are. Goodbye.'

*

Fredie sat down to lunch in very good spirits. 'The Frogs are as good as done for. Now for the Tommies. What's new in the village?'

'Just imagine, a woman called Frau Raab approached me. Out of the blue! What a nerve those Jews have! Said her husband was here in the camp, and could I take him a bottle of wine for their thirtieth wedding anniversary? Well, I brought the wine back with me. What do you think?'

She had struck the right note. Fredie nodded.

'Raab is a special case. What's for lunch?'

'Veal schnitzel *au naturel* with cream sauce and rice. And green beans on the side.'

'Schäfer can take you to Raab when we've eaten. Incidentally, I have to go away for a couple of days, to compare notes with my colleague at Buchenwald. Not a very inviting prospect, they say his wife is a terrible cook. Hurry up, Jana. I'm ravenous.'

Oberscharführer Schäfer was waiting for Marlene at the door beyond the yew hedge. He had taken off his peaked cap and was mopping his brow. 'A hot day, isn't it?' The bristly-headed man attempted a smile. He looked like

290

the doorman of a second-class hotel hoping for a tip. He did not look like a murderer. That was the thing that made the executioners of Blumenau so terrible: they were ordinary men and women who smiled, perspired, made love, went to the lavatory and looked forward to pay day.

Schäfer hit the corrugated iron with his stick. It made a hollow sound like a drum in the African bush announcing some misfortune. The guard opened the door at once and stood to attention. 'That's all right, my boy,' the Ober-scharführer thanked him jovially. 'This way, Frau Neubert.' He trudged towards a bungalow that stood outside the camp itself, like the office and infirmary buildings. Here too, gravel paths and well-tended flower beds would give visitors the impression that the atmosphere was one of calm and beauty. Inside, the bungalow was clean and cool. Polished, pale-grey linoleum muted the sound of Schäfer's hobnailed boots. There was a door at the end of a corridor. 'Visitor for you, Raab. In you go, Frau Neubert.'

A room flooded with light, a cross between a workshop and a laboratory. A chubby little man with a white coat over the coarse, cotton uniform worn by inmates. He was wearing a Helmholtz mirror on a band around his fore-head. He folded the mirror up, revealing intelligent brown eyes, and stood stiffly to attention, which looked rather comic. 'Prisoner 48659, Heil Hitler,' he said in a quiet and friendly voice.

'Are you Herr Raab?'

'In an earlier life I was Dr Raab. Professor Georg Raab.'

'I'm Frau Neubert.'

'I know, madame.'

'My congratulations on your thirtieth wedding anniversary, and greet-ings from your wife.' Marlene handed him the bag with the bottle in it.

'Mascha came here?'

'I saw her down in the village. I'm afraid it wasn't possible for her to get a visitor's permit. She's looking fine, she's in good health. A beautiful woman.'

'Oh yes, she is indeed beautiful.' An expression of reverie appeared on his face. He took the bottle out of the bag. 'Wonderful, a 1934 Chablis. To think such things still exist! I shall allow myself a glass at supper. It would be better in company, but I mustn't ask too much.'

'Don't you have to go back to the huts at night?'

'I have a comfortable little bedroom here, my own bathroom with a lava-tory, and the same meals as the guards.'

'As an inmate of the camp?'

'They need me. Please sit down, madame.' He pulled out a chair for her. 'Your husband has let you visit me, so he obviously has no objection to your knowing what I'm doing here, even though it's top secret.'

'That sounds intriguing, Professor!' A touch of the old Berlin accent crept back into her voice.

'A genuine Berliner, and a particularly pretty one too!' Raab rubbed his hands, delighted. 'We live in Köpenick, in the Wendenschloss district, if you happen to know it.'

'Sorry, no.'

'A pretty place. You should visit us there some time.' He bowed his head and added quietly, 'They've let Mascha stay on in a little room in our house.'

He picked up a sheet of white paper, put it in the printer's block by the window, and turned the handle of the wooden spindle until its leather pad pressed the paper down on the plate. He took the paper out and held it up. 'Would you like to see?' Marlene could make out ornate black lettering on a white background.

'A banknote for twenty pounds sterling. The paper and the watermark will stand up to any examination, it's almost as well printed as the original There's a tiny flourish on the C of the words "Chief Cashier" still missing. I'm about to add it. Well, what do you think?' There was a touch of pride in Raab's voice.

'Forgeries?'

'Forgeries that even the Bank of England will take for the real thing. Once they're put into circulation in their millions, they're expected to wreck the British currency. A project devised by the SS Office of Economic Affairs, at Himmler's instigation.'

'You're a forger?'

'Oh, a dedicated forger. Also former professor of art history at Berlin University, now dismissed, and a former member of the Prussian Academy of Arts. In addition I'm a trained engraver, both copperplate and woodcuts. Even eminent international art experts have fallen for my Dürers and Piranesis. Until recently I pursued my hobby for fun and never made any money out of it. Now it's paying off. They let me stay alive a little longer, and they spare my Mascha.'

'You're very frank with me, professor.'

'Mascha trusts you, that's enough for me. And furthermore, they need me. So long as Himmler's pince-nez look kindly on me, I have nothing to fear . . .'

'And when you've finished your work?'

'Oh, there's plenty more to be forged yet. We're working on dollars and Swiss francs, for buying armaments. Passports of all countries are in preparation for the secret services, ID papers, military marching orders, certificates of appointment . . . I have originals of all those documents here in my wall safe. They're already combing the prisons for capable people to work with me. Oh, there you are, Herr Siebert.'

The young Untersturmführer wore a laboratory coat over his uniform. 'Hello, Frau Neubert. What an honour for our witches' kitchen! Professor, we've raised the nickel content of the security thread by 0.03 milligrams. I hope that was right.' She was surprised to hear the SS man speaking to a prisoner with such respect.

'Thank you, Herr Siebert. Excuse me, madame, I want to get back to that flourish. Will you visit me again?'

'And me too?' Siebert was clearly always eager for a little flirtation.

Marlene ignored him. 'Yes, indeed, Professor. Good day, Herr Siebert.'

'I'll find you a cushion to make you more comfortable, Professor,' she heard Siebert say as she left. A thought went through her head: in other circumstances, would the SS man kill Raab out of hand?

*

'A one-pot dish, the kind of thing the Führer wants to see on every German lunch table once a week. With water from our well. And as dessert, fruit bottled from our own harvest. We are proud of our simple, nourishing food.'

'Oh, don't talk such garbage!'

Fredie was nervous. Reichsführer Himmler had announced a visit. He wanted to inspect the forgery project personally. It went under the cover name of Needle and Thread; the Bank of England was in Threadneedle Street.

'A beef, pork or mutton one-pot dish?' inquired Marlene.

Fredie's old bent for sarcasm surfaced. 'Chicken. After all, the man used to be a chicken farmer.'

'I'll tell Jana.'

'Good German women make their own one-pot dishes. Help in the kitchen in this second year of the war is a luxury the nation can't allow itself. Oh, and remember that good German women don't smoke. No lipstick either.'

'Anything else? Maybe a wheatsheaf on the table and place cards in Germanic runes?'

'Send Jana back to her tribe in the gypsy hut.'

'So Frau Werner can torment her? No, I won't have it.'

'I've told everyone to go easy on the day of the visit. Seems our guest is rather squeamish when things move from theory to practice.'

'What, a day without beatings and murders? The camp won't feel like home to you, Fredie.'

'Oh, shut up,' he said angrily.

*

They had dressed Professor Georg Raab in a brand-new, striped prisoner's outfit, with a matching round cap. He stood outside the laboratory-cum-bungalow with Fredie and Untersturmführer Siebert. Like a teddy bear in a zebra skin, thought Marlene, watching the scene through a crack in the corrugated-iron door. She had not been allowed to attend the official viewing.

Two heavy, open Mercedes rolled into view. Out poured men in caps bearing the death's head badge, dove-grey uniforms and shiny black riding boots. Marlene recognized the pince-nez under the peaked cap leading them. Fredie stood to attention as he made his report. His uniform jacket was a little tight around the waist these days. An Iron Cross from the Great War, which he had dug up in some junk shop, was resplendent on his left breast pocket. '*Mundus vult decipi*', had been his casual comment. Marlene had got Professor Raab to translate it for her. 'The world likes to be deceived.'

Showing off, the lot of them, she thought dismissively, looking at all those boots. Never ridden a horse in their lives. She saw through these men and despised them, just as she saw through and despised herself. The yew hedge split her life in two. On one side their comfortable everyday life in the house and garden. On the other, the camp, torture and death.

The pince-nez and its retinue disappeared into the bungalow. For the umpteenth time Marlene checked that everything in the kitchen and dining room was in order. In half an hour's time she expected to see her unwelcome guests at lunch.

'Heil Hitler, Reichsführer. Your visit is a pleasure to me and a great honour to my house.' The words slipped smoothly past her lips. His hand was limp in hers. The eyes behind the pince-nez avoided her glance, seeking to dwell somewhere else. Why, he's scared of women, she realized in surprise.

He thanked her quietly, and turned to Fredie. 'I'm impressed, Obersturmbannführer Neubert.' He sat down, and everyone else followed his example. They waited for the man of power to speak again. He remained silent and reached for the jug of water. Fredie tried to anticipate his wishes and pour him a glass. The result was a collision. The jug slopped over, water spilled on the most distinguished of all SS uniforms. Its wearer got some splashes on his nose and his pince-nez. He looked a little foolish.

Marlene spluttered. The company around the table froze. Fredie turned pale. The end of his career hovered before him. Then the man on the receiving end of the water mopped his nose and his pince-nez with his napkin — and laughed, at first soundlessly, then with a kind of bleat. There was general relief. Fredie breathed again. The cup, or rather the jug, had passed him by.

The bleat of laughter stopped as suddenly as it had begun. Marlene served the one-pot dish. The quiet voice continued. 'I am impressed by what I've seen. Operation Needle and Thread will be a great success. And its guiding hand deserves commendation. The prisoner has hardly any Semitic characteristics. Very likely most of his ancestors were Aryan, which would explain his outstanding abilities. I would like the man to continue his work with your full support, and to lack for nothing.'

'Perhaps he could be given leave from imprisonment, and the laboratory might continue its work outside the camp as an SS research institute, under his direction,' Noack suggested.

'Oh no, the requirement for secrecy and security rules out any such thing, Dr Noack. That's why the prisoner must be eliminated at the end of the operation. Your chicken one-pot dish is delicious, Frau Neubert.'

And I hope the chicken bones stick in your throat and bloody choke you, you bastard, she thought. 'How very kind of you, Reichsführer,' she replied.

That evening, Fredie was lounging comfortably in breeches and check slippers on the couch. He was pleased. 'That went splendidly. Come here, darling.' He pushed up her dress and took her panties down. She hadn't the strength to resist, but she paid attention to what was going on inside her, unable to believe it. The hated orgasm didn't come. She felt nothing. A sense of triumph took hold. The spell that had lasted so many years was broken.

In the morning she woke with a start. Something was wrong. There was no familiar aroma of coffee and clatter of china in the kitchen. Of course. Jana wasn't there. Marlene quickly showered and dressed. She must get the girl back into the house before any cruel ideas occurred to the appalling Frau Werner. She hurried past the office and infirmary buildings, and passed through the gate in the barbed-wire fence and into the camp itself. 'Find me Jana,' she told an old woman outside the gypsy hut.

The woman gave her a strange look. 'Jana not here.'

'Where is she?'

'Here, no dawdling around.' Oberscharführer Schäfer pushed the woman back into the hut with his stick. 'Heil Hitler, Frau Neubert. What an unusual honour! I'm just doing my rounds, can I help you in any way?'

'I'm looking for my housemaid.'

'Jana, is that right? I've no idea where she is.'

'Is with doctor,' the old woman hissed through the door.

All was quiet in the infirmary. Marlene went into the first room. The surgical instruments glittered in their glass-fronted cupboards, just as they had on her first visit. 'Is anyone there?'

The swing door to the next room moved slightly in a draught. Marlene pushed it open. Invisible, giant hands clutched at her chest and constricted it. The sight was so unimaginable that her brain refused to take it in.

Five human heads stood on a shelf. Jana's was second from the left. Marlene came closer. 'Jana . . .' she whispered. She touched the cold cheeks, tenderly stroked the short hair, looked into the black gypsy eyes that had been so beautiful only a little while ago. Now they were a clouded, milky blue.

'An interesting series of experiments. I am injecting organic pigments.' Dr Engel took the girl's head off the shelf. 'I use healthy young specimens. Frau Werner is a great help to me in selecting them. I shall soon be in a position to change the dark iris so foreign to our race into a Nordic blue. Aren't you feeling well? Wait a minute, I'll get you a glass of water.'

'No, thank you,' she heard herself say.

'Then I'll take my lunch break. They have knuckle of veal in the canteen today.'

Marlene felt nothing, didn't know who or where she was. Everything seemed to be extinguished. She slowly came back to her senses as cold water rushed down on her, and found that she was crouching fully dressed under the shower in her bathroom, screaming like an animal. The lash of the cold water forced her back into the present. She stripped off her wet clothes, dried herself and dressed. Then she searched in the wardrobe until she found what she was looking for. She took a spade from the garden shed.

She met no one on the way to the infirmary. She took the head off the shelf and wrapped it in Grandmother Mine's white lace scarf. She dug a hole in the rose bed outside the door and laid the head in it. 'Pretty roses,' she could hear Jana's voice saying as she levelled off the little grave.

'Sleep well, my dear,' she said huskily.

*

It was more than most people could have come to terms with, but Marlene was tough, a child of Rübenstrasse. Her grief and horror gave way to cold fury. 'If this gets out,' she told her husband, 'you'll all be for it – you, Engel, Noack, all the others. Not forgetting Reichswhatsit Himmler. And you know something? I'll be laughing while I bloody watch them hang you all.'

Fredie kept calm. 'Take it easy, darling. I can understand you're angry, stranded without a maid.' He fetched himself a beer from the kitchen. 'You should be glad Dr Engel isn't putting in an official complaint for the sabotage of a series of experiments conducted under the auspices of the Racial Hygiene Research Institute. Well, never mind that. A good, strong seventeen-year-old girl came with this morning's transport of Jews. Take a look at her and see if you think she could do the housework.'

'I'm going to Berlin to do some shopping. Has my lord and master any objection?'

'Get me a bottle of Petrol Hahn from the Kaufhaus des Westens, would you?'

She bought his hair lotion, and some underwear for herself. It was a pretext. Her aim was to see Frank Saunders. The monstrous discovery she had made must reach the public.

The *New York Herald Tribune* office was in Friedrichstrasse. A peroxide-blonde secretary was hammering away on an Underwood, her fingernails painted red, a cigarette between her heavily made-up lips. She acted very American. 'How can I help you?'

'You can speak German to me, Fräulein. I want to see Mr Saunders.'

Evidently insulted, the blonde ignored her remark and continued in English. 'Mr Saunders is now in our Paris office. Mr Wilkins will be back in half an hour. Would you like to speak to him?' Marlene would not like to speak to Mr Wilkins. He didn't know her and wouldn't believe a word she said. In fact no one's going to believe you, my girl, she told herself.

Carefree people in summer clothes sat in the terrace of the Café Vienna on the Kurfürstendamm. A couple of good-looking young officers were flirting with their girlfriends. A paper boy was shouting out the headlines of the *BZ am Mittag*. German paratroopers had expelled the Allied forces from the island of Crete.

There you sit, eating ice cream while they're cutting people's heads off in Blumenau, she thought grimly. Something had to be done. She just didn't know what. She was helpless, a prisoner herself, although one who could move about freely.

She spent the night at the Pension Wolke, where the windows were blacked out with cardboard and drawing pins in case of air raids. Frau Wolke remembered her. 'You spent a few days with us here.' No, the land-lady didn't know what had become of Fräulein von Aichborn. 'Probably married a posh fellow, a count or something.'

Once she got home, the first thing Marlene did was pick up the field tele-phone to tell Fredie she was back. She was surprised to hear voices, and then remembered that there was something wrong with the line. She had forgot-ten to mention it to Fredie.

She recognized Noack's voice. '. . . among other things, we're keeping our eye on all foreign newspaper correspondents.'

'Of course, Standartenführer.'

'Including the *New York Herald Tribune* office. Their secretary is one of our informants. She tells us that a woman called Marlene Neubert went there yesterday wanting to speak to Frank Saunders. Obersturmbannführer Neubert, your wife is in touch with the foreign press.'

A brief silence. Then Fredie spoke again. 'Saunders was once a . . . a guest of hers.'

'Once, yes, never mind that. But now? Neubert, this is one hell of a mess.'

Fredie's voice sounded strained. 'She found her housemaid's head in the laboratory. Dr Engel had selected the gypsy girl for a series of experiments. My wife was rather upset about it, but I didn't think anything much of her reaction.'

'What reaction? Out with it, man.'

'She threatened to make Engel's experiments public.'

'By making them public she meant going to that American newspaper correspondent. Neubert, that's high treason. It could have unfortunate consequences for you.'

There was no emotion at all in Fredie's voice. 'Herr Standartenführer, I shall petition for the immediate dissolution of my marriage.'

'It does you credit, Obersturmbannführer. I'll set things in motion for you. Don't let your wife notice anything. Act the same as usual, understand?'

'Yes, Standartenführer.'

'What shall we do with her? I'd prefer a solution that won't attract any attention.'

'We'll transfer a prostitute named Marlene Kaschke to the camp at Theresienstadt. She's an immoral influence on national morale.'

Fredie, you absolute bastard, thought Marlene without any particular surprise. She hung up. Time to get out of here, she decided for the third time in her life.

Fredie didn't let his intentions show. If anything, he was more agreeable than usual. He opened a bottle of Mosel at dinner. 'Because it's Wednesday,' he joked.

You certainly have chutzpah, she thought.

After dinner he yawned. 'I'm going to bed.'

'I don't feel tired. Any objection to my visiting that old Jew in his witches' kitchen? He has such interesting stories of the old days to tell. Just think, he even met the Kaiser once.'

'If you like.' Fredie went upstairs.

The guard on night duty opened the gate for her. The glaring beams of spotlights shone down from the watchtowers, casting a harsh light on the gravel path leading to the camp.

Professor Georg Raab was engraving a copperplate under a strong lamp. His garland of white hair shone in the otherwise dim light. He looked like the kindly grandfather Marlene had never had.

'Professor, I have to leave this place.' She told him everything. 'I don't know where to go. Please advise me.'

'You have great confidence in me, madame.'

'I've no one else to turn to.'

Raab continued working on the plate. 'There could be a way out.'

'I'll do whatever you suggest.'

'I could make you a pass allowing you to leave the country, a Swiss transit visa, and an entry permit to France signed by the German military governor. You can go to Paris by way of Munich and Geneva. The direct route over the Franco-German border is barred to civilians.'

'You know a lot about current affairs for a camp inmate.'

'They let me have newspapers and the radio. The BBC is an invaluable source of information.'

'Why Paris?'

'Because you can be sure no one will look for you there. And because I know someone in Paris who will help you. Do you have a passport photo? A fairly old one would be best.'

'I have five if you want them. The Photomaton doesn't do less than six at a time. I needed one two years ago for my new ID papers, and the others are with my sewing things in my workbox.'

'Bring them to me tomorrow morning. From now on Marlene Neubert is Helene Neumann. That's close enough for you to remember it easily. We'll leave your date of birth unchanged. You're on this trip to inspect buildings for their suitability as the headquarters of the Paris branch of the Nazi Women's Association. It sounds so crazy that no one will check up on it. And if anyone does, you'll be able to show a document to that effect from the Party leadership in Munich. I've made a good job of their letterhead, particularly the Nazi eagle. It squints slightly.' The little professor chuckled.

'Who is the person you know in Paris?'

'An old friend. His name's Brunel, Aristide Brunel. Ask for him at the Louvre.'

'Where's that?'

'Any Parisian will tell you the way. Ask Brunel if he's managed to tell the two Canalettos apart yet. He'll find you somewhere safe to stay, and then you just have to wait.'

'For the Final Victory?'

'For the inevitable victory of reason and humanity.' The stout little man with the white coat over his striped camp uniform thought for a moment. 'You'll need money. The first series of Swiss francs is in production now — I'll print off enough of those for you at the same time. Don't change too many at once.' He hesitated. 'There's just one problem, though. Siebert is always looking over my shoulder while I work.'

'How long will you need?'

'An hour a day for a week.'

'I can keep Siebert off your back for an hour every afternoon.'

'How will you do that?'

'Better not ask.'

Sex with young Siebert wasn't particularly exciting, but Marlene liked the thought of being unfaithful to Fredie with his subordinate in his their conjugal bed. They did it daily from three to four in the afternoon when the commandant was on his rounds of the camp. She made sure that Frau Werner got wind of these sessions too. Someone had to tip Fredie off, after all, or it wouldn't be half as much fun.

So for a week she had sex with Siebert in the Neubert bed, generously making him feel that he was an incomparable lover. Then the professor had finished his forgeries. 'With a new birth certificate thrown in. The best of luck, my dear.'

She put her hand on his sleeve. 'Just a moment, Professor. What about you? We must both go. I have to go because they want to send me to Theresienstadt. You have to go because that man Himmler has ordered you to be liquidated once Operation Needle and Thread is over.' She deliberately adopted a light tone. 'You're not going to wait around for that, are you? You can't! Forge yourself some good papers, and we can make off together, laughing at the thought of their faces when they find out.'

Raab looked at her sadly. 'I wouldn't get further than the gate. There's no escaping one's fate. Mascha will follow me when she hears the news. Our death is of no importance. What are two more dead Jews in two thousand years of the history of a monumental misunderstanding? You must live to tell the world about these appalling things. Now, please go, quickly.'

'You stupid idiot, you bloody stupid Jew!' she cried, giving vent to unspeakable grief and despair. She turned and ran, her face streaming with tears.

She had shut herself off from her fellow travellers behind *Vogue*, but she wasn't reading it. She was suspended in that state between waking and sleeping, when the body and mind can't agree on time and place. The last twenty-four hours had been too much, even for the born survivor from Rübenstrasse. Her headlong bicycle ride to Blumenau station, suitcase on the back of the bike. The early train that was late. Her fear of missing her connection in Berlin. The endless train journey to Munich. Changing to the Geneva train. Her heart thudding every time tickets were inspected. The official at the German border who told her, 'Come with me' – and then, confused, she realized it was the conductor of the train, who had found her the seat in a no-smoking compartment that she had requested. The relief when Germany was left behind her and Switzerland by night was slipping by, no checkpoints, windows brightly lit. The sleep of exhaustion that blotted out everything, only not the noise of the wheels on the tracks that became the sound of a hundred decapitated heads rolling away.

'*Votre passeport, s'il vous plaît.*' Marlene woke with a start. It was early morning. A French passport inspector was in the compartment, a German military policeman behind him. My name is Neumann, went the words in her head, Helene Neumann . . .

The French official leafed through Professor Raab's work of art. The military policeman read it over his shoulder. 'Where to?' he asked.

'Paris.'

'What for?'

She took the letter from the Party leadership out of her handbag. The military policeman read it. He obviously didn't understand a word. 'Thanks, all in order.' He gave her the letter back.

'*Bon voyage, mademoiselle.*' The passport inspector handed her papers back and turned to the next passenger.

A French steam engine had taken over from the Swiss electric locomotive and puffed away fast, staccato, until its flywheels took hold and the train slowly moved away.

The Gare de Lyon was a peaceful scene, one that a few German soldiers lounging about could not disturb. Passengers in a hurry. Porters bustling about. Brightly coloured kiosks. A man playing the accordion. A dog lifting its leg against the advertising pillar bearing the Picon ad. And hovering over everything its own particular mixture of smells, a compound of soot, cheap perfume, Gitanes and pastis. Marlene breathed it all in. No different from Lehrter station, just not the same, she thought with her best Rübenstrasse logic.

Bicycle taxis were waiting outside the station. Gasoline was in short supply. Marlene put her case in one of these vehicles. 'To the Louvre, please.' She enjoyed the swaying ride through the city, little damaged by a few weeks of war and twelve months of ceasefire. '*Attendez*,' she asked the cabby when they reached her destination.

Outside the Louvre a group of German officers had gathered around a tourist guide who was explaining something in terrible German. '*Mon dieu, non, c'est intolérable. Parlez français, s'il vous plaît*,' a captain told the guide in fluent French.

A major left the group and came over to Marlene. She put her case down to get her papers out of her handbag. I expect they check up on you here even if you want to go to the loo, she thought crossly.

'*Vous permettez, madame?*' The major was after her case, not her pass-port. '*Où puis-je vous la porter?*'

'Up there, please.' She indicated the steps up to the entrance.

'You're German?'

'You can hear I am.'

'Visiting the Louvre?'

'You can see I am.' A German officer was the last thing she needed just now.

He was not to be shaken off so easily. 'Major Achim Wächter, if I may introduce myself. Perhaps we could see each other again?' He was about forty and had some grey in his hair. He was sizing her up.

Now he's wondering out how easy it would be to get me into bed, she thought. 'Thank you for carrying my case.' She left him standing there and turned to the museum attendant in the entrance. '*Je cherche Monsieur Aristide Brunel.*'

'*Vous êtes la dame allemande?*'

'Any objection?'

'*Allons.*' The man went ahead of her. A small side door. A narrow passage. A spiral staircase. A long corridor. Tall double doors. An imposing desk. A white-haired man in a dark, double-breasted suit. '*La dame allemande, Monsieur le directeur.*'

'Our visitor from Munich.' The white-haired man spoke German. 'From the Alte Pinakothek, am I right? The restorer? *Bonjour, madame.*'

'I don't have anything to do with restaurants. I'm to ask if you've been able to tell the difference between the two Canalettos yet.'

Brunel's face brightened. 'How is my friend Georg Raab?' he asked, delighted.

'In a terrible way. And as long as he's in a terrible way he's all right because he's still alive. But don't ask me for how much longer.'

'Is it that bad?'

'Worse.'

'What about you, madame?'

'I managed to get away. With his help. He says you'll find a safe place for me to stay.'

Brunel made a call, speaking quietly and fast. Marlene couldn't make out a word. He hung up. 'You were never here, and we'll never see each other again. In the unlikely event of a chance meeting we don't know each other.'

'I understand. So now?'

'Go downstairs, and the rest will follow.' He kissed her hand. '*Bonne chance, ma chère.*' He escorted her to the top of the spiral staircase.

The group of German officers had disappeared. The bicycle taxi was waiting at the foot of the broad flight of steps. Marlene stopped short. It wasn't the same cabby, but a dark man with a moustache, who silently indicated that she should get in.

Jerkily, they set off. They rode fast through the city; Marlene had no idea for how long or where to. The cyclist had to tread hard on the pedals as they went uphill. 'Montmartre,' he told her, out of breath. Next moment they were coasting downhill again towards an entrance. BERTRAND'S

VELOTAXIS, she read over the gate as it clanged shut behind them. There was darkness all around.

So now what, she thought, more baffled than alarmed.

'*Votre nom?*' said a voice in the darkness.

'Helene Neumann.'

'*Votre vrai nom.*'

'Look, I don't understand. My French is strictly limited, if you know what I mean.'

'We want your real name,' the voice demanded.

'Let's have a bit of light in here first so that I can see you.'

A quiet murmuring, then a pause, and the creak of shutters. Light dazzled her, and traced the outlines of three people. She raised a hand to shield her eyes. She recognized the man with the moustache. A young woman stood beside him, wearing a brightly coloured summer dress and fashionable wedge heels. Her long black hair was caught up and turned under in a roll. She was sizing Marlene up.

'We want to know who you are, what your real name is and where you come from.' The speaker was a tall, dark man of around thirty with a craggy chin. His German was fluent. Marlene, whose own native Berlin accent was returning to her, thought she heard the trace of a dialect that she didn't recognize.

'Why do you want to know all this?'

'*Parce que vous êtes allemande et les allemands sont nos ennemis,*' said the young woman sharply.

'Very well, if you must know, my name's Marlene Neubert. I've come from Blumenau camp near Berlin. A friend of your friend Monsieur Brunel helped me get out with forged papers. The papers say my name is Helene Neumann and I'm in Paris to find a suitable building for the Nazi Women's Association. Here's my passport, and a letter from Party leadership – that's a fake too.' She handed the papers to the speaker. 'So now maybe you'd be kind enough to introduce yourselves.'

'My name is Armand, this is Yvonne, and this is Bertrand.'

'*Nos noms de guerre,*' the woman added.

'And you'll be Madeleine from now on,' Armand told her. 'We're all on first-name terms here. What happens if the Germans check up on you?'

305

'Nothing at first. But if I'm identified back in Berlin I'm done for. They'll kill me or send me to Theresienstadt, which comes to the same thing. Any more questions?'

'Yes. Are you prepared to help us fight the Germans?'

'The Germans, no. The SS, the Gestapo and the Nazis, yes.'

'C'est la même chose,' said Yvonne, her voice filled with scorn.

'You mean I'm the same as that bunch of murderers? No, mademoiselle, you'll have to put that differently.'

'Drop it, Yvonne,' Armand told her. 'Notre nouvelle alliée prend le même risque que nous. As she can prove in her first operation,' he added thoughtfully. 'Show Madeleine her quarters.'

There was a glasshouse in the overgrown yard, used until recently as an artist's studio, its windows half-covered with linen sheets to give the occupants a little privacy. The artist had gone to Provence. His abstract works were everywhere, and there was a smell of oil paint and turpentine. An unfinished female nude stood on the easel, with breasts at odd angles and an eye instead of a navel. 'What a sight,' Marlene said.

'Armand sleeps in the next room. You'll leave him alone, d'accord?'

'Don't you worry. I've had enough of the lords of creation to last me quite some time.' Marlene inspected the little spirit stove in the kitchen corner and made herself a coffee, ignoring Yvonne, who went off in a huff.

Armand was out almost all the time, returning only to sleep. The other members of the group, about a dozen in all, lived scattered around Paris. Bertrand's Velotaxis gave them freedom of movement and a perfect cover for their Resistance operations. There was a battery-powered transmitter in one of the vehicles, which moved constantly, thereby avoiding German tracking devices. They had it tuned to London, from where orders for the Resistance workers came. Marlene learned all this over the next few days. There was much hectic coming and going, indicating that an operation was about to take place. What role was she to play?

Meanwhile, she was bored. She didn't dare venture out into the streets; she wouldn't have known where to go. The group had no time for her, although Yvonne kept a suspicious eye on her, particularly when Armand came back in the evening.

Men were just about the last thing Marlene had on her mind. Bastards, the whole lot of them, was her summary of her many years of experience. Well, almost all of them. Old Herr Eulenfels had been all right. Frank Saunders too, in his way. She thought of Franz Giese, and suddenly had an odd feeling in the pit of her stomach. Longing? She didn't know. But she did know one thing, she'd been off her head back then. If you'd said yes you'd be Frau Giese today, and you'd have been spared all that shit, she told herself. Then she realized that she alone would have been spared. Nothing would have been different for Jana, for the little professor, for all the wretches in Blumenau.

On the third day after her arrival a large red Panhard limousine with Paris number-plates drove into the yard. A German officer got out. Marlene was horrified. When she recognized Armand she breathed a sigh of relief. He was in the uniform of a Wehrmacht colonel, and he had brought a German Red Cross nurse's uniform for Marlene.

Marlene wrinkled her nose. 'Stinks to high heaven.'

Armand laughed. 'Our Maghrebi tailor finds inspiration in garlic when he's copying German uniforms.'

Their orders had come from London. The Germans had shot down an RAF plane on a reconnaissance flight. The pilot and his observer had parachuted to safety and were taken prisoner.

'We're not interested in the pilot,' Armand told her. 'It's the other man we want. Lieutenant-Colonel Colby is the RAF's chief strategist. He knows all the bomber targets from Bordeaux to Berlin. He broke his arm coming down, and now he's in the German officers' hospital in Neuilly. The Gestapo have got wind of their patient's identity, and they've sent him Edelgard in the role of a nurse.'

'Edelgard?'

'Edelgard Bornheim is a trained psychologist. She likes to think she can make anyone talk. She was transferred to Gestapo headquarters in Paris because of her perfect French, and her English is just as good. A dangerous opponent. She'll use any means she can. She can be sympathetic, under-standing, sweet as sugar. If it serves her ends she'll sleep with her victim, whether it's a man or a woman. She'll try to win Colby's confidence, and we have to get him out of there as fast as possible. Here, take this, just to be on the safe side.' He gave Marlene a small pistol. 'A 6.35 Beretta. Deadly at close quarters. If you have to use it on yourself, the best way is to put it in your mouth and pull the trigger. It won't hurt. Come on, Bertrand will drive us.'

Bertrand was wearing black chauffeur's livery and a peaked cap. 'A German officer in a French limousine with a French driver?' she wondered aloud.

'All part of our camouflage. Get in, Nurse Magda,' Armand told her.

'How do you come to speak such good German?' she asked as they drove through the streets of Paris.

'I'm from Alsace. I first saw the light of day as a subject of His Majesty Kaiser Wilhelm II, but I grew up as a citizen of the *République*. My heart belongs to France. Now I'm German again and due to be called up. If they catch me they'll shoot me as a deserter.'

'In such a case the best way is to put your pistol in your mouth and pull the trigger. It won't hurt,' said Marlene, unimpressed.

The German officers' hospital was housed in a large villa in Neuilly park, dating from the time of Napoleon III. An ornate gateway led to an inner courtyard. 'If they close the gate we won't never get out,' said Marlene, her accent reverting to her Berlin roots.

'Pick up the raincoat and follow me, Nurse Magda,' Armand cut her short. A lance-corporal orderly jumped to his feet and saluted. 'I'm Colonel Klemens. Who's in charge here?'

'Medical Officer Fahrenkamp.'

'Take us to him.'

'Yessir.' The lance-corporal hurried ahead, brushing past several nurses, and flung open a double door. 'Colonel Klemens, Dr Fahrenkamp, sir,' he announced.

'And this is Nurse Magda. She'll be looking after our patient,' Armand introduced her.

'Colonel, Nurse Magda . . .' The medical officer clicked his heels. 'Which patient do you mean?'

'Haven't you recived a telex from the Führer headquarters, then? I don't believe it! Well, we can go into this bungling incompetence later. Now let's get the Englishman ready to travel.'

'Lieutenant-Colonel Colby?'

Armand lowered his voice. 'This is secret state business. Colby is a close relation of the British royal family. We have orders to take him to Schloss

Südmaringen, the internment camp for VIPs. It could be that we'll exchange him for Hess, but remember, you never heard that.'

'Of course not, colonel.' The medical officer sniffed in surprise.

Armand grinned. 'You'll have to forgive us, Dr Fahrenkamp. Nurse Magda and I were dining on snails with garlic butter last night. Now, back to business. We mustn't attract any attention in moving the patient. Hence my French car and its French chauffeur. We've brought a raincoat with us, for Nurse Magda to put over his uniform.'

'Can I see my patient now, please?' Marlene was very much the energetic nurse.

'Lance-Corporal Fink, take Nurse Magda to our prisoner. May I offer you an Armagnac meanwhile, colonel?'

'No thank you, there's no time. Hurry up, will you, nurse? The Luftwaffe won't keep that plane waiting for ever.'

The lance-corporal led Marlene to a bright, pleasant room. A thin man in a khaki shirt and braces rose from the edge of the bed, and reached for his uniform jacket. 'You must excuse me. I didn't expect visitors.'

'I'm Nurse Magda. Let me help you.' She helped him to fit his right arm into its sleeve, and draped the jacket over his left shoulder so that his arm in its plaster rested comfortably in the sling. 'We're going to get you out of here. Please trust us,' she said in a low voice. 'And now your raincoat.' She was about to put the raincoat round him when the door opened.

Here comes trouble, she thought.

The woman who entered the room was good-looking, around thirty. She wore a stylish, blue tailored suit and a starched nurse's cap. 'I see our patient has a visitor,' she said, smiling. 'I'm Nurse Edelgard. How do you do?'

'Nurse Magda,' Marlene introduced herself.

'Glad to meet you, nurse.' Edelgard offered her hand with natural friendliness. 'Are you new here?'

'We've come to collect the prisoner. He's being transferred to Schloss Südmaringen.'

Armand came in. 'Colonel Klemens,' he introduced himself.

'How do you do, Colonel,' the Englishman replied formally, and winced. He was clearly in pain.

'Nurse Magda has painkillers in her bag. She'll see to your arm on the way,' Armand told him.

'A fracture of the femur,' said Nurse Edelgard. 'It will soon heal. Let me make you a cup of tea before you go.' She opened the door of a cubby hole, where a gas boiler and kettle stood on a table – as well as a field telephone with a line leading out through the open window.

'Draughts won't do our patient any good.' Marlene closed the window.

Edelgard was filling the kettle at the sink. 'They say Südmaringen is a very pretty place. How nice for you, lieutenant-colonel. Tea will be ready in a moment.' She was about to close the door of the cubby hole behind her.

Armand's right hook came quick as lightning. With a sigh, Nurse Edelgard collapsed on the floor. 'She was only going to make tea,' said Marlene reproachfully.

'She was going to raise the alarm.' Armand closed the door of the tiny room and pocketed the key. 'The femur is the thigh bone. Any real nurse would know that. The phone is connected to Gestapo HQ.'

'Was connected,' Marlene said, showing him the two ends of the telephone wire that she had broken as she closed the window. 'A temporary field connection like that isn't very stable, someone once told me.'

'Jolly good show,' said the Englishman appreciatively.

'And now to get out inconspicuously.' Marlene put the raincoat round his shoulders and led him out of the room. Armand brought up the rear. On the stairs, the medical officer joined them and accompanied them to the car. 'All the best, lieutenant-colonel,' he said to Colby.

'Thank you, doctor.' The red Panhard started up. Colby turned to Armand. 'Now what?'

'You'll be back in London in a couple of days' time.'

They stopped in the middle of Neuilly park, behind some dense bushes. Bertrand put two fingers to his mouth and gave a shrill whistle. Two bicycle taxis raced over the grass. Armand left his cap and uniform jacket in the car, Marlene added her nurse's cap to them. She helped the Englishman into one of the vehicles and squeezed in beside him. The rider stepped on the pedals. 'I like your Resistance. It's fun,' she called, in high spirits.

'Only as long as they don't catch us,' said Armand, quelling her exuberance.

No one's going to catch me, thought Marlene, eager to do something. She asked Yvonne, 'Where do you go shopping around here?'

'At Printemps or the Galeries Lafayette. Or the Place Vendôme if you have enough money.'

One of the bicycle taxis took her into the city. At the Crédit Lyonnais they changed her forged Swiss francs into French francs without demur, giving her enough for a pretty dress and a coat of inimitable Parisian chic to go with it, as well as a pair of divine shoes with high heels and a matching handbag in the Place Vendôme, as well as silk underwear and stockings from Madame Schiaparelli's boutique in the Ritz Hotel.

The muted sound of voices rose in the hotel bar. She sat down at one of the little tables. A couple of high-ranking German officers were drinking aperitifs with their women. Some French businessmen were pouring RICARD over a cube of sugar in a glass. The world was going to the devil in style. She ordered a glass of champagne.

Two men were drinking whisky at the bar. Marlene saw the backs of their tweed jackets. One of them was watching her in the mirror. It was Frank Saunders. He nodded at her with an inquiring glance, and she inclined her head. He picked up his whisky glass and strolled over to her.

'Changed your hunting grounds?'

'What, with all the local competition?' She adopted his own light tone as if they'd last met only yesterday.

'You have no competition at all.' He kissed her fingertips. 'How about it? I live just around the corner.'

'Going there at once, are we, or can I finish my drink?'

'Hey, sweetheart, you never used to be so touchy. Tell me, what are you doing in Paris?'

'It's a long story. Are you still with the *Herald Tribune*?'

'In charge of our office here. Fascinating job. As a neutral I have freedom of movement.'

'I have something for you. Where can we talk undisturbed?'

'Like I said, I live just around the corner.'

'Not to fuck, Frank. To talk.'

'The pianist at Harry's plays so loud you can hardly hear yourself speak. It's only a step away.' Saunders waved to the waiter and paid. 'See you tomorrow, Ernest.' He clapped his tweed-clad companion on the shoulder as he passed. 'A colleague. Reporter for the *New York Times*, writes novels on the side.'

Harry's New York Bar was in the rue Daunou. A piano tinkled a metallic staccato as they entered. 'Two glasses of Scotch in the back room,' Saunders ordered. 'OK, shoot,' he said.

'Which bit would you like to hear about first? Skeletons with skin stretched over their bones starving on watery soup? Guards beating helpless prisoners to death with their cudgels? Human subjects with their heads chopped off for use in experiments? Or just being kept in a cellar where the rats gnaw off your toes? The place is called Blumenau. It's one of their camps. They torture and murder human beings there.'

'Sounds damn improbable. And what are you, a German civilian, doing in Paris in the middle of the war? Where did you come by this story? Are you sure of the details? Convince me.'

She talked without stopping for half an hour. In spite of the horrors, she didn't forget to mention the forged money. Saunders pushed his whisky glass back and forth. He thought about it. 'Yes, this is what we must do,' he finally said. 'Listen. My secretary Nancy is blonde like you. With horn-rimmed glasses you'd resemble her passport photo. We can take the plane from Lisbon over the Azores to Florida and fly on to New York. As soon as we land I'll introduce you to the press and radio.' His enthusiasm was growing as he talked. 'Ex-wife of concentration camp commandant tells all. What about that? Good, don't you think? Sweetheart, it will be *the* sensation of the year, with your sex appeal. You'll get a fabulous fee. And most important of all, you'll be safe.'

'As simple as that.' Her tone conveyed the despair of all the maltreated people for whom there was no escape.

'Nancy's hair is shorter than yours. Go to the hairdresser.'

'Telephone!' called the barkeeper, holding up the receiver. After a brief conversation, Frank Saunders returned to their table.

'I don't want to go to America,' said Marlene quietly. 'I want to stay here. And when the whole bloody thing is over I want to go back to Berlin.'

'You'll be able to do that sooner than you dared to hope. That call was from my office. Hitler's declared war on the United States. The poor stupid sod doesn't know that means he's lost the war, of course. Sorry, I must go and pack. They're giving us just a few hours to leave the country.'

'Will you publish the story?'

'It's worth nothing without you there in person. You can't sell that kind

312

of thing at home without sex appeal. Sorry, sweetheart. Try the Swedes. They have a gloomy Nordic taste for horror stories.'

She walked away without a word. There was nothing more to say.

She ran into Major Wächter outside the Café de l'Opéra. It was too late to avoid him. 'You're not going to turn me down this time, are you?' he asked.

'Very well, a cup of coffee.'

'I don't even know your name.'

'Helene Neumann. I'm from Berlin. I'm here looking for suitable quarters for the local headquarters of our Women's Association.'

'I'm from Nuremberg. A toy manufacturer. I get around Paris a good deal as adjutant to the city commandant.' He waited for her reaction. 'We could have a lot of fun together,' he said.

Still doesn't know how to win me over, she thought, analysing his advances to her.

'Adjutant to the city commandant – that must be an interesting post,' she said non-committally.

'Paradise for a lover of French food and wine. The French are paying court to the victor. I accompany the general to dozens of receptions and banquets. Though sometimes I'd rather have a couple of good Nuremberg sausages and a beer.'

She rose to her feet. 'Thank you for the coffee.'

He leaped up. 'Shall we see each other again, Fräulein Neumann?'

'Perhaps. I quite often come here for a cup of coffee. Good day, Major.'

'I'll take you home. Just let me call an official car.' He was making for the nearest public telephone.

Marlene beckoned to a bicycle taxi. 'Montmartre.' With a sigh of relief, she fell into the seat.

'Spy, traitor, *sale Boche!*' hissed Yvonne. Someone had seen Marlene with the major.

'You'll have to explain,' said Armand calmly.

'He spoke to me outside the Louvre the day I arrived, absolutely insisted on carrying my case. Name of Major Achim Wächter. I ran into him by chance at the Café de l'Opéra today. Was I supposed to run away? I accepted his invitation to a coffee. It wasn't easy to get rid of him.'

'What do you know about him?'

'Only that he's a toy manufacturer in civilian life, and at present he's adjutant to the city commandant.'

'It's all a lie. She's working for the Germans,' cried Yvonne in agitation. 'Can't you see how cleverly she's wormed her way in with us? Joins in a couple of operations for the sake of camouflage. Then she'll turn us in to the Gestapo.'

Armand was thinking out loud. 'The German city commandant's head-quarters are at the Palais de Verny. The Marquis de Verny built it in the fifteenth century. We have a plan of the layout of all the rooms from the cellars to the attics, got it from the city archives. We know from the French staff that the general works in the library, and his secretariat is in the music room next to it. Intelligence has its offices on the second floor. The Military Police conduct operations from the south wing. What we don't know is the precise location of the cells down in the vaults where they hold people they've arrested until they hand them over to the French or German police, which is to say the SS. Madeleine, I'd like you to meet the adjutant again. The success of an operation to free detainees might depend on the answer.'

So she drank her coffee in front of the Café de l'Opéra every afternoon. She had to wait a week for the major to reappear. 'I was on leave, a quick visit home. Ilse and the boys just didn't want to let me go. I hope you're not going to run away again today. I have the evening off. Would you give me the great pleasure of dining with me?'

He had ordered a suite in the George V hotel, with a silent waiter who poured the champagne and served dinner. There was freshly smoked Loire salmon, consommé of Limousin beef, and snipe with wild peaches.

There he goes spending a fortune, and I'd get between the sheets with him for nothing but a sausage! She grinned to herself. She had decided to take the direct route. The direct route was by way of bed, and she knew from experience that it usually got her where she wanted. She ate with a hearty appetite, ignoring the culinary refinements. As a child of Rübenstrasse she knew that you don't live to eat, you eat to live.

She let him seduce her for the sake of appearances. He fumbled and went to work on her as clumsily as most men. She gave in, with a sigh, as soon as she decently could. He didn't last long, and she was glad of that.

'Do you always entice ladies into such expensive beds?' she teased him.

'We're not allowed to entertain ladies at HQ.'

'Even during the day?'

'We could meet at a hotel in the day.'

She drew a line with her finger from his breastbone to his navel. 'What can you be thinking of?' she cooed. 'That's not why I asked. I mentioned that I've been sent to Paris to find a suitable building for our Women's Association, didn't I? I'm an architect, so I'm interested in historical buildings. I know the Palais de Verny, I've studied the building plans and countless illustrations. I'd just love to get a close look at the way they built their foundations five hundred years ago. The architects of the past were ahead of us in many ways.'

'Our safety precautions have been stepped up since we caught a burglar in the Grand Salon a few days ago.'

'Please, Achim.' She blew into the curly hair on his chest and then went down lower. Her lips aroused him again. She rode him, her pelvis circling, and this time she could be said to have earned her dinner.

'Come to my office on Tuesday,' he said as they parted. 'I'll see what can be done.'

Tuesday was cold and wet. Marlene wore her new raincoat and elegant rubber galoshes, both from the Galeries Lafayette, for the first time. She slung her bag over her right shoulder as usual. Bertrand took her to the commandant's HQ by bicycle taxi. He said he would wait – 'Just in case' – and lit himself a Caporal.

An NCO took her to Achim Wächter, who was on the phone. 'What nonsense. Of course the man's not a British intelligence agent, just an ordinary burglar after the table silver. It's a bad mark for our Military Police that he got as far as the Grand Salon. The general's given orders for him to be handed over to the French police. No, of course we're not sending him over to the Gestapo. If you absolutely insist on interrogating the prisoner you'll have to come here, and make it nippy, if I may say so. The French are coming for him this afternoon. Your big boss in person, you say? You can send Himmler himself for all I care. Over and out.'

He slammed the receiver down angrily. 'Forgive me. Our friends in the Gestapo want everything handed to them on a plate.' He kissed his visitor's hand. 'Frau Neumann, how kind of you to come. I told the city commandant what you wanted to see, as a qualified architect, and he gave permission. Corporal Lehmann, take the lady to Gaston.'

'Yes, sir.'

'Gaston is the caretaker here; he knows every nook and cranny. Please excuse me. I have business to deal with.' He stood to attention and clicked his heels. 'When shall we see each other?' he asked quietly, so that the NCO couldn't hear.

'Soon.' She gave him a promising smile.

Gaston was a bent little man with silver hair and a big nose. '*Bonjour, madame. Je suis entièrement à votre disposition.*' He greeted Marlene with an old-fashioned bow. He had obviously been given his instructions, for he hurried assiduously ahead of her up the curve of the marble stairway.

It was a severe test of her patience. They had to go down the mile-long gallery of ancestors from portrait to portrait, and tour over forty rooms. Only after two hours was Gaston's repertory exhausted. '*Et maintenant j'aimerais voir le sous-sol. Les fondations m'intéressent.*' The oldest part of the foundation walls was beneath the south wing, she was told. They were Roman catacombs which later became part of the medieval fortifications.

In the south wing, an officer from the Military Police met them. 'Frau Neumann the architect? Major Wächter said you'd be coming. I'm Captain Grosse. Down here, please.' Worn stone steps led down into the depths, where a brick vault opened up with passages running into it from right and left. An iron grating had been let into the mouth of the right-hand passage. 'The cells for prisoners are in there,' the captain told her. 'There's an interrogation going on in one of them at the moment, but don't let it bother you.' The guard by the grating saluted. 'Stand at ease, lance-corporal. The lady's an architect, she's going to look around down here a little.'

'Yes, captain.'

'It's a real labyrinth. Don't lose yourself, ma'am.'

'I hope my tourist guide knows his way around. Thank you, Herr Grosse.' The captain disappeared up the steps. The young lance-corporal opened the grating for her. All going swimmingly, she thought.

'The Frenchman can't come in here,' the guard said.

'*Monsieur Gaston, attendez.*'

The passage went round a bend that took her out of sight of the guard. Three steel doors, as recently installed as the grating. The detention cells! She memorized their location. The door of the middle cell was half-open.

A chair. A man sitting on it, his hands tied with a cord behind the back of the chair. A camp bed, and lying on it, carelessly tossed down, a dove-grey uniform coat, a peaked cap with the death's-head badge, and a belt with a pistol holster. Their owner was standing in front of the prisoner.

'We can handle this in a civilized manner. So once more – who are you? Secret Service? British Military Intelligence?'

'*Je ne comprends pas, monsieur.*'

The interrogator swung his arm back, ready to strike. It froze in mid-movement, Marlene too stood as if paralysed.

Fredie was the first to recover. 'Hello, darling, what a surprise. Who'd have expected to meet you here? Well, never mind. Some things sort themselves out.' Marlene looked at the cell door. 'Don't bother. You'd get no further than the foot of the steps. You just stay here and listen. I could send you to Auschwitz on the next transport. Or much nicer, arrange a date for you with the executioner. I must tell you that Monsieur de Paris, as they call him, works fast and with precision. Of course if you like he can strap you to the board slowly and elaborately. That'll pass a few chilly minutes until the blade finally falls.' Fredie was relishing every word.

She had got control of herself. There was total contempt in her voice. 'Still the same old bastard, Fredie.'

'Brigadeführer Neubert, if you please. That is to say major-general. Blumenau is a thing of the past. They've appointed me head of the Gestapo here in Paris. Now and then I conduct interrogations personally.' He gave a nasty grin. 'So as not to get out of practice.' Her glance fell on his belt and holster. 'No, darling. You're not quick enough for that.' With one stride he was beside the camp bed.

The couple of seconds were enough. She got her hand on the Beretta in her shoulder bag. Armand had practised the movement with her. She shot right through the leather. The bag and its contents muted the sound of the shot. Fredie fell on his knees. He looked up at her imploringly, about to say something. Her second shot hit him in the middle of the forehead.

She acted fast and with circumspection. She undid the cord, and the prisoner rubbed his wrists. In her excitement she spoke in German. 'Quick, put this on.' She threw him Fredie's coat.

The man understood. He buttoned the coat up to his chin, buckled the belt round it and put on the cap with the death's head. Luckily he was wearing grey trousers and black shoes. 'You keep quiet, I'll do the talking.' He seemed to understand that too.

They approached the grating. 'I'll see the rest down here another time. Come along, Herr Brigadeführer. We must celebrate meeting again like this.' Marlene kept up an uninterrupted flow of talk. 'How's your wife? It seems for ever since I last saw Nina. *Monsieur Gaston, allez.*' The little caretaker trotted after them. 'And your sheepdog Harro?' Up the steps, not too hastily. Marlene forced herself to keep calm. 'Such a nice creature.' One step at a time, over the black and white stone flags of the ground floor and so to the open double door. Another guard. 'What do you say to a glass of champagne in the Ritz, Herr Brigadeführer? It's not far on foot, and we can have your car follow us.' Out in the street at last. Stroll calmly on. Then a dive round the corner. A sigh of relief.

The man she had rescued dumped his disguise in a doorway. Bertrand's bicycle taxi skidded into view on the wet carriageway. They were safe.

*

Sleep, sleep was all she wanted. After twenty-four hours Armand broke the silence in the glasshouse. 'Get up, Madeleine, you have to get out of here. They're looking for you everywhere. You not only killed the head of the Paris Gestapo, it so happens that you rescued one of our most important men in the process. We're taking you to Provence. You'll be safe there until the war is over.'

They played marches, Resistance songs, and over and over again the Marseillaise. The Parisians hailed the soldiers who had liberated them. The tall, thin general stood on a podium above the jubilant crowd. Armand, in the uniform of a colonel in the Free French forces, stood beside him. '*Madeleine, mon général,*' he introduced her. The tall, thin general embraced Marlene and pinned an order to her blouse.

She climbed down from the podium and stood in line with the others whom the general had decorated. The woman next to her had been given the cross of the Légion d'Honneur too. She wore American uniform. 'What's your name? Where are you from?' she asked in a husky voice.

Marlene reverted to her native accent. 'I'm Marlene. Berlin born and bred.'

'Me too,' said her neighbour.

'The general is greatly impressed by your story,' Armand told her. 'He'd like to know if there's anything that we can do for you.'

Marlene didn't even have to think about it. 'I want to go home.'

The DC3 with French markings on its fuselage and wings made a bumpy landing. There were great cracks in the runway and only some of the bomb craters had been filled. The Americans had occupied their sector of Berlin a few days earlier, taking over Tempelhof airport. As yet the French had no airfield in their sector.

Marlene climbed out of the plane. An elegant Spahi officer was waiting for her. 'Capitaine de Bertin, madame. I'm to look after you while you are here. We've put you up in the guest house at our headquarters, and you can decide when you want to return to Paris.' Capitaine de Bertin put her case in the big staff car.

'I don't want to go back to Paris. I want to go to Rübenstrasse.'

'What, madame?'

'Rübenstrasse, please.'

The captain was a veteran of many diplomatic missions, but this complicated task was executed only after much discussion with the driver, and with the aid of several German workers. At last they set off, passing ragged men and women making for unknown destinations. Others were busy clearing rubble. Children with hungry faces reached their hands out to the car. 'Chocolate,' they begged. 'Chocolate.' There were ruins everywhere.

Marlene wept. This was her city.

There was no Rübenstrasse any more, only a lunar landscape of broken bricks and rubble, with a single chimney rising from it three storeys high. Oh well, she thought, and wiped her tears away. '*Arrêtez, s'il vous plaît.*' They stopped. 'I must go on from here alone.'

Capitaine de Bertin gave her a card. 'You can reach me any time at this number.' He helped her out of the limousine and saluted. 'Goodbye, madame. You are a very brave woman.' The car disappeared in a cloud of dust.

Marlene took her case and set off. She knew she had made the right decision.

Only the entrance of the building in Schöneberg was left. '*The Reich family now in Lichtenrade*,' someone had chalked on the charred wood of the door, adding the address. A dozen tenants had left similar information. Franz Giese was not among them.

Marlene clambered over the ruins to the place where the stairs had led up into his building. Dandelions grew among the rubble. Something glinted gold among the broken bricks and scraps of mortar. It was the rutting stag in the autumnal wood. She picked the last splinters of glass out of the frame and stuck the picture under her arm. Now what? Obvious. Look for Franz.

She slept in the park. She had a dried sausage in her case, and ate some of it for breakfast. A hydrant supplied washing water in the morning. 'Tastes horrible, but it's drinkable,' an old man told her, slurping it noisily from the hollow of his hand.

EMPLOYMENT OFFICE – the notice hung on a side door of the Schöneberg town hall which was still almost intact. She joined the end of the long queue. After two hours she reached a table.

'Name?'

'Kaschke, Marlene.'

'Papers?'

She gave the man her old passport, the one she had kept through the years.

'It's expired.'

'I'll get a new one before my next luxury trip round the world. Now I need work and somewhere to live.'

'The Housing Department deals with accommodation. I can register you as looking for work, but we don't have anything at the moment.'

'Do you speak English?' an elderly lady asked.

Marlene was surprised. 'A little. Why do you want to know?'

'You should try the American employment office in Lichterfelde. They wouldn't take me, I'm too old.'

'How old are you, Fräulein Kaschke?' The head of the German–American Employment Office could see it in her passport, but he was testing her English.

Marlene did her sums. 'I was born in 1912. Now we are in 1945. That makes me thirty-three years old, right?'

'Your English is OK. Let's see what we have for you. What are your legs like?'

'I beg your pardon?'

'Raise your skirt.' The man spoke German with a heavy American accent.

'Anything else?' she asked indignantly. 'If you're looking for tarts for an army whorehouse you've come to the wrong address, mister.'

'Nonsense. The usherettes in the Uncle Tom cinema wear short dresses. Our boys like to see girls with pretty legs. Well, what about it?'

'Usherette? That's fantastic!' She couldn't raise her skirt fast enough.

He inspected her legs. 'All right, they're in order. We pay a hundred and twenty marks a week. You get army food and half a CARE parcel a month. Now go for your medical. Your address, please.'

'Third bench in the park. Just back from the East. I was working on the land there,' she lied. 'My apartment's gone.'

'Sorry, no job without an address.' The American wrote something on a piece of paper and rubber-stamped it. 'Take this to the Zehlendorf Housing Department office.'

Is he doing this because he wants to get me into bed? Marlene wondered. But Mr Chalford took no more notice of her, just lovingly stroked the black marble obelisk on his desk. 'Looks like a big toothpick,' she said.

'That,' Mr Chalford told her, sounding offended, 'is a genuine Barlach.'

A British bomb had torn away a third of the front of Number 198 Argentinische Allee. The bizarre cross-section of floors was reminiscent of a doll's house. The bedroom, kitchen and bathroom in the third-floor apartment on the left were intact, including the furniture. The door to the living room went nowhere. One step through it and you were on the brink of the abyss. Marlene unpacked her few things. She put the cross of the Légion d'Honneur on the chest of drawers, with the rutting stag behind it.

'Pretty picture.' She swung round, startled. The man in the doorway had plastered his yellowish strands of hair across his skull, and wore shabby trousers and check slippers. 'The name's Mühlberger. I live next door. My wife's in the West.' He scratched his crotch. 'And you are . . . ?'

'Marlene Kaschke. They've allotted me this place. And next time you call please knock or ring, Herr Mühlberger, or better still don't call at all.'

'Oh, hoity-toity, are we? Well, if the lady thinks she can manage without masculine protection . . . a woman's not safe around here, so they say now, specially at night.'

'I don't think there'll be a problem – so long as I don't come across you,' she shot straight back at him. With a dirty laugh, he disappeared.

She found a hammer and nails in the kitchen and hung the stag above the chest of drawers. She knew Franz would be glad she'd found the picture. Her face cleared. 'Now for the cinema.'

It was like a dream. The dimly lit auditorium with the curving rows of seats. The heavy, silvery blue curtain that would open any minute for Hans Albers, Willy Fritsch or Heinz Rühmann. First the man who played the Wurlitzer would climb out of the depths and accompany the colourful slides of advertisements with his magical, swelling organ music. Marlene remembered every detail of her past visit to the Onkel Tom cinema.

The manager was a pale corporal called Pringle, who was sitting in the office drinking coffee with his pallid German boyfriend. 'There'll be no playing around with the boys. Gisela will get your dress.'

Gisela was a strong-minded redhead who advised her, 'Do as I do, wear four pairs of panties on top of each other. They're always bloody pinching your arse. Here, this should fit.' She helped Marlene into the short lilac taffeta dress with its frilled sleeves and tied a large bow, also lilac, in her hair. Then she steered Marlene to the mirror and stood beside her. 'Designed and made by Corporal Pringle. The taffeta cost him four cartons of Chesterfields. He and Detlev just love to sew. Well, at least those two don't pinch you, the little darlings.' The two young women looked at each other and spluttered with laughter.

Marlene was given a torch and a tray slung around her with chocolate bars, bags of popcorn and a small chilled container for ices on a stick. Her territory was the left-hand aisle. A doll-faced, black-haired girl paraded up and down the right-hand aisle, and Gisela took the middle one.

There was no Wurlitzer now, there were no ads, there was no documentary. The loudspeakers played swing, while slides warned you about sexually transmitted diseases. Instead of the screen heroes of the pre-war UfA, Terra and Tobis studios, the cinema was showing a Metro-Goldwyn-

Mayer movie with Clark Gable. Admission was from eight, and the movie began at twenty to nine.

All went smoothly. She managed to elude the bottom-pinching to some extent. Clark Gable radiated raw masculinity, and predictably won Loretta Young. The cinema closed at eleven, and the girls changed. 'Never, for heaven's sake, forget your Yank pass,' Gisela warned. 'Or they'll take you in for being out after curfew.'

'Got it here.' Marlene slapped her shoulder bag with the flat of her hand.

'Hey, there's a hole in your bag. Listen, my Erich works with leather goods. Bet you he's got a patch of leather somewhere he could mend it with for you.'

'No, I want to leave the bag like that, as a memento. But thanks for the offer. See you tomorrow.'

She didn't have far to go: past the Yank guard, out of the prohibited zone, right into Argentinische Allee. The war meant that the second carriageway had never been built, and so a broad strip of sand overgrown with weeds ran parallel to the street. She crossed it to reach the buildings on the other side, and had to be careful not to stumble in a rabbit hole.

A motorbike came rattling through the dark. Right in front of her, its headlight flared. She swerved aside just in time. 'You lunatic,' she swore as the rider moved away. The headlight was switched off. The motorbike turned. She could hear it coming back towards her. This time it roared past without any light on, only just missing her.

She didn't wait for it to turn again, but raced over the pavement to the nearest building. The front door was not locked. Gasping, she leaned against it from the inside. She gradually calmed down, and became aware that someone else was breathing heavily. She switched on her torch. An American soldier and his girl were standing on the stairs. The girl was a step above the man, leaning against the wall. She had pulled up her dress and wrapped one bare leg around his hip. She was moaning in time to his movements.

'Sorry.' Marlene made her escape. All was quiet outside now. She reached the door of her building unmolested, and opened it.

'Rather late home, lady.'

She jumped. She knew that voice. Quickly, she climbed the stairs. He followed her. It seemed an eternity before she got the door of the apartment open. 'Goodnight, Herr Mühlberger.' She slammed it shut. In the bathroom, she ran water into the washbasin – thanks to the Americans, the water mains were functioning in the Onkel Tom quarter – and dipped her face into it. The chorine stung her eyes.

She fell asleep, exhausted. She dreamed. Franz had put a protective arm around her. 'Go ahead . . .' she murmured happily.

*

Mühlberger seemed to guess her comings and goings. He always happened to be in the stairwell, scratching his crotch and making suggestive remarks. 'And so little to say for himself when his wife's around!' Frau Müller from the second floor showed a tiny gap between thumb and forefinger. 'All the same – don't you have anyone to look after you?'

'Of course I do.'

'Mine's in Russia.' Frau Müller didn't expect an answer.

Was Franz in Russia too? She remembered how she had last seen him, tied to a post in the cellar, being tortured by the Gestapo. She didn't like to think of it.

'Franz Giese: please get in touch. Lene is living in Onkel Toms Hütte, 198 Argentinische Allee, 3rd floor,' she wrote on the once-white lid of a shoebox. She fixed it to the entrance of the apartment building where he'd lived.

The lid of the shoebox followed her into her dreams. Suppose Franz didn't pass the door of his old building any more because he'd long ago found another place to live? Or suppose someone had torn the message down? Rain could have washed the writing off. Wind could have blown the cardboard away.

Every other day she set off for Schöneberg. The message still hung in its place, unchanged and obviously unread. Her secret hope of finding a note stuck behind it with his answer, with a brief explanation of why he hadn't been able to visit her yet, began to fade.

On Wednesday, yet again, she went home disappointed. The tram was overcrowded, as usual. The man behind her was rubbing his penis against her hip. She turned round, which wasn't easy. 'Here you are, then.' She rammed her knee into his crotch. His face went pale with the pain.

A woman got in at the next stop. She had hollow cheeks and wore a head-scarf. Her eyes wandered over Marlene and the other passengers, and then, incredulous, returned to Marlene. Her voice was quiet and hesitant at first, as if she had to convince herself. 'Frau Camp Commandant Neubert, isn't it? What a surprise!' The voice grew louder. 'So where's your riding crop, Frau camp commandant?'

Marlene understood. The woman was mixing her up with Gertrud Werner, the appalling Hauptsturmführerin. In her tormented memory, the similarities between them were blurred. For her, Marlene and Frau Werner were one and the same person. Assurances and explanations would do no good. She'd get out at the next stop.

Accusingly, the woman turned to them all. 'She used to beat you mercilessly until you couldn't even whimper.'

The other passengers pricked up their ears. A few showed signs of sympathy. Most turned away. They didn't want anything to do with this kind of thing. But they were all listening.

'She enjoyed strapping you into a chair, then her doctor colleague could root about until your insides burned like fire. She'd lever your teeth apart and pour chemicals down your throat so that her criminal friend with his doctorate could study their effects. If you were lucky you didn't die, you just developed a few harmless symptoms.' The woman tore the scarf off her head. Her skull was bald and fiery red. 'Allow me to introduce myself, ladies and gentlemen,' she cried. 'Lilo Goldblatt, doctor of medicine, formerly a guinea pig in Blumenau concentration camp. Do you remember me, Frau camp commandant?'

'Ought to be hanged!' trumpeted the man who had been molesting Marlene. 'Turn her in to the police!' shouted someone else.

I have to get out of here, thought Marlene — how many times in her life had she told herself that? She took a deep breath and jumped from the moving tram. The hedge between the tracks and the pavement cushioned her fall. She picked herself up and ran as she used to run in Rübenstrasse, when you had to be first to the corner to get a bit of bread from the Salvation Army's barrow. She'd been eight then. She noticed her breath coming faster and her legs moving more slowly. She was thirty-three now.

When she saw the cemetery gate she put on a final spurt. She came to a halt in the middle of a company of mourners beside an open grave, and smiled apologetically at the pastor. She had nearly knocked him into it. The man of God bowed his head with Christian forgiveness, and continued his sermon.

For the moment, she was safe from her pursuers. But now what? She considered her position. Suppose they went on looking for her, and ended up finding her? She'd have to offer long explanations. She didn't need to explain anything in Paris. A call to Capitaine de Bertin would be enough. But you can't do that to Franz, an inner voice told her.

The pastor was holding the Bible before him in both hands, praising the character of the dear departed, while Marlene looked around. She seemed to be in the clear. The word Führer kept coming up in the priest's address. 'One of our very best . . . always on the alert, ready to make decisions . . . always keeping his eye open for signals . . . now let us pray . . .' But Führer, of course, her confused mind registered, meant all sorts of other things, including a train driver, and this was a train driver's funeral. As the mourners left the cemetery an old gentleman, taking her for one of the party, shook her hand with fervour. 'One of the best engine drivers we ever had.'

Marlene shook his hand vigorously in return. 'He was indeed. Listen, how do I get back from here to Onkel Tom?' She was given a long description, with many alternatives, and chose the simplest.

There was a letter waiting for her at home. The postal service had been running again for the last few days. When she saw the sturdy handwriting on the envelope she uttered a cry of joy. She tore it open, took out the sheet of lined paper, and read:

Dear Fräulein Lene

I found your message and now I am answering it. So we are both still alive, which is more than can be said for many. I was a soldier in the war in Denmark, except that it wasn't really a war there, which was fine by me, I had quite enough of war with the first one. After a few weeks as prisoners they let us go, and now I'm in Berlin again, in Ruhleben, I'm working as a driver for the British. I will come and see you on Sunday. Is four o'clock all right for you?

With warm regards
Franz Giese

She laughed and wept, because he was alive and coming to see her on Sunday, and he was the only person she really knew, none of the others counted. She thought of the haulage business with the three-wheeled van, and maybe a bigger truck later. It's going to be all right, she thought.

'Good news?' asked Gisela on Saturday as they were getting into their lilac taffeta dresses and fixing the horrible bows in their hair.

'Very good,' Marlene beamed. 'He's coming tomorrow afternoon. Do me a favour? Ask Rita to take my shift.'

'OK, lover.' Gisela had picked that up from Mae West.

'Corporal Pringle doesn't have to know that I'm playing hooky on Sunday.'

'Don't you worry. He's got eyes only for Detlev and the new knitting pattern.'

Marlene put the sling of the refreshments tray around her shoulders. This was her turn for the centre aisle, which meant twice the work, because she had to show the audience in on both sides, left and right. She put up with a couple of pinches. Nothing could trouble her today.

A tall, lanky captain bought two bags of popcorn and gave one to the woman with him. Marlene showed them to their seats. The captain thanked her with a smile, which his companion didn't seem to like at all. Don't worry, I'm not aiming to take him away from you, thought Marlene in high spirits.

She had pocketed a chocolate bar from her tray. It would buy her a couple of briquettes from the fuel merchant who supplied the shopping street and the cinema. She put them in the bathroom stove late on Sunday morning, and soon it was bubbling comfortably away. The Camay soap came from the cinema toilets. It smelled divine and foamed wonderfully.

A bottle of sparkling wine was cooling under running water. It had cost most of her half of a CARE parcel, but would go very well with the army ration of canned bacon. She had wrapped the bacon around prunes from an earlier distribution. Crackers and peanuts completed the luxurious tidbits.

She put on Madame Schiaparelli's diaphanous underwear and the expensive silk stockings. She'd quite forgotten that she had a good figure and long, slender legs. The high-heeled shoes set them off beautifully. The elegant Printemps dress was as good as new. Parisian chic in Onkel Toms Hütte. How Franz would stare!

The clock showed four on the dot when he knocked. With every step to the door, her anticipation grew. She slowly opened it. He had a pot of geraniums under his arm, and swallowed with embarrassment.

'So there you are.'

'Good day, Fräulein Lene,' he said stiffly. 'How are you?'

'Fine, thanks. Now, let's forget the formalities. Come on in.'

He put the pot of geraniums down. 'Pretty place here.'

'Yours in Schöneberg was prettier. Well, we can make up for all that. We're still young, aren't we?' She poured the sparkling wine. 'Cheers, Franz.'

'Cheers, Lene.' His awkwardness was melting away. He sat down. 'I still can't believe the two of us are here.'

'The three of us.' She pointed at the rutting stag over the chest of drawers. He looked at the picture as if he were seeing it for the first time. She drank in the sight of him. He had rounded out a little, and it suited him. The dimple in his chin was slightly deeper. His hairline had receded a bit. His brown eyes were the same as ever. They bent a calm and honest gaze on the world.

'It's been a while, hasn't it?' she said.

'You came to me because you wanted to get away from that man Fredie, and I took you to the Pension Wolke. That's the last time I saw you.' He bent his head. 'But I told them where you were. It was cowardly of me, but I was scared. It's a funny thing, I never understood why they suddenly left me alone. Most people would have ended up in a camp. Did they leave you alone too?'

'Of course,' she lied. 'We were both lucky, that's what.' She moved to face him. 'Stand up, Franz, and kiss me properly at last.' She pulled him up by his dyed British uniform tunic until their faces were very close. Then they were just a man and a woman, and everything was clear between them.

He was large, and hard. Her moistness made him a supple messenger of love. The afternoon wasn't enough for him, or the evening either. They didn't talk much as they rested in between times, probably because there was too much to say.

Just before ten he got dressed, so as not to miss the last U-Bahn train before curfew. She took one of the flickering candles off the chest of drawers. 'So you don't fall down the stairs.' They said no elaborate goodbyes. He'd be back tomorrow.

'And then we'll talk about the future,' he promised.

'The future,' she repeated, because at last she had one.

Elated, she went into the bathroom. The stove was still warm. The fine spray of the shower set off an indescribably sensuous tingling of her skin. She directed the hand-held jet on her mount of Venus, and came to climax at once. It was like the full stop to a wonderful first chapter.

She was just wrapping herself in her dressing gown when she heard a faint knocking. She tied the belt and took her torch from the wardrobe in the corridor. 'Franz?' Had he missed his train? Outside stood a figure in goggles and a leather cap. It held a clinking chain between two raised gauntlets. 'Here, what's the idea?' she said angrily.

She had no time to feel afraid. The figure forced her back into the apartment. Cold metal went around her throat and cut off her artery. The lack of oxygen to her brain set off euphoria.

A heavenly peace filled her, peace that no earthly pain could penetrate. She was floating weightlessly towards a sunny Rübenstrasse, full of bright houses and happy people, with a laughing Franz leading them all.

'Watch out, everyone, here comes Lene!' she cried happily.

CHAPTER SEVEN

THE DISTRICT COUNCILLOR'S large, walnut-veneered Superhet radio had survived air raids, Russians, and Inge Dietrich's pressing requests to let her exchange it for food at Frau Molch's. Not even the prospect of a few packets of Yugoslav Drinas, more affordable than American cigarettes, could make Dr Hellbich change his mind. 'One has to know what's going on in the world,' he stated, and he listened to the news when the power was on.

There was a good deal going on in the world during that early autumn of 1945. Japan had surrendered in the face of America's atom bombs, and was allowed to keep its Emperor. A largely unknown British general had fired the equally unknown new mayor of Cologne, Konrad Adenauer, for incompetence. In Hollywood, Greta Garbo was making her fourteenth movie. The Scotsman Alexander Fleming won the Nobel Prize for discovering some kind of miracle medication.

'Made of mould, would you believe it?' commented Hellbich.

'Can we listen to AFN?' asked Ralf, when the news was over and the announcer was threatening to play merry operetta tunes.

'You can do that when I'm not home.' His grandfather hated the 'tuneless tootling' of the American Forces Network.

The radio had a graduated tuning scale which glowed a mysterious green and bore names like Tripoli, Hilversum and Brindisi. They appealed to Ben's dreams of distant places, not that he really wanted to go anywhere except perhaps America, where the longest cars and the sharpest gentlemen's fashions were to be found. A GI had left the latest issue of *Esquire* lying in the U-Bahn. Ben leafed through its sterile world of sexless glamour and deceptive glossy advertising, where a bottle of Johnnie Walker was praised to the skies as if it were holy water. At the back of the magazine he found a coloured ad for the Buick Eight. This quality limousine was still top of his list. Its driver was leaning casually against the radiator, wearing a double-breasted suit, which presented Ben with a dilemma. Would it be better to opt for a button at pocket level, as shown here, which would mean he could have longer lapels, or was the waist-level button which he had hitherto favoured the only real thing? He'd have to discuss it with Rödel. After all, the master tailor was an authority in the field.

Above all, however, he must get twenty cartons of Yankee cigarettes out of Clarence C. Brubaker by playing on his hopes for the greatest journalistic scoop of modern times. Only then would the coveted suit and suede shoes be within his reach. The Führer's right-hand man would be a help. Ben grinned happily to himself, because now he knew how to bring it off.

That afternoon he was trotting along the villa-lined streets behind US headquarters. Brubaker's car was in the drive. The aspirant to the Pulitzer Prize had had his Ford sent over from Hackensack at US government expense.

Ben did not press the doorbell as usual, but walked round the side of the house and tapped softly at a window pane. Brubaker was hunched over the sheet of paper in his Remington. With a conspiratorial air, Ben signalled for him to open the back door.

Brubaker opened it. 'What's happening?' he asked in surprise.

'I've been followed. But I managed to shake them off.' Ben injected a touch of Humphrey Bogart into the part he was playing. He had just seen *The Maltese Falcon*.

Hackensack's star reporter didn't understand. 'Who followed you?'

'*Them*, of course. They got wind of it. We must hurry. He's waiting for you. Do you have the cigarettes?'

'Fifteen cartons. I knew you'd do it.' Brubaker was obviously pleased.

'Chesterfields?' Ben checked, and wondered how he could raise the price to twenty. After all, this wasn't just some ordinary Nazi like friendly little Herr Adler, who crept round his own former premises with his head hung low, as if he were a war criminal. And all he'd done was run the National Socialist People's Welfare Office for the Onkel Tom area, giving the housewives who were always short of ration coupons a few extra on the sly. No, this was a top quality Nazi, and as such he had his price.

'Lucky Strikes,' said Brubaker apologetically. 'Chesterfields were sold out.'

Ben saw his chance. 'Well, I don't know. He usually only smokes Chesterfields. Perhaps he'll make an exception for you if you add another five cartons.'

'Five cartons of Philip Morris, my own stock,' agreed Clarence P. That made sure of the crêpe-soled suede shoes. 'Where do I meet him?'

'He's going to a secret meeting of the Werewolves today.'

Brubaker was delighted. 'Dick Draycott of United Press was saying recently – and rather condescendingly too – that the Werewolves were only the brainchild of small provincial reporters, mainly from Hackensack, New Jersey. This'll show him, the arrogant bastard! So the Hitler Youth is still alive and kicking?'

'You bet,' Ben assured him, squinting at the cartons of cigarettes piled high on the table.

'I suppose you don't happen to know just what they do in more detail?'

'They sing,' said Ben, drawing on personal experience.

'Nazi songs?'

'Sure.'

'Do you know any?'

'*Hoch auf dem gelben Wagen*,' remembered Ben, although he was not quite sure whether this ditty was tainted by the past like poor Herr Adler. 'High on the yellow car,' he translated to the best of his ability. Brubaker faithfully wrote it down. '. . . I sit in front with my brother-in-law,' Ben continued, and the man from the *Hackensack Herald* noted that the words were an expression of typical German family feeling. 'I can sing it if you like,' offered Ben, unfolding the potato sack he had brought with him to hold the cigarettes.

'Some other time. Let's go,' urged Brubaker.

'We must leave the cigarettes in his hideout first or he won't agree to talk to you.' Ben was anxious to make sure he had them. He hid his treasure in the shed behind his grandparents' house, under cartons full of empty preserving jars, and shrugged off any vague feelings of guilt. It wasn't his fault if the Yank was such a fool, was it?

'No one's following us,' he announced as they went on. Brubaker was driving the Ford in the happy expectation of his secret meeting. There was a journalistic sensation in the offing.

At Ben's command, he left the car in an unused driveway, and followed him by tortuous routes leading, as he failed to notice, several times around the same corners. After the third circuit Ben raised a hand to halt him and crept through a gap in the hedge, going ahead. From there they went on over six plots of land and twelve fences. They could easily have reached their destination from the road, but for twenty cartons of cigarettes the man had earned the right to a dramatic scene. Ben ducked down behind a laurel bush. Brubaker got into cover too. He considered giving an owl's hoot by way of camouflage – he had learned this trick years ago in the Hackensack Boy Scouts – but first, owls don't hoot in daylight, and second, Ben had laid a warning finger on his lips before wriggling the last few metres to the back of the Zehlendorf GYA Club on his stomach. Clarence the Boy Scout imitated him. He was tingling unbearably, although that had less to do with suspense than with the ants in the garden.

Ben had worked it all out precisely. Sergeant Allen would be reporting to the Signal Corps colonel, Corporal Kauwe would be helping the girls with their doll's house. The coast was clear. He pushed Brubaker towards the cellar door. You could get a good view of the drama group's rehearsal stage through its barred window. The timing was perfect. The 'robbers' were just singing, at the top of their voices, 'We live a life of liberty'.

'The Werewolves' battle song,' whispered Ben. 'They sing it before any major operation. Better not go so close to the window. They shoot on sight. See that man under the stairs? That's him.' Ben pointed to the caretaker.

'Hitler's right-hand man,' murmured Brubaker, much impressed.

Appel was emptying a couple of mousetraps. 'We beat the drum, we all rejoice, to hear the weeping maiden's voice,' sang the robbers' chorus, while Herr Appel set his traps, this time with popcorn. Heidi Rödel was sitting on the front of the platform swinging her bare legs and watching with a bored expression.

'They have girls in the Werewolves?' said Brubaker, surprised. 'And very pretty girls too.'

'That's Dynamite Heidi. She carries out special operations.' Ben cheerfully continued to spin his yarn. He was enjoying this more and more.

'Can I speak to him now?'

Ben had thought this out carefully in advance. 'Slink over to that garden summerhouse, keeping under cover, and wait for us there.' He watched with interest as Brubaker wriggled his way from shrub to shrub in his best Boy Scout manner, and covered the open stretch of lawn between the last forsythia and the summerhouse with a racing dive, making use of his training in the Hackensack High School baseball team. His body was much quicker off the mark than his brain.

Ben went into the cellar. Heidi was still dangling her legs. 'You didn't come the other evening.' She pushed herself slightly forward on the edge of the stage, and her dress rucked up a little further.

'What, skinny-dipping with the entire bunch?' Ben snorted with derision.

'What about with just me?'

'Dunno.' He looked at her brown thighs and wondered what they felt like.

Gert Schlomm clapped his hands. 'We're going back two pages. Moor kills Amalie. Come on, Heidi, and die a bit more slowly this time.'

Ben did not wait for the deadly blow, but strolled back to the caretaker between the improvised rows of seats. 'Hi, Herr Appel. Do you have a moment? There's a Yank out there, he's a newspaper reporter and he wants to write something about German allotment gardeners.'

An American taking an interest in Appel's kohlrabi! The caretaker hid his delight behind a reluctant, 'S'pose I can take a look at him.' He did not stop to wonder just how the man from overseas knew about him and his allotment. 'Does he speak German?'

'Not a word of it, but I can interpret.' Ben steered him into the summerhouse. 'This is Herr Appel.'

Brubaker had his pencil and notepad ready. 'The Führer's right-hand man, is that correct?'

Although Herr Appel spoke no English, he would certainly understand the word 'Führer'. Ben reacted like lightning. 'Is it true that the Führer took a great interest in German allotment gardeners?'

Herr Appel's eyes bulged a little more. 'Could be. Him being a vegetarian and all, he only ate vegetables. But I can't say any more for sure. I was never in the Party, I'd like to say that loud and clear.'

'I was always at his side,' translated Ben.

'Where is he now?' Brubaker was trying to make these earth-shattering questions sound casual.

'What's your own favourite vegetable?' Ben interpreted.

'Cauliflower. *Brassica oleracea argentinensis*, the Argentinian variety. Grows almost of its own accord, delicious with black butter. Ha, butter, did I say?' Herr Appel gave a brief bark of laughter.

'Dead. Or maybe in Argentina. Or both,' Ben translated the gardener's culinary observations.

'If he's alive, would you by any chance know his address?' Brubaker persisted.

'Baked with a topping of breadcrumbs?'

'No,' said Herr Appel.

'No.'

Outside, a whistle was blown. Sergeant Allen was back, and summoning his baseball team. 'Got to get back to work,' Herr Appel grunted. 'Don't forget to write how difficult it is for us German allotment gardeners to protect our crops from thieves these days. Only last week, for instance . . .'

'The alarm signal. They've got wind of our meeting. I have to leave at once,' Ben translated, pushing the Führer's right-hand man out of the summerhouse door.

Another verse of the robbers' song drifted over from the building. *'Mercury's the god for us, a trickster, he was ever thus . . .'*

'Inspector Dietrich with his witness, sir,' Gertrud Olsen told her boss. 'To look at the card index.'

Curtis S. Chalford glanced out at the corridor. The visitors were waiting at the end of it. 'I'm busy. You see to it, Gertrud. Show them the card index and then get them out of here. We really do have better ways to spend our time.' He shut his office door.

Gertrud put two boxes of index cards on the table in the outside office. 'There you are, gentlemen. Hurry up, please. Mr Chalford's not in a very good temper. All the same – would you like a coffee?'

'No thank you, Frau Olsen,' said Dietrich, much to Mühlberger's disappointment. 'We don't want to strain Mr Chalford's temper unduly.' They went through the card index. Mühlberger proudly pointed to his own photograph, and Dietrich also recognized the picture of Ziesel the garbage truck driver. But he was out of contention as the murderer now.

The inspector pulled the card index of women employees towards him, although it was not really of any interest in this context. Under A he found

Henriette von Aichborn's card. There was a black † after the name. 'The boss marked the other four with a cross too. He's very meticulous that way,' explained Gertrud Olsen, noticing Dietrich's surprise.

'Respectful sort of fellow,' said Mühlberger with heavy irony. 'Can we go now?'

'I'll drive you home.'

Chalford, watching from his office window, saw the wood-gas Opel lumber into motion. 'What is it, Gertrud?'

'Frau Weber is here.'

'Show her in.'

Jutta entered the office. 'Good morning, Mr Chalford. You sent for me?'

'Yes, it's some time since we saw each other.'

'Not since you hired me, in fact.'

'Sit down, please.' Chalford indicated a chair and got back behind his desk. 'I hear that Sergeant Panelli is very pleased with you. He praises you a lot, says you're a damned good cook, Frau Weber.' He stroked back his thin fair hair. 'I'm always happy when an arrangement I've made proves successful.' When he moved from English to German, his heavy American accent made his German seem clumsier than it really was. 'So what delicacy are you serving for lunch today?'

'*Königsberger Klopse.*'

'*Kounigsboorger Klapse,*' he tried to say, and laughed at his own mispronunciation. 'What's that?'

'Something like your own meatballs. Served with caper sauce and boiled potatoes. This is the third time the boys have written it on the board where they can say what they'd like. It's all ready, and Sergeant Panelli is going to finish the cooking. I have a couple of days off.'

'Wonderful. Then I'm sure you'll have time to dine with me — this evening, perhaps?'

'Thank you so much for the invitation, but I'm going to see my parents in Köpenick.' She was glad that she didn't have to invent an excuse.

If he was disappointed he didn't show it. 'Frau Weber, it's because of your cooking skills that I asked to see you. Mr Gold of the State Department is looking for a first-class cook. In his position, he often has important guests to dinner. You'd have many privileges, but a good deal of overtime too. How about it?'

It would mean less time with John. 'I'm sure that's an interesting offer, Mr Chalford, but I'm happy where I am.'

'Well, I can't force you, Frau Weber.' He accompanied her to the stairs. '*Königsberger Klopse*,' he repeated with amusement.

'Well done. You said it without any accent at all that time,' she told him encouragingly.

She cycled home to fetch her overnight bag. On the stairs, she met a thin woman in a hat and coat, carrying a shabby suitcase. 'Hurry up, do,' she called to someone, without deigning to glance at Jutta. Jürgen Brandenburg came down the stairs with his white stick. He was wearing an ancient, ankle-length loden coat that made him look even shorter than he was, and a black Mao cap pulled well down over his ears. He looked pathetic and pitiable. He pushed past Jutta, and seemed about to say something, but decided against it.

In the apartment, an agitated Herr König greeted her. 'That Brandenburg! Just a conman! A fraud! Fighter pilot my foot! And he never won the Knight's Cross! His sister says their mother had measles when she was pregnant, and he was born blind. Fräulein Brandenburg tracked him down through the ration-card distribution centre. She came from Klein Beelzen to take him home so he can't do any more damage. He swindled a general's widow in Potsdam out of her last ring for an expensive operation to restore a war hero's sight. He'd been talking us into the same kind of thing. Ilse was on the point of sacrificing her platinum brooch for him. Well, now he can go back to weaving baskets under his sister's eye, the rogue. I always had a funny feeling about him, you know.'

'Of course you did, Herr König.' Jutta picked up her bag. 'Well, better luck with the next wearer of the Knight's Cross.'

John Ashburner was stowing a carton full of cans and bottles in the jeep, a present for Jutta's parents. 'Oh, please don't, John. They might feel it was charity.'

Shrugging, he carried the carton back into the kitchen. 'How did you do with Chalford?'

'He offered me a different job, but I said no. And he asked me out for a meal.'

'Oh, so he has his eye on you. What do you think of him?'

'He's a nice guy, but as a man he doesn't appeal to me at all.' She stood on tiptoe and put her arms around his neck from behind. 'Anyway, I already have one who wants to marry me. A girl doesn't let someone like that get away in a hurry,' she whispered in his ear.

Ashburner consulted the map. The Köpenick district was in the Soviet sector, and was best reached by driving right across the city. In these early post-war days, the borders between the four zones of occupation were of purely symbolic significance. Allies and Germans alike could move freely all over Berlin.

They drove through the ruinous landscape of the Mitte district. 'Until now going to see my parents was like a journey round the world.' Jutta leaned her head on his shoulder. 'I didn't know a tall good-looking American with a jeep then.'

'What are your parents like?'

'Mutti is hopelessly old-fashioned. "He's married," was the first thing she said when I told her about us.'

'What about your father?'

'He's unhappy with the way things are these days – but basically it's more himself he's unhappy with.'

'A Nazi?'

She sat up. 'Are you marrying him or me? Still, if it sets your mind at rest, Vati is inclined to be nationalistic, but he was never a Nazi.'

Two burnt-out German tanks stood one on either side of the street. Ashburner was about to drive between them when a dirty brown jeep with a red star blocked the way. The captain braked hard. A man with a stubbly head and a lieutenant's shoulder straps got out of the jeep. He put his cap on and checked its angle in his rear mirror before approaching. '*Propusk*,' he demanded. Ashburner guessed that it meant 'Papers'. He saluted very correctly. 'Captain John Ashburner, United States Army. According to the agreement of our high commands, Allies in uniform don't have to produce papers.'

The Russian barked something as incomprehensible as it was unfriendly in tone, which helped neither side to get any further.

'Let's turn back, darling,' Jutta said quietly.

'I can't do that, if only on principle. I have a right to drive through freely. Let us pass, lieutenant.' He gestured to the Russian to move his vehicle out of the way. The man shouted something over his shoulder.

Three Red Army soldiers standing by the vehicle trod out their *papyrossi* and unslung their Kalashnikovs. The fourth man, who wore a blue mechanic's overalls and a worker's cap tilted at an angle, climbed out and approached at a leisurely pace. 'Do you understand German?' he asked.

'My name is Weber, and I'm a German myself,' said Jutta. 'Please can you explain to this man that he has no right to stop an American officer.'

'Storch,' the man introduced himself. 'Secretary of the Communist Party, Köpenick district, back in my homeland with the victorious Red Army.'

'How nice for you, Herr Storch. Now we'd like to drive on.'

Storch spoke to the lieutenant in Russian. 'Your pass,' he asked her. She did not want to aggravate matters, and handed him the ID indicating that she was an employee of the Americans.

'What's going on?' Ashburner asked impatiently.

The interpreter spoke to the Russian. 'The American can drive on. The German woman comes with us for questioning.' He kept her pass.

'John, they want to take me with them.'

Instinctively, Ashburner reached for the Magnum at his side, but luckily he had left it in the office. 'My companion does not leave this jeep, is that understood?'

Jutta translated it into German, and the interpreter translated it into Russian. The lieutenant shouted an order. The soldiers loaded their Kalashnikovs.

'This doesn't look good,' muttered Ashburner, reaching for the field telephone. 'Let's hear what HQ has to say.'

The lieutenant drew his pistol from its holster, shouting, '*Ne svonyit*'!'

'Very well, my friend and ally, I get the idea,' Ashburner mollified him, switching the device to Off. He unfolded the latest number of *Stars and Stripes* and leaned back. 'He'll get tired of this after a while,' he soothed his girlfriend.

'They have radios too.'

'Yes, darling?'

'Your Russian friend. The one with the white sports car. Do you think he could help us?'

'Maxim Petrovich? My clever angel, that's the idea of the century. Tell that German Bolshie to get his Red liberator to phone General Bersarin's office and ask for Major Berkov. And tell him he'll be in deep trouble if he doesn't.'

Jutta beckoned to the district secretary. 'Oh, please, Herr Storch, we need your help.' She explained. 'Major Berkov will take responsibility, and then your lieutenant will be in the clear.'

Storch spoke to the Russian. He took off his cap and scratched his stubbly head. 'Da,' he decided. He took paper and pencil out of a card case dangling from a long strap and handed both to the interpreter.

'I'm to write down the American's name and rank in Cyrillic script,' he told Jutta. She spelled out the information he wanted.

The lieutenant returned to his vehicle. He spoke into the microphone, gesticulated, and kept pointing to the jeep. 'Seems like he has a lot to report,' commented Ashburner calmly.

Twenty minutes later the white BMW drew up beside their jeep. Major Berkov got out. 'John, how are you?'

'Thanks, very well. Apart from a little trouble with your excitable colleague here.'

'We'll soon deal with that. Won't you introduce me to your fair companion first?'

'Major Maxim Petrovich Berkov – Jutta Weber,' said John Ashburner, relieved.

Jutta shook hands with the major. 'We've seen each other before.'

'I remember it with pleasure.' Berkov did not conceal his interest. 'John, what seems to be the problem?' Ashburner explained. 'Leave it to me.' The major went over to the lieutenant, and after a brief exchange of words returned. 'He has orders to check all military vehicles passing this way – but only our own, of course. You must forgive his excess of zeal. Here you are, madame.' He gave Jutta her pass back. 'What brings you to our part of the city?'

'We're visiting my parents in Köpenick. They run the Red Eagle bar and café.'

'Well, I wish you a pleasant afternoon.' A long, appreciative look. 'A pity we won't be meeting again. I've been recalled to Moscow.' The major got into his sports car. 'Goodbye, John.'

'Thanks, Maxim Petrovich. You were a great help. It's been nice to know you.'

Berkov replied with a casual little wave of his hand. The BMW raced away. As he started the jeep, Ashburner made the four wheels spin, and left five coughing figures in a cloud of dust behind them. Fifteen minutes later, they had reached their destination.

The emblematic bird of Brandenburg itself was the sign above the door of the Red Eagle. A few hungry children surrounded the jeep. Jutta distributed chocolate bars that she had taken out of John's carton. A man in his sixties came out of the house. Jutta hugged him. 'Vati, this is John Ashburner. John, this is my father Ludwig Reimann.'

In honour of the day, Herr Reimann was wearing his dark-blue suit with a silver-grey tie, and in his buttonhole the little black and white ribbon of the Iron Cross, First Class, from the Great War. He shook hands with Ashburner. 'Pleased to meet you, captain.'

'Just John, sir, please.'

'Come in and let me introduce you to Mother.' He led the guest inside, through the empty bar and straight to the kitchen. Her hair freshly arranged, Frau Reimann stood by the stove lowering large dumplings into simmering water with a perforated spoon. 'Mother, this is John Ashburner. And this is my wife Else.'

Else Reimann wiped her right hand on her apron before offering it to the visitor. 'Do you like braised beef with potato dumplings? And for a starter we have zander fillets from the Müggelsee with shrimp, and a beef bouillon in between. Thank goodness for our old coal-burning stove. The gas connection is wrecked, and you can't get a proper meal cooked on the electric plate. Even if the power's on. My husband has put some Mosel to chill for the fish, and we have burgundy for the braised beef, and then chocolate pudding with vanilla sauce.'

She's excited and rather confused, thought Jutta as she interpreted. Suddenly she realized what unattainable delicacies her mother had been itemizing.

Her father said, in his rudimentary English, 'The bar is closed today. So we're on our own. A glass of sparkling wine, captain – I mean John.' Reimann opened the bottle, with a loud pop. It was not any old sparkling wine, but a 1940 champagne from Duval-Leroy. Where had her parents found all these marvels?

'You're late.' Ludwig Reimann reached for the watch in his waistcoat pocket. But only its pendant was hanging from the gold chain. 'Oh, I forgot, it's being repaired,' he murmured, embarrassed. Then Jutta realized: her father had sacrificed his gold watch to give his guest a proper welcome.

John Ashburner looked round the bar. The worn, wooden tables with clean, shiny ashtrays on them were meticulously arranged. The tablecloths at the back of the room were starched and well ironed. Everything here was simple and clean. Only the window frames didn't fit the picture. They looked as if woodworm had been at them. However, the marks were the pricks of countless drawing pins, a memento of the evening blackouts during the war years, when black paper had to keep any ray of light indoors. Reimann explained it to his guest, concluding gloomily, 'It cost our neighbour his head, because he was acused of giving light signals to enemy bombers. The poor fellow just forgot to black out his toilet window one evening. And that night of all nights he had the trots and kept running to the lavatory.'

'Why are you doing all this?' Jutta asked her mother in the kitchen. 'John and I didn't come to stuff ourselves with food.'

'We have our pride too.' Her mother tasted the broth. 'Jochen brought me flowers when he was courting you. "Jutta and I are for life," he said.' Else Reimann's eyes filled with tears. 'And now you're being unfaithful to him.'

'I suppose you'd rather I committed *suttee*.' At the same moment she realized that her irony was beyond her mother's grasp. In a more conciliatory tone, she added, 'Of course I can't forget Jochen just like that. John knows and understands.'

Her mother pursed her lips. 'And does he know what those brutes did to you?'

'I've told him I was raped twice, and almost raped a third time, and I said I'd no intention of letting that ruin my love life.'

'He isn't even divorced yet.'

'That's enough, Mother. Don't spoil the day for us.'

A couple of pennants of the local football club and a team photo hung on the walls. 'Cheers, boys.' Herr Reimann raised his glass to the picture. 'There's none of them left alive, except the outside left.' John Ashburner looked thoughtfully at the eleven young men in their football strip. Although he didn't like to admit it, the idea of a war in which he had not fought and which was so much more than he could imagine made him feel confused and upset.

'Come and eat!' Jutta took his arm and led him into the room next to the bar. He held her out mother's chair for her, earning a shy smile.

Reimann poured the Mosel. 'A Wehlener Sonnenuhr. Our German wines have rather flowery names. This one reminds me of the professor who lived in one of the villas at Wendenschloss. Professor Georg Raab, an art historian. He often looked in for a glass or two of Mosel. His wife wasn't supposed to know, he was a diabetic.'

'Jutta, do you remember how he used to draw you?'

'Yes, he did fourteen drawings of me. They were all nudes.' She cast her mother a challenging glance.

Else Reimann, embarrassed, changed the subject. 'They took the poor man away, like most of his kind. They spared his wife. She was only half-Jewish. All the same, she insisted on wearing the Jewish star. They let her keep a little room in her villa, and you saw her going about the place looking terrible, half-starved. Half-rations were the most those people got. In the end she hanged herself.'

'You could have slipped her something on the sly,' Jutta said soberly.

'What, and put us all in danger? What are you saying, child?'

'The truth.'

Her mother, looking injured, brought in the fish.

'What do you think about the Jews, John?' Ludwig Reimann asked.

At a loss, Ashburner shrugged his shoulders. 'I don't really know. There aren't any back home in Venice.'

'I can't say I particularly like them. Not that I ever wished them any harm. That was Hitler's big mistake, killing them instead of sending them to Madagascar. He roused all the Jewish financiers of America against him, and they put pressure on your President Roosevelt until the United States joined in the war. Without America on the other side we'd have won. I'm an old soldier of the Great War, I know what I'm talking about.' Reimann put his forefinger on the ribbon of his order. 'Cheers, my dear fellow.' He was getting animated. He emptied his glass and refilled it at once.

'Your zander is getting cold, Father,' Jutta said, to get him off the subject.

'Have they caught that dreadful murderer yet?' Her mother turned the conversation in what was hardly a more cheerful direction.

'We're getting close, ma'am. I have a very capable German colleague.' John Ashburner sipped the Mosel. 'Wonderful wine. Many thanks. And thank you for the invitation too. It's very important that you get to know me. After all, I want to take your daughter across the Atlantic.'

Else Reimann gave a loud sob. 'There, there, Mother,' her husband soothed her. 'Better times will soon come, and then we'll visit the two of them. I've always wanted to go to America.'

'Very nice people, your parents,' said John as they left.

He's only being polite, thought Jutta. Mother's tearful, as usual, and Father hasn't really understood the war. But he knows enough to run this place in Köpenick.

John got his long legs into the jeep. 'How long are you going to stay here?'

'Until Wednesday. I want to help Mother a bit in the garden. She has trouble with her back.' She bent down to kiss him. 'You know something? Mrs John Ashburner doesn't sound so bad.'

Rödel tore the sleeve away from the armhole. The ugly ripping sound went right through Ben. He looked at himself in the mirror, clad in a construction vaguely reminiscent of a jacket, with horsehair sticking out all over it. Tacking thread distorted the clear lines of the classic Prince of Wales check.

From the veranda workshop, he could see through the living room and into the bedroom. Heidi, naked to the waist, was sitting at her dressing table, brushing her hair. Her breasts rose and fell with every stroke of the brush. She must have failed to notice that the door was ajar.

The tailor ripped out the right sleeve too. Ben seemed to feel actual physical pain. 'Do you have to?' he protested faintly. The pale, pink-tipped girlish breasts were swaying in rhythm.

Rödel continued his work of destruction, unmoved. 'Another two fittings and you'll have a suit like something out of Baron Eelking's gentlemen's magazine, Herr Dietrich.' He had taken to calling Ben Herr Dietrich now that he was one of his esteemed customers.

Heidi rose to her feet. She had wrapped a towel around her hips, and it fell to the floor as she stood up. She went over to the chest of drawers. Her buttocks rubbed against each other.

'We'll leave the button at waist height. You don't want to take those dreadful Americans as your model.' Heidi opened a drawer and took out a white sports shirt. She reached her arms up in the air and pulled it over her head.

'What do you have against the Yanks, Herr Rödel?'

'What do I have against the Yanks?' Heidi's breasts disappeared under the sleeveless shirt that barely reached her navel. 'I have something against half-savages who want to destroy our culture, that's what. Only you can't say that out loud these days or someone gets straight up and calls you a Nazi.'

Ben didn't know why, but she looked more naked in the short sports shirt than without it. He tried to concentrate on the suit. 'When will it be ready?'

'We'll have another fitting next week. Let's say in two weeks' time.'

Spellbound, Ben stared at Heidi's dark bush, with a glow of pink between the curly hairs. A singing sensation rose in his groin.

'Do you have shoes, gentlemen's socks, a good shirt and a tie?' asked the tailor. 'Without the proper accessories you can forget about the suit.'

Heidi turned her back to the door and bent to tie her gym shoes. Ben's eyes remained glued to the mysterious shadow between her thighs until she put on her black gym shorts.

'I'm getting my suede shoes from the Dutchman, and I have the rest already.'

Heidi came into the workshop, a ball under her arm. She patted it to the floor with the flat of her hand and neatly caught it on the bounce. 'I'm going to play handball. Coming?'

'No time.'

She gave Ben a sly look. 'What a pity. I like to have spectators.' And he realized that she had known that he was watching her.

*

Herr Mühlberger, in a state of great agitation, propped his bicycle against the fence and stormed into the Zehlendorf CID office. 'He's back!' Sergeant Franke was busy bashing his poor typewriter. Police headquarters had demanded for a full account of all office materials used over the last few months. 'Who's back?' he asked without much interest, and typed:

APRIL: *500 sheets typing paper scattered around the area by pressure blast of a bomb. 64 sheets retrieved, of which 14 intact, 26 slightly soiled, 11 badly damaged, 13 charred. The search for the missing 436 sheets continues.*

345

MAY: *box of 100 sheets of carbon paper stolen by looting mujiks. Considering their state of civilization, probably to wipe their arses.*

JUNE: *1000 paperclips exchanged for 2 typewriter ribbons.*

JULY: *1 typewriter ribbon exchanged for 3 pencils.*

'The murderer. The one with a dimple in his chin,' Mühlberger cried. Franke went on typing:

AUGUST: *3 pencils given to the neighbours' children for school.*

'Where?' Franke asked when he had finished his task:

SEPTEMBER: *2 sheets typing paper and 1 envelope wasted on this Goddam list.*

'He's prowling round the building. It's clear as day, sergeant. The murderer is drawn back to the scene of the crime.'

'Herr Mühlberger, well, here we are together again sooner than I expected,' said Inspector Dietrich, who had been listening in from the next room. 'The car, Franke.'

'In the workshop, sir. The ignition's done for.'

'Oh, all right. You get more out of life riding a bicycle. You hold the fort here, Franke. Come with me, Herr Mühlberger.'

Twelve minutes later they had reached their destination. 'There, that's him in the entrance,' whispered Mühlberger, although it was impossible for the man to overhear him at this distance.

'Hold my bike.' Klaus Dietrich left the road and crossed the sandy strip to Number 198. The man was sitting on the front step outside the door. 'Inspector Dietrich, CID. What's your name?'

The man stood up. 'Giese. Franz Giese. I was meeting Lene, I'm a bit early. So I'm just waiting for her.'

'For Marlene Kaschke?'

'We've waited years, Lene and me, and now we've found each other again at last, it was the day before yesterday, and we swore nothing would part us again.'

'You were here the day before yesterday?'

'At four in the afternoon. She made some nice titbits for us to eat, and we drank sparkling wine. We made love till late.'

'You stayed all evening, Herr Giese? Till when?'

'Till the last U-Bahn left.' Mühlberger pushed the bicycles closer. Dietrich waved him away. Giese sat down on the step again. 'She's a good woman. She's been through a lot, even if she doesn't talk about it.' He paused for a while, as if there was no more to be said. Then he looked up at Dietrich, with torment, despair and hopelessness in his face. 'Who did it, inspector?'

Klaus Dietrich had seen soldiers' bodies torn to pieces and hanging in Russian birch trees; he had heard the screams of tank crews burning to death in their vehicles, and the whimpering of dying women and children in blazing cottages. But it wasn't wartime any more, where even the worst horrors became routine, and this grown man's quiet, grief-stricken voice moved him more deeply than anything he had seen. He laid his hand gently on Giese's head, he didn't know why. 'We'll find him, I promise you, Herr Giese. You can help us. Come and see me at the police station. This is the address. Good day, Herr Giese.'

Mühlberger had moved the two bicycles within earshot, and didn't let a word escape him. The inspector went to take his own bicycle back, but Mühlberger clutched it. 'Put that murderer behind bars!' he urged shrilly. 'You want to lock him up, you do!' Dietrich angrily liberated his bike from the man's grip and rode off.

Sergeant Franke struck his hands together in dismay. 'You let him go?'

'I asked him to come and see us in the next few days.'

'And you seriously believe he'll accept your invitation?'

'He'll come. He's not the murderer.'

'Mühlberger saw him in the stairwell at almost exactly the time of the crime, inspector. There can't be that many men with dimples in their chins.'

'He saw Franz Giese coming downstairs, that's true. Giese himself doesn't deny being with Marlene Kaschke from four in the afternoon until just before curfew. Two lovers, Franke, who had found each other again. Tenderness in the air, and the hope of a wonderful future together. And the murderer arrived only a few minutes later.'

'Who, sir? Who was he?'

'I don't know. But I have a kind of feeling that we know him.'

Hendrijk Claasen lived four houses away from Ben's grandparents. He was cleaning his Triumph in the front garden.

'Evening, Herr Claasen,' Ben greeted him politely. He tapped his school bag. 'Five cartons of Philip Morrises, is that OK?'

The Dutchman put the sponge down on the saddle of his motorcycle. 'Come in.' They entered the house. Claasen disappeared up to his shoulders in the sideboard and came out again with a pair of shoes. 'Brought them back from Nijmegen on my last trip. Try them on.'

Ben cautiously stroked the velvety brown suede and pressed the thick crêpe soles, testing them. 'Oh, wow!' he groaned, overwhelmed. The fact that the shoes were half a size too big did not lessen his delight. Claasen cut insoles out of several layers of newspaper. Ben slipped the shoes on. Doing up the laces was like a ritual act. The first steps were a revelation. He walked across the room as if on cotton wool. Carefully, he took the shoes off again. They would get their baptism at the same time as the suit. Only two more weeks, Herr Rödel had said.

CHAPTER EIGHT

THE CRIMEAN ORANGE crop was particularly good this year. Consequently, the manager of the Red Sun *kolkhoz* arranged a celebration in honour of the victorious Red Army, and after delivering a stirring speech, which was followed by some rousing songs performed by a choir of Young Pioneers from Odessa, he sent a cart full of the deliciously aromatic fruits on its way 'to our brave sons in the conquered capital of the Fascist enemy'. His calculated move was noticed by the Soviet press and inflated out of all proportion. Soon the word was that a dozen freight trucks of oranges were on their way to the West — a welcome alibi for the manager, who then sold the lion's share of the harvest on the black market at a hundred times its proper price.

The single cart of citrus fruit did in fact reach Berlin. By that time half the oranges were rotten. The Soviet city commandant had the other, edible half distributed to soldiers with families. Two crates ended up in the hands of the cultural officer, Lieutenant-Colonel Talin. He was not a family man, but was very fond indeed of a young blond dancer, a soloist called Heinzotto Druschke, and gave him one of the crates.

Druschke had survived the Hitler era in the bed of a high-ranking SS officer, thus preserving himself from the concentration camps. 'Pure self-defence. The man had shocking bad breath,' he drawled to friends after the liberation of the city. As a victim of Nazi persecution he received an apartment on Eschershauser Weg in Zehlendorf, where he exchanged the oranges with his neighbour Frau Molch for two bottles of cherry brandy. He intended to use the sweet, sticky alcohol to pull young boys.

The crate of oranges, along with two smoked hams, ten hundredweight of coal briquettes, three hundredweight of potatoes, five litres of cooking oil, and two kilos each of pearl barley, dried peas and haricot beans were the price paid for Frau Hermine Hellbich's Persian lamb coat. 'I have my good, thick-wool coat,' she explained, embarrassed. 'The boys need something hot and nourishing in winter, and it won't do the rest of the family any harm either.' She had even acquired six packets of Stella cigarettes for the district councillor.

She put five of the oranges in a bag. 'Take that to your father at the police station,' she told Ralf. 'The vitamins will do him good.'

Ralf hurried off. Perhaps he'd get to see a handcuffed criminal at the police station. But Papa was just sitting at his desk. He took the oranges with pleasure. 'What a nice surprise. Have one yourself, Ralf. And sit quiet in the corner until we're finished. Would you like one?' The inspector offered the bag to Sergeant Franke. 'So what else is new?'

'Orders from the top brass, no raid on those black marketeers at Schlachtensee station like we planned. Seems they're displaced persons and we can't touch them. Riff-raff, if you ask me, inspector.'

'Looks as if our hands are tied there. So let's keep concentrating on the search for our man.' Klaus Dietrich put a segment of orange in his mouth, pressing it against his palate with his tongue until the cells burst. The delicious, refreshing juice ran down his throat. 'Another one, Franke?'

'Thanks very much. I'll take it home to my wife.' Franke tied the precious fruit up in his handkerchief. 'Take my word for it, inspector, when we find that motorbike we'll find the murderer too.'

'I admire your perspicacity. So can you also tell us where to look for the motorbike?'

'In Frau Kalkfurth's garage,' said a voice from the corner.

Klaus Dietrich was startled. 'What did you say?'

Ralf flicked an orange pip into the waste bin with precision. 'Her cat was sitting on an old eiderdown. It was covering up a motorbike.'

'When was this?'

'Couple of days ago.'

Franke was sceptical. 'So the bike was just standing in the garage where anyone could see it?'

'You have to get past a whole lot of old junk first, and it's pretty dark in there,' Ralf told him.

'Is there any other way into the garage?' his father asked.

'Yes, a door out the back.'

'Come here.' Klaus Dietrich put his hands on his son's shoulders. 'Why didn't you tell me this before?'

'Didn't know you were looking for it. Did someone nick it?'

'Listen, son. What we've been discussing here is strictly secret. Police business. You're not to say a word about it to anyone else. Even Mama or Ben.'

Ralf's chest swelled with pride as he walked home. He was in on strictly secret police business!

Franke was convinced. 'So the Kalkfurth son wasn't killed in Poland at all. He survived the war and now he's killing again. His mother's hiding him and the motorbike. Why don't we put the lady through the wringer? A few hours in the cells will soften her up. We can find some excuse.'

'Take it easy, sergeant. If there's anything in what you say we'd be giving him advance warning. And we have no evidence.'

'He's alive and he's killing, I feel it in my guts,' Franke insisted. 'What do you suggest, sir?'

'We keep a watch on the garage. If our suspicions are right, he'll come out some time or other with the motorbike and go hunting again.'

Franke was sceptical. 'And we chug along behind in our wood-gas racing car?'

The inspector picked up the phone. 'Hello, Captain Ashburner. Dietrich here. I think we're on the trail.' He passed on Ralf's information, concluding, 'We're going to watch the garage. The problem is, if something happens how do we follow the motorbike? Our mobile stove does fifty kilometres an hour at the most. Of course, if we had a jeep . . .'

'You can dismiss that idea from your mind, Inspector. The Military Police isn't a car-hire firm. And since by now it's clear you're after a German killer, and he's been thoughtful enough not to murder any American girls, I have strict instructions to confine myself to an advisory function.' Ashburner looked at the silver-framed photograph on his desk. 'All the same, it's possible I might be able to help you. I'll call you back tomorrow. Goodbye.'

The captain straightened the photograph; the cleaning lady had knocked it out of place while she was dusting. The picture showed him and Jutta, arm in arm outside the door of the Wilskistrasse building. They had taken it with the delayed action shutter release, much to Jutta's amusement, because he looked so funny racing back from the camera on his long legs to stand there beside her. To him, it was more than just a snapshot. It was a public statement of his love. Even Sergeant Donovan, not noted for sensitivity, refrained from making a comment.

Colonel Tucker was less tactful. The city commandant's adjutant clicked his tongue. 'Pretty blonde Fräulein. Nice little morsel for the Uncle Tom killer, don't you think?'

'Keep your tasteless comments to yourself, Tucker.'

'Only a joke. You know what I hold against that damn murderer most, captain? Killing our Helga. Myra's back on the gin bottle now.'

'The German police have picked up a fresh trail.'

'General Abbot will be glad to hear it. But that's not the reason for my visit. You must help me, John. It's about Senator William Bullock from Washington. He's seen the Brandenburg Gate, he's bought a black-market Leica, and he's assured the local press that the eyes of the free world are on Berlin. The Senator's own eyes are more on the young women of Berlin, particularly a voluptuous redhead called Waltraud. Bullock's flying to Frankfurt today, to meet the military governor there for dinner. After that exhausting programme he'd like to relax for a few days in the Taunus, at our guesthouse there, once a German luxury hotel, in the company of the aforesaid lady. General Abbot wants nothing to do with the business and has offloaded it on me.'

'A delicate diplomatic mission, sir,' said the captain with heavy irony. 'How can I help you?'

'I need someone to pick the lady up in Steglitz and take her to the airplane. A captain in the Military Police would be above all suspicion.'

'In fact that fits in rather well, sir. I have to go to Tempelhof anyway. My wife is arriving today, in the plane that will be going on to Frankfurt with the senator.'

'All we need is a plausible explanation as to why this German girl has permission to fly AOA.'

'No problem, sir. We'll say she's a witness in the US case against some Nazi armaments company, and they want to question her in Frankfurt. Last week we had to fly a former state secretary to Frankfurt to give evidence, so it's not the first time. No one's going to check up.'

'Perfect idea, John. I'll have the necessary papers made out at once. Thanks a lot. I owe you one.'

The voluptuous redhead was called Waltraud Sommer and lived in Albrechtstrasse. She obviously enjoyed having a genuine US captain to carry her case and help her into the jeep. 'Does the plane shake about a lot?' she asked, more in anticipation then anxiety.

'Not in fine weather,' he told her.

The Arrivals and Departures of American Overseas Airlines were temporarily accommodated in a side area of Tempelhof airfield, which had been two-thirds destroyed. The rest of the space belonged to the US Air Force. Civilian air traffic had resumed two weeks earlier. There were few flights, and they were taken only by relations of the soldiers stationed in Berlin and a few official visitors.

Senator William Bullock was a massive man in a white Stetson. He stood surrounded by reporters, uttering a few platitudes. 'There he is! Hi, Bullie darling!' Waltraud sailed towards the senator with arms outstretched. With great presence of mind, Ashburner turned her round and gently but firmly pressed her down on a seat. 'You don't know the senator,' he quietly informed her. 'He'll come over to you.'

'OK, I get it. So no one notices and tells his old lady.'

They were sitting back to back with two passengers waiting to fly out. 'Hitler's right-hand man a Berlin allotment gardener!' Ashburner heard one of them say behind him. 'They were taking you for a ride, Clarence Preston Brubaker, and a good long ride at that.'

'A mistake, Dad, I admit it.'

'If I hadn't flown straight over and told Dick Draycott of UP to check the story out, right now the *Hackensack Herald* would be the laughing stock of the press. Cost me a pretty packet of dollars getting Draycott to keep his mouth shut, I can tell you.'

'I'm sorry, Dad.'

'You'll be even sorrier when I tell you there'll be no more foreign assignments for you. In future you can stay home and run the Puzzle Corner of the paper.'

'Yes, Dad. Here comes our plane.'

John Ashburner watched with mixed feelings as the silver bird flew in between the ruined buildings at the Neukölln end of the makeshift runway. Ethel had announced that she was coming in a few brief lines. Her letter said not a word about divorce, and without her consent he stood no chance. The laws of Illinois were on Ethel's side. He had not told Jutta that his wife was coming, and he felt very bad about that.

'Don't move until your flight is called,' he told the girl beside him. 'And stay away from the senator. Have a good journey.' He rose.

'All clear. And thank you very much.' Ashburner made off before Waltraud could clasp him gratefully to her opulent bosom.

As he passed, he took a look at father and son. Dad had a fat, jowly face. Brubaker Junior was colourless as a glass of water. The captain opened the newly glazed door of the lounge and stepped out into the open air. Nearby lay the burnt-out skeleton of a four-engined plane. 'The last Lufthansa flight from Barcelona,' a young air-force sergeant told him. 'A Junkers 290. An incendiary bomb hit it after it landed. That was back in April.'

The DC4, with its port engine roaring, came in under the badly damaged suspended roof of the arrivals area. Two men rolled the steps out. A stewardess appeared at the top of them, looking out over the smoke-blackened remains of the former central airport as if it were a sunny, fairy-tale landscape. With routine civility, she said goodbye to the few passengers who made their way down the steps, then returned to the shelter of the cabin.

Ethel was wearing an old trench coat and an all-weather hat. She never had bothered much about her appearance. 'So there you are.' He took her travelling bag and case.

'Are you getting enough to eat?' She had read about the starvation rations in Germany.

'Oh, you can get all you need in the PX. Or I go and eat dinner at the Harnack House.' He put her baggage in the jeep. The day had turned hot. A cloud of dust drifted over from the ruins on Berliner Strasse.

'People really might clean the place up a little better,' she grumbled as they drove through the rubble.

'If the German Luftwaffe had reached Venice you wouldn't talk such nonsense,' he snapped, and realized with surprise that he was defending the city and its inhabitants. He braked, because a horse-drawn cart, laden with rubble, was crossing the road.

'How primitive. Don't they have any trucks?'

'No,' he said crossly. At the same moment he realized that he was showing more hostility with every word he spoke. He changed the subject. 'Tell me, dear, what's new at home?'

354

'They brought in Jesse Rollins as pitcher for the Chicago Cubs.' Ethel was an admirer of the baseball pros.

'Is Rollins still having a relationship with the mayor's wife?'

'He's having a relationship, yes, but not with Millie Walker.' She giggled as if she had heard a good joke. For the rest of the drive she talked about the neighbours. 'Liz Lunnon's expecting her fourth. Folks say it's not her husband's. Dick and Ella Jarwood are getting divorced – because she wants to leave Venice and he doesn't. Vanessa King's at loggerheads with the mayor. She says America is a free country and she won't take that *Lady Chatterley* book out of her window.' She chuckled. 'I read it. All that about the gardener fellow sticking flowers everywhere . . .'

He listened, and thought of Jutta. Would she be bored in Venice, like the lively Ella? Maybe not if she made friends with Vanessa. She was a bookseller too. But Ethel still stood between them, and so far she hadn't said a word to indicate what she thought of their divorce.

They stopped at the entrance of the US enclave. 'Uncle Tom's Cabin,' he explained.

'I wept over that story when I was a little girl.'

'I don't mean the book – it's the name of the U-Bahn station and the area round about, right, Ted?'

'Yes, sir.' The young military policeman grinned and raised the barrier. Ashburner turned right at the corner.

'Acacias, how pretty,' she cried, delighted. 'They cut them all down at my parents' in Springfield when the telephone line went underground.'

He carried her case and bag into the bedroom and put them down beside the bed. 'It has clean sheets on it,' he told her, earning an amused glance. 'I'll be sleeping on the sofa next door. Can I make you a coffee or a tea?'

'I'd rather have a drink. Any bourbon here?' She settled comfortably in the armchair, kicked off her flat loafers and stretched her legs uninhibitedly. She reminded him of the athletic, tomboyish high-school girl he'd married ten years earlier.

He poured two whiskeys. 'How was your journey?'

'Endless. The bus to Chicago, then the "Century" to New York. Six hours' flight from New York to Newfoundland. Refuelling in Gander. They have to be full up to reach Shannon in Ireland. That's the shortest way to Europe, the stewardess told us. Ten hours over the Atlantic, just imagine.

Not to mention four hours going on to Frankfurt and almost two hours to Berlin.'

'You must be exhausted.'

'I never felt more awake, and I'm ravenously hungry. I'll just shower, and then let's go and have dinner in your Harnack House, OK, Johnny?' That was what she'd called him in the first years of their marriage.

'OK.' He admired her energy.

She was fresh and slightly pink from the shower, which suited her, like the way she'd pinned up her damp, shining brown hair. She wore high heels and a full-skirted summer dress, blue with white spots and a blue bolero. He hadn't seen her look so chic in a long time. She pulled the dress up to her thighs to adjust her suspenders.

Limousines and army vehicles were parked outside the Harnack House. A band was playing inside. 'Capt. & Mrs Ashburner', he wrote in the visitors' book. That was the rule, like showing his ID card. Germans could come in only accompanied by Allies.

Harold Tucker and his wife crossed their path. Myra Tucker was obviously tipsy. 'All go smoothly at Tempelhof, John?' asked Tucker.

'Yes, sir. This is my wife Ethel. Colonel and Mrs Tucker.'

'Hi, Ethel. Just call me Myra,' babbled Mrs Tucker, seeking support on her shoulder.

'Delighted to meet you, Mrs Ashburner. You and John must visit with us sometime soon,' said the colonel, trying to gloss over the difficult situation. 'Come along, Myra.' He led his swaying spouse away.

'Seems to have a problem, poor woman,' said Ethel dryly.

Ashburner pulled her chair out for her. The waiter brought the menu. They chose veal goulash with rice, and a Rhine wine to drink, with apple tart and vanilla ice to follow. Ethel talked vivaciously about trivialities. When they reached coffee, he couldn't contain himself any longer. 'You did get my letter?'

'Swing, that's great!' she cried, clapping. 'Come on, Johnny!' She led him away from the table to the nearby nightclub. Engineers had converted the horseshoe-shaped auditorium of the Harnack House, turning the rising tiers of seats into terraces with little tables. The bar was at the top. Down below, where Max Planck had once delivered his lectures, they were dancing to swing.

356

There was a table free by the dance floor. 'Champagne,' she demanded. That was something new, too.

He played along; he had to keep her in a good mood. 'Cheers,' he said, raising his glass to her.

'Cheers, Johnny.' She emptied her own. 'Let's dance again.' He had no choice. Luckily the slow foxtrot kept her high spirits within bounds. But she pressed so close to him that at every step her knee came between his thighs.

'Hey, you're not drinking,' she cried when they were back in their seats. He emptied his glass in a single gulp. Another followed when they returned from the dance floor for the third time, feeling heated, and then another too. On the way home he realized that he had drunk a little too much.

'How about talking now?' he asked in the bedroom.

'Tomorrow, Johnny.' She let her dress slip to the floor beside the bed. She looked very sexy in her suspender belt and panties.

'OK, tomorrow, then.' He took a blanket from the cupboard and went to settle down with it next door.

'Will you help me off with this?' He waited for her to turn round so that he could undo her bra. 'It fastens in front.' He groped clumsily between her breasts until they leaped out at him. Suddenly it dawned on him that she had planned this all along. Now they were closely intertwined, just as they had been on those hot Sundays at the beginning of their marriage, when they couldn't get enough of each other.

'So what's your new girl like?' she asked later, in the dark. 'I've heard these German girls are good in bed. Congratulations.' She laughed softly. 'Our goodbye fuck, Johnny. I hope it was fun for you. I'm going to Chicago with Jesse Rollins. We want to get married. I came to sort out all that divorce stuff with you.'

'You devil!' He turned her over and took her wildly.

Inge Dietrich wrapped up two sandwiches for her husband. He put them in the briefcase that he strapped to the carrier behind his bike. 'Coming home the same time as usual?'

'I don't know. Don't wait up for me.' He kissed her; his thoughts somewhere else entirely. That indefinable feeling wouldn't let go. A feeling that he'd missed something important. He'd run right into it and never noticed. He had lain awake half the night, searching for something he couldn't grasp.

Towards morning the answer had seemed close enough for him to reach out for it, before it ran through his fingers again.

Inge was worried. She knew that the murders of those women pursued him into his dreams. He had taken up the gauntlet thrown down by the sinister killer. To him, it was a man to man fight that he had to win.

She cut bread for the others. It was grey and sticky; the baker had stretched the dough with minced potato peelings. Yesterday she had been to Frau Kalkfurth's for a special ration of syrup made from the waste left after processing sugar beet. Her father trickled the thick, dark brown goo on a slice of bread. 'I'm worried about your husband. He's been asking when the security services firm will be starting up again.'

'He wants to go back to his old job once these dreadful crimes have been solved.'

'I wouldn't if I were him,' the district councillor said. 'If he stays with the CID they'll take him on in the police force officially, and that'll give him pension rights. You have to think of the future.' Hellbich helped himself to another spoonful of syrup.

Ben bit into his second slice of bread and inspected the semi-circle stamped in it by his teeth. There was no more, but that couldn't dampen his high spirits. The suit was waiting for him. In half an hour's time he could take that tailor-made dream home.

His mother appeared in headscarf and jacket. 'The pharmacist has peppermint tea off the ration. It'll make a change from the chestnut coffee, and it's good for the bronchial tubes.' In fact no one in the house had bronchial problems except for her father, who was plagued by a permanent smoker's cough, but she liked to look on the bright side of everything. It was her way of countering the bleak misery of everyday post-war life.

The district councillor reached for his hat. Ralf put his school bag under his arm. 'Coming, Ben?'

'You go ahead,' called his brother from upstairs. From out the window, he saw his grandfather, Ralf and his mother leave the house. He took the suede shoes out of their hiding place. His socks had holes in their left toes, but the shoes hid them. The collar of the shirt he'd worn for his confirmation was two sizes too small and wouldn't do up, but the striped tie from Father's wardrobe held it together at the neck. He tucked the shirt into his trousers and put his sweater over it. He deposited his school bag in the garden shed.

He entered the veranda workshop on Ithweg, filled with anticipation. 'Just a moment, please, Herr Dietrich.' Rödel was busy brushing a heavy ulster. 'I forgot about it all these years, it was hanging in mothballs at the back of the storeroom. Professor Simon, the distinguished surgeon brought it in to be pressed in '38. They took him and his family away next day.' Ben was hardly listening. His eyes were searching the workshop. 'I'll mothproof the coat again afterwards, just in case Herr Simon has survived. A few have come back from the camps. Little Rademann from Schmidt's drug store, for instance. He doesn't talk about it, but it must have been terrible. Now they're trying to turn it against him, but he was only the commandant's orderly. Heidi – Heidi! Bring Herr Dietrich's suit.'

Heidi took her time. Through the open doorway Ben could see her tidying her hair in front of the mirror and undoing the top button of her blouse, perhaps because it was quite a warm day. She disappeared from his field of vision, and soon afterwards came into the workshop with the suit over her arm.

'Hi.' Ben put out his hand, but Heidi was too busy putting the jacket on the black tailor's dummy. She handed Ben the trousers and stood there waiting.

'Heidi, please!' Her father gestured impatiently. She tossed her hair back with a challenging air and went out.

The trousers were long and narrow, with sharp creases in them, high turn-ups, and a perfect fall to the velvety brown suede shoes. Ben felt like whooping out loud, but a man of the world didn't break into cries of delight just because of a pair of well-fitting trousers. He coolly noted that the jacket was A1 – the prefix which since time immemorial had distinguished car registration plates in the capital from those of lesser beings in the provinces, a synonym for all that was first-class and metropolitan.

'A masterpiece. You don't see this kind of thing every day.' Herr Rödel helped Ben into the jacket and straightened his tie. 'Finest pre-war horsehair and ivory-nut buttons. My last reserves.' The tailor looked in a drawer.

Heidi reappeared. Another button on her blouse had undone itself. Ben could see the pale glimmer of her breasts. 'Suits you really well.' She came close to him and stroked the lapels. 'Aren't they soft?' Her warm, sweet breath wafted over his face. 'Sunday at two in the hollow by the lake,' she said softly. Ben took a deep breath. His suit seemed to have finally routed Gerd Schlomm's short lederhosen.

Rödel had found what he was looking for. 'Here, a little extra.' He tucked a decorative silk handkerchief into the breast pocket of the jacket. 'And please recommend me elsewhere, Herr Dietrich.' Ben got into his old clothes. The master tailor wrapped the suit in a grey cloth and draped it over the boy's arm.

Once home, Ben got upstairs unseen and hid his treasure in the locker in the attic. Even his fertile imagination wouldn't have stretched to devising an explanation for this surprising addition to his wardrobe that would satisfy his parents. The suit disappeared behind the district councillor's black frock coat, last worn for his son's funeral. Lance-Corporal Werner Hellbich had died in a German field hospital of burns suffered while training a *Volkssturm* civil defence brigade. A seventy-year-old conscript had aimed the rear fire-jet of his bazooka at him by mistake.

Grandmother Hellbich was polishing the hall floor. 'You're early home today,' she said in surprise

'Our maths teacher is off sick,' he lied. 'I'm going to the barber's.'

'Tell him to cut it shorter this time, will you?'

'Medium length with a parting,' Ben told Herr Pagel. The barber had moved his business premises to his own apartment. His salon was out of reach, in the American prohibited zone at Onkel Toms Hütte U-Bahn station. A GI from Brooklyn was giving his comrades crew cuts there.

'Yes, sir. Want a magazine to read?' Herr Pagel had salvaged several years' issues of the *Berliner Illustrierte*. Ben picked an old number celebrating the first flight to New York of the airship Hindenburg.

'And a packet of condoms,' he added casually as he was paying for the haircut.

'Top quality peacetime wares. Guaranteed not to split.' Herr Pagel pushed what he wanted over the table. 'To keep the most precious part of you warm.' He winked at Ben, who pocketed the box and got out of there. He would have liked to ask a couple of questions about how to use the condoms, but he felt embarrassed. He hoped there were instructions with them.

Inspector Dietrich had ordered several officers to keep watch on Frau Kalkfurth's garage round the clock. No luck. 'Killers like our man have a sixth sense,' said Franke gloomily.

'More likely he goes through some macabre cycle of compulsion.' Klaus

Dietrich had been reading several works of criminal psychology covering similar cases. 'He'll be back when the mood takes him again.'

Vollmer put his head round the door. 'Captain Ashburner, sir.'

'Come in, captain. How are you?'

'Fine, thanks.' Ashburner put a small, gleaming metallic box down on the desk. It was about the size of a matchbox. 'Know what that is?'

'No idea.'

'Come on, I'll show you.'

There were two jeeps parked out in the road. Corporal Miller was sitting in the front vehicle smoking a pipe. Ashburner bent down and fixed the box under Miller's jeep. 'A magnet. Sticks like glue. OK, corporal, drive on.' Miller stepped on the gas. Ashburner strolled over to his own jeep. 'Get in, inspector. Here, take this.' He handed Dietrich a canvas bag.

'Would you tell me what's going on?'

'Open it.' Ashburner drove off.

The bag contained a rectangular grey object the size of a cigar box, with switches and buttons, rather like a radio. 'A radar device?'

'Not a bad shot, inspector. Throw the left-hand switch and turn the middle button to the right.' Loud beeping was heard, and soon became weaker. 'That's the little transmitter under Miller's jeep. The corporal's driving faster than us. The signal gets weaker as the distance increases. So let's step on it a bit.' Ashburner accelerated. The beeping tone grew louder, and then suddenly softer again. Ashburner braked. They reversed a little way and turned into the side street they had just passed. The beeping was more and more insistent. They stopped. Miller's jeep was waiting for them, concealed in the entrance to a building. Ashburner bent down and fished the little box out from under the other jeep.

'Amazing.' Dietrich was enthusiastic.

'A loan from our strategic services people. They're already working on a smaller version, one you can stick under a suspect's shoe.'

'No one's going to believe this.'

'And it's no one's business to know about it either. My role as an adviser doesn't stretch to helping out the German police with electronic toys.' The captain put the little transmitter in the bag with the receiver. 'There's a pair of headphones in there too. You put them on and throw the right-hand switch. OK, I'll take you back to the station.'

'There's no need. A little walk will do me good.'

'Well, good luck, inspector.'

Dietrich took the bag by its shoulder strap and got out. Ashburner, shaking his head, watched him go: a thin, prematurely grey-haired man in a suit too big for him, dragging his left leg slightly.

'And he thinks he's going to catch a killer,' said Corporal Miller, putting his superior officer's thoughts into words.

'I want to get into the garage and look at that motorbike unobserved. Any ideas?'

'Diversionary tactics,' said Vollmer, and came up with some suggestions.

'Excellent,' the inspector praised him. 'Tomorrow morning here at eight-thirty, then.'

At nine they were at Am Hegewinkel. Vollmer went knocking on doors, making out that he was an inspector from the power station making sure no one was illegally tapping into the electricity. Dietrich and Franke, meanwhile, were behind the buildings collecting bits of wood. The inspector wore an old parka and a greasy sailor's cap. Franke had got himself up in a sweater full of holes and was pulling a small handcart. They were slowly approaching the Kalkfurth property.

'Get to the back of the line,' said the queuing women crossly as Vollmer pushed past them into the shop.

'Berlin Electricity.' Vollmer showed an official-looking piece of paper. 'Show me all the power points you have in the place,' he told the well-fed Winkelmann, who was serving hungry customers.

'You go with him. I'll take over here.' Martha Kalkfurth steered her wheelchair round behind the counter. 'Well, what'll it be, Frau Krüger?'

Dietrich looked at his watch and nodded to Franke. The gate in the fence was no obstacle. A few steps and they were at the back door of the garage. Franke took a bunch of skeleton keys out of his pocket. Minutes later he had cracked the simple lock.

The light inside was dim. Two metres ahead of them lumber towered up to the ceiling, barring the way to the front of the garage. On the right, a garden hose hung on the wall, and a lawn mower was propped against it. On the left you could just make out the shape of a motorbike under a shabby old eiderdown. The inspector raised the quilt. A 1936 NSU 300 was revealed.

The tank was half full, and several damp leaves clinging to the front tyre showed that the bike had recently been used.

Dietrich bent down, as if checking the number plate, and fixed the little metal box under the back mudguard. It was his own personal weapon in his duel with the murderer, and there was no need for the others to know about it.

'What did I say, sir?' asked the sergeant triumphantly once they were outside.

Dietrich grinned. 'You said you'd help to deliver any wood we collected to my home. Which is just around the corner.'

Vollmer was back in the police station soon after them. 'Huge long line of customers outside the shop, Frau Kalkfurth and her assistant Winkelmann inside,' he reported. 'I made out I was examining every power point from the cellar to the attic, and I took a good look around the place. There's no sign that anyone is living in that house except for Frau Kalkfurth, or that anyone's been hiding there.'

As usual he waited for nightfall. Night was his hunting ground. He went into the garage around ten and switched on his torch, took the quilt off the motorbike and stopped short. Something was different. The top of the fuel tank! He always screwed it on so that the maker's logo was vertical. Now it was over to one side. It didn't take him a minute to find the little metal box under the back mudguard. Wondering what to do, he turned it back and forth, fitted it to the lawn mower, took it off again and thought. Grinning, he put it in his pocket. He got the message. He did up the chinstrap of the leather helmet and put his goggles on.

'They're on your trail, son,' said a voice through the lumber.

He laughed dryly. 'The inspector's thought up something special. He thinks I don't know.'

'They'll find you wherever you hide. I can't help you now. Times have changed. Leave your motorbike here, son, and get out before they chop your head off. Though that might be best for both of us.'

'Mother, you're going too far,' he said, indignant.

Klaus Dietrich slung the bag containing the receiver over his shoulder and cycled out into the dark, a rather odd figure. The headphones gave him an owlish look. This was the third night, and Inge was wondering anxiously how long his exhausted and undernourished frame could keep it up.

His route took him first to Am Hegewinkel, where on the last two nights a steady beeping tone had told him that the motorbike was in the garage. Tonight there was no beep. The killer was on the prowl.

Her father's self-righteous monologues and her mother's constant complaints got on Jutta's nerves. She set off for home two days earlier than she had planned. It took her for ever to get from Köpenick to Berlin Mitte. The total collapse of the capital was just four months in the past, and the transport system still left much to be desired. But from Wittenbergplatz on, the U-Bahn ran normally. The line had hardly been damaged at all in the western suburbs.

On the way she thought about John. She felt a shameless, delicious desire for him. She imagined taking him by surprise, and felt herself get damp. The elderly man opposite gave her a little wink, as if he guessed her thoughts.

She reached Onkel Toms Hütte on the last train, hurried up the steps and left the station down the narrow alley lined with barbed wire that the Americans had left for Germans to use. At the barrier, she showed the guard her pass. Full of happy anticipation, she entered the brightly lit prohibited zone. The music of Benny Goodman was swinging from a window somewhere, accompanied by laughing voices. She pressed the bottom bell outside Number 47 Wilskistrasse.

What seemed like endless seconds of waiting heightened her excitement. She thought she could already feel his firm body and her tongue between his lips. At last the door opened. She had the words 'John, darling' on the tip of her tongue. But the woman in the doorway got in first. 'John, darling,' she called over her shoulder.

She instantly knew the identity of this woman in the housecoat standing in front of her, hair rather dishevelled, a glass in her hand, and she knew the woman had come to claim her property. Like a wounded deer, Jutta turned and ran.

John Ashburner came out of the bathroom. Ethel was amused. 'Rather impulsive, your young lady.'

'I'm going after her,' he said firmly.

The inspector turned into Argentinische Allee. His stump hurt every time he pushed the pedals down. The bicycle rattled quietly. Candlelight flickered in a few windows, as if Christmas had come early. But it was October, the electricity was off, and there was a murderer cruising somewhere, through the mild, starlit night. He listened to the headphones as if expecting them to answer his question.

He went through the week's events in his mind. Where had he been? What had he been doing? Captain Ashburner had shown him the beeping transmitter. He had been to Mr Chalford's office with Mühlberger to ask about the card index of employees. He had searched the garage in secret, and tampered with the motorbike. He had been on cycle patrol for the last three nights. Somewhere and at some time during the past week, an idea had occurred to him. He had filed it away in his subconscious, and now it was lying there, refusing to be dredged up to the surface.

A faint beeping chirped in the headphones and soon grew stronger. Dietrich braked, laid his bicycle flat on the pavement, and ducked down behind a switchbox beside the road. The motorbike roared past not two metres from him, the rider's goggles reflecting the clear night sky.

Getting on his bicycle, Dietrich followed the fading beep, which showed him that the motorbike was moving away. He had no chance on his old bike. But to his surprise, a minute later the signal grew stronger again, swelling to a fortissimo. His adversary must be very close.

He stopped, looked all round – and saw the small box with the metallic gleam. It was stuck to the lamppost in front of him. His enemy had tricked him.

Something came rushing toward him with concentrated force from the nearby main road. The NSU 300! A dull thud flung him to the ground. His enemy swerved around and returned to the attack. Dietrich rolled aside, but not fast enough. There was an ugly crunch, as if all his bones were breaking. The motorbike raced away.

He lay there helpless. Suddenly revelation struck him like a thousand-volt electric shock. There it was, the connection he had desperately been trying to make for days on end. He tried to get up. He failed. The tyres of the heavy motorbike had crushed his prosthesis, and now it was hanging at a bizarre angle from the stump. Turning up his trouser leg, he unstrapped it.

A jeep was approaching, its searchlight sweeping the pavement. Dietrich raised an arm and waved, but just before the jeep reached him the searchlight switched to the other side of the road. His calls were drowned out by the sound of the engine. The hell with it, I have to get to my feet somehow, he thought. To my foot, he corrected himself.

He turned over and crawled on hands and knees to the street light where his bicycle was lying. It was barely three metres, but it seemed like miles. He hauled himself up by the lamppost. Only at the third attempt did he succeed in picking up his bike. Grasping the handlebars with both hands, he put his half leg over the middle bar and got himself into the saddle. He pushed off with his sound foot. For a few seconds he thought he would tip over, but he soon found out how to keep his balance. Pushing down the pedal, he brought it up again with his instep. It worked better than he'd expected. He got up some speed. There was no time to lose. He hoped the guard would let him telephone the American prohibited zone. And then he had an appointment with the killer.

Benny Goodman and the laughing voices mocked her, and the bright glow of the floodlights burned Jutta's eyes. She pulled herself together. She mustn't let go. She wasn't going to give the other woman the satisfaction.

There was no electricity on the other side of the barrier. She strode energetically forward. She was furious with herself and with John. He'd lied to her. A nice little adventure to see him through until Ethel arrived, that was what he wanted, and silly goose that she was, she'd served it up to him on a silver salver.

She stopped and breathed deeply. The night air did her good. She remembered all that lay behind her. The nights of air raids. The Red Army hordes. The unspeakable humiliations. And here she was getting upset over an American to whom, after all, she had given herself willingly! 'Let's forget it!' she heard Jochen saying. It was what he'd said after their first marital tiff, which led to a delightful reconciliation in bed. She smiled.

A sound brought her back to reality. Jutta turned. A figure emerged from the darkness, arms raised. A chain came around her neck, clinking. Breathing hard, her attacker tugged at her dress. She was gasping like a landed fish. Her hands clutched empty air. The chain cut off her breath.

Violet squiggles danced before her eyes. In the last few seconds before death by strangulation you see your whole life pass before your eyes again, she thought; now where did I read that?

JUTTA

WAS IT A dream or reality? She felt his weight on her and his prick deep between her thighs. His face was hidden in the darkness. Jochen? Or the other man, the man she hadn't yet met but would meet some day? He did exist, this man, how else could she dream of him? Her heart was thudding persistently, as if it were Mutti knocking on the door.

It was Mutti. 'Seven o'clock, child!' she cried. Reluctantly, Jutta hauled herself out of bed. She was all hot and damp between her legs. She would have loved to go back into her dream and see his face. His blurred features were still before her as she stood under the shower. In the kitchen she spread her usual breakfast roll with butter, watching a fly crawling over Kaiser Wilhelm's nose. The old gentleman with his mutton-chop whiskers hung on the door of the pantry. Jutta's great-grandfather, very much the loyal subject, had pinned him up there long ago.

Mutti poured coffee from the big, blue enamel pot that stood on the cast-iron stove. Its coals glowed even at night. A couple of workers were talking in loud voices over an early beer in the bar. Vati laughed approvingly at some remark. He often laughed like that, a short and almost surprised burst of laughter. It saved him the trouble of keeping up a conversation. Mutti put the pot back on the stove. The black brew would stay warm there in case a guest ordered coffee. 'Do we expect you home this evening?'

'It all depends.' She had no idea what it all depended on, she was fending off the questions that Mutti would ask next: why didn't they finally get married? Spending the night with a man, even your fiancé, was improper. Jochen should know that too, as an educated man who was aware of his responsibilities.

'I must be off.' She avoided the bar and left the Red Eagle through the kitchen garden. It was ten minutes' walk to Köpenick station.

368

In the train she took Hans Fallada's new novel out of her briefcase. As a future bookseller she had to keep up to date. Today she had the last pages of a depressing story about a hopeless hero in a penitentiary to read.

When she had finished the book she played at guessing what kind of people the other passengers were, with their grave, cheerful, indifferent, friendly or hostile faces. A gentleman in a Homburg hat, his waistcoat stretched tight over a rounded paunch: a jeweller, insurance agent, teacher? He hid his Party badge behind the *Lokalanzeiger*, and Jutta read the newspaper headlines for this day in July 1934. 'Austria's Chancellor Dollfuss Assassinated – Hans Stuck wins German Grand Prix for Auto Union – Marie Curie Dies.' The old woman opposite, who had a basket full of eggs, a ham, two sausages and a bunch of rhubarb, must come from Rahnsdorf, Zeuthen or even further out in the country, bringing good nourishing food for city children. The lady in the hat and cotton gloves was surely on her way to have a comfortable gossip over coffee at Kranzler's or the Café Schilling with other ladies in hats and cotton gloves. The air force major with his white summer cap and battered leather case was probably on the way to his desk in the new Reich Aviation Ministry.

Also new to the general appearance of the city were the swastika banners on post offices, and the notices in some shop windows: 'Under Aryan Management'. The familiar Prussian blue of the police uniform had changed to an ugly green that even forestry officials disliked.

The Berliners took all this in their stride. It hailed from distant southern provinces that no one took seriously. They were all agreed: this Austro-Bavarian circus would soon close down again.

The man in the boots and brown shirt at Heidelberger Platz, where Jutta changed from the S-Bahn to the U-Bahn, was also a Berliner first and an SA man second. 'Give generously! The Führer needs warm underclothes,' he shouted, rattling his collection tin for the Nazi Winter Charity fund. 'You wearing brown underpants too?' asked a cheeky boy. 'Only when I got the trots,' was the cheerful answer.

Jutta took the U-Bahn to Onkel Toms Hütte. A few years earlier the architect Doering had built a modern shopping centre there on the sandy soil of the Brandenburg Mark around the station. It was on the same level as the U-Bahn tracks, and thus lower than the street.

The bookshop was in one of the two shopping streets that ran parallel to

369

the two long sides of the station platform. On its left was Zabel's soap shop, on the right was Fräulein Schummel, gentlemen's outfitter. Further right, Herr Müller and Herr Hacker sold and repaired radio sets, while to the left of the soap shop a smell of the North Sea wafted from Ehlers the fish-monger's.

There was a smell of freshly brewed coffee in the bookshop. Jutta's boss drank it all morning, in tiny coffee cups, smoking Egyptian cigarettes with it. In the afternoon she took tea. She was sitting in the back room as usual, reading. Diana Gerold was in her thirties, with short, black hair and a healthy glow from all the tennis she played at the club on Hüttenweg. 'Like a coffee too?'

Jutta poured herself a cup. They opened at nine, which gave her another ten minutes. She pointed to Diana's book. 'A new publication?'

'No, old stock. Stefan Zweig's novellas. Twenty copies, unsaleable because they've just been banned. Degenerate and un-German, apparently. Although there's hardly a greater master of the German language than Zweig. Unlike the clumping style of one Herr Beumelburg, whose wartime prose the German Book Trade Association so warmly recommends. His publisher is reserving us fifty copies of the latest, with the gentle hint that it wouldn't look good if we take any fewer. Outrageous blackmail, that's what it is.' Diana Gerold had talked herself into a rage.

'Time I opened up.' Jutta dealt with sales and the lending library, while the owner of the shop usually stayed behind the scenes.

Herr Lesch was already waiting: Ewald Lesch, widower, retired post-office official, a regular customer of the library. 'Good morning, Herr Lesch. We have a new Lord Peter Wimsey in,' she greeted him. Lesch loved English detective stories. She took the Dorothy L. Sayers volume off the shelf.

'I hope it's not a let-down like that Edgar Wallace book. I thought *Sanders of the River* would be a crime story. Didn't know the man writes about Africa too. I'm not interested in African stories.'

'You could have a nice Agatha Christie,' Jutta said, to mollify him. 'What about Hercule Poirot?' Herr Lesch went away, a satisfied customer. At the door he passed a well-dressed, youngish man, who came in and looked rather helplessly around the shop.

'Good morning, sir. Are you looking for anything in particular?'

'Yes, Hitler's *Mein Kampf*.' He seemed embarrassed about it.

'Cloth-bound or half-cloth?' asked Jutta in a business-like way.

'Leather-bound, please. Russian leather or morocco. Gold-stamped. India paper if possible.'

'I'm afraid we don't have a de luxe edition like that in stock, sir. Maybe if you tried one of the big bookshops in the city centre . . .'

'I can order what you want by phone.' Frau Gerold had come into the front of the shop. 'The book distribution people will send it with tomorrow's delivery. Meanwhile, take the half-cloth edition to read. We won't charge you.'

'I don't want to read the damn thing. I need a handsome edition for the desk in my new legal offices.'

'Of course, as a good German and an upright National Comrade one likes to have the great work of our Führer and Reich Chancellor always to hand.' Diana Gerold's mouth twisted in a mocking smile.

He gave Jutta his card. 'For when the order arrives.' He was Dr Rainer Jordan, a lawyer. She could tell that he liked her. 'As I said, I'm new around here, and a bachelor. Would you think it too forward of me to ask you to drink a glass of wine with me after work?'

'Not at all forward, Dr Jordan, I take it as a compliment. But I already have a date this evening.'

'Well, anyway, I hope you have a good day.' He raised his hat.

'Congratulations, an admirer,' said Frau Gerold from the back of the shop.

'And a very nice one too,' said Jutta happily, putting *Sanders of the River* back in its place. She thought of Jochen.

On the dot of seven, when the shop had shut, she was up at the public clock. She could hear the hammering of the engine from a long way off. The little Hanomag, called the Loaf of Bread by the people of Berlin for its shape, turned the corner, hiccuped and stopped. Jochen's hair was untidy as usual, and his tie was crooked as usual too. 'Hello, bookworm,' he cried cheerfully.

'Good evening, teacher, sir!'

Isabel was sitting beside him. Isabel Severin, dark-blonde, grey eyes, tall, slim. She and Jochen were soon to take the state examination, Jochen as a future public-school teacher of German, English and history, while Isabel was going to teach French and geography at the Lyceum.

Never a day without Isabel, thought Jutta crossly. 'Move up a bit.' She squeezed in. 'How was the uni today?'

Jochen started up. 'My viva is going to be about the Merovingians. Isabel winkled that out of Professor Gabler's assistant.'

'I showed him a bit of knee and he turned talkative.' Isabel had legs well worth seeing. 'Will you drive me home?' She sub-let a room in Lynarstrasse. Her mother had died when Isabel was born, her father had married again and gave her an adequate allowance. Apart from that he took no notice of her, and she had no other family, and this was why she had attached herself to Jochen and Jutta. Attached herself rather too closely for Jutta's liking.

She was relieved when Isabel got out. Now she could look forward to the evening with Jochen in his unusual home in an old railway car.

'I'll look in on you two later,' said Isabel, casting a damper on her anticipation. 'I'll bring the transcript of Gabler's lecture on the new national awareness of history. You should slip a little of it into your viva, Jochen. That'll flatter him.'

'Can't we ever be on our own any more?' Jutta complained later.

'Working with her matters to me. She gives good advice.'

'Next thing we know she'll be sitting on the bed with us giving good advice.'

'She sacrifices a lot of time for me, so don't be so touchy.'

'Oh, take me to the S-Bahn, please. I'm going home. Have fun with Isabel,' she said sharply.

The de luxe edition of *Mein Kampf* was delivered on Friday morning, along with several cookery books and the threatened fifty copies of Beumelburg. 'Put one of them in the window,' said Frau Gerold. 'You can hide it behind *French Cuisine*.' The telephone rang. 'Your fiancé.' She handed the receiver to Jutta.

'Hello, bookworm, how's the printed word today?'

'You read it and you wonder at all the heroic garbage that gets published.'

'That's the trend of modern times.' He sounded perfectly at ease.

She had made up her mind not to bear a grudge. 'Will you collect me at seven this evening?'

'That's why I was calling. The state library stays open late this evening.'

Isabel and I can look up a lot of material there. Then we're working right through Saturday and Sunday at my place. I'll pick you up as usual on Monday.'

'Well, I do hope you have a really nice weekend.' She tried to sound superior, but succeeded only in conveying a miserable acknowledgement of her jealousy.

'Isabel is fabulous at testing me on the right questions.' It was meant to be both an explanation and an apology.

'Fabulous in other ways too?'

'Don't talk nonsense. We keep going by dosing ourselves with Pervitin.'

'They say that's a stimulant,' she said. It was a snide remark, but he had already hung up.

'Get us a bag of cherries for lunchtime, would you?' her boss asked.

'Right, then I can take Dr Jordan his order at the same time,' she said very casually, earning herself a long look from Diana.

It was only a little way, out of the back of the shop, up the alley which gave delivery vans access to the shops, and into Wilskistrasse. A brass plate on Number 47 said: DR. JUR. RAINER JORDAN, ATTORNEY. The buzzer on the door let Jutta in. The legal offices were to the right on the ground floor, and Jordan opened the door himself. 'My secretaries are out at lunch. Do come into my office.'

'I brought your order. The invoice is in with it.' Jutta put the parcel down on his desk. Dozens of legal works covered the wall behind it. She didn't take her eyes off him as he unwrapped the book. There was something about him that for safety's sake she ignored, because she knew just how humiliatingly fast she might fall for it. On the other hand, it was an alluring thought, and set off a tingling below her navel. Typewriters started clattering next door. A telephone rang, and she heard a woman's voice.

'Ah, the ladies are back.'

'I won't keep you any longer, Dr Jordan. You're obviously extremely busy.'

'You noticed?' He sounded pleased. 'Come and take a look.'

The three doors in the outer office were labelled WAITING ROOM – SECRETARY'S OFFICE 1 – SECRETARY'S OFFICE 2. Jordan opened them one by one. Behind the opaque-glass door of the 'waiting room' was a kitchen. 'Secretary's Office 1' was the bathroom, and 'Secretary's Office 2' was empty but for a gramophone which stood on the floor, playing a recording of the staccato sound of a typewriter, the ringing of a telephone bell and busy voices talking.

'Was one of your ancestors by any chance called Potemkin?'

'Advertising is all part of the trade. If a client really does find his way to me then I'm a very busy lawyer. So far I've had only a plumber who wants me to sue for payment of his invoice. Otherwise I live like most beginners in my line, on meagre fees from providing legal aid.' His glance rested on her sky-blue pullover. 'Would I get the brush-off again if I invited you to a glass of wine this evening?'

She thought of Jochen and Isabel. 'You would not.'

'Seven o'clock at Brumm's?'

'Ten past seven, if that's all right.'

'On that note I shall take my well-deserved siesta.' He folded down the wall of books behind the desk, and not a single volume fell out – they were the spines of books glued to the partition. An unmade bed appeared.

'As soon as I'm a successful lawyer representing prominent people, as I fully intend to be, I shall have offices in the best location and a Kurfürstendamm apartment. May I pay for *Mein Kampf* next week? I'm a bit short of cash for the moment.'

'I'm sure my boss won't object. Have a nice siesta.'

She bought cherries from Frowein's fruit and vegetable shop, plump, red and yellow fruit grown in Werder, and ate them with Frau Gerold in the back room of the bookshop. 'He has a bed behind a partition with the spines of books glued to it, and a gramophone in another room instead of a typist,' she told her boss. 'Didn't you mention that you sometimes need a lawyer?'

'Not at the moment, though.' The bookseller put an arm round Jutta's shoulders. 'You like him, don't you? Watch out, things might get complicated.'

Brumm's was right opposite the U-Bahn station. In the bar on the left, the clerks and minor civil servants of the quarter drank beer and played skat. In the middle was the bakery and cake shop. On the right was the café-restaurant. The young lime trees in the front garden glowed gold in the evening sun.

Rainer Jordan was there already. He pulled a chair out for her. 'How about a Mosel? It would go well with fresh zander from the Havel. The plumber called in this afternoon – his customer knuckled under when he got my letter, and I've been paid my fee.'

'Which is no reason for throwing money around.' In her mind, she totted up her ready cash. It would just about stretch. And in the last resort she could turn to her father. 'I'm going Dutch.'

'You're very generous.'

'Just practical.'

'Annie!' He waved to the waitress, a pretty blonde with blue eyes. 'We'll have the zander and a bottle of Mosel.'

'Two zanders, one Mosel. At once, doctor.'

'So you've made friends around here already?'

'Only as a paying customer. But it's a fact that some men come just because of Annie. You know Kalkfurth Sausages? The owner's son sits over there for hours every Sunday, ordering endless portions of coffee and cake.' He grinned. 'The boy should try his luck with a few of the family products as a sign of his devotion. Waitresses like good hearty fare.'

'Speaking from practical experience, doctor?' she teased him.

'Modesty forbids me to say more. How definitely are you going steady?'

'Why are you interested?'

'Because I like you a lot.' He skilfully dissected his fish.

It was beginning to get dark. The gas lamps along the street flared on. A Line-T bus puffed diesel vapour out from the nearby bus stop. Some of the passengers got out to hurry home or change to the U-Bahn. 'What about you, Dr Jordan?'

'Bachelor with a bit of a past. Marion was very chic, very spoilt. A manufacturer's daughter. She liked to keep a poverty-stricken student as a lapdog. When he took her to expensive restaurants she'd hand him her purse under the table. A point came when she tired of him and said goodbye with a pair of sinfully expensive cufflinks. He sold them to finance the rest of his studies. Since then, well, it's been a couple of fleeting relationships, if you really want to know.'

She watched him as he spoke. She liked his frank face; when he raised his eyebrows he reminded her of a clumsy puppy. She felt that tingling below the navel again, and relished it without shame.

'Unattached, then. Shall we have an ice for dessert?'

'Two ices, please, Annie.'

'And the bill,' she added. 'Half and half, remember.'

'My uncle is going to find me a job at the UfA studios. He's a movie director. Theodor Alberti. Maybe you've heard of him?'

'I'm afraid not.'

'Never mind. Uncle Theo thinks I should try the legal department of a big film studio. After one or two years I could set up on my own with a lucrative clientele from the movie world and earn a lot of money. I'll invite you out properly then. Shall I take you to the bus stop or the U-Bahn?'

Jutta spooned up her ice. Isabel and Jochen would be sitting bent over great fat books, quite close together, of course. How far would they go? And how far would she go?

'Coffee?' she suggested.

He raised his hand. 'Annie!'

'I meant at your place.'

She enjoyed his surprise, and was equally surprised herself.

'Coffee at my place then. With pleasure, but I'm afraid I don't have any milk and sugar.'

'The pleasure will do.' She was enjoying this more and more. She was just going to take things as they came – there'd be time for remorse later. At least, if there was anything to feel remorseful about, she told herself.

A car with dipped headlights was waiting by the pavement outside Number 47 Wilskistrasse. A uniformed man got out. 'Dr Jordan?'

'Yes, that's me.'

'Police Superintendent Kuhlmann. It's about your client Paul Belzig. He's hanged himself in remand custody. We need you as a witness. Someone from the public prosecutor's office is on his way already. Purely a matter of form, doctor.'

'Oh, how dreadful,' Jutta exclaimed.

'A small-time burglar,' said Jordan. 'Offended for the sixth time. According to the new guidelines that makes him what they call a danger to national morale, and after serving his sentence he was likely to be sent to a camp for preventive detention. These days that means for life. A life that he's now cut short.' She sensed his anger. He controlled himself. 'I'm really sorry our evening has to end like this.'

'Not your fault.' She gave him her hand. 'Goodnight.' The rear lights of the car disappeared around the corner, and with them the answer to an unspoken question.

It was too late to go home now. She had keys to the bookshop. In the back room, she got out the folding bed that Frau Gerold sometimes used for her siesta. Is Isabel sleeping with him? she wondered, surprised to find how she could ask herself that question with such objectivity.

On Saturdays the shops closed at one. Anja Schmitt came to collect Diana Gerold. Anja was a graceful, ash-blonde woman with cropped hair. Today she wore a tennis dress. The two women were going to play in a match at the club. It had taken some time for it to dawn on Jutta that they lived together as a couple.

'Doing anything interesting this weekend, Fräulein Reimann?' Anja asked politely.

'Weeding the garden in Köpenick. My parents don't have time for it, with all the customers they get in their bar these days. And my fiancé is busy studying for his exam, so he doesn't want me hanging around.'

The emblematic bird of Brandenburg shone in the sun over the door. Jutta's great-grandparents had opened the Red Eagle in 1871. At the time, the little town of Köpenick was not yet part of Berlin, and the cobbler Wilhelm Voigt had knocked back his beer there long before he became world famous as the impostor Captain of Köpenick.

Vati was carefully drawing off beer into glass jugs behind the counter. His face showed contentment. He nodded to his daughter without stopping what he was doing, and jerked his head in the direction of the kitchen. Her mother was frying dozens of meatballs in a huge, black, cast-iron pan. 'Drain those eggs, would you?' she told Jutta by way of greeting. Jutta took the pan off the stove and carried it over to the sink. Steam rose as she poured the boiling water away. She turned the brass tap on and ran cold water over the eggs before shelling them one by one, twenty in all. They joined the meatballs under a protective mesh cover on the counter of the bar.

She spent all afternoon weeding the vegetable beds and tipping the weeds off the wheelbarrow on to the compost heap by the fence. She couldn't help thinking about Jochen Weber, Rainer Jordan, and the inevitable Isabel Severin. She had to talk to someone.

377

Professor Georg Raab was a member of the Prussian Academy of Arts and professor of art history at the university. He and his wife lived in a large, comfortable villa dating from the 1870s in the Wendenschloss district. Now and then he came into the Red Eagle for a couple of glasses of wine. Jutta had known him since childhood.

Roses were wafting their soft scent in the front garden. On the slate slabs of the path leading from the wrought-iron gate to the villa, a long-haired, slender Borzoi leaped to meet her. 'All right, Igor, stop that,' she said, fending him off, and climbed the steps to the front door.

It was opened by Professor Raab's wife Mascha, a beautiful woman of forty with slender hands and dark, velvety eyes. 'Jutta, how nice. My husband will be so pleased. He's in the studio, just go down.'

She had been the same way countless times. Through the spacious hall, past the massive refectory table which always had fresh flowers glowing on it, straight to the dark oak panelling at the side of the steps, from which a door led down.

The bright basement room was both workshop and studio. In the middle of it there was a printing press with a huge spindle. Shelves filled with dozens of different kinds of paper rose along the walls. The sturdy work-bench, bearing the traces of decades of work, stood at one of the two barred windows through which you saw the garden at eye level. There was a char-coal sketch of Igor on the easel beside it.

The professor was bending over a block of wood, carving fine shavings from its smooth surface with a tiny knife. 'This one's going to be a Dürer woodcut. Still life with cabbage and potatoes, supposed to be a previously unknown work by the master. I shall print it off on paper of the period. I've bet Max Liebermann that the new curator of the national gallery here will fall for it twice over. First he'll miss the fact that it's a forgery at all, second he'll fail to notice that potatoes didn't reach Germany until a hundred years after Dürer. So far the good curator has put his limited knowledge of his subject to hunting for "degenerate art". Liebermann's masterpieces, which all the world admires, fall into that category.' The professor chuckled like a naughty schoolboy. 'Know what the curator said? "I can't eat as much of it as I'd like to throw up again."' He went on working with the knife. 'I expect to be thrown out of the academy any day and fired from the university. All of a sudden we Jews aren't German enough. Well, Mascha's looking forward to my early retirement. She hopes she'll have more of me to herself. And how are you, Jutta, my dear?'

'Very well, professor.'

'But not as well as you'd like to be.' The stout little man with the wreath of grey hair put his knife down. 'You're prettier than ever, and you've grown up since our last sitting. There must be more than one man interested in you, and that's why you're here.'

'I don't know what I should do. I'm engaged to Jochen. But this girl Isabel keeps coming between us, and now I've met an interesting young lawyer. I think he likes me.'

'You mean you like him. As much as your Jochen? Better? Or as an instrument of sweet revenge?'

She hadn't seen it as clearly as that. 'I think because of the revenge.' She pouted. 'But not entirely.'

Raab sat down on the stool by the window and propped a large sketch-pad on his knee. 'Will you get undressed?'

'Of course.' Unselfconsciously, she stripped.

'Last time you were sixteen, and before that fourteen.' The professor began working with a soft pencil. 'Do you remember our very first sitting?'

Mascha appeared with a tray of lemonade. 'She was five then. You insisted that her mother must come too. How is she?'

'Thank you for asking. Mutti has the house and kitchen well in hand.'

'You were seven when you came alone for the first time. Do you remember, Mascha darling – the child absolutely didn't want to get undressed. Why not is a mystery to me to this day.'

Jutta laughed. 'Because I had a brand-new dress on, red with big white spots. I thought I looked truly beautiful in it. How often have you drawn me, Professor?'

There were fourteen nude drawings. Raab took them out of their folder after the sitting and looked at them, pleased. 'From little girl to pretty young woman. All of them good. They'll be yours after my death. Will you go on modelling for me?'

'As long as you like.'

'Unless we have to go away,' Mascha said, with an anxious look.

'Nonsense, dear heart, no one will actually harm us. They'll remove me from my position, that's all. A kind of early retirement. We can live with that.'

'Time for your insulin, Georg.'

'And I must go and help Mutti in the kitchen.' Jutta said goodbye.

The professor showed her out. 'Make yourself desirable for your Jochen.' He smiled slyly. 'And introduce Isabel to the lawyer.'

As always, hasty footsteps could be heard along the two shopping streets shortly before closing time. A babble of voices rose from the shops. Office workers were buying their supper on the way home from the U-Bahn. Jutta bought half a pound of freshly churned butter in the dairy, and quarter of a pound of sliced meat in Lehmann's butcher's shop.

'Hello, bookworm,' Jochen greeted her by the public clock.

'Good evening, teacher, sir.'

'Hop in.' He took a half-eaten apple off the passenger seat. 'Want a bite?'

'Thanks, no. I had breakfast ages ago. Was the weekend with her fun?'

'Oh, don't be silly. We worked damn hard. Isabel's a good companion, that's all.' He pulled her close. 'You're the only one I love.'

'When?' She let the tip of her tongue play in his ear.

'Later, you immoral girl. Off to school first.'

The Hanomag set off, making a comic rattling sound. They stopped in the Dahlem district, outside a large building with a double roof. A mighty clock tower rose above the broad entrance. The wings of the building adjoined the central section to right and left.

'The Ernst-Moritz-Arndt Gymnasium, my future place of work as teacher of German, English and history. Qualified Schoolmaster Weber. Sounds good, eh?'

'Provided you pass the exam,' she said cautiously.

'The last test was this morning. They handed out the certificates this afternoon. I passed the whole thing. What do you say now, bookworm?'

'Three cheers!' she cried so loud that a pedestrian turned to stare. She hugged him hard. 'Why didn't you say so at once? I thought you wouldn't know until next week.'

'So you'd quake with anxiety on my behalf? Well, it's over and done with now.'

'You're a genius,' she said happily.

'Lucky, more like. I shone with those Merovingians in my history viva, thanks to Isabel's knee.'

'You were cheating, then!'

'No worse than Armin Drechsel. Professor Gabler himself hinted that he'd be asking him about Charlemagne.'

'Gabler's favourite?'

'Gabler's Party Comrade.'

'Does he still go about the place in silly short trousers with his knees braced rigid?' Jutta had met Drechsel a couple of times, and hadn't really taken to him.

'Drechsel is high up as a Hitler Youth leader. He's going to teach maths, so we'll be seeing each other daily in the staff room. I have to get on with him as well as my other colleagues. Isabel's coming round later with sparkling wine. We're going to celebrate our success.'

'Not a day without Isabel.'

'Don't be a spoilsport. She's a nice girl. Come on, let's look at my new workplace. The caretaker knows we're coming.' They ran hand in hand up the steps to the porch. Inside was a vestibule with pseudo-Romanesque columns, and between them a roll of honour of former pupils who had fallen in the Great War.

Jutta read aloud. 'Imperial Count Kuno von Schweinitz – Baron Artwig Schreck zu Cadelbach – Prince Heinrich XXIII von Selb. Not a single ordinary Schulze, Meier or Müller. It's pure *Almanach de Gotha*.'

'All of Prussia sends its sons to board here,' Jochen said. 'A Prussian Eton. The headmaster was tutor to the imperial princes.'

'What a snob you are!'

'So why do you think I want to marry Princess Jutta von Köpenick?'

'Do you really want to?'

'You bet I do, princess. Come along, I'll show you a classroom and the big hall. The caretaker locks up at eight on the dot.'

After the guided tour they chugged away again. Twenty minutes later they parked the little car at the end of Trabener Strasse. There was no wind, and it was sultry. A storm was in the air. Jochen put up the convertible's roof to be on the safe side.

The man on duty at the turnstile to the Grunewald railway yard greeted them. They climbed over rusty rails and clinker with thistles growing in it. Their destination was an old saloon car, out of service and in the sidings, which the Mitropa rail company rented out cheap. Jochen had made himself comfortable here with his books, a spirit stove for cooking and a paraffin stove for heating. Jutta enjoyed this idyll two or three times a week.

She wound up the portable gramophone and put a record on. '*I don't have a car or a manor house, I'm not rich . . .*' The hit of the season echoed from the box, which was covered with black artificial leather.

'Where are we off to today, then?' Jochen inquired.

'The Riviera. We'll ride from Menton to San Remo and on to Genoa.' She went into the sleeping compartment. He followed her soon afterwards. She leaned out of the window. 'How blue the sea is! Oh, look at that big white ship!' she cried, inventing scenery for them to pass. She was still wearing her blouse, but from the waist down she was naked. She cried out with delight as he entered her. They called this 'going on our travels', and it was their favourite game.

Isabel came picking her way across the tracks with two bottles of sparkling wine in a net bag. She looked up with interest at Jutta, whose flushed face spoke volumes.

The gramophone was idling to a halt as they went to the front of the saloon car. Jochen switched it off. Isabel was lounging on an upholstered seat. 'Hello, you two,' she murmured lazily.

Jutta put water on. She had wrapped herself in her dressing gown. When the water came to the boil she turned the flame down and put half a pea sausage in the pan. 'Something hot every day, that's what my mother insists on. And there's sliced meat too.'

Jochen sawed slices of bread off a loaf and unwrapped the yellow butter from its greaseproof paper. The smell of pea soup rose from the pan. 'Pea sausage,' he told them. 'Steamed pea-meal mixed with fat, salt and spices and pressed into a sausage shape. The recipe was developed for the Prussian Army during the Franco-Prussian war to save on weight for transporting supplies, and to enhance its keeping quality.'

'The things you know,' said Isabel admiringly.

He spread pâté on some slices of bread and put cooked ham on the rest. He opened a bottle of sparkling wine and poured three glasses.

Jutta handed Isabel a cup of soup. 'Did you pass too?'

'Not as brilliantly as your fiancé.'

Jochen indicated the letter beside his plate. 'Mail from Africa. My parents send their love. They'd come and meet you if it wasn't so far from Windhoek.' Jochen's grandparents had emigrated from Mecklenburg to German South West Africa at the end of the last century, to raise cattle. His parents had remained there, breeding cattle even after the end of German colonial rule. They sent their younger son to school back in the home country, so Jochen had grown up with relations in Naumburg.

'Why not go there on honeymoon?' Isabel suggested.

'And of course you'll come too,' Jutta said mockingly.

'If you like.' There was no throwing Isabel off balance. She took a good bite of her bread.

After supper, they listened to the Berlin Philharmonic under Furt-wängler. The programme included Mendelssohn's Fifth Symphony. 'Better push the window up,' Isabel warned them. 'The composer's just been banned.'

'Do you seriously think anyone over in the signal box can tell Felix Mendelssohn from Paul Lincke? And what if it turns out that Lincke has a Jewish great-grandmother? Will his "Little Glow-worms" be banned too? Do we really have to go along with this idiocy?' Jutta was furious.

Jochen kept calm. 'Don't get so worked up, bookworm. We're not the ones who make the rules.'

'We keep them, though, like a flock of sheep.' Jutta tucked her knees under her chin and immersed herself in *French Cuisine*; she had asked her boss to let her borrow the book. 'Did you know that they put fox meat in a real *daube provençale*? They wrap a piece in muslin and add it for the flavour.'

'No, I didn't know.' He yawned. 'We'll drink the second bottle another time.'

'Fine. Goodnight, lovebirds.' Isabel disappeared into the dark.

Jutta sighed. 'A little less Isabel would be a little more welcome.'

'She doesn't have anyone else.'

She slept nestling close to Jochen. Even the storm didn't wake her. In the small hours she dreamed of riding through Africa by train. Rainer Jordan sat beside her. He was wearing a topi and looked very handsome. She enjoyed the rhythm of the wheels on the tracks and the characteristic smell of soot and steam which, to her, meant the glamour of distant places. Just before Windhoek the locomotive whistled so shrilly that she woke with a start. It was early, not yet six in the morning. Outside, the signal box that had always stood at the far end of the railway yard was gliding past. They stopped with a jolt. 'What's going on?' Jochen was still half-asleep.

Jutta got into her dressing gown and leaned out of the window. Down below stood men in railway uniforms. 'Hey – what d'you think you're doing in there?' one of them barked up at her. He had silver braid on his cap.

'We were sleeping peacefully until a moment ago. Now we're going to make breakfast, if you don't mind.'

Evidently the man with the silver braid did mind. He stormed into the old railway car. 'This is no place for the homeless,' he shouted at them.

Jochen got to his feet. 'I don't like your manner, sir. May I ask what you want?'

'I'm Reich Rail Officer Schmitz,' barked the man with the silver braid. 'You'll have to clear out of here. This carriage has been handed over to the Grunewald SA as a meeting place.'

'But I'm the legal tenant.' Jochen searched his case. 'Here's my rental agreement with Mitropa. Here's the police registration. My fiancée Fräulein Reimann is visiting me.'

'This car has been transferred to us by Mitropa, so the Reichsbahn is now its owner. We're not interested in your agreement. You'll have to be out by the end of the week. Heil Hitler.'

'Same to you,' Jochen snapped back. 'Darling, what are we going to do? Apartments are very hard to find.'

'We'll have breakfast first,' said Jutta. 'Then we'll go and see our lawyer.'

'I didn't know we had one,' he said in surprise.

The ubiquitous Isabel was already sitting in the Hanomag. 'You'll take me with you, won't you?' She didn't seem to mind where they were going. Normally Jutta would have minded a great deal, but today it suited her plans nicely. 'We're calling on Dr Jordan. An interesting man and a lawyer. He's going to sort out Jochen's rights to his place. You can come and listen.'

She enjoyed Isabel's reaction when she introduced her to Jordan. Isabel was cool, but never took her eyes off him. Jochen explained the situation to the lawyer. 'If the Reichsbahn throw me out I'm homeless. Of course I could go to my fiancée and her parents in Köpenick, but that's not a permanent solution, particularly in the eyes of the school board which is my future employer. I'm starting as a teacher at the Arndt Gymnasium in Dahlem after the summer holidays.'

Rainer Jordan was in good spirits. 'Fräulein Reimann, Herr Weber, you've come at just the right moment. No need for any argument with the Reichsbahn. I'm starting in the legal department of UfA next week, and moving to Babelsberg to be near the film studios. Why don't you just take over this apartment? I believe you're soon getting married, and I'm sure a married schoolmaster will be welcome as a tenant to the owners – they're a big real estate company. I'll be happy to introduce you to the property manager. Bring the necessary documents with you.'

'Can we look round?' Jochen asked.

'By all means. Two rooms, kitchen, bathroom, if that's enough for you.'

As they walked around the apartment, Jutta heard Rainer Jordan making a date with Isabel. She smiled quietly to herself.

The tiny, modern kitchen was all electric, a rarity in the Berlin of 1935. There was even an electric water heater. Jutta used it every day. The toaster, however, a construction of Bakelite, heated wires and tin that was apt to burn your fingers when you opened its side flaps, was plugged in only on Sundays. It was a wedding present from Rainer and Isabel Jordan. They had managed to get married before Jochen and Jutta.

Outside, a rainy November day was dawning. Water dripped from the bare branches of the acacias beside the road. A wet mongrel dog was lapping water from a puddle on the pavement. 'Filthy weather. I'll take the bus.' Jochen usually cycled to school. 'When we have a car again . . .' he day-dreamed out loud. The Hanomag had died of old age.

'With a chauffeur, of course,' she teased.

'A car's not as far beyond our reach as you may think,' he told her. 'You save five Reichsmarks a week, and if you do that for three years you can order the car. Then you pay the remaining two hundred and seventy-five marks on delivery.'

Jutta did some quick mental arithmetic. 'A car for a thousand marks? You don't believe that yourself.'

'The Führer guarantees the price. The first Volkswagens will be delivered next year.'

'Five marks a week is twenty marks a month, and they have to be earned first.' Jutta was a realist.

'Drechsel gives private maths coaching. He's recommended me to the parents of a pupil who needs coaching in English. It was very kind of him.'

'You think so?' Jutta disliked Jochen's colleague as much as ever. 'We could do with the money, of course,' she conceded. 'Listen, I found a furniture store in Klein Machnow. All modern pieces from the People's Workshops. They'd be just what we want.'

'We have all we need.'

'Oh, do we?' She pointed to the sideboard, dining table with six chairs and bookcase, all in ugly walnut veneer. There were two worn, leather club chairs too. Parents and friends had equipped the young couple. She hated the furnishings, including the heavy green velour curtains. So far their combined salaries had run only to bedroom furniture in pale birch. Jochen's desk was in the bedroom too; there wasn't room for it in the living room.

'Two marks per coaching session. Two or three pupils a week. That'll get us the car. I'll make sure we have the savings book for it, anyway.'

She cleared the breakfast table. 'Would you bring me up some coke?' He carried a scuttle of coke up from the cellar and filled the boiler in the kitchen that piped heating to the four radiators. If you turned the air supply right down it would last until evening. They hugged and kissed. Only Jutta's reminder, 'Take your umbrella,' kept them from a passionate return to bed which would have made them both late. At five to nine she closed the door of the apartment behind her. Herr Vollmer was just opening up the apartment next door. 'Good morning, Frau Weber.' He politely raised his hat.

'Morning, Herr Vollmer. Any air raids likely soon?' Jutta mocked gently.

The Reich Air-Raid Defence League had rented the apartment next door as its Zehlendorf office. It was run by Herr Vollmer, a friendly man of fifty who didn't really know why they were supposed to be defending themselves from enemy planes when there was no war in sight. 'You'd have to ask Hermann Göring. I'm just responsible for collecting the contributions of our National Comrades. I wish you a pleasant morning.'

It passed quickly, what with sorting out the card index for the lending library and drinking coffee in the back room. There was a light on to cheer up the grey day. Frau Gerold was cross because of some official letter she'd had. 'Today's my afternoon off,' Jutta reminded her. Once a month, Jutta had the afternoon off to do her housework.

'That's fine. There's not much going on in this weather anyway.'

She changed the bed, dusted and washed the dishes. Then she took a long bath. At three the doorbell rang. A boy was standing outside. He stared. Jutta quickly closed her dressing gown, which had been flapping wide open. 'Sorry, I was still in the tub,' she apologized. 'I'm Frau Weber. Come on in.'

The boy was standing beside the bookcase when she came into the living room, now dressed. He wore shorts and knee socks. His bare thighs were red from the cold, wet weather outside. He didn't seem to mind. He was a strong lad with dark, curly hair. 'Oh, look, Karl May!' he said reverently. Jochen had kept all twenty books of May's stories from his youth. They were on the shelves between the Brockhaus encyclopaedia and the Muret-Sanders dictionary.

'What's your name?'

'Paul Grabert.'

'How old are you?'

'Eleven.'

'In your second year at the school?'

'Yes.'

'And you've come for English coaching?'

Jochen arrived, putting an end to the laborious exchange of questions and answers. 'The meeting went on longer than planned,' he apologized.

'Well, I'll leave you two alone now. Goodbye, Paul.' She shook hands with him.

'Goodbye, Frau Weber.' He bowed.

'A nice lad.' Laughing, she told the tale of her open dressing gown over supper.

Jochen didn't make an big issue of it. 'Well, at least he has something pretty to think about while he's masturbating.'

'Do all boys masturbate?'

'Most of them.'

'And men?'

'Sometimes.'

She went around the table and put her arms round his neck. 'Will you

387

show me?' she whispered in his ear. It was the signal for passionate erotic games. She couldn't get enough of them.

They got new furniture a year later. Pale wood, modern, just what Jutta liked. Frau Gerold had given her a rise. Her parents had contributed too. Jochen was saving hard for the Volkswagen.

'Save up for our son instead. A child costs money.'

'We'll have a big vacation in the new car first.' He was already planning that for the summer of 1939, three years away. He'd got brochures and maps from the Italian travel agency in Friedrichstrasse. 'We'll conceive our son beside Lake Garda, and then of course you'll give up work.' He took another slice of roast beef, and beer from the siphon he fetched from the bar every Sunday.

He isn't even asking me, she thought in amazement. He just decided it all ages ago. She watched him pour gravy over the roast meat. He liked it rich and well-seasoned.

After dinner they spoke English for half an hour. Jochen needed the practice for his weekly conversation lessons with the class taking its school-leaving exam. Jutta used the opportunity to improve her own schoolgirl English. She enjoyed it, and it took her mind off other things, like her anxiety about herself and Jochen.

For he had changed in these last few months. Not so much outwardly, although he had put on some weight. She could put up with his no longer being the passionate lover of their early days together. They led a satis-factory married life and could still enjoy some good times. You couldn't ask too much.

No, it wasn't that. It was the comfortable complacency he had begun to show, which threatened to include her too. What she missed was a challenge.

When Jutta went to buy rolls for breakfast on Tuesday morning, the front garden at Brumm's was filled with agitated people. 'Dead, strangled, right there at that table. Blood all over the place,' she heard. 'No, not the redhead, the blonde. Annie, that was her name.'

'Strangled?' someone repeated. 'Nonsense. A haemorrhage. She had TB. Imagine someone like that serving in a cake shop!'

Rumours about a serial killer of women didn't last long. Since the newspapers published nothing, it seemed that no crime had been committed. Anyway, the Olympic Games held everyone spellbound. Illustrated books about previous Games sold like hot cakes. Frau Gerold couldn't get them delivered to the bookshop fast enough.

'Drechsel and his *Pimpfs* are going to form the guard of honour outside the Führer's box,' Jochen told his wife, impressed.

Jutta felt anxious. 'I hope those poor children don't keel over in the heat.'

'Oh, they'll hold out.'

'Little Müller too?' Dieter Müller was one of the pupils Jochen coached, a slight lad who was known as Didi. Jutta had a soft spot for him.

'He's as tough as the others. The young people of today aren't mollycoddled the way they used to be.' His tone was new to her.

'Tough as leather and hard as Krupp steel,' she quoted Hitler's saying with irony. 'Sorry, I forgot – fast as greyhounds too, of course. Specially your head *Pimpf*, Drechsel. Has it ever occurred to you that he isn't exactly the living image of the ideal young Germanic male?' Jochen's colleague was a thin man with a vacant, infantile face and sandy hair.

'Drechsel's all right. He's offered to back my application to join the National Socialist party. As a Party Comrade I'll get promotion faster. We could do with the salary of a teacher on the next stage up the scale – what do you think?'

'I think you're a good teacher anyway. Your pupils and your colleagues like you. You'll get promotion without the Party.'

She was right. Jochen was duly promoted. It happened just before the summer holidays of the year 1937, when the former King Edward VIII of Great Britain married Mrs Simpson after abdicating, when the Japanese conquered Peking, and the airship Hindenburg exploded on landing at Lakehurst near New York. There was lively discussion in Frau Gerold's bookshop. Was it an accident or an assassination attempt? Herr Lesch knew who to blame. 'The Americans, of course. It wouldn't have happened if they'd sold us helium gas. But instead we had to fill the buoyancy cells with highly explosive hydrogen, and then a spark was enough.' Where that spark came from, Herr Lesch couldn't say.

He knew who to blame next year, too. 'Joe Louis's Jewish promoter, of course. He put a horseshoe in the black's left boxing glove. Otherwise our

Max Schmeling would never have been knocked out, he'd be world champion now.'

If Jutta had been asked what event she remembered most vividly from the last years before the war, she would immediately have said the German Book Trade Association ball in the summer of 1939. Jochen had hired tie and tails from Koëdel in Kantstrasse and looked fabulous. Her own long, white evening dress was a dream.

Jutta's boss had invited the young couple. She and her ash-blonde girlfriend went entirely in black. They created quite a sensation, and several gentlemen showed an interest in them, but Diana Gerold and Anja Schmitt had eyes only for each other. 'All we need is for them to dance together,' Jochen said mockingly.

'You're getting more narrow-minded all the time,' she exclaimed. Injured, he was about to say something, but the orchestra started to play. Jutta clapped her hands, delighted. 'The Lambeth Walk – the latest thing from London. Isabel showed me how you do it.' She led her husband on to the dance floor. Jochen soon got the hang of the simple steps – somewhere between the Tiller Girls and a Prussian military march – and enjoyed the dance. Suddenly he was the carefree young man she loved again.

Then Kurt Widmann and his band played a hot foxtrot. 'Oh, wow, wonderful jazz, or degenerate Negro music to you!' cried Jutta exuberantly. To Jochen's relief, her words were drowned out by the percussion. Some things were better left unsaid.

Frau Gerold bought them each a ticket for the sweepstake. Drinking sparkling wine and eating lobster mayonnaise, they waited in suspense for the draw. Diana Gerold laughed till she cried. She had won a book by Beumelburg. Jochen won a Waterman fountain pen.

'And now, ladies and gentlemen, for the main prize. A red fox fur donated by Kaiser Furriers. If you please . . . Nadja Horn!' The popular actress, laughing, put her hand in the tub and told the announcer the number of the ticket she had drawn. He spoke in a theatrical voice: 'And the big prize, ladies and gentlemen, please listen carefully now, the big prize goes to number 1481. I repeat: one – four – eight – one. Who has the winning number 1481?'

'I do,' said Jutta, barely audibly. She let her arm droop feebly.

Jochen kept cool. He took the ticket from her hand. 'You're right. I think you have to go up there now.'

It was like a dream. Past the applauding guests, up the four steps to the platform, the announcer kissing her hand, the actress congratulating her as she helped her into the coat with sisterly feeling, more applause. They were delighted at her table. 'I think I know someone who'll be looking forward to colder weather,' Diana Gerold teased her.

Jutta hugged her. 'Thank you, Frau Gerold, thank you for your wonderful present.'

They went home, happy and slightly tipsy. Jochen helped Jutta up the few steps to their apartment door. When he came into the bedroom she was lying naked on the fox fur on the floor. They made love as passionately as they had back in the Mitropa railway car, and didn't find their way to bed until early on Sunday morning.

Jutta went home at twelve-thirty to make lunch. Frau Gerold stayed in the bookshop, lunching on a little fruit. 'See you tomorrow,' she told her assistant.

Jochen called at two. They had just got a telephone. 'Don't wait for me for lunch. Someone from the air-raid defence league is coming to check that the school building's fireproof. As the youngest member of staff it's my pleasure – I don't think – to show the gentleman round.'

She sat under the sun umbrella on the balcony with a plate of risotto. The window boxes of begonias shielded her from prying eyes. After lunch she allowed herself a Juno. She didn't inhale, but blew the smoke into the air. The packet of twenty would last her a whole year. Feeling relaxed, she dozed in the sun until Herr Schnorr, who was hard of hearing, turned his radio to full volume. The lunchtime concert from Reich Radio, conducted by Otto Dobrindt, rang out pitilessly from the open window. No one dared complain. Herr Schnorr was a long-standing Party member, an 'Old Campaigner'. It was said that he had almost entirely ruined his hearing in street fighting against the Communists. Jutta closed the balcony door. She'd talk to Jochen about the noise. They didn't have to put up with that kind of thing, even from someone like Schnorr.

Little Didi Müller rang the bell at four. He came for coaching every Thursday. 'Oh, goodness, I entirely forgot you. My husband is late today. Do you want to wait?' Didi didn't answer. He seemed upset. 'What's the matter, Didi? Aren't you feeling well? Go into the kitchen and I'll make you a peppermint tea.'

The boy obediently went ahead of her. She saw blood on the seat of his trousers. 'My God, Didi, did you hurt yourself?' The twelve-year-old shook his head. 'Don't you want to tell me what happened? Have you been fighting with the other boys? No, what am I saying? I know you've been having coaching with Herr Drechsel.' Didi sobbed. Jutta stroked his hair. 'What happened? You can tell me. I won't tell anyone else, word of honour.'

The boy was rigid as a board. Only after a good deal more encouragement did he relax slightly. Hesitantly, he said, 'He told me to take my trousers down.'

Jutta was shocked. She wouldn't have expected Drechsel to resort to the cane. It was taboo, particularly among the younger masters. And to cane the boy until he bled was barbaric. She got some disinfectant and cotton wool out of the bathroom cupboard. The boy bent his head. 'Don't want to. I want to go home.' Something told her that it was better to let him go.

That evening she told Jochen what had happened. He dismissed it. 'Drechsel doesn't beat the boys, I could swear to that.'

'"He told me to take my trousers down." That's what Didi said. He didn't pluck those words out of thin air.'

'I'll ask Drechsel what happened.'

He brought it up at lunch next day. 'I knew it would be perfectly innocent. Drechsel was just as worried as you, so he told Didi to take his trousers down. Not a trace of blood. The boy had been eating too many sour cherries. They colour the stools red. He'd dirtied his pants.'

A suspicion crept into her mind that this explanation wasn't right. The cherry season was over, and she had never heard of them having that effect.

She met Dr Ohlsen on Saturday in her parents' bar, where he was drinking a beer. 'Hello, Jutta, we hardly ever see you these days.'

'You know I've been married two years. We live in Zehlendorf.'

'Is having babies forbidden there?' the old family doctor teased her. 'Or do you need medical instructions?'

'Neither. Can I ask you something, doctor?'

'Go on.'

She told him about the discoloration of the stools.

'It can happen if someone eats too much beetroot. Out of the question with cherries,' was the medical reply. So Drechsel was lying. In her mind's eye, she saw childish buttocks criss-crossed with bloody weals.

Outside, brakes squealed. A truck drew up, its engine idling. There were loud shouts, and then police officers brought four people out of the house opposite. SA men in brown uniforms lifted the father, mother and two little daughters up on the open flatbed of the truck, which was already crowded with a great many men, women and children. 'They're taking the Jews away all over Berlin,' someone said. 'It's Köpenick's turn today.' The truck slowly moved off again, the valves of its diesel engine ringing.

My God, the professor, though Jutta in dismay. She ran as if the devil were after her. She knew all the short cuts in the neighbourhood, but she was still too late. Professor Georg Raab was already standing in the truck, clutching a small case. 'A single to Jerusalem!' mocked the fat-necked man in front of her.

The professor's wife Mascha, apologizing courteously, forced her way through the onlookers. Her tall figure in its simple, tweed suit, her distinguished face and velvety, dark eyes, the hair caught in a knot at her neck all made her stand out from the naïve, gaping crowd. An SA man barred her way.

'Let me by, please. I'm going with my husband,' Jutta heard her calm voice.

'Hey, ever here the likes of this? Here's one actually volunteering to go!' shouted the SA man.

'My husband is a diabetic. It's his blood sugar. He needs my help.'

'Don't you fret, we'll give him blood sugar!' The SA lout looked around for applause. His companions roared with laughter.

A police officer moved in front of Mascha Raab to protect her. Jutta knew him. He was from the local station, and quite often came to the Red Eagle for a beer. 'Sorry, Frau Raab, they don't take half-Jews,' he said regretfully. He seemed unaware of the absurdity of his remark. He made a path for her back to the gate and steered her carefully through. Igor greeted her in the front garden, wagging his tail. She absently tickled him behind the ears, her gaze directed over the heads of the crowd and at her husband.

Jutta stood wedged in the throng. 'Where are the people going, Mama?' one little boy asked. 'To Palestine,' his mother told him. 'It's always sunny there, and oranges grow on the trees.'

'That brown riff-raff, they want hanging,' muttered the man behind them. 'Hush, be quiet, Egon,' his wife warned.

Jutta shook off her paralysis. She worked her way forward, climbed on the truck, flung her arms round the little man with his wreath of grey hair and kissed him on the cheek. 'Hey, let's take the Jew's whore along!' shouted one of the SA men angrily.

The Köpenick policeman lifted her down. 'You come down to the station with me!' he shouted harshly, grabbing Jutta's arm. 'Are you crazy?' he whispered. He let her go at the next corner. 'Those SA bandits aren't from around here, and I never saw a thing. You go home, quick.'

There were loud celebrations in the bar. The local football team had beaten Adlershof. She went round behind the counter to help her father. 'They've taken Professor Raab away,' she shouted to him through the noise.

'It was three-nil,' he shouted back with enthusiasm.

Rainer and Isabel Jordan came to visit one Sunday morning in August 1939. They would have created a sensation even without their open Mercedes with its long, long radiator and chrome-plated compressor pipes, Isabel long-legged in a sporty foal-skin coat, her dark-blonde hair tousled from the breeze, Rainer in his smart, fluffy, teddy-bear coat. Their car brought people crowding into the usually peaceful Wilskistrasse. The four friends watched with mischievous pleasure from the living-room window.

Jutta looked at Rainer's profile: his rounded chin thrust slightly forward, his full lips, the strong eyebrows over the straight nose. He had hardly changed at all, was still youthful, if not as carefree as on the day they'd first met. His physical proximity set off that old tingling below her navel.

'Rather *nouveau riche*,' she teased.

He grinned. 'The fruits of hard labour. I'm working away, day and night. Right now I'm working for Metro-Goldwyn-Mayer, haggling with the Propaganda Ministry over every Hollywood film that doesn't fit with our sound German national feeling, Shirley Temple excepted. A Swiss watch or a gold tiepin for the head of the relevant ministry department works miracles, along with a couple of cuts in the movie for form's sake. I get paid pretty well by MGM, of course. I'm legal adviser on rights to Tobis Films. And then there are the divorces. You'd be amazed how many would sooner part with their Jewish wives than their movie careers. Rühmann's in a particular hurry. On the other hand, I'm also creating a legal precedent for a wonderful union. Hoppe and Gründgens are supplying each other with male and female playmates, all under cover of their wedding rings.'

'I don't remember you as being quite so cynical,' Jutta marvelled.

'Pure self-defence. Is there a beer anywhere around here?'

'Sure, in the kitchen.' Jochen took his arm.

Isabel stayed in the living room with Jutta. 'How's life with you two?'

'I think Jochen's happy. He throws himself into his work body and soul, he's a born teacher.'

'I can hardly believe I ever wanted to be one too. Sorry, I didn't mean to sound stuck-up. How about you, Jutta?'

'I have Frau Gerold and the bookshop.'

'What about your marriage?'

'In bed, you mean? Well, it's kind of OK there. Reliable.'

'You fancy a change?'

'Yes, I guess so. But I'm not really on the lookout for an opportunity. Too lazy, too cowardly – probably both.'

Isabel nodded understandingly. 'We sometimes ask a nice couple round to our place.'

'Heavens, Jochen would never go along with that.' Jutta offered Isabel a Juno, but it was refused. She laughed dryly. 'The most erotic thing he can imagine is a Volkswagen. I guess he has that in common with our beloved Führer. Except that I don't suppose the Führer has to stick savings stamps in a book. Jochen is financing his by giving pupils extra coaching. And about coaching, by the way – Drechsel does some coaching too. He beats the boys. He drew blood from little Didi Müller, though of course he denied it when Jochen asked him.'

'That doesn't really fit the picture,' said Isabel. She sounded as if she knew.

'What do you mean?'

Rainer and Jochen came back from the kitchen, each holding a bottle of Engelhard lager. Jochen was unusually animated. '. . . You unbend the metal clips and pull the closure out of the bottle neck. It works with bottles of pop too. You remove the porcelain stopper. Then the wire's a perfect skeleton key. We used one on the sly at my public school in Naumburg to open the teachers' toilets and spread honey over the loo seat.'

'Sounds a sticky business to me.'

'Herr Wetzer, our teacher, sat on a wasp. You should have heard him yell.'

The two of them shook with laughter. Rainer was gasping for air, Jochen's face was red. Like two naughty boys, thought Jutta. Isabel winked at her, obviously thinking just the same. 'What shall we do now?' she asked her husband.

'I'm inviting us all to Brumm's.'

'Sommerfeld's now,' Jochen told him. 'That's what the place is called these days.'

They got the last free table. The café was popular. The continuing economic upturn allowed many people the modest luxury of eating out at lunchtime. Herr Vollmer from the Reich Air-Raid Defence League waved. He was sitting with his wife and son, eating jugged hare. The boy, about twelve, was struggling desperately with the little bones left after the meat was eaten, which kept slipping off his fork before he could deposit them on the side of the plate.

'I once had an excellent zander here. The Mosel was just as good, and the company was entrancing.' Rainer Jordan looked at Jutta with a tiny smile that escaped the others. 'But sad to say, nothing came of coffee afterwards.' She was surprised to feel herself going moist. She pressed her thighs together, which intensified the sensation and was not at all unpleasant.

Zander wasn't in season at this time of year, and no one would have wanted it. Instead they ate an excellent Viennese goulash with dumplings, and drank Franconian wine. 'How's Armin Drechsel doing?' Isabel asked. She gave Jutta a meaningful glance.

'His pupils shine in their maths exams,' Jochen said enthusiastically. 'They say he'll get early promotion to senior status. He's a very gifted teacher.'

'And a very gifted Hitler Youth leader,' said Jutta dryly. 'Does he teach the boys' lessons in shorts too?'

'Armin takes his responsibilities in the Hitler Youth very seriously,' her husband told her. Isabel pouted, and gave a scornful snort.

'I'm going for a spin in the car with Jochen,' said her husband. 'Order coffee for us, will you?'

'To get back to the subject of Drechsel . . .' said Jutta impatiently, as soon as she and Isabel were alone.

'I was going to do just that, so listen. No, it's not the cane. Armin doesn't beat little boys. Armin abuses them.'

'What do you mean?'

'I found out by chance at the uni. I hadn't seen the 'Out of Order' notice on the door of the Ladies' room. Armin was in there with his trousers down and the caretaker's twelve-year-old son in front of him. I never told anyone. You don't like to get a fellow-student into trouble. But I realize now that it wasn't just a one-off.'

'He indecently assaults children?' Jutta was horrified.

'Boys. He has plenty of opportunity. First it was the *Wandervogel* hikers, then the Pathfinders. Later he attached himself to the Hitler Youth. His position as teacher in a boys' school fits the picture too. He's always around places where boys gather together. On a long-distance hike, camping out in tents, in your school. You can guess where the blood on little Didi's trousers came from.'

They were interrupted by the return of the men. Jochen was in transports of delight. 'Rainer let me take the wheel. That engine – such sweet music! And the acceleration . . .'

'It has four wheels, like any other car,' said Isabel, puring cold water on his enthusiasm. 'Darling, we must go home and change. We're expected at the Trencks' for cocktails at six.'

That evening Jutta smoked another of her rare Junos on the balcony. Jochen watched its smoke mingle with the yellow light of the street lamps. It was warm, peaceful late-summer weather, although dark events cast their shadows before them. The newspapers and radio had been full of bad news for days.

'Will they call you up if there's a war?'

'Teachers will be what they call a reserved occupation. I know that from Armin Drechsel. He has good connections with the authorities.'

'I suppose that's why no one puts a stop to his activities.'

'Still not satisfied?' he snapped.

Jutta was not giving in. 'He was involved with the *Wandervogel* and the Pathfinders, then he went on to the Hitler Youth. Drechsel's been around wherever he can find a lot of boys gathered together. Including your school.'

'Look, I did what you wanted and spoke to him, and he had a perfectly satisfactory explanation.'

'Try asking him about the university caretaker's son. Isabel says she caught Drechsel at it with the boy in the toilets.'

'He'll deny such a slander and hit back, and then it'll be us in trouble. Drechsel has a long arm. I can already see myself stagnating in the provinces. And you with me.'

'You're a coward.'

'There's no proof.'

'What about little Didi? You talked to the abuser, so now why not talk to his victim?'

'Very well, I'm taking the class for our annual outing on Tuesday. We're going to the Kaiser Wilhelm Tower in the Grunewald. We'll have a picnic and play some fun games. The boys are looking forward to it. I'll have a word with Didi then, just to set your mind at rest once and for all.'

'And if you do find out that something happened – will you cover up for Drechsel?'

'Do you really think I'd do a thing like that?'

'I don't know.' And she genuinely didn't. He often seemed so strange to her these days.

Jochen was already home when Jutta came back from work that Tuesday evening. He was sitting at the table, exhausted, staring into space. His voice was barely audible. 'You were right. I'm a coward, I've been a coward far too long.'

'Did you get any information out of Didi?'

'Drechsel has been abusing him and other boys for years.' Jochen looked up. He had tears in his eyes. 'Do you know what the boy said to me? "It doesn't hurt so much now when Herr Drechsel does it to me".'

Shattered, Jutta did not reply. At last she pulled herself together. 'You must report him. Didi will have to give evidence, no matter how unpleasant it is for him.'

Jochen closed his eyes. 'I took the class up the Kaiser Wilhelm Tower. There's a wonderful view from up there. And when we got to the top of the tower Didi jumped off. He died instantly.'

When Jutta thought about it afterwards, she was painfully aware that this was the moment she lost her innocence. It was replaced by a sense of helplessness. She was helpless as she stood by the open grave, listening to the priest who spoke, without knowing the truth, about the confusion of adolescence. She was helpless as she noted that Drechsel had been promoted and moved to Schwerin and the National Political Education Institute, with a personal commendation from the Gauleiter. She watched, helpless, as a war that she did not want began. Helpless, she learned a few days after the outbreak of war that Jochen was being called up, although teachers were supposed to be a reserved profession. He had tried to get other boys in the class to talk. Forty-eight hours later he was at the Front, with practically no military training.

'"It's against all usual practice. Someone must have pulled a hell of a lot of strings to get rid of you, my dear fellow," said my battalion commander, looking at me as if I were some exotic animal,' Jochen wrote. It was his first letter home, and his last. A Polish sniper caught him on the latrine. No one had told him it was advisable to keep your head down when you answered the call of nature. Jutta received a handwritten letter:

> *Your husband Private Joachim Weber fell at the battle of Rydcz on 6 December 1939 doing his military duty, true to his oath of allegiance to the Fatherland. May the knowledge that your husband gave his life for the nation, the Führer and the Reich be a comfort to you in your great grief. With regards and sincere condolences,*
> *Kuntze, Captain and Company Commander.*

She sent the news on by way of the Red Cross to Herr and Frau Carl Weber, Boescamp Farm, Windhoek, South West Africa. Drechsel killed Jochen and Didi and I shall kill him in return, she swore to herself.

She put Jochen's things away and remembered. It was her way of mourning. She couldn't help laughing when she came upon the photograph of herself leaning out of the window of the railway car, looking flushed, with Jochen's intent face behind her. Isabel had taken it with her little Kodak, in perfect innocence, or so she'd made out. Shaking her head, she put away the savings book for the car, where there were only three tokens missing.

They were to have taken delivery of their brand-new VW in October. It was now probably driving around on war business somewhere. The Waterman was full of blue ink. Jochen had left it behind in the desk. Lost in thought, Jutta drew a couple of hearts on the blotting paper.

Gradually, everyday life began again. The world of Onkel Toms Hütte, still intact, won the upper hand. Jutta seldom left it. Her days flowed calmly on, divided between Frau Gerold's bookshop and the little Wilskistrasse apartment. The war was going on its victorious way, fortunately far from the Fatherland itself. Even the blaring fanfares of the Reich Radio brought it no closer. What did were hitherto unknown delicacies from allied or conquered countries. Frowein's fruit and vegetable shop was suddenly selling persimmons; no one knew how to eat them. And they had artichokes on sale, and fresh figs. Familiar foodstuffs were available in abundance; only tea and coffee were in short supply. Diana Gerold got both from a woman she knew at the Swiss Embassy.

They closed the shop at one on a Saturday. Then Anja Schmitt came to fetch Diana to play tennis. 'And we're going to the pictures afterwards. The Zeli is showing a new movie with Zarah Leander. Want to come with us?' But Jutta was going into the city centre. Isabel had promised to bring her back a pair of shoes from Rome.

The Jordans were living on the Kurfürstendamm, just as Rainer had predicted. He opened the door himself. 'Jutta, you've come at just the right moment. I'm cooking an early supper. I brought spaghetti back from Italy, parmesan too, and we'll have genuine Chianti with it.' The UfA studios had sent him to Cinecittà for negotiations over some films. 'Isabel is staying on in Rome for a couple of days.'

She knew the apartment from earlier visits with Jochen. The big drawing room had modern furniture: pale calfskin leather, white oak, Plexiglas, a few antiques, and as the crowning touch a television set. It looked like a radio with a kind of opaque-glass pane beside the loudspeaker. 'One of the few in private ownership,' said Rainer proudly. 'It cost me six hundred and fifty Reichsmarks. The other forty are in the Berlin field hospitals. They don't show much except for army reports and a Sunday programme with the pretty title *Transmitting merriment, bringing joy*'. Seems they're going to expand programming after the war – they'll even show feature films.'

He put a few drops of olive oil in boiling water and fed the hard spaghetti in until it softened and folded under the water. Tomatoes, garlic and tarragon were simmering in a saucepan.

As antipasto, they each had a can of tuna, calamari and olives in a

400

piquant sauce. 'It's the most delicious thing I ever ate,' Jutta told him enthusiastically.

'They have all these things fresh in the Cinecittà canteen.' He poured Chianti. 'They're filming very interesting things there. Some of it's trash, of course. The latest sentimental piece has Beniamino Gigli singing and languishing as a Roman taxi driver. It's sure to be a hit here too. I was supposed to be negotiating a co-production. Hans Albers and Alida Valli as a German-Italian couple. With a dear little Japanese girl as their adopted daughter. The Berlin-Rome-Tokyo Axis bears some strange fruits.'

'And the Italians go along with this tosh?'

'They politely suggested I might approach the Spaniards. They'd rather work with the French. Conrad Jung is not best pleased. He was to direct, although he doesn't speak a word of Italian.' Rainer grated parmesan over the spaghetti, frowning over the task and looking delightful, as usual. And there was that tingling again.

He had brought back an espresso machine that you had to turn upside down as soon as the water rose in it. The brew was pitch black and very hot. Jutta drank it, sipping carefully. She put her cup down. 'We never got as far as coffee that time, did we?'

He knew what she meant. 'We never got as far as anything that time.'

'Let's make up for it.' She began to undress.

'Don't forget I'm an elderly gent in my mid-thirties.' He unbuttoned his trousers.

'I'm twenty-five and I want you.'

She draped her legs to left and right, over the arms of the chair. He knelt between her thighs. His erect penis turned slightly upwards; he guided it with one hand, rubbing the glans against her clitoris with circling movements. She relished the sensation that promised fulfilment as it grew stronger, but went on and on. The glans moved further and lingered between her lips. He did not move, and by that very fact brought her to the verge of a pulsating orgasm that she didn't want just yet, much as she was responding to him. He withdrew, and then thrust right into her. His staccato movements shook both her body and the chair, making its springs squeak. She looked down at herself, saw his hard prick parting her blonde pubic hair again and again as it thrust in, heightening her desire until it was intolerable and release came — but there was more to come.

When she came out of the bathroom, fully dressed, he was standing by the window in his dressing gown. 'Unfinished business – we had to deal with it sometime,' he said, without turning round.

'Once and for all,' she agreed.

'No repeat performances.'

'Of course not.'

*

The glass of the shop window was miraculously intact. Jutta stood among the books in her stockinged feet. She opened the third little window of the Advent calendar. Outside, two small girls were pressing their noses flat against the pane, counting the days till Christmas. Only the children could still look forward to it. Adults were in a state of anxiety, somewhere between dwindling hope and growing fear. The incessant Allied air raids made Berlin purgatory in the days leading up to the Christmas of 1944. Hell itself still waited in the wings.

She put the calendar back between Rudolf Binding's *On Riding: For a Lover* and Goethe's *Elective Affinities*, books which she had decorated with a few sprigs of fir and some tinsel. Yawning, she climbed out of the window. A British air raid had kept her in the cellar all night, and she hadn't had a wink of sleep. She was also tormented by toothache. A filling had fallen out, and there were no dentists left in Onkel Toms Hütte. The younger ones were with the forces, and the one old dentist who had come out of retirement fled to his sister in the country soon after re-opening his practice.

'Perhaps they'll have some aspirin in the pharmacy.'

'Take a Eumed, Jutta, that'll help just as well.' Diana Gerold offered her the tin tube of tablets. 'And do go and see my dentist.'

Diana had been urging her to go for days. Jutta kept putting it off. Dr Bräuer's practice was in the city, which meant three-quarters of an hour by U-Bahn. No one liked to leave the deceptive security of their immediate surroundings, including the generally inadequate air-raid shelters.

'Well, if you really insist.' She wound her silk scarf round her neck and put on the fox fur. The lined ankle-boots had been donated from Frau Gerold's wardrobe. She went up the slight rise of the shopping street to where the ground ran level, bought a return ticket and climbed down the wide flight of steps to the platform. The train came in. She got into one of

402

the yellow no-smoking carriages. The smoking carriages were red. Four small children were chasing noisily around a man home on leave. He looked well-fed and content. He was stationed in Norway. His wife looked anxious and worn out. She was wearing a brightly embroidered, sheepskin coat that looked as if it didn't belong to her; it was obviously a present her husband had brought home.

Fresh snow had fallen overnight, turning the suburbs into a landscape dusted with icing sugar. In the city, it had already turned to a dirty-yellow slush that was being cleared away by horse-drawn snow ploughs.

Dr Bräuer had his practice on the second floor of an apartment building in Budapester Strasse. The secretary at reception was expecting Jutta. 'Frau Gerold rang to say you were coming. There's another patient still to see the dentist before you. Please would you wait in the next room.'

The other patient turned out to be Armin Drechsel. He had grown fat. His brown Party uniform was stretched over a paunch. His sandy hair was sparser than five years earlier, and his pale, infantile face fuller, but as expressionless as ever. 'Heil Hitler, Frau Weber,' he greeted her without showing any surprise.

Her stomach cramped. She could have thrown up there and then, but she controlled herself. 'Good day, Herr Drechsel, what a coincidence.'

'A wisdom tooth. What about you?'

'I'm having a filling replaced.'

'It's a long time since we last met. I'm head of the Political Education Institute in Schwerin now. How are you doing?'

Dr Bräuer appeared, a kindly, white-haired gentleman with gold-rimmed glasses. 'Herr Drechsel, please.' She was glad when the door closed. A dull physical pain filled her, slowly giving way to icy rage.

Dr Bräuer brought the patient back into the waiting room shortly afterwards. 'A few minutes, please, until the injection takes effect. Would you come in now, Frau Weber?' She had to pass very close to Drechsel. If I had a weapon now, she suddenly thought, and there was no melodrama in her mind, only deadly determination.

'Please rinse,' the dentist told her when he had replaced the filling. At that very moment the sirens howled. The first bombs dropped very close. 'They don't warn you in good time any more,' said Bräuer crossly. 'Come on, down the back stairs is quickest.' He hurried ahead, white coat flying.

403

Down below, candles cast a little light in the cellar. More and more of the tenants of the building arrived and sat down on the rough-hewn benches. Dr Bräuer's receptionist took knitting out of her big bag. Drechsel was nowhere to be seen.

The anti-aircraft shells sounded like the kind of theatrical thunder you make with sheets of metal. The flying fortresses of the US Air Force droned ten thousand metres above the city. The blast from the bombs shook their targets even before they made impact. So far the bombers had spared the west of the city; their targets were the workers' quarters. The plan was to make the working classes rebel against the Nazi regime, although the Allies had miscalculated. The woman next to Jutta put what they were all fearing into words: 'It's our turn today.'

Confirmation followed within seconds. The roar of five hundred kilos of exploding Amtex 9 paralysed them all. A bomb had hit the roof and detonated before it could pass through the floors below. Part of its force was muted.

Hits close by shook the foundations of the building. The cellar was full of people, screaming, coughing and whimpering. The beam of a torch lit up the dust like car headlights penetrating fog. The receptionist sat like a white marble statue, still knitting.

An acrid smell of phosphorus grew stronger. 'They're carpet bombing us, and we're right in the line of fire!' someone shouted. 'We must get out of here!'

Blindly, Jutta groped her way through the thick smoke. She stumbled on the bottom step of a staircase and crawled up, on all fours. No one followed her. Obviously the tenants of the building knew another way out.

The plaster of the ceiling in the hall had come down, blocking the entrance to the building and revealing the sky above. Acrid smoke from the burning buildings came in through a hole in the wall on the first floor. Someone was gasping for air. She vaguely made out a figure in the lift. A heavy beam had fallen in front of the grating. She tried to raise it – and looked into the infantile face that was usually incapable of showing emotion. Now it was distorted by fear.

Girders were glowing up on the fourth floor. Burning phosphorus flowed stickily down the lift shaft and ran over the linoleum on the floor of the cabin, making the man inside tread from foot to foot like a dancing bear on a hot iron surface. 'Help me out of here,' he croaked.

A hit nearby flung her to the floor. She picked herself up. The pressure had burst the door of the porter's lodge open. There were holes which had once been windows in the living-room wall. It was a way out! Behind her, the man imprisoned in the lift desperately rattled the brass bars. She didn't need to kill him, she could just have let it happen. An offer from the devil himself.

It seemed like a betrayal of Jochen and Didi, but she couldn't do it. She couldn't let him burn to death. She braced herself against the beam. Her shoulder hurt, but she kept pushing. Slowly she got the beam upright. One last effort, and the force of gravity sent it falling the other way. She opened the folding door, and the man staggered out past her.

Outside, burning rubble was raining from the rooftops. People were protecting themselves with wet blankets, getting the water from burst hydrants. Fragmentation bombs cut down dozens of fugitives. Then the bombers moved away. Jutta stood in the middle of the street. Her red fox fur looked like the skin of a mangy dog. Animals from the nearby Zoological Gardens were wandering around, disorientated. A female gorilla was carrying her infant in the charred stumps of her arms. The phosphorus had burnt her hands off. Drechsel lay dead on a black heap of snow on the pavement. His brown uniform had been shredded by bomb splinters, and one of the zoo's jackals was licking his empty, infantile face.

'They won't drop bombs at Christmas.' Frowein the greengrocer had heard it from a customer who had heard it from her dressmaker, whose brother knew someone in counter-intelligence. 'And they have people close to the enemy, believe you me.'

'Not spending Christmas in the cellar would be nice,' Jutta sighed. She put the pound of apples and the few nuts to which she was entitled in her shopping bag along with a red cabbage. Next door in Otto's: Coffee Roasters, which had had nothing to roast for ages, there was a special ration of real coffee and even a few ginger biscuits. She hung her net bag in the back room of the bookshop, where her boss was unwrapping something. A bony object came into view. 'What's that supposed to be?' asked Jutta, surprised.

Diana Gerold was slightly nettled. 'A goose, of course.' Her friend in the Swiss Embassy had proved useful yet again. 'Rather a thin one, I'll admit, but it will do for the three of us. Can we have Christmas dinner at your place, Jutta? Our stove isn't working. A bomb hit the gas mains.' She opened the *Morgenpost*. 'Electricity supply guaranteed for Christmas,' it said on page two. 'We can roast the bird in your electric oven. Anja still has a bottle of cherry brandy left from last Christmas. But we'd have to stay the night, there'll be no transport running late.'

'I can contribute a bottle of burgundy from Father's last stocks.'

The shop door opened. Herr Lesch was returning two library books. 'Time this mess was sorted out,' he grumbled. 'Not a new Hercule Poirot to be had anywhere. Do you think Agatha Christie is still writing?'

'We'll find out after the Final Victory.'

'Do you believe in that?'

'What, in Agatha Christie?'

Herr Lesch muttered something and left the shop. Outside, he peered in through the display window, which had been cracked in many places and repaired with sticky tape, and watched Jutta open the last little window on the Advent calendar. It was 24 December 1944.

Anja Schmitt came at midday, wearing a black cloth coat with a grey astrakhan collar in honour of the occasion, along with fur cap and boots. She looked like a pretty Cossack boy. 'From my Petersburg nights,' she laughed. She had once had an affair with a White Russian princess. Diana Gerold preferred her loden coat and hunter's hat, which made her resemble the mistress of a country estate. Jutta had restored her red fox coat to its former glory with shampoo and a hairdryer. You had to ignore the bare, burnt patches. Pretending was part of survival.

'So let's shut up shop.' Frau Gerold bolted the shop door on the inside and put the security bar in front of it. They left the bookshop through the back door. Here too she closed all three locks, which she never usually did. Jutta watched in surprise. 'Shall we go the long way round through the Fischtal park? We never get any fresh air these days.'

Fresh snow had fallen, giving the area something of a Christmassy look. The fir trees in the park were dusted white. Ice crystals glittered in the late afternoon sun. Children slid down the slope on their toboggans, squealing. A lad of fifteen in the uniform of a 'Luftwaffe auxiliary' passed them on one ski. He had turned up his empty trouser leg.

The sun sank red in the haze. It promised to be a bright, cold night. The three women walked faster. Freezing, Jutta pulled the fur close around her. 'We'll soon warm up at home. I have a little coke left in the cellar.'

An organ rang out from the church by the U-Bahn station. Professor Heitmann was playing Bach. The interior of the brick building was crammed. Held, the sexton, had opened the main door wide so that those left outside could share the service and the organ music. Pastor Gess was preaching the Christmas sermon. The birth of Our Lord was an innocuous subject; even the Gestapo spy in the third pew couldn't find anything objectionable in it.

Now it was winter Jutta didn't go to the trouble of taking the blackout paper off the windows when she left the apartment in the morning, so she could switch the light on as soon as she got in without having the air-raid warden yell, 'Lights out!' She opened the flap of the boiler in the kitchen and poured in plenty of coke. 'We won't be mean with it today.'

'A cherry brandy to warm us up? Find me some glasses, Jutta.' Anja poured the liqueur.

Jutta raised her glass to the others, and turned on the oven. Then they prepared the goose, peeled apples and potatoes, and cut up the red cabbage, which was simmered with the remnants of some bacon rind.

The candles in the living room were generally used as emergency lighting when the power was off. Jutta held a fir twig in their flames. The sharp scent of its ethereal oil had something festive about it, and soon mingled with the smell of the roast. Anja poured more cherry brandy, and Jutta retreated into Jochen's armchair with her glass. She wanted to be by herself for a moment. Then the telephone rang. It was her father with good wishes for Christmas, asking if she wouldn't come round to them. 'It's not seven yet, and you could be in Köpenick at nine if there isn't an air raid.'

'I have visitors here, and a goose in the oven. We're going to drink your burgundy. Happy Christmas, and to Mother too.' She hung up before her mother could take the receiver. She couldn't bear her mournful remarks just now.

Anja was looking at the photograph of the 1938 class expedition beside the balcony door. 'He was good-looking, your husband. Do you miss him very much?'

'It's all so long ago.' She didn't want to talk about it.

'Shall we sacrifice a little of the wine for the gravy?' Diana changed the subject, guessing how she must feel.

'I still have a stock cube. We can dissolve it in boiling water and use that.'

The goose was tough and had no flavour. The red cabbage tasted considerably better. Jutta had put a few cloves in it. 'Happy Christmas,' she toasted the other two.

'Same to you,' said Anja cheerfully.

They enjoyed the full red burgundy and chewed the goose with resignation. 'Could have been worse,' Diana comforted her fellow diners. They had ginger biscuits and coffee for dessert. Jutta switched on the People's Radio, and then switched it off again. The Vienna Boys' Choir singing 'Silent Night' was just too much. Instead, she wound up the portable gramophone and brought some long-forgotten records out of the bookcase. She put on a Charleston and danced skilfully through the room with it. Anja followed her example. Diana watched, smiling. When the gramophone played a tango she took Jutta in her arms and led her through the steps.

They drank cherry brandy, and became cheerful. Anja had found a record of Don Cossack music, and did a Cossack dance with her knees bent. 'And after that, at the Princess's, there was vodka and caviar and lots of Russian soul stuff,' she remembered.

'We don't plan to hang around for any of that this time,' said Diana, turning to Jutta. 'Anja and I are going to Hesse tomorrow. My brother has a farm there. We'd rather be at the American end when they roll in. Why not come with us?'

'I can't leave my parents on their own.'

'If you feel like carrying on with the bookshop . . .' Diana Gerold put the keys on the table.

The candles had burned down, the bottle of cherry brandy was empty. Christmas was over. Jutta switched the ceiling light on. It had a sobering effect. 'I'll make up the bed for you two, and I'll sleep on the couch.'

'There's room in the bed for three,' said Diana.

Jutta lay there between the two friends, abandoning herself to their gentle caresses, but she felt lonelier than she had ever been.

One bright February night in early 1945, hundreds of British Lancaster bombers carried out an air raid on Berlin, killing several thousand women, children and old men. His Britannic Majesty's Air Marshal Arthur 'Bomber' Harris was rehearsing for Dresden.

The firestorm swept through the ruins of Berlin Mitte. Those who were not vaporized in the heat were torn apart by bombs. In the cellar of Number 47 Wilskistrasse, the inferno sounded like a distant earthquake. Suppose it came closer? Fear knotted Jutta's stomach. Frau Reiche from the first floor left was clinging to a bag containing the family papers. Frau Fritz from next door held her two small children in her arms. Lieutenant Kolbe, first floor on the right, came down the cellar steps. In civilian life he was an architect, and he was now on leave. 'This you have to see. Come on up with me. It's all quiet outside.' His wife fearfully shook her head.

Jutta plucked up courage. The sky in the east was pulsating and blood red. To the north, the velvety, black sky was a background for the bright 'Christmas trees', the light markings set by pilot planes. Kolbe lit a cigarette. 'They're sparing the suburbs. They don't want to destroy their own future quarters.' He threw the cigarette away and took Jutta by the hips. 'A little quickie standing here? Just to cheer us up?' His prick pressed against her thigh.

'Please don't, Herr Kolbe.'

'My wife puts it about more generously than that. I suppose you know better than I do how many uniformed visitors she has. Makes you glad to get back to the Front.'

'I don't know what you're talking about.' Jutta freed herself and went back down to the cellar. She could have spared herself the journey. The siren on the roof opposite sounded the all clear.

Her apartment was cold and inhospitable. The coal merchant had held out the prospect of a few briquettes at the weekend, but she hated standing in line almost as much as she hated shivering in a strange cellar if the alarm sounded for an air raid while she was there. She switched on the lamp. It flickered a couple of times and went out. Power cut.

Luckily the water in the electric storage tank was still warm. She took a candle into the bathroom and ran the tub full. The hot water warmed her freezing body and gave her a feeling of safety. She wrapped herself in a big bath towel and went to bed. I'll open the bookshop again tomorrow, she thought as she went to sleep, but she knew that she wouldn't.

Spring arrived, and with it the hesitant green of the acacia trees, and mild temperatures. The people in the cellar of Number 47 Wilskistrasse were frozen, but with fear rather than cold. They were eating potatoes left behind by a fellow tenant who had long ago fled to the country. Herr von Hanke, a cultivated man of seventy, always with a tie and a silk handkerchief in his breast pocket, divided them up. 'Please, dear lady, be reasonable,' he told old Frau Möbich. 'Who knows how long they'll have to last?'

'But I'm so dreadfully hungry,' sobbed the old lady. Jutta gave her a few potatoes from her own ration. They cooked the tubers on a burner they had found in her locker in the cellar along with a few sticks of white coal. Mementoes of those Bohemian days in the railway car with Jochen.

'They could be here any time. Then what?' wailed the old woman.

'Well, I don't suppose you have anything to fear yourself, ma'am.' Lieutenant Kolbe smirked.

Herr von Hanke cleared his throat, embarrassed. 'The Russians are civilized people like us. I know them well. I was attaché to the Imperial German Embassy in St Petersburg in 1912, and made many friends there. As it happens I speak Russian, although French was the language preferred in high society.'

'You'll have a chance to try both out soon,' Jutta laughed.

The thunder of artillery over the last few days had grown fainter. Instead, they could hear the tack-tack-tack of machine guns. 'Time I changed my clothes,' announced Lieutenant Kolbe. 'What does a man of the world wear to receive the Russians?'

'A suit in sober colours. No dinner jacket until after six in the evening,' Jutta suggested. The telephone in her apartment was still working. She dialled her parents' number. Her father, in great distress, answered. She could hear yelling and shooting in the background. 'Jutta? This is dreadful – they're here.'

'Listen, Vati, you must keep calm and be friendly. Do what they ask, and don't show any fear. It won't be all that bad. I'll call again when it's over.'

It hadn't even begun yet in Onkel Toms Hütte. Low-flying aircraft roared over the district for two days, and still nothing happened. The rattle of tanks could be heard. Three T34s crawled up Riemeister Strasse and came to a grinding halt outside the U-Bahn station. Their gun turrets swivelled menacingly back and forth. Someone on the top floor of Sommerfeld's café waved a white sheet on a broomstick. Pillow cases, towels and napkins followed suit from the windows of the surrounding buildings. The hatch of one of the monster vehicles was raised, and a round face under a leather helmet came into view. The tank soldier waved, laughing. There was applause from behind the white flags. The soldier disappeared, the hatch closed, the colossus started moving again.

They heard the applause down in the cellar. 'Well, there we are,' said Herr von Hanke, and he pulled out his white silk handkerchief and went up the steps. Jutta and a few of the others hesitantly followed. Old Frau Möbich ran past them. 'They have fresh vegetables at Frowein's!' she cried, her expression ecstatic.

A jeep stopped, and a personnel carrier behind it. An officer jumped down from the jeep, a dark, stocky man with short legs. Herr von Hanke addressed him courteously in Russian. It was the Russian of the Tsarist period: a deadly insult. The officer drew his pistol and shot the old man in the forehead. He kicked the corpse aside with his boot. Then his gaze fell on Jutta. He shouted an order. Two soldiers grabbed the struggling woman, dragged her to the jeep, threw her across the hot radiator bearing the red star and held her firmly there, grinning. Panting, the officer writhed on top of her. He stank of vodka and garlic. She felt nothing, convincing herself that she wasn't the one being raped, it was some other woman, a stranger. The officer finished quickly, let her go and got back into the jeep. He drove off without a moment's thought as she fell into the road.

A soldier helped her up, a boy with a friendly smile. She thanked him, smoothed down her dress, turned to go back to the others. He held on to her, saying something in a halting voice; it sounded like a request. 'Another time, right?' she promised, just for something to say. His eyes narrowed. He struck her in the face and dragged her into the bushes in front of the building. This one took a long time. The rapist forced her into more and more contorted positions. He was enjoying his victory to the full. Afterwards, she staggered into the building, exhausted. 'At least you've got it behind you,' Frau Reiche consoled her.

'You think so?' said Jutta. Swaying, she made her way into her apartment and tore her clothes off. She stood in the bathtub and turned on the shower. A trickle of brown fluid was all that came out. 'Oh, bloody shit!' The bad language did her good. She rubbed herself with a towel and the pathetic remnant of some eau-de-Cologne. It gave her the illusion of being clean.

Frau Reiche appeared with a rubber sheet. 'Memento of Grandpa. He wasn't entirely leak-proof at the end,' she said, trying to strike a humorous note. She spread the rubber sheet on the bed. 'Now, lie down.' She had brought an enema syringe and a bottle of seltzer water with her. 'My last. It may help.' There was a pop as she opened the bottle. 'Open your legs.' The seltzer water was cold, and the carbonic acid prickled like little pins. After the douche Jutta felt better.

The motorized advance party was followed by shaggy little horses pulling carts, and soldiers stiff with dirt. Even their own generals saw them not as men, but as primitive human material to be sacrificed in their thousands in achieving some insignificant strategic advantage, or driven into the minefields, clearing a path as they were blown up. Thin cows trotted behind the carts, and chickens cackled in wicker cages. The convoy stopped. Soon smoke was rising from fires built in the road. A pockmarked Asiatic soldier sawed the head off a chicken and let the blood drain from the flapping body before he plucked it. Another cut thick slices of black bread and handed them out to the hungry children. Then he picked up his accordion and began to play.

Jutta dressed: long trousers, a tight belt, a high-necked sweater. As if that would be any use. She put a sharp kitchen knife in her belt. 'I'm going to kill the next one,' she said.

'Then here's your chance,' said Frau Reiche. A mujik with a bristling moustache burst in. His cap was perched perilously on the back of his head, and he was carrying a basket of potatoes encrusted with earth. He made his way through the apartment in search of something. His eye fell on the lavatory. There was water in the bowl. He tipped the potatoes in to wash them, and then, out of curiosity, pulled the chain. The cistern was still full of water. Astonished, he saw his meal disappear.

Jutta laughed out loud. It was a rare moment of complete relaxation. The whiskery man laughed aloud too and went away. Frau Reiche's voice was trembling. 'That could have gone very wrong indeed.'

The women of Berlin smeared their faces with soot, dressed in dirty rags, rolled in filth. It made no difference. Their liberators were perfectly used to dirt and smells. They couldn't read, but they obeyed the vicious orders of the infamous Ilya Ehrenburg writing in *Pravda*. 'Take their women without mercy. Break their Germanic pride.' The soldiers stood in line, faces expressionless, until it was their turn. There were often thirty men or more.

Towards morning all fell still. The screams of the rape victims had died down, the campfires in the streets were burning out. The liberators lay unconscious in their vodka fumes. Jutta saw it all from the balcony. It was the only time she had ventured into the fresh air. In two or three hours the horrors would begin again.

'Hey, you up there,' a voice whispered. 'Is this Number 47?' She leaned forward. The man wore a black raincoat buttoned to the neck, the kind that fastened with clips instead of buttons and had been fashionable before the war.

'The front door's open.'

A thin, grey-haired man with a pale face and tired eyes appeared. 'Colonel Werner Lüddeke, Army High Command,' he introduced himself. 'I'm asked by an old lady to tell the tenants of Number 47 that Frowein doesn't have any vegetables after all. Her last words. I think she wasn't quite right in the head any more. She died a few minutes ago. Internal haemorrhaging would be the natural assumption. Those animals shrink from nothing.'

'Frau Möbich. My God, she was eighty.'

The colonel opened the clips of his raincoat. He was in uniform under it. 'Anything here I could wear? I got away from those Nazi butchers, I don't intend to fall into the hands of the Reds coming after them.'

Jutta gave him Jochen's old track suit and stuffed the uniform into the stove that provided central heating for the whole floor. 'What will you do?'

'Try getting through to the west as a French labourer. I got the papers from a real Frenchman, or rather from what little they'd left of him.'

'Suppose you're caught?'

'Open your fingers.' He dropped a small capsule on the palm of Jutta's hand. 'Bite the glass and pray,' he told her. 'Cyanide takes direct effect on the mucous membranes. It's all over within fifteen seconds. I must get going as soon as it's dark. Will you take the old woman down when it gets light again? Those brutes have nailed her to the church door.'

At dawn they laid the wrinkled old body on the altar: Jutta, Frau Reiche and young Frau Kolbe, whose husband had long ago run for it. 'How often?' Frau Reiche asked the young woman. 'Five times,' was the indifferent answer.

'Let's say a prayer,' Jutta suggested, 'and then we'll put her in the bomb crater behind the sacristy. And then for heaven's sake let's get home before those bastards wake up.' After praying, they put the dead woman in the crater and loosened the soil from around the edge. It soon mercifully covered the abused body. One by one, they left the church.

A new day, thought Jutta. Perhaps my last. She clutched the little capsule in her pocket.

There were splashes of blood on Dr Liselotte Dorn's white coat. 'You'll have to forgive me, but my household help hanged herself after the fifteenth liberator, and I don't have time to do any washing. My card index is up the spout too. It's Frau Weber, isn't it? Don't you come once a year for a check-up?'

'Yes. Jutta Weber, 47 Wilskistrasse. Another tenant in the building was very helpful, she gave me a douche, but I'm afraid it didn't work.'

'In the sixth or seventh week, right? You're the fourth this morning. Most of them in their sixth or seventh week. I was spared – seems they respect a doctor in Russia too.'

There was a view from the surgery window of the flowers in the garden and further away of the Fischtal park, cheerful in the summer weather, where a couple of Russian soldiers were flirting with their girls. Marshal Zhukov had withdrawn the bestial rapists and murderers of the early days, replacing them with slightly more civilized troops. It was safe to venture out again.

'Place your legs there.' The doctor strapped Jutta's knees into the supports. 'Just so that you don't get in my way. I have no anaesthetic for you.'

'The first two Russkis didn't have any for me either.' The dry scraping of the curette in her uterus went through her body like fire. It hurt horribly.

'And the third?' Dr Dorn spoke in a conversational tone as she withdrew the sharp instrument from inside Jutta and introduced the next size up.

'My third was a clean, well-shaved sergeant. One of the better sort.' Talking helped with the pain. 'He dragged me into Lehmann the butcher's cellar. He had whips, knives and other pretty things ready there. I had to undress. He wanted to tie me up to a hook with my hands above my head. Will it take much longer?'

'We're on number six.' The doctor turned the curette back and fourth. 'Number eight is the last.'

Jutta was breathing hard. The pain was almost unbearable. She forced herself to go on talking. 'There was only one way to stop him.' She screamed.

'Number seven,' said Dr Dorn in a matter-of-fact voice. 'So how did you do that?'

'I did it to him with my mouth – that kept him quiet. Then I pulled him down to me. He thought I was going to get astride him. I stroked his cheek. I had the capsule in my hand, and I rammed it up his nostril and hit it with my fist to make it break. The colonel was right. The mucous membranes of his nose absorbed the poison at once, and in fifteen seconds he was dead. The longest fifteen seconds of my life.'

'Finished.' The doctor straightened up. 'You were very brave.'

Jutta laughed bitterly. 'Aren't we all?'

'The bleeding should stop in a few hours' time. If it doesn't, please come straight back here. And by the way – in a few days' time we'll have the Western powers in the city too. The Yanks, the British and the French are each getting a part of Berlin as what they call an occupied sector. I heard it on the radio.'

'That's the best news in a long time,' said Jutta in English.

'You know English?'

'It was one of my husband's subjects. He taught at the Arndt Gymnasium. We spoke it once a week at home.'

'I just hope they'll bring us medicaments.'

'We have the water back on already, and sometimes the power too. I'll wash some of your white coats for you. And thank you very much, doctor.'

On the first Thursday in July 1945, the armoured reconnaissance vehicles of the 1st US Airborne Division rolled from the Brandenburg Gate over Hitler's East-West Axis through the devastated Tiergarten, and symbolically took possession of its sector of the city. Few Berliners watched the spectacle. They had seen more than enough military marches and parades. In the Onkel Toms Hütte district the new masters made their presence felt with surveying troops who drove around fast in jeeps making marks everywhere, no one knew what for.

Jutta kept her windows open all day and gave the apartment a thorough clean. The old Protos vacuum cleaner howled, there was still a little Vim scouring powder for the kitchen, and Frau Reiche's green, soft soap took care of the rest. Copies of the *Völkische Beobachter* containing reports of the heroic battle for Berlin were no longer the latest news, but the newsprint was excellent for cleaning windows. A couple of Red Army soldiers had drunk the last of her methylated spirits. The apartment and its furnishings were as good as intact. More than half the window panes were still there, or only cracked. She neatly stopped up the others with cardboard and painted it white. She had found a pot of paint in the cellar.

Airing, cleaning and painting were an act of liberation. You could breathe again and make plans at last. It was true that public transport was only sporadic. 'But I'll make it to Köpenick somehow,' she said with optimism.

'Do you really want to go there? Köpenick is in the Russian sector.' Frau Reiche was chewing something with concentration.

'I absolutely have to see my parents. I can't phone them now. What's that you're eating?'

'Peppermint-flavoured chewing gum. Would you like a piece? A Yank gave me a packet, nice man. Showed me pictures of his family. His name's Sergeant Backols, he said. Took me a while to work out that that's how the Americans say Buchholz. His grandfather was from Königswusterhausen.'

Jutta tried the chewing gum. The flavour was refreshing, but the gum wasn't really satisfying because you couldn't eat it. She switched on the People's Radio and turned the tuner. Lively swing came from the loudspeaker. 'This is AFN Berlin, the American Forces Network,' said the announcer. 'And now "Frolic at Five" with George Houdac.'

Goodbye Otto Dobrindt, Jutta thought with satisfaction.

She went down to the shopping street. In the first few days hordes of Reds, dead drunk, had kicked in the doors and looted the interiors of the shops. Now that things had calmed down some of the owners were beginning to clear up. Thomas the watchmaker was putting a few old alarm clocks in his broken window. 'Just so it won't look so empty.' Frowein and his wife were scrubbing their shelves. 'Looking forward to the first bananas,' joked the greengrocer.

Jutta had been here only once since the end of the war, to secure the bookshop door with a padlock and chain. In spite of her efforts, many books had been torn from the shelves, but most were still in good condition. She set about sorting them out.

'You can save yourself the trouble.' A man with a hat and briefcase came in, followed by two American officers. 'Wacker, District Office,' he introduced himself.

The older officer said a polite good day. The younger man, a lieutenant, looked Jutta up and down and whistled appreciatively. 'Hello, Fräulein, *wie geht's?*' he asked. How's things? It was obviously the only German sentence he knew.

'What can I do for you, gentlemen?' she asked with reserve.

'Herr Wacker will explain.'

There wasn't much to be explained. The US Army had requisitioned the entire Onkel Tom quarter from the shopping street to the Fischtal. All tenants of apartments and proprietors of shops must move out within two days.

'What about the books here and my furniture at home? I live at Number 47 Wilskistrasse.'

'If you can get the books taken away by the day after tomorrow that'll be all right. You can take only your clothes and other personal items from your apartment,' Herr Wacker told her.

'And mind you hurry, Fräulein,' the lieutenant snapped.

'Looks as if you're not much better than the Reds,' Jutta fired back at the two Americans.

'I'm sorry,' the older man apologized.

'The District Office will find you accommodation,' Herr Wacker said, raising his hat.

Troops from the US Engineers had already begun putting up tall posts and erecting a barbed-wire fence several kilometres long around the Onkel Toms Hütte quarter.

Jutta was upset. She had thought everything was going to be better now. A new life would begin. The word 'future' would mean something again. And now these Americans had nothing better to do than drive humiliated and starving people away from the last few things they possessed.

She went to bed to shut out the ugly truth. Warm night air moved the curtains. The sheets were cool. In her mind's eye she saw faces. Jochen, little Didi, the appalling Drechsel, old Frau Möbich. They were all dead. And what about me? she asked herself in the dark, afraid. Am I not dead too?

CHAPTER NINE

HEADLIGHTS CUT THROUGH the darkness. With a grunt of annoyance, the killer dropped his victim and disappeared into the night. John Ashburner jumped out of the jeep. He knelt down beside Jutta, loosened the cattle chain and put the back of his hand to her carotid artery, desperately seeking her pulse. A motorbike started up nearby.

'I was a long way off,' she murmured, her eyes closed.

'You're back now,' he said, overjoyed. Very carefully, he picked her up and carried her to the jeep.

Dr Möbius examined the purple strangulation marks on her neck. 'They won't leave any trace,' he assured her. 'You were lucky. Thirty seconds longer and you'd be on the autopsy slab like the others. I'm going to keep you in until tomorrow. Your blood pressure is right down – not surprising, with the shock you had. Nurse Dagmar will get you into bed.'

The lanky figure of John Ashburner stood in the background. He had taken her straight to the nearby Waldfrieden hospital, and spent an anxious half-hour waiting until he was called into the examination room. 'Can I talk to her, doctor?'

'Two minutes.'

'There's nothing to talk about,' said Jutta defensively as he sat down on the side of the bed. 'You can talk to your wife.'

'Ethel? Sure. About our divorce. That's why she's here. She wants to marry this Jesse Rollins. She thinks you're very nice, by the way. Maybe a bit too impulsive.'

'Like this?' she said, flinging her arms around his neck and kissing him.

Nurse Dagmar appeared in the doorway. 'Could you get your car to shut up? It's yelling its head off, disturbing the patients.'

'See you tomorrow, darling. Goodnight, nurse.'

Ashburner hurried out to his jeep. Sergeant Donovan's voice was echoing from the loudspeaker. 'Call in, boss, for God's sake! It's bloody urgent.'

He was disappointed. She'd granted him nothing but a brief rattle in the throat, and then she withdrew before he could possess her. Spoilsport, he thought, feeling injured. He leaned his motorbike up against the kerb somewhere and patted the tank as if it were a horse's flank. It had helped him to get that persistent inspector out of the way. Now it was no more use to him. Feet dragging, he made his way home. In the kitchen, he carefully peeled himself an apple and bit into it. 'Too sour,' he muttered disapprovingly.

Glass splintered. Suddenly the large pane in the French window leading from the kitchen to the garden was shattered. Bewildered, he saw the inspector clambering clumsily through the window frame. Klaus Dietrich had broken off a plank of wood from a fence somewhere, and was using it as a crutch.

'I should have seen it days ago. Your secretary handed it to me on a plate, never suspecting, and I didn't notice. "The boss marked the other four with a cross too," she said. The other four cards in the card index, making five in all, right? And with that cross on the fifth card you were anticipating Jutta Weber's death. Only the killer could know she'd be the next victim.'

Chalford picked up the knife on the kitchen table. 'An unfortunate mistake, inspector. I assumed you were a burglar, so then I stabbed you.' Hand raised, he made for Dietrich.

Dietrich shifted his weight to his sound leg. He could keep his balance for only a few seconds, but it was enough. Putting his full weight into it, he brought the piece of wood down against the back of his attacker's knees. Chalford collapsed. The inspector swayed and fell to the ground beside him.

'And we'll take care of the rest.' Captain Ashburner, followed by Sergeant Donovan, climbed into the kitchen, crunching over shards of broken glass. He helped Dietrich up and found him a chair. The sergeant handcuffed Chalford and hauled him up by his collar.

'Take him to the station and lock him up. And don't take your eyes off him for a second,' Ashburner told his sergeant. 'Inspector, you'd better rest for a little. Meanwhile I'll take a look around here.'

Klaus Dietrich was exhausted. He had caught the killer. He felt neither triumph nor satisfaction; he was just glad to have done the job. Back to the security services firm, he thought with mild humour.

'Inspector, take a look at this,' Ashburner said. Dietrich reached for the plank of wood and hauled himself up by it, breathing heavily. Ashburner had forced open the cupboard in the study next door. Behind them, someone screamed in horror. Chalford's housekeeper was staring past them at the open cupboard. A washing line was stretched across its interior, with four pairs of bloodstained panties hanging from it.

Inge Dietrich had accompanied her husband to the hospital, the Oskar-Helene-Heim. He needed a new prosthesis. They waited until it was his turn.

'We've impounded the black-marble obelisk from Chalford's desk. A genuine Barlach, he used to tell visitors. There's no doubt that he used it to torture his victims.'

'Oh, be quiet, Klaus, I don't want to hear about it.' Inge went to the reception desk. 'Will it be much longer?'

'Your turn will come in due course,' the nurse told her.

She sat down again. 'What will happen to Chalford?'

'There *is* no Curtis S. Chalford. Only Kurt Kalkfurth, the trainee butcher, who was murdering women in Onkel Toms Hütte before the war. The Americans will be happy to hand him over to the German judicial system.'

'And his mother?'

'Martha Kalkfurth is as guilty as her son. She's known he's a pathological killer since he committed his first murder in 1936. She could have prevented all those other deaths by turning him in. Instead, she bribed an employee in the American consulate to grant him an emigration visa. Shortly before the outbreak of war, Kurt Kalkfurth disappeared. His mother spread the story that he'd volunteered for the Motorcycle Corps and fell during the invasion of Poland. She paid for her infatuation with a stroke and the paralysis that followed it. I'm sure she was secretly hoping he'd come home sometime, because in spite of her physical disability she looked after his motorbike and kept it hidden all through the war.'

'You've questioned her?'

'She can't talk any more. A second stroke, the day before yesterday.

But she confirmed my accusations by blinking her eyes – that's all she can still move.'

'And Chalford – I mean Kalkfurth?'

'He lay low in the United States. Not unusual for a pathological killer of his kind. He was completely fixated on Onkel Toms Hütte. When the American government was handing out jobs in defeated Germany, he took the opportunity to come back there.'

'Suppose someone had recognized him?'

'In American uniform? Not very likely. All the same, he accepted the risk. He couldn't help satisfying his urge again in the old neighbourhood.'

The nurse called their names. The orthopaedic workshop was at the end of a polished corridor. The technician took a basic wooden leg from the shelf. It had a rubber tip and a couple of straps at the top. 'I'm afraid I can't offer you anything better just now, Herr Dietrich.'

'Oh, just throw in a parrot for my shoulder and I can play Long John Silver.' Dietrich had decided to take this lightly.

'A parrot?' The man had never read *Treasure Island*. 'As soon as I get the materials I'll make you a better lower leg, but it could take some time. What with all the demand, and these bloody awful circumstances . . . excuse my language, ma'am.'

'The main thing is for you to be mobile. We'll strap the thing on somehow.' Inge helped him. 'Can you manage to get home with it?'

He took her arm. 'I can manage anything with you.'

They had invited Jutta Weber and John Ashburner round. 'A kind of engagement party for you,' said Klaus Dietrich, rather awkwardly. 'And, well, because we've known each other a while now.'

John Ashburner had brought a couple of bottles of wine, and cigarettes for the district councillor. He listened patiently to Hellbich's version of the story, according to which he, Hellbich, had of course suspected Chalford all along.

The women had only one thing to talk about. 'When's the wedding?'

Jutta beamed. 'In four weeks' time. We're getting married in the Evangelical church near the U-Bahn station, and then having the wedding breakfast at Club 48. You're all invited. Sergeant Panelli is already working on a wedding cake with four tiers.'

'You'll have your new leg by then too, inspector. I've had a word with General Abbot, and he's given the go-ahead for the military hospital to make you one.' Ashburner pointed to the window. 'Take a look out there.' A tricycle stood outside the house, with Sergeant Donovan beside it. 'He made you that in his free time. Know what he brought himself to say about you? "That darn Kraut, he's the right sort."'

'I hope he'll like the lunch. Find another plate, Inge.' Klaus Dietrich limped to the front door and waved to Donovan to come in. Expectantly, the family and their guests gathered around the table. There was good pea soup with fried onions and large cubes of bacon, courtesy of grandmother Hellbich's Persian lamb coat.

'Coming to lunch, Ben?' called Inge Dietrich.

'I'm not hungry. Keep some for me,' replied a voice from the steps. All eyes were on the soup tureen. Unobserved, Ben slipped out of the house.

Riemeister Strasse was dozing in the sun. Its inhabitants were at lunch, if they had any, or dreaming of better times on their verandas. Someone was listening to the radio with the volume right up and the window open. A neighbour opposite shouted, 'Turn it down!'

Ben breathed deeply in and out, straightened his back, held his head high and put his left hand flat in the jacket pocket. He left his thumb outside; the new suit called for upright but casual bearing. To his great grief, he met no one to show respectful amazement at his inimitable elegance. Only an old lady shuffled past with her head bent.

Where Riemeister and Onkel-Tom-Strasse came together to trace the rest of the long way to the Kurfürstendamm, the Grunewald began, now much sparser because of the bombs and shells. It was five minutes from the outskirts of the wood down to the lake.

The Krumme Lanke lay dark silver in its marshy setting. It was a part of the chain of lakes that had once been an arm of the Havel running through the Grunewald, navigable until the middle of the sixteenth century. Elector Joachim II of Brandenburg had been able to bring the building materials for his hunting lodge in the middle of the forest along the river. Ben had learned that in history at school. At the moment, however, he was more interested in Heidi Rödel than in princely architecture. 'Sunday at two in the hollow by the lake,' she had said, which showed that she knew how to appreciate a well-dressed man.

Laughter and shouting came up from the water. These hard times could not spoil the pleasure of the bathers. Ben kept away from the bank so as not to be hit by someone's wet ball, but just close enough for the public to be able to react with speechless admiration to the appearance of the gentleman in Prince of Wales check. Public reaction was not very forthcoming. 'Hey, aren't we posh!' someone called after him. Ben replied with what he hoped was a scornful smile hovering around his mouth.

'Rather overdressed, eh, kid?' grinned an elderly man in a towelling wrap, but Ben loftily ignored him. Nothing anyone said could affect his suit. It symbolized a world in which everything was all right, where there were elegant people and enough to eat. He skirted the puddles left by last night's rain; they would have done the suede shoes no good. The fenced clearing rose gently from this bank of the lake. Ben avoided the bramble bushes and slipped through the young birch trees which could do no harm to his suit.

He didn't see Heidi until he had almost reached the hollow. She was sunbathing in a two-piece, blue bathing suit. Ben saw her full, half-opened lips, which she had quickly moistened as he approached, and her breasts rising to an amazing height with every breath she took. She had closed her eyes and appeared not to have noticed him. He cleared his throat. 'Oh, it's you,' she murmured sleepily, as if she were not very interested.

Ben was hurt. 'I can always go away again. Though we did have a date.'

'I know.' Suddenly she was wide awake. 'Looks really good, your suit.' She invitingly patted the ground beside her. He sat down, arms folded behind his head, and looked up at the sky. He had never been so close to her before. She smelled of walnut oil with a faint lily-of-the-valley fragrance, the pharmacist Schmidt's own concoction.

What happened next? Did she expect him to kiss her? Or would she rather they talked, and if so, what about? Perhaps she'd like a cigarette? He still had a packet with a couple of Stellas in it. On the other hand, you weren't allowed to smoke in the wood.

Suddenly her face was very close. She pressed her lips to his. He wondered how long she would keep them like that without taking a breath. She didn't go that far, but told him, 'If you open your teeth it works better.'

He did as she wanted. Her tongue darted out like a little snake and felt for his. He got the idea and let his own tongue wriggle vigorously. It set off a pleasant tingling feeling somewhere else entirely.

'Much better than Gert Schlomm,' she assessed his efforts in a pause for breath. 'Do take your suit off or it will get all crumpled . . . and then there's the grass stains . . .' These were convincing arguments, particularly as he had his bathing trunks on underneath. Minutes later the precious garments were hanging on a young birch tree and the suede shoes were lying on the moss. Leaves rustled somewhere; it was probably a deer.

He pushed her down in the grass, and they went busily on exploring each other's mouth with their tongues. The top half of her bathing suit had slipped, because she had carefully unhooked it. Her breasts were warm and soft, a little slippery from Herr Schmidt's sun oil, but all in all very pleasant.

'It's much nicer with nothing on,' she whispered, slipping the bottom of her bathing suit off too. He removed his bathing trunks, hesitantly, because he felt ashamed of his erect penis. She took it in her hand with interest. The deer was rustling in the background.

He stroked her mound of Venus. The little hairs were silky soft. Only five minutes before he would never have believed he'd touch her there. He did it with a heart beating fast, and she seemed to like it. Her hand gently rubbed him. 'Did you ever do it before?'

Something told him that this was a moment for honesty. 'Not really, no,' he admitted. 'But I know what you do.'

'I know too.'

'I mean, did you ever . . . ?' He swallowed. 'With Gert Schlomm, for instance.'

'What, with the ridiculous way he carries on?' she exclaimed, her hand rubbing harder to encourage him.

Ben knelt between her thighs. 'Help me a bit.' She showed him the way. He felt her damp warmth – and slid out. Patiently, she helped him in again. He tried once more, in vain. His sheer anxiety to do it properly had made his prick go soft. 'Oh, shit,' he muttered.

Heidi was disappointed. Was this going to be all? No, certainly not. Instinct guided her. She bent over him. Between her lips he grew large again. Ben let her do as she liked. As she sat astride him, and he found his way back into her with amazement, he realized that he had made a start. He braced himself against her, moving in time. Her little squeals spurred him on. It got better and even better, and the world around ceased to exist, including the sounds of the rustling leaves and cracking twigs which, as it happened, were not made by a deer. Afterwards they lay there flushed, holding hands.

'Was it good for you too?' whispered Heidi.

Ben was his old non-committal self. 'It was OK.' He thought of the condoms. Should he put one on now? 'So that most precious part of you doesn't catch cold,' Herr Pagel had said, as it easily might now after what had happened. The box was in his jacket pocket.

He stood up to get it, and froze to the spot. His suit and shoes were gone. The young birch tree swayed innocently in the October wind.